INFERNO

ROAD TO THE BREAKING
BOOK 9

CHRIS BENNETT

Inferno is a work of historical fiction. Apart from well-documented actual people, events, and places that figure in the narrative, all names, characters, places, and incidents are the products of the author's imagination, or are used fictitiously. Any resemblance to current events, places, or living persons, is entirely coincidental.

Names: Bennett, Chris (Chris Arthur), 1959- author.
Title: Inferno / Chris Bennett.
Description: [Spokane, Washington] : [CPB Publishing, LLC], [2024] |
Series: Road to the breaking ; book 9
Identifiers: ISBN: 978-1-955100-10-6 (trade paperback) | 978-1-955100-11-3 (ebook)
Subjects: LCSH: United States. Army--Officers--History--19th century--Fiction. | United States-- History--Civil War, 1861-1865--Fiction. | Confederate States of America. Army--Fiction. | Women spies--Southern States--Fiction. | Freed persons--United States--History--19th century--Fiction. | Shenandoah Valley Campaign, 1864 (May-August)--Fiction. | LCGFT: Historical fiction. | BISAC: FICTION / Historical / Civil War Era. | FICTION / Sagas.
Classification: LCC: PS3602.E66446 I54 2024 | DDC: 813/.6--dc23

To sign up for a
no-spam newsletter
about
ROAD TO THE BREAKING
and
exclusive free bonus material
visit my website:

http://www.ChrisABennett.com

Inferno [ĭn-fûr′nō] noun:
1. An extremely large, intense, and uncontrolled fire; a conflagration.
2. A place or condition of fiery heat or destruction, suggestive of hell, especially with respect to human pain, suffering, or death.
3. Hell; the infernal regions.

DEDICATION

To
Travis Tynan
our very excellent
(so much more than a)
proofreader
— an invaluable member of the team
that helps make good books great!

Contents

"Breaking the established norms of warfare will only instigate a downward spiral of mindless brutality and destruction — a path of blood, pain, and death leading straight to hell. Makes me think of Billy's old Indian story ... about the merciless war that raged when everything civilized fell apart, resulting in a nightmarish inferno ... the time he called 'The Breaking.'"

– *Colonel Nathaniel Chambers*

Shenandoah Valley Campaign Battles of 1864

Chapter 1. Bitter Defeat and Sweet Victory

"Defeat is not bitter
unless you swallow it."
- Joe Clark

Monday May 30, 1864 – New Market, Virginia:

Nathan and Tom stared down into the dark pit, the remains of an old, abandoned rock quarry. Tom glanced over at Nathan and saw the look he'd expected: a grim visage such as usually presaged a violent outburst. But in this case, the subject of Nathan's anger was no longer present—the aggressive response would have to wait.

Tom looked back down into the hole and tried to make a count of the bodies it contained, nearly all missing their shoes, jackets, and other articles of clothing. He estimated fifty at least, though likely there were many more, covered by the large rocks haphazardly dumped in on top of the bodies. But despite their lack of uniforms, based on the treatment of the dead, there could be no doubt as to who these men were: Union soldiers killed in the recent Battle of New Market.

Tom looked back up as movement to his right caught his eye. Their commanding officer, Major General David Hunter, was striding toward them, followed closely by his staff officers. The general and his men had not yet reached the edge of the pit, nor seen its grisly contents.

General Hunter stepped up to Nathan, but the latter didn't turn nor acknowledge his superior's presence—a response that would normally be considered a severe breach of military protocol. But Hunter seemed to sense that something was terribly amiss, and instead of chastising his subordinate officer, he stepped up to look at what had so captured his colonel's attention.

Hunter gazed into the pit, seeing nothing at first as his eyes adjusted to the darkness. Then he muttered a curse under his breath and frowned. Tom thought the general's usual stern demeanor looked angrier than usual. Even more so than Nathan's, if that was possible.

The day had started with a satisfying return to the very battlefield at New Market where they'd been defeated and humiliated just two weeks earlier while under the command of the incompetent General Franz Sigel. This time, the rebel force that'd been left behind to hold the town had been quickly routed and driven from the field by the Twelfth West Virginia and other elements of General Hunter's command.

But the discovery of the burial pit had changed the mood of the federal soldiers from celebratory to downcast. The Confederates' disrespectful, unconscionable treatment of the Union dead, depriving them of the common decency of a simple burial, cast a pall over the men.

"*The barbarians…*" Hunter growled, and then turned to face Nathan, who finally looked up to meet his dark gaze.

"Chambers, we'll make camp here tonight, that we may properly inter our dead. Please make the necessary arrangements for the burial detail."

Nathan nodded, "It will be done, sir." But the two men did not exchange a salute as Tom had expected. Instead, they locked eyes for a long moment.

Finally, Hunter nodded. "This too shall be avenged, Colonel."

"Agreed," Nathan answered, then turned back to gaze into the dark hole, before taking out a cigar, sticking it in his mouth and biting down hard.

৯১৩৫৯৩৩৯৯১৩৫৯৩৩৯৯১৩৫৯৩৩

Friday June 3, 1864 – Cold Harbor, Virginia:

Union Captain James Hawkins of the Seventh West Virginia infantry regiment, part of the Gibraltar Brigade, led his depleted rifle company of forty-six men up over the Union earthworks in the pre-dawn darkness. Though it was still too dark to see much, he knew the remainder of the brigade was also moving forward as part of a large-scale assault by Major General Hancock's II Corps.

Despite the Union Army's great advantage in numbers, Hawkins was feeling a great deal of trepidation as he stepped cautiously forward, moving out toward where General Lee's army was well dug in some eight hundred yards away and up a slight rise.

He'd decided to leave his infantry officer's sword behind in favor of a standard-issue infantry rifle, complete with mounted bayonet. After eyeing the rebel earthworks the night before, he'd decided it would likely be *that* kind of battle. No gallant, sword-waving charge this time—more likely it would be a slow, methodical, hard-fought slog. He inwardly groaned at the thought. Many men would die; he had no illusions about that.

But as he moved cautiously across the open field, he began to feel a glimmer of hope; the swirling morning mists seemed to conceal the movements of he and his men from the prying eyes of the enemy's scouts, and they were able to cross nearly three-quarters of the distance required without meeting any resistance.

But then as Hawkins led his men down a short slope into what looked like tall grass in the dim light of dawn, he suffered a sudden shock when he sunk up to his knees in murky water, which sent an icy chill up his spine. And he knew that the slogging, stumbling, and cursing of the men could not fail to give away their position. Then he heard it, the unmistakable distant popping sound: enemy rifle fire. Bullets zipped past and plunged into the water around them. Some projectiles found their marks, and a few soldiers fell screaming. Other men fell with only a splash after a hard, wet smack to the face or chest.

"Move out at the double-quick!" Hawkins shouted, "We've got to get out of this swamp, or they'll cut us to pieces!" He surged forward with all his strength, but the wet muddy earth beneath the water seemed to pull at his feet like lead weights, making his progress nightmarishly slow.

He could now hear massive rifle fire all down the rebel line, and could see flashes of light sparking in the near distance.

After several hundred more grueling yards, the Seventh reached the edge of the marsh, and immediately went to ground on the backside of a slope leading up to dryer land. To their credit, the men of the Seventh immediately began returning fire, despite their frigid soaking and near exhaustion.

To his satisfaction, Hawkins now heard heavy gunfire coming from all along the advancing Union lines to the left and right. Though the federals were taking a pounding, they were at least fighting back.

But then he heard the sound he'd most feared and dreaded: the deep rumble and boom of artillery coming from the rebel earthworks directly to his front. He ducked his head even as something shrieked past him, so close he could feel the sharp, concussive wind from its flight. *Cannister shot! Damn it ... this is going to be bad.*

He peeked up to survey the ground ahead, then immediately ducked back down. The field ahead was almost entirely devoid of vegetation, and sloped slowly up to a long wall of dirt and logs, from which a cloud of gun smoke slowly rose.

"Stay put, men ... nothing good will come of us trying to go any further now," he called out.

Then he turned to the sergeant lying next to him and said, "We try to advance from here ... it'll be just plain murder. Let's see if some of the other units might flank them ... or at least our artillery might silence those big guns."

"Yes, sir ... Seems prudent," the sergeant nodded, even as he pressed his head against the dirt to hide as much of it as possible.

A half hour later, to Hawkins' chagrin, the Union assault seemed to have stalled completely. Though he could still see nothing more than the rebel earthworks less than two hundred yards away, he no longer heard any significant rifle fire, save possibly far off to the north where General Burnside's IX Corps was deployed. The inevitable screaming of the wounded men was now more noticeable than any gunfire.

Another half hour passed with no action, and Hawkins was about to nod off where he lay in the dirt, despite his soaked uniform, when a sudden tremendous cacophony roused him with a start.

A great volley of gunfire had erupted from the rebel earthworks, followed once again by the pounding of their big

4

guns. But from the Union side, there was only a smattering of rifle fire in response. He wondered what it might signify. Why would the rebels pour so much lead into such a minor Union attack?

As none of the incoming fire appeared to be directed his way at the moment, Hawkins decided to risk a quick look out to his left where he'd heard the most gunfire from the rebels. He grabbed his binoculars, stood to his feet, panned the field out in that direction, then dropped back down with a gasp. What he'd seen had shocked him, veteran fighter though he was, and it sent a chill of fear all through his body: blue-uniformed soldiers lay wounded or dead all across the field, as far as he could see. Thousands upon untold thousands, too many to count, and so thick one could hardly see the green grass between them.

And at that moment, as the ultimate irony in what he could only imagine must be the greatest Union disaster of the war, a young lieutenant came slogging through the marsh behind Hawkins and plopped down on the ground next to him. After taking a moment to catch his breath, the lieutenant gasped out, "Sorry I'm late, sir ... The swamp slowed me. I am from General Hancock's command, with orders that the Seventh join the general assault against the enemy's position..."

Hawkins just stared at him, mouth agape. "Lieutenant ... are you not paying attention?"

"I ... don't know what you mean, sir."

"Listen, Lieutenant ... what do you hear?"

"Uh ... nothing much, sir."

"Neither do I, Lieutenant ... Neither do I. Nobody is advancing. They're either all dead, or simply refuse to move further into that inferno."

"But, sir ... your orders are to advance. I have it straight from the general, who received his orders from General Grant himself."

"Well, right now I don't care if those orders came from God Almighty, Lieutenant. I'm not ordering my men to advance. This battle is over ... and we've already lost. Getting all my men killed is not going to change that."

෪෩෫෬෭෪෩෫෬෭෪෩෫෬

C.S.A. Captain Jubal Collins crept cautiously to the top of the rebel earthworks, a good two feet above the firing loopholes his men had just used to such devastating effect. Though it was a dangerous move, and very likely to get him killed, he simply had to see for himself what was happening out in front of their position. The Union assault had suddenly grown silent, and he needed to know what it meant—likely, they were regrouping for another attack. He felt responsible for his men, the soldiers of the old Stonewall Brigade, and wanted to be prepared for whatever was coming next.

Jubal, who'd been unceremoniously promoted to captain only a week earlier, still had a hard time believing he was now the highest-ranking officer of what was once the mighty Stonewall Brigade. From its high of nearly 3,000 officers and men at the beginning of the war under Stonewall Jackson, the remnants of the brigade now numbered just 249 survivors. They'd recently been consolidated with remnants of other depleted units under the command of Brigadier General William Terry.

He raised his binoculars to his eyes, and slowly rose up over the top of the berm. At first, he thought the field glasses were smudged or had been damaged somehow, for all he could see was a great smear of blue, wherever he gazed. So he lowered the glasses and gazed out with his naked eyes. What he saw was so unexpected and horrific, he could scarcely take it in. He suddenly felt out of breath, and felt a burning sensation rising up from his stomach.

He turned his back to the scene, and slowly slid back down into the trench.

"What is it, Captain?" the sergeant next to him asked, his eyes widened by the expression on his commander's face.

But for several moments, Jubal could not speak; he felt shaken. He took a deep breath, closed his eyes, and wiped his hands across his face before opening them again.

He finally looked at the sergeant. "They're dead, Sergeant. The Union soldiers ... they're dead."

"Oh ... but that's good, ain't it, sir? Which units do you suppose they was?"

"All of them, Sergeant … *all* of them."

Union Commanding General Ulysses S. Grant sat on his horse on a low rise and gazed out at the Cold Harbor battlefield in utter disbelief. Blue-clad bodies lay everywhere. Demoralized and defeated soldiers streamed away from the fight, refusing their officers' orders to continue the advance, never even noticing their commanding general sitting on his horse right next to the road they were trudging down. *What happened here? It wasn't supposed to be this way. How could this have happened? What has become of my army?*

After months of fruitless maneuvering, and frustratingly slow, grinding progress against a rebel army that had become adept at defensive battle tactics and avoiding a devastatingly costly head-on confrontation, Lee had finally drawn up his army for a real fight at the strategic crossroads of Cold Harbor, Virginia.

Grant had been elated. To the Union commander, it had seemed a golden opportunity, too good to pass up. With one swift blow, the numerically superior, better fed, and better equipped Union Army would crush Lee and end the rebellion.

Grant slowly shook his head. *What happened?* he asked himself again. His first instinct had been to blame the failure on the overly cautious ineffectiveness that was typical of some of his subordinate commanders, Meade in particular, who'd famously squandered the opportunity to destroy Lee after Gettysburg.

But now that Grant had seen the disaster firsthand, he realized there was no one to blame but himself.

He shook his head and silently scolded himself for his hubris. He'd believed Lee's skill as a commander was mostly at swift maneuvering, wily deception, and bold unexpected assault.

But here at Cold Harbor, Lee had simply lined up his army behind a pile of sticks and dirt and opened fire when Grant attacked. No bold moves, no deception. Just Lee understanding that a well dug-in veteran army on good defensible ground with modern rifles and artillery was almost completely immune to a head-on assault. *They could stand there all day, fending off anything we could throw at them with relative ease, and almost zero casualties.*

And then Grant realized with a twisting knot in his stomach that Lee had just played him. *Like a cat playing a mouse ... only in this case, the mouse is playing the cat! Lee knew I was overly eager to draw him into a fight. So he gave me exactly what I wished for; set me up, then utterly destroyed me.*

Grant slowly shook his head, a new respect and grudging admiration for his enemy growing in his breast. But also, from the depths of his despair, a new resolve grew. *Never again! Never again, Mr. Lee, will I underestimate you. Never again will you beat me at this deadly game. This I swear ... on my life!*

ଈୠଔୠ୧ଔ୧ୠ୧ୠ୧ୠ୧ୠ୧ଔ୧ଔ

Sunday June 5, 1864 – Piedmont, Virginia:

Nathan gazed through his brass spyglass out toward the dug-in position of the Confederates under Brigadier General William "Grumble" Jones. Jones had positioned his defensive line along a ridge at the edge of a deep wood, which faced a roadway that Union forces would have to cross to attack them. The two forces now met just outside the small town of Piedmont, and the rebels had already repelled a head-on assault by a federal brigade under the command of Colonel Augustus Moor.

The Twelfth West Virginia and the other regiments of Colonel Thoburn's brigade were positioned on the left flank of the Union force and had not yet been involved in the action, awaiting General Hunter's order to advance.

Nathan watched with satisfaction as the last of the rebel artillery burst into flames after a devastatingly accurate bombardment by Union artillery commanded by Captain DuPont, the same officer whose courage and efficiency had recently helped extract the Twelfth from potential annihilation at the Battle of New Market. DuPont was aided in his efforts by the ever-present Captain Carlin and his Wheeling Battery.

By directing each battery to target the rebel guns one at a time, DuPont and Carlin had succeeded in completely destroying the enemy's artillery, seriously degrading their defensive capability.

With the rebel guns silenced, Colonel Moor launched another attack, but once again the rebels held firm and the attack stalled.

This time, however, General Hunter had already ordered Nathan and the rest of Thoburn's brigade to attack the enemy's right flank even as Moor was hitting the center of their line.

And by good fortune, as Nathan and Tom trotted up the hill toward the rebel lines, sabers drawn, followed closely by the men of the Twelfth, bayonets fixed, they noticed their advance was shielded from the enemy's view by a long slope that ended in a hump near the enemy's lines.

As Nathan reached the top of the rise and hopped up onto a stump, the sight that greeted his eyes was a thrill that officers dreamed of but rarely experienced: he found himself gazing straight down the enemy's defensive line from only a few dozen yards away! They'd caught the enemy formation entirely by surprise and had completely flanked them. The rare opportunity to roll up the entire enemy column in one attack was now laid out before Nathan, if only he was able to seize it.

He could hear his heart pounding in his ears, and not just from the exertion of the climb. He turned back toward his men, cupped his hands around his mouth, and shouted, "Twelfth West Virginia—*charge!*"

Nathan unholstered his left-hand pistol, raised his saber in his right, and sprinted forward with Tom at his side. Nathan was greeted by the gratifying sight of shocked rebel soldiers turning to behold this new unexpected danger. Some of the rebels scrambled to reposition themselves and face the threat, while others began to pull back.

The Twelfth West Virginia and the other two regiments of Colonel Thoburn's brigade hit the Confederate right flank like a hammer, driving the rebels in toward their center in panicked disarray.

Nathan hacked with his saber and fired the Colt at anyone standing in his path. Off to his right, he noted Zeke had pushed even farther ahead, leading Company D with his Henry rifle, wielding the precious weapon as if it were a club, having apparently already fired off all seventeen rounds in the magazine.

Within moments, the rebels were streaming away, and suddenly Nathan had no one in front of him to fight. He paused and gazed across the battlefield, spotting the rebels' commanding general, Grumble Jones, his dark full beard and grim visage unmistakable even several hundred yards away. Jones was up on his spotted gray horse, shouting and pointing—already rallying his troops, turning the panicked soldiers back around to face their oncoming enemy with the sheer force of his will.

As Thoburn's brigade pushed forward, the rebels' defense stiffened, and the Union attack slowed.

Nathan had a new grudging respect for General Jones. The rebel commander was no shrinking political officer, ready to wilt at the first whiff of danger; the man had backbone and clearly knew how to lead men amidst a desperate battle. But Nathan didn't need to remind himself that Jones was the enemy and needed to be beaten.

And even as Nathan was considering how best to counter the rebels' sudden stiffening, Billy stepped up beside him. Nathan turned and looked at his scout expectantly, sensing he had something he wished to say.

Billy smiled incongruously, and asked a question Nathan found odd, even for his enigmatic Indian scout: "Captain ... would you like to win this battle ... right now?"

Nathan looked at Billy questioningly, wondering if he'd heard rightly through the ongoing cacophony of battle. "What?"

"Would you like to end this battle now, and defeat these rebels?"

"Well ... yes, of course but—"

Billy nodded, chambered a round into his Henry rifle with the lever, trotted off a few yards to the right, and climbed up a section of the abandoned rebel earthworks. He stood still like a statue, ignoring the chaos, gunfire, and smoke swirling around him, aiming his rifle out toward the enemy.

Nathan realized his own mouth was hanging open and snapped it shut. He turned and lifted his spyglass to see what Billy was targeting. He saw General Grumble Jones upon his horse, waving his saber above his head, shouting encouragement to his troops.

Nathan heard the report of Billy's rifle. A second later, Grumble Jones tumbled from the saddle.

Billy trotted back over to Nathan, grinned and said, "Now this battle is over."

Nathan slowly shook his head, then turned to look back out toward the battlefield. The effect on the Confederates of the sudden death of their commanding general was immediate and devastating. The rebels were already turning and fleeing the field en masse. The Union soldiers raced after them.

The rout was on; the battle was won.

❧☙❧☙❧☙❧☙❧☙

C.S.A. Lieutenant Colonel Elijah Walters had watched the Battle of Piedmont through his binoculars from atop his horse. His Thirty-Sixth Virginia Cavalry Battalion had been positioned in the thick wood to the back of the Confederate defensive line. They'd been ordered to stay in reserve until they received further orders from General Jones.

At first, the battle seemed to be going well, despite the odds against them being at least two to one. The rebels were well dug in, and the first two Union attacks had been repulsed with relative ease.

But as time wore on, Walters sensed that their chances were quickly deteriorating. The Union artillery officer was one of the most efficient Walters had yet seen, quickly taking out the Confederate guns one by one, seriously undermining their ability to hold the position.

And then they were hit by the sudden surprise Union attack to their right flank. Walters watched as the line crumpled, and Grumble Jones scrambled to rally the troops. It crossed Walters' mind that if he were a truly dedicated fighting officer, he would order a charge to help General Jones push back the Union soldiers.

But Walters was *not* that type of officer, and had no such pretenses. He was, however, intelligent and resourceful when it came to self-preservation. He quickly realized the battle was already lost, regardless of how heroically Jones fought. So, rather than order an advance, he ordered his battalion to fall back through the forest toward the river. There, they would immediately ford to the other side and escape the doomed battle.

But as he turned his horse to follow his troops back into the forest, he paused, turned toward the battlefield, and took one last look through his binoculars. He panned his view across the advancing Union lines, then suddenly paused and refocused. A tall, dark-haired officer stood upon a rock, gazing across the battlefield with a brass spyglass.

Walters cursed, *"Chambers …"*

ℰℴℛℭℰℬℴℰℴℛℭℰℬℴℰℴℛℭℰ

The evening after the Piedmont battle, the feeling in the camp of the Twelfth West Virginia was as uplifting and joyful as any Nathan could remember, and that feeling was echoed throughout the Union camp. Though the Twelfth had no band, several other regiments did, and raucous, patriotic songs could be heard across the camp, making for a festive, holiday-like atmosphere.

The Twelfth, despite its superior officers and equipment, and excellent training, had suffered a long series of defeats and non-victories through no fault of its own—always outnumbered and outgunned, and often out-generaled: Winchester, Hagerstown, Falling Waters, and finally, New Market. Each a bitter pill, despite courage, skill, and heroism on the part of the men and officers.

But today, everything had changed; today, they'd finally held the advantage in numbers and in guns. And they had made the most of it.

The overwhelming victory had been stunning in its speed and efficiency. Grumble Jones's command had been decimated, with over six hundred killed or wounded and another thousand captured.

On the Union side, though Colonel Moor's brigade had suffered heavy casualties during their two failed frontal assaults,

Colonel Thoburn's brigade, which included the Twelfth, had escaped almost unscathed, for which Nathan said a quick prayer of thanks.

He was especially grateful in that regard, on account of the continued absence of the regiment's head surgeon, William Jenkins. Though William had returned to the regiment after his escape from Libby Prison, he'd made the painful decision to remain behind when the present campaign had commenced.

Nathan recalled the conversation before their departure. William had been distraught, unable to decide between two hard choices: to remain behind and continue treating the Twelfth's seriously wounded from the New Market battle, including Stan, Jim, and Harry the Dog, or to march with the regiment in the upcoming campaign so that he'd be on hand to care for any new casualties.

"I feel more torn than ever in life," William said, slowly shaking his head, his eyes becoming watery. "I fear if I am not here to supervise, Stan and Jim's injuries may fester, and they could die. And I am nearly certain the surgeons will ignore the hound entirely—he most likely would not recover. There are a half dozen more of our men in similar straits.

"But on the other hand, if something were to happen to *you*, sir … or to Tom, or Zeke … and I wasn't there to help you … how could I live with myself after?"

Nathan's heart ached for his friend, knowing the conundrum was beyond William's ability to decide. So he took pity on him, saying, "You must stay here, William. Your duty is to tend to those who are already wounded, not those who may never be. If it helps, consider that an order from your commanding officer."

The look of relief on William's face had been immediate, and his thanks effusive and sincere.

Nathan just prayed it had been the right choice. *So far, so good.*

❧❧❧❧❧❧❧

Colonel Ira Grayson of the C.S.A. Signal Corps, known to his clandestine contacts simply as "Mr. Gray," removed his uniform hat, hanging it on an iron hook on the wall as he entered the rough, stonewalled room in the basement of the Mechanic's Institute building that served as the Confederate War Department offices. The small room, originally meant for cold storage, featured a heavy iron door but no windows. Grayson next removed his fine butternut-colored leather riding gloves and gray uniform tunic, laying them carefully over the back of a simple but sturdy wooden chair sitting near the door.

He then turned toward the prisoner, a dirty, raggedly dressed man of around forty years, with graying hair and beard, who stood against the far wall. Grayson decided that the man looked like he ought to be very uncomfortable, with his shirt stripped off and his hands stretched above his head via a set of shackles that'd been threaded through an iron ring on the wall.

But the fellow seemed surprisingly calm—*considering*—making easy eye contact with Grayson as he approached.

Grayson shrugged and slowly rolled up the sleeves of his shirt as he approached the prisoner. When he was within a few feet, he stopped, still locking eyes with the man. "I am Colonel Grayson of the Confederate Signal Corps."

He lashed out and punched the prisoner hard in the stomach with his left fist, followed immediately by a punch to the face with his right.

The man groaned and grimaced in pain, hanging his head and sagging on his chains. But he said nothing. *Interesting* ... Grayson decided.

But to Grayson's satisfaction, the man no longer had the audacity to look his better in the eye as if they were equals.

Grayson pulled up a second rough chair and sat in front of the dangling prisoner.

"Now ... I have properly introduced *myself,* but you have me at a disadvantage, sir, as I don't yet know *your* name ..."

The man nodded, "Name's Joseph, Your Honor ..." he answered.

"And do you have a surname, Joseph?"

"Yes, Your Honor ... *Smith* ... Joseph Smith."

"Hmm ... not your *real* name, I'll wager. But ... no matter ... you'll soon be begging me to allow you to spew out everything you know. So, if you're comfortable," Grayson grinned, "shall we begin? First, I wish to know the names of the people you report to ... especially the name of one nefarious traitor commonly referred to as ... *the Employer* ..."

※✿❧☙※✿❧☙※✿❧

At the end of a very long day, with only a short break for Grayson to eat his lunch while the guards splashed cold water on the prisoner to shock him back to consciousness, the colonel had to admit defeat ... for the moment. Grayson was growing tired, and hungry, and his knuckles were feeling sore from punching the man, not to mention his legs, which were becoming weary from all the kicking the job had required. The old wound in his leg ached painfully from the exertion, and likely his usual limp would be worse come the morrow. He decided he'd have to use less strenuous but more painful methods going forward.

Despite the punishment, the prisoner had stubbornly insisted he was only a poor vagrant, who'd been hanging around the Confederate Army defensive lines south of Petersburg only for the purpose of begging food from the soldiers. He adamantly insisted he was no spy, and that he had no use for "them devil Yankees."

But Grayson was certain the man was lying. For one, the fellow looked a little too well fed to be a real street beggar; even folks who earned an honest wage in Richmond were no longer able to purchase their normal rations and were taking on a decidedly lean appearance.

And for another, a real beggar wouldn't have stood up to the abuse this fellow had received for hours on end, without crying, screaming, or begging for mercy. Any self-respecting vagrant would've long since made up any number of lies and made all sorts of promises to try to placate his tormentor. But not *this* fellow.

"Well, Mr. *Smith* ... I'm afraid our little ... *conversation* ... has come to an end for the evening, as it's time for dinner. Oh ... not *yours,* I'm afraid ... only mine. Yes, I expect to have a fine meal: ham, sweet potatoes, beans ... and likely something sweet for dessert. Washed down with a fine snifter of cognac, I should think.

"You, on the other hand, will enjoy a nice quiet evening, scratching at lice, fending off rats, and otherwise *starving* with your Yankee comrades ... in Libby Prison.

"But have no fear, we'll resume our little talk first thing tomorrow. I have faith that I can come up with some new and even more persuasive arguments to bring you around to my way of thinking, come the morning. And I trust a night spent in Richmond's finest accommodation will put you in a humor to be more ... *forthcoming,* shall we say?"

Grayson smirked, but if Smith had any thoughts on the matter, he kept them to himself, hanging his head, though his blinking eyes showed he was still conscious.

৪৩৯৫৫৯৫৬৪৩৯৫৫৯৫৬৪৩৯৫৫৬

"Come, Margaret—they've arrived, and the surgeons need all the help they can get," head Matron Phoebe Pember called out as she poked her head in the door to the hospital ward, one of more than forty converted army barracks housing patients at Chimborazo Military Hospital in Richmond.

Margaret looked up at the young soldier and smiled. "Sorry, Billy, duty calls. I shall return and finish writing your letter when I may."

The young private, who'd lost an eye and his right arm just above the elbow, managed a grin and a nod. "That'd be just fine, Miss Margaret. Much obliged." She returned the smile, then set the pen and paper aside, stood, and stepped outside.

She'd been volunteering as a nurse at the hospital for more than a week now after telling Phoebe that she wished to help out as repayment for the kindness of the nurses during her own recent convalescence from an accidental gunshot wound. At first, she'd felt uncomfortable being around the deathly ill, and especially the horribly maimed and suffering. But by now, she'd become more accustomed to it.

And fortunately, up to this point they'd not asked her to do anything too demanding in that regard; her duties had mostly consisted of serving out medicines, meals, and water to the patients and emptying out bed pans. She also spent a lot of her time providing the men with the common comforts of writing letters to their loved ones, or reading aloud newspapers or books, or just sitting and talking. Occasionally, one of the men would ask for a song, and though she had no special talent nor great confidence in her own singing voice, she did her best, for which they always seemed grateful.

It never failed to amaze her how polite and respectful these young, rough, crude fighting men were, despite everything they'd been through. Even in the dark of night, surrounded by more than forty soldiers in a ward, she never felt the least bit threatened or uncomfortable. And she could feel the warmth of the soldiers' gratitude for her services almost as a tangible thing.

So now as she strode across the hospital grounds toward where the ambulances would be arriving, she felt confident she was ready to start doing her part as a *real* nurse, aiding the surgeons working on the wounded. And then … she discovered that she wasn't.

As Margaret turned the corner of the last of a long line of ward buildings, a sight of absolute horror met her eyes. Men were being unloaded from dozens of wagons, packed to overflowing with the wounded. Blood was dripping out from the floorboards onto the dirt, making dark puddles beneath the wheels.

The wounded were being lifted from the wagons by the hospital's soldiers. She saw one man dropped when the soldier tried to lift him by the arm, and the arm came completely detached just below the shoulder, spewing blood all over the soldier. Another man was pulled out but had no legs for the soldier to hang onto, so two men had to grip the tail of the man's shirt to carry him.

And the moaning and screaming of the horribly maimed men was so heartrending that Margaret felt tears streaming down her cheeks and bile burning the back of her throat.

The wounded were being laid out on the ground where the surgeons were examining them in what had come to be known — crudely, in Margaret's view — as a "triage," separating them into those who could most benefit from immediate treatment, the highest priority; to those who could wait for treatment, the lesser priority; and then to those who were dying or already dead, who would likely receive no treatment at all.

The nurses were rushing to and fro, applying bandages where needed and then directing the soldiers to lift the wounded onto stretchers and move them to the appropriate places as directed by the surgeons.

Margaret felt light-headed like she was going to faint, and she had to move to one side, leaning over, hands on her knees, trying to catch her breath. And then she suddenly felt sick, and to her horror, could not keep from vomiting right there on the ground.

One of the nurses called out, "Just sit down a spell, dear. There's no shame in it. Happens to everyone at first."

Margaret didn't even look her way, but nodded, and sat down right on the grass, careful to avoid the mess she'd just made. She pulled her knees up under her chin and tucked in her face. But shortly after, she had to cover her ears to shut out the cries and screams of the patients.

※☆☆☆☆☆☆☆☆☆☆☆

Joseph watched through half-lidded eyes as Grayson moved to the door, pulled it open, and leaned out into the hallway, "Has the detail from Libby arrived yet? Ah ... good; send them in."

The colonel stepped back into the cell, wiped his hands on a bloody rag he kept on a small table in one corner, then donned his tunic and hat and tucked his gloves into the uniform pocket.

After a few moments, a Confederate captain stepped into the room and saluted the colonel, who returned it half-heartedly. The captain was accompanied by two privates with rifles on their shoulders.

"Captain Bob Hill from Libby Prison, Colonel," the officer announced.

"Captain Hill, you will accompany this prisoner to Libby, where you will place him in one of your solitary cells—those down in the basement, as I recall. Give him no food, nor any other comforts, though he should have water … I do need him alive, for now."

Captain Hill turned and looked at Joseph, then frowned. Joseph immediately looked down at the floor, not daring to risk angering another short-tempered Confederate officer.

"Just have him back here in good order at morning's first light, if you would, Captain."

"Begging the colonel's pardon," the captain began hesitantly, "but … the fellow seems in no condition to walk the dozen or so blocks back down to the prison, and I wasn't told to bring an ambulance … why not just leave him here, sir? This cell seems perfectly adequate."

"I would do just that, Captain, and save us all the bother. But," he shrugged, "our commanding officer apparently doesn't wish to use his tight budget employing guards for overnight *guests*. So we're not allowed to house them."

"Ah … I see …"

"Never fear, Captain, he's not suffering any broken bones—at least not any that will prevent him walking. And I'm sure your privates can prod him along with their bayonets as necessary." The colonel turned and graced Joseph with an evil leer as he placed the key to the shackles in the captain's hand.

"Very good, sir," the captain saluted again as the colonel turned and departed.

Joseph closed his eyes and steeled himself for the pain he knew was coming the moment they released the shackles from their ring and he was forced to bear his own weight. A few moments of the guards fumbling with the keys in the lock, and then he was free, slumping to the ground with a gasp, enduring a shocking wave of anguish that nearly made him lose consciousness.

But then, to his surprise, the guard captain held a canteen of water to his lips. Joseph looked up at the man and nodded in appreciation before taking a sip.

The captain frowned, then shrugged and said, "He did say you could have water …"

The privates then came and helped him to his feet.

"Can you walk?" the captain asked. "It'll be easier on all of us, you included, if you can make it on your own two feet."

Joseph tried a couple of slow steps, then nodded.

"Good … Then let's go. I'd prefer we were back at the prison before it gets too late and we're all stumbling about in the dark."

ಬಿಂಚಿ ಅಂಚಿ ಬಿಂಚಿ ಬಿಂಚಿ ಅಂಚಿ ಬಿಂಚಿ ಬಿಂಚಿ ಅಂಚಿ

Captain Bob Hill felt a knot of disgust in his stomach; that his present duty as captain of the guard at Libby forced him to participate in such inhumane abuse of prisoners sickened him. He'd left Elijah Walters's employ and joined the army in the first place as a sort of penance to restore his guilty conscience from all the evil he'd done on behalf of his old master.

And now … after all the hard fighting and self-sacrifice he'd endured as a member of the Stonewall Brigade … he was stuck back in a job that required him to participate in the most despicable treatment of fellow human beings imaginable. Starvings, beatings, entirely unnecessary deaths due to simple lack of medicines … and now this intentional, prolonged torture. *Despicable and unconscionable.*

He sighed heavily at the thought as he walked at a slow but steady pace down Capitol Hill on the sidewalk alongside Ninth Street.

The prisoner shuffled along directly behind him, coughing and gasping in pain every few steps. Bob grimaced at the sound, assuming it meant the unfortunate fellow had suffered broken ribs during his beating. At one point, Bob heard the prisoner stumble, and turned around just in time to catch him before he hit the ground.

The man grunted in pain as Bob eased him slowly to the ground, then offered him another drink from his canteen.

20

After taking several swallows, and a moment to catch his breath, the prisoner looked up at Bob and nodded. "Thank you, Captain," he said in a croaking voice.

"Come ... I will help you up, but we must keep moving," Bob ordered. Then he waved to one of the privates to come assist, and in a moment, they had the man back on his feet.

As they continued once more down the street, Bob debated with himself whether or not to file an official complaint against the Signal Corps colonel for his illegal and immoral treatment of this prisoner. On the one hand, Bob knew it would do no good — none of his previous reports had, after all. They'd only served to get him in hot water with his superiors. On the other hand, it was the *right* thing to do, and might help ease his conscience ... somewhat.

He even briefly considered setting the fellow free. But he immediately discarded the notion. The privates would likely resist the order, and even if they complied, would immediately report it upon arrival back at the prison. Then the poor fellow would likely be recaptured in short order, and all that would've been accomplished was for Bob to join the fellow in the rat hell of Libby's dungeon ... *though I would have a clear conscience.*

The sun had already set, and shadows were darkening in the doorways and alleyways they passed. Street traffic was beginning to thin out, and pedestrians were few and scattered. Bob had to resist the urge to walk faster, knowing it would only add more suffering to the poor soul he escorted.

They reached Carey Street and turned left, continuing on toward the prison. They'd passed Tenth Street and were halfway down the block, approaching the alleyway on their left that led back up the hill toward American Hotel on Main Street, when a group of six men stepped out of the alleyway. And if there were any doubts about the intentions of these men, they were quickly resolved by the bandanas on their faces and the pistols gripped in their fists.

The newcomers surrounded Bob, his prisoner, and the two privates. They'd appeared so suddenly and unexpectedly that

21

Bob hadn't even thought to unholster his revolver, and the two privates never had a chance to unshoulder their rifles.

Bob raised his hands slowly as a man of medium height stepped up to him, aiming a revolver at his midsection. The man reached forward, unbuttoned Bob's holster, and snatched out the gun.

The other men grabbed the rifles from the privates, who immediately followed their captain's lead, raising their hands in surrender.

"You would rob armed soldiers right on the street in Richmond ... just blocks from the War Department?" Bob asked, more out of incredulity than anger. "That's either very bold, or very desperate. Or perhaps both..."

Despite the bandana around the lower half of his face, Bob could see that the man in front of him held a dark frown, and his face was turning red.

"This is no robbery," the man growled. "And for what you've done to our man ... I ought to shoot y'all down right here, like the spineless dogs you are!" And though he spoke in anger, his voice betrayed him as an upper-class Virginian—clearly *not* a street thief, to Bob's surprise. To emphasize his intentions, the man raised his pistol, aimed it right a Bob's face, and pulled back the hammer.

"*Peace!*" a hoarse voice called out, and the prisoner shambled out to stand between Bob and his assailant. "This officer has done me no harm. In fact, he has treated me kindly, under the circumstances. So, please ... lower your weapon, my good sir."

The man in the mask continued to glare, but Bob could see that his features had softened. "Very well," he finally said, then he lowered the pistol and uncocked it.

The prisoner turned to Bob, "Now, Captain, as thanks for your compassion, I would offer you a deal—" But before he could continue, he coughed, doubling over as if in great pain.

After a moment, he straightened back up and continued, "If you will turn and face the other way, then give your word, as an officer and a gentleman, to count to one thousand before turning back around, we will leave your weapons down the street. There you may retrieve them once we're gone."

Bob considered this proposal for only an instant—for a soldier, losing one's weapons, especially to civilians, was a disgrace that no veteran wished to endure. But Bob also had his own reasons for consenting...

"Agreed. On my word of honor, we will turn away and I will count to one thousand before turning back around or moving from this spot."

"Very good, Captain. In that case, I shall bid you farewell."

The three Confederate soldiers turned their backs to their assailants, and Bob started counting.

"One, two, three, four, five—"

"Slower, Captain ... if you please..."

"... six ... seven ...eight..."

"Much better, thank you..."

Bob continued counting for several minutes, with the two privates standing next to him. All three were still holding their hands in the air when a civilian—an older gentleman in a fine suit—stepped up to address Bob. "Captain ... those men who accosted you ... they are gone, sir. Fled up the alleyway. You needn't count any longer."

"Five hundred, sixty-five ... five hundred, sixty-six ..." Bob shook his head and continued counting.

"Did you hear what I said, Captain?" the man held a puzzled expression.

Bob paused in his counting, "Yes, my good man, and I appreciate you pointing it out. But ... I gave my word of honor as an officer and a gentleman that I would count to one thousand before turning around, and I mean to keep my word."

He did, however, lower his hands so he'd be more comfortable while he counted, and he ordered the privates to stand at ease until he finished.

"Five hundred, sixty-seven ... five hundred, sixty-eight..."

As the civilian turned to depart, shaking his head and muttering to himself, Bob couldn't suppress a slight grin; the entire incident had worked out perfectly, to his way of thinking—

the prisoner would no longer be abused by the despicable Signal Corp colonel, and Bob would not have to file a complaint, nor suffer a guilty conscience. And he could hardly be blamed for the incident as nobody had warned him to expect an attempted rescue of the man—if they had, he would've brought more men, and had them walk dispersed with weapons in hand. *Yep, all in all, I'd say that worked out very well indeed,* he decided.

ഇരുട്ടുഇരുട്ടുഇരുട്ടു

Joseph's rescuers escorted him up the alleyway toward the American Hotel. He moved as quickly as he could manage, but his legs had been battered and bruised, and his cracked ribs stabbed painfully anytime he breathed too deeply.

Fortunately, the men leading him were sympathetic, and if they were anxious to hurry him along, they resisted saying so, for which he was grateful.

When they neared the stables at the back of the hotel, he could see a dark, shiny carriage waiting. The curtains on the windows were drawn, but he thought he saw someone peeking out, though in the fading light he could not make out a face.

The leader of the rescue party trotted up to the carriage and opened the door, gesturing for Joseph to enter. When he shuffled up to the step and hesitated, the man reached out and took his arm, helping to lift him up onto the step and into the carriage.

Joseph was not surprised when the leader hopped up into the carriage and sat opposite him while the other men hid their pistols under their coats, removed their masks, and strolled away casually, each in a different direction.

He was also not surprised when the man removed his mask to reveal he was Jonathan Hughes, *the Employer* himself. Though Jonathan rarely participated in this type of operation, Joseph had recognized his voice when he'd spoken with the guard captain earlier.

Joseph *was* surprised, however, by who was awaiting him in the carriage: Evelyn reached across from her seat and embraced him gently before leaning back, gazing at his battered face and scowling, even as the carriage lurched forward and sped off down the street.

"Hello, Evelyn. Nice of you to arrange a ride home for me..." he said, but when he started to chuckle, a stabbing pain made him double over and cough instead.

"Oh, Joseph ... you poor dear. Look what they've done to you. The monsters!" She shook her head slowly, continuing to frown. She pulled out a handkerchief and dabbed at his bleeding nose and lips. He resisted the urge to flinch at the additional pain her well-meant ministrations were inflicting.

"But you're safe now. Angeline has a bed prepared for you, and a physician standing by to tend to your wounds. And I'm sure Margaret will volunteer to serve as your nurse, should you need one."

"Margaret?" Joseph managed before stifling another cough, "She's barely healed herself. What does she know about nursing?"

"Oh, didn't you know? She's been feeling well enough to volunteer at Chimborazo Military Hospital, as a way to pay back Phoebe Pember for regularly sending nurses to the house during her convalescence. Margaret is so intelligent and capable ... if I know her, by now she's probably the best nurse they have."

"Hmm ... you two make quite the pair in that regard. But I'm sure I won't be needing any nursi—" Joseph's sentence was cut off by a sudden, excruciating bout of coughing. "All right ... maybe a *little* nursing," he managed to choke out with a wan smile.

"Anyway, you can rest and recover at Angeline's house until you're feeling better. And then ... no more spying for *you*, sir!"

But now it was Joseph's turn to scowl, "*No*, my dear lady ... though I can no longer count on my vagabond disguise, I have many others I can use."

"But Joseph, be reasonable. Clearly, you've been badly injured—you could've been killed."

"Yes, true ... All the more reason to continue." He coughed again, then gave her a dark look. "Besides ... now they've made it *personal* ... now I'm going to do whatever it takes to bring them down. And … as soon as I'm feeling well again, I am going to personally murder that son of a bitch Signal Corps colonel who beat me—if it's the last thing I do."

Jonathan grinned at this statement and gave Evelyn a questioning look. The two of them had often debated the merits of assassinating enemy officials, a notion Evelyn had always firmly resisted.

She gazed at the Employer for a moment, then nodded and turned to Joseph, "For once, I agree. After what that vile man has done to you … I'll even help."

ՏՕՇՇՅՕՏՕՇՇՅՕՏՕՇՇՅ

Pull yourself together, Margaret … You've dealt with horrible things before … Walters beating slaves … Henry strangling that soldier … Phinney losing his arm … you can do this.

Through force of will, Margaret raised her head and gazed back at the bloody, chaotic scene in front of her. But she saw it was now beginning to show some semblance of order; pairs of soldiers with stretchers held between them trotted off to the surgery wards as the nurses ministered to those still laid out on the grass in neat rows. Margaret saw men off to one side who were not neatly laid out but appeared to have been dumped somewhat haphazardly: the dead, she realized. She quickly looked away.

After a few moments, she noticed a large group of wounded soldiers laid out by themselves. At first, she thought that these must be more dead men, as no nurses or surgeons seemed to be paying them any mind. But then she noticed several were moving, and that these soldiers wore blue uniforms!

The realization that there were Union soldiers here also, and that they were not yet being tended, prodded her into action. She rose and walked over to where the Union wounded men lay.

As she approached, one of the men reached out toward her, "Water … please …" he pleaded, in a voice that was weak and raspy.

"Oh … oh, dear. Yes, of course," she turned and raced to the well, grabbing a bucket that was already filled along with a water dipper sitting next to it. She hefted the heavy load and moved as

26

quickly as she could without sloshing the water out. It felt awkward, and she realized her genteel, city upbringing had ill-prepared her for such tasks. But she managed it, and was soon moving among the Union men, holding up their heads and doling out desperately needed swallows of water with the dipper. When she'd made the rounds to all thirty or so soldiers, she went looking for bandages.

She approached one of the nurses, and asked, "Where are you getting the bandages?" The nurse glanced at her for a moment, then pointed over to a table that'd been set up outside one of the hospital ward buildings. She approached the table, and the nurse looked up at her.

"Bandages, please?"

The nurse reached under the table and pulled out a stack of clean, neatly cut pieces of cloth. Margaret grabbed the pile and raced back to the Union soldiers, and went down the line, applying the cloth as best she could to the horrific wounds she encountered. She suppressed a shudder when she noticed that one of the soldiers she'd given water to only moments before had died in the time it took her to fetch the bandages. She looked back toward the other groups of men, and noted the surgeons seemed to have completed their examinations, and most were now gone, having headed off to the surgical wards to perform whatever amputations and other procedures might be necessary to save the lives of the incoming patients.

But none seemed interested in looking at the Union soldiers. Margaret could feel an anger building up inside herself, and she trotted over to the nearest surgeon, who seemed to be having a casual conversation with one of the nurses.

Margaret stepped up in front of him, "Excuse me, sir."

He looked over at her, "Yes, nurse, what is it?"

"There are men over there who've received no treatment whatever, and ... you are a surgeon ... Will you not tend to them?"

He looked over where she pointed, and shrugged, "Damned Yankees ... We'll get to them as time allows. Or not."

Margaret put her hands on her hips and scowled, "You should be ashamed of yourself! You call yourself a doctor? A man who has sworn a sacred oath to aid those in need? How *dare* you, sir!"

The surgeon frowned at her, "You are out of line, nurse. You have no right to speak to me in such a saucy manner. I'll do as I see fit, and if I choose not to treat these murderous Yankee villains, then so be it!"

Margaret was trying to think of a truly biting, vile insult to hurl back when a commanding voice said, "No!"

Margaret, the surgeon, and the nurse he'd been talking with looked up and saw a man striding toward them. Margaret recognized the newcomer as Surgeon-in-Chief Dr. James McCaw. Though she'd never spoken with him, she'd seen him often at various places around the hospital grounds, and he had a reputation as an excellent doctor, and an extremely competent administrator.

"*No*, doctor, the nurse is right," McCaw said, then turned to Margaret, and asked, "Miss...?"

"Margaret, sir. Margaret Chambers."

"Miss Margaret is *right*. You *will* treat the Union wounded, same as our men. We are doctors, and they are fellow human beings in need of our services. Our Hippocratic Oath requires us to render aid, regardless of government affiliation. They will be triaged and operated upon to the best of our abilities. Is that clear, doctor?"

"Yes, sir. But the surgical wards are overwhelmed, and the convalescent wards are overflowing ..."

Dr. McCaw was thoughtful a moment, then nodded, "They will have to wait until our soldiers are treated first ... but not one moment later. And we can put them in the Sibley tents after. For now, do what you can for them. You too, nurse."

McCaw then turned and ordered the other nurses to start tending the Union wounded. Finally, he turned back to Margaret, and nodded, "That was admirably done, Miss Margaret. I thank you."

Though she still felt sick and shaky, and was beginning to feel utterly drained by the event, she managed a smile, "Thank you, Doctor McCaw."

CHAPTER 2. TAINTED VICTORY

*"Disappointment is the gap
that exists between
expectation and reality."*
- John C. Maxwell

Monday June 6, 1864 – Staunton, Virginia:

The day after the Piedmont victory, Nathan was surprised when General Hunter ordered the army to turn west and occupy the town of Staunton, which had been abandoned by the rebel commander after having heard of the Confederates' devastating defeat the previous day.

Nathan had assumed the army would move southward, pursuing the shattered remnants of the late Grumble Jones's rebel army, now under the command of Brigadier General John Vaughn, then continue toward the campaign's immediate objective of capturing Lynchburg, Virginia. Capturing Lynchburg would cut the rebels' critical rail line supplying Lee's army at Richmond via North Carolina.

Several other officers Nathan talked with were feeling the same confusion. There was speculation Hunter had sidetracked in order to wait for reinforcements, a column of 12,000 infantry and cavalry, expected to arrive at any moment and led by General George Crook, with General William Averell in command of the cavalry. But no one knew for sure why Hunter had decided upon his present westward course.

As expected, the rebels offered no resistance, and the army marched into town in parade formation, regimental bands playing. After reassuring a delegation of local residents that he would not burn down their town—though he couldn't guarantee the behavior of individual unruly soldiers—Hunter proceeded to free all prisoners from the local jails, including a few who claimed to be Union soldiers.

The next day, rather than advancing toward Lynchburg, Hunter remained in Staunton and ordered the destruction of all of the town's Confederate military installations, equipment, and transportation facilities, including the train depot. Though the delay made him uneasy, Nathan thought the destruction of rebel materiel prudent, and in keeping with the generally accepted practices of waging warfare in enemy territory.

But Hunter went on to order the burning of the jail, a woolens factory, stables, a steam mill, wagon shops, and various storehouses. There was also widespread looting by Union soldiers, which had not been ordered nor sanctioned by the commanding general, but which was nearly impossible to prevent.

Though he wasn't enthused with what he considered excessive and wasteful destruction, Nathan shrugged it off. After all, anything material could potentially provide aid and succor to the enemy, so depriving him of it could be helpful, one might argue.

But Nathan's opinion was about to change…

ℬ)ℭ℞ℭℱℬ℧ℬ)ℭ℞ℭℱℬ℧ℬ)ℭ℞ℭℱ

Tuesday June 7, 1864 – Staunton, Virginia:

Billy stopped in his tracks and knelt to the ground, listening intently for the sound that had caught his attention. Even as he quieted his breathing and concentrated on all the subtle sounds in the woods around him, he reached down and silently drew his Colt revolver from its holster at his right hip.

He heard the sound again, then let out his breath, re-holstering the pistol and standing up. To his relief, the sound had not come from a rebel picket or scout quietly preparing to put a bullet through his head, but rather from the flapping of a bird's wings. He turned toward the sound and listened again. A few seconds later, it repeated—not the normal sound of a bird in flight, but rather the frantic flapping of a creature in distress.

Curious, he moved in the direction of the sound, hoping it might be a wounded chicken, or perhaps even a pheasant, which would make a nice meal and pleasant change from the usual bland army rations. He came to a place where the thick woods gave way to a wide pasture of waist-high grass, which was already midway through the process of transforming from the bright green of spring to the ripe golden brown of summer.

As he stepped cautiously into the open field, allowing his eyes a moment to adjust to the brighter light, he spied the object of his search. A few dozen yards away, a three-strand wire fence line stretched between rough-hewn wooden posts. Dangling upside down by one of its legs tangled in the wire was a very large bird.

But as he stepped forward, he realized, to his disappointment, that this was no chicken, nor any game bird. It was a red-tailed hawk. He knew from experience the meat of such a bird would be tough, stringy, and gamey. Only in the direst state of starvation would he attempt to eat such undesirable meat. And today, he did not feel that sort of hunger.

He stepped up to the bird and examined it more closely. He decided this hawk was a female of the species, though that would not have been obvious to the untrained eye, the plumage of the two genders being identical. But the females were significantly larger than the males, and this was an especially large specimen.

Slipping his hunting knife from his belt, he intended to quickly put an end to her suffering. He could see the hawk was exhausted, and nearly spent; the twisted wire bit into her leg mercilessly, and blood oozed out around it.

He knelt down, and gently turned the creature so she was facing him, thinking to either cut her throat, or finish her with a quick thrust to the heart. But as he turned the bird, he was met with her stern gaze. Something about her eyes made him pause … He found himself impressed by the ferocity and defiance he saw there—a look he could relate to. Then the hawk squawked at him and again thrashed her wings, never losing eye contact.

Billy switched his attention to the hawk's wings, and after a few moments' examination, concluded they were most likely not damaged and that the creature might fly again, if only she were free of the wire.

So he re-sheathed his knife, turned the bird around and secured her wings, then began untangling the wire. In a few moments, her leg was free, and he was able to gently set the bird on the ground, still holding her wings in place. He let the bird loose and stepped away, moving parallel to the fence so the hawk would feel free to fly in a direction that would not send her immediately back into the wire.

The bird looked at him again with the same stern, hard eyes, then turned, flapped her wings, and ... *nothing*. The hawk simply could not get off the ground. After several flaps, she paused, then made one last attempt, but to no avail. She lay with her chest to the ground, wings spread wide, gasping for breath.

Billy stepped around in front of her, knelt down, and again looked in her eyes. He sighed, "How long have you been hanging there, fierce little one? Dying of thirst by now I expect ... and likely starving too." He slowly shook his head, "What am I going to do with you?"

And then he shrugged, and silently answered his own question. He had already decided he couldn't bring himself to kill such a fierce, defiant warrior in such a pitiable state of helpless need. And he knew if he left her here, she would either slowly die of hunger and thirst, or fall prey to the next predator that came along. So he reached down, once again secured her wings, then lifted her from the ground, setting her taloned feet on his left arm while wrapping his right arm around her wings. She looked at him again, but this time he thought he detected a softening of her gaze, and perhaps a hint of curiosity. *Or maybe I'm just making too much of it?* he wondered.

Billy trotted back into the woods, then turned in the direction from which he'd come, back toward the camp of the Twelfth just outside the town of Staunton. Fortunately, there'd been no sign of the enemy for days, despite a wide screen of pickets and cavalry patrols. And General Hunter seemed disinclined to be in any hurry to march, being more interested in burning and destroying Confederate infrastructure, equipment, and property in and around the town. So Billy's outing had been more for the sake of finding something to do rather than any military necessity.

Nobody would know or care if he came back to camp early with his odd new companion.

ℬ𝒟𝒞𝒮𝒞𝒯ℬ𝒰ℬ𝒟𝒞𝒮𝒞𝒯ℬ𝒰ℬ𝒟𝒞𝒮𝒞𝒯

Since Billy only used a tent in the most severe weather, preferring to sleep outdoors, typically in a different location each night, the men of his scout company were surprised and amused when he ordered several of the privates to erect a tent for him.

And if they were curious about the hawk he now held perched on his arm, nobody asked. Though the men respected Billy's unmatched skills at scouting, skirmishing, and fighting, he had a reputation for odd behavior and an unusual sense of humor. To his men, the hawk was just another of his peculiarities—likely some sort of Indian tradition, which the white soldiers could not fathom.

When the tent was in place, no one was surprised that Billy placed the hawk inside, gave orders that no one disturb it, then walked away.

ℬ𝒟𝒞𝒮𝒞𝒯ℬ𝒰ℬ𝒟𝒞𝒮𝒞𝒯ℬ𝒰ℬ𝒟𝒞𝒮𝒞𝒯

Billy returned a few minutes later with a handful of raw meat; scraps from the evening's meal preparation.

But if he'd expected the hawk to attack the meat with the enthusiasm of a famished soldier, he was quickly disappointed.

When he'd first put the hawk inside the tent, he'd attempted to give her some water in a small bowl. But despite her obvious need, she seemed strangely disinterested. Then he remembered his grandfather telling him once that such birds preferred to get their water from the prey they ate, rather than drinking from a pond or stream. So he'd gone in search of meat.

But now she also seemed unwilling or unable to eat the meat. She poked at it for a few moments with her beak, then turned away. He knew from hard experience that sometimes starving men were entirely unable to eat, their stomachs having been deprived for so long that they were cramped up such that nothing could be kept down. So, after a few moments, he stepped forward, grasped her head, pried open her beak, and shoved a small chunk

34

of meat down her throat with his finger. She swallowed with a gulp, then glared up at him angrily. But he shrugged. "You may not like it, but it will keep you alive," he answered her unspoken reproach.

He repeated the action several more times, until he decided she'd likely had enough for the moment. *Don't want to overdo it,* he thought, remembering how starving men had been known to die suddenly from ingesting too much food all at once. He wondered about that, and decided he'd have to ask William about it, if and when they ever saw him again.

Billy sat cross-legged on the dirt floor of the tent, watching until the hawk's eyelids flickered several times and she appeared to drift off to sleep. Then he rose and silently slipped out of the tent, heading off to procure his own evening meal.

The next morning, Billy returned to the tent after breakfast, again having obtained a few scraps of raw meat from the cooks. Though the hawk still seemed drowsy and lethargic, this time when he picked her up on his arm and offered her meat, she accepted it, and swallowed the chunks on her own.

He took it for a good sign. "A few more days of this, and you will be as good as new, fierce one," he told her as he turned toward the tent flap. This time, he was certain that her previously fierce glare had softened to one of curiosity. She now tilted her head when he spoke to her, as if trying to fathom the meaning of the sounds.

That evening, when Billy returned to the tent thinking to repeat the successful feeding from the morning, things did not go as planned. As he entered the tent, he immediately noticed she looked more upright and energetic. And based on the large, white droppings scattered around the floor of the tent, he could tell she'd been moving around a lot more.

He bent down and scooped her up on his left arm even as he'd done that morning, meaning to once again feed her. But the moment he stood, he gasped, suffering a sharp, agonizing pain in his left arm, as if someone had stabbed him with multiple knives all at once.

He flinched his arm back, his mind in confusion, not grasping what was happening. But as he pulled his arm away, the hawk came with it, and the pain became ever more intense, as if the knives had now struck bone.

Billy fought against the instinct to pull away, absorbing the sudden realization that moving away would only make the pain worse. He also resisted the urge to lash out, to strike down his attacker, anything to make the pain go away. After going to all the effort of rescuing and reviving the bird, the last thing he wanted to do was injure or kill it.

Then, as he often did when in great agony, he recalled his grandfather's training—embracing the pain rather than fighting it, calming his mind, and thinking of a solution. He took a deep breath, then stepped forward, pushing the hawk back toward the wall of the tent. When the bird's back hit the canvas, he continued to push, forcing the creature's talons up against her own breast. This simple maneuver weakened her grasp, allowing him to extract his arm. The hawk flapped her wings, landing softly on the floor of the tent, gazing up at him, the fierce glare having returned.

Billy resisted the very natural urge to rub his aching, wounded arm, refusing to show pain in front of an adversary, even this small non-human one. And he felt no anger toward the creature; she'd only given in to her natural instincts—her inborn fear of men overwhelming any benevolent feelings she might've been experiencing due to his kindly treatment.

He looked at her another moment, shrugged his shoulders, and said, "Well ... seems like you are well now. Time to go."

He stepped back, opened the tent flap, and stood to the side, allowing the bird an open portal to the outside.

The bird gazed out at the opening, but then seemed to hesitate for a moment, once more looking over at Billy. Then with a great beat of her wings she was up off the ground and sailing out the door.

And despite the throbbing pain in his left arm, and the blood dripping off it from multiple punctures, Billy smiled, nodded, and headed out of the tent.

When Billy arrived at camp the next morning, all was astir, with tents being dismantled and gear being stowed into the supply wagons. Word had come down during the night that they were moving out in a few hours. This didn't surprise Billy; he'd spoken with the Captain the previous day, and Nathan had been certain a new march toward Lynchburg was imminent.

But Billy *was* surprised when one of the privates stepped up to him and said, "Sergeant Creek, sir … what do you want us to do about your tent?"

Billy was confused, and answered, "Why not break it down and pack it into one of the wagons with all the others?"

"But what about your bird, sir?"

"Oh, *that* … the hawk is already gone, Private. You needn't concern yourself about that anymore."

But the private tipped back his hat and scratched at his scalp thoughtfully, "Well, sir … not to contradict a superior officer or anything, but … there's a large bird sitting on the top of your tent even now … look for yourself, sir."

Billy turned and looked across the camp to where his tent stood. Sure enough, a great bird sat perched on the very peak of the roof, preening its feathers.

"Oh," Billy said, then moved off toward the tent, not bothering to answer the private's original question.

As he stepped up to the tent, he saw the hawk watching him. He came to a stop in front of the tent, still gazing up at her. "Thought you were done with me," he said.

Then to his shock, in answer, the bird launched herself toward him. He instinctively held up his now-bandaged left arm to fend off her attack. But when she reached his arm she alighted there, and this time she did not dig in her talons, only clutching his arm hard enough to maintain her perch.

He slowly lowered his arm, and the two once again stared into each other's eyes, this time only inches apart. For a moment, Billy was perplexed, and couldn't think of why she would come back now that she could fly again. But then something in her look answered his question; he realized she once again appeared to be tired and weak. It occurred to him that she had still not been fully recovered when she'd left the day before. And likely, with a large army roaming about the countryside, harvesting every squirrel, rabbit, and game bird in sight while frightening the rest into hiding, the hawk had had a very difficult time finding a meal.

"You're hungry again," Billy said, and once again she gave him the curious look he'd seen once before when he'd spoken to her. "All right. Let's go see if there are any scraps left for you to eat."

Moments later, the hawk was gulping down small pieces of burned meat and strips of gristle that'd been tossed aside from breakfast, while still perched on Billy's arm. An amazed cook stood by, mouth agape, watching the strange, unexpected spectacle.

The cook's shocked look triggered a thought in Billy, and when the bird had finished her meal, he immediately went to seek out the Captain.

As Billy approached the regimental command tent, Tom Clark stepped out on his way to perform some unknown duty. When he saw Billy he smiled and said, "Ah ... good morning, Billy. What've you got there? A new pet?"

But Billy just shrugged and said, "Yes ... maybe. Is the Captain in?"

"Yes ... finishing up some paperwork before we move out. I'm sure he'll appreciate an interruption, if you have a mind."

Billy nodded, but hesitated. "Sergeant Clark," he said, using Tom's old Texas rank, as was his habit. "Would you be willing to ask the Captain to step outside? I'm afraid *she* may not wish to enter the tent..."

Tom looked at Billy, then over at the bird on his arm, "Oh! Oh, yes, of course. Just a moment..."

Tom ducked back into the tent, and a moment later Colonel Chambers stepped out, with Tom right behind him. "Billy, Tom says you wanted to see me ... Oh! What's that you've got, Billy?"

"She's a red-tailed hawk, Captain."

"Well, yes, I can see that, Billy, but … why is she sitting on your arm? And why is your arm bandaged? Have you been wounded?"

Billy tilted his head to one side as if contemplating how best to answer. "She is sitting on my arm because she was hungry, and I have just fed her. I am wounded because yesterday she was … unsure of my trustworthiness, and I think … maybe wanted to make it known that she was not afraid of me."

Nathan nodded his head and grinned, looking thoughtful. He pulled a cigar from his pocket and stuck it in his mouth, but apparently thought better of lighting it in the presence of the animal.

"Well, if anyone else had shown up with such a creature I'd be shocked, but with you … well, somehow it seems normal. Was there something you wished to speak with me about, Billy, or did you just want to show me this peculiar bird?"

"Both, Captain. The hawk … I rescued her from a certain death a few days back, and now … well, she seems to have attached herself to me. I have come here to ask you to issue an order to the regiment … and beyond, if possible. To tell the men not to shoot at birds in the sky, especially large birds — eagles, hawks, ravens, and so on. If she continues to seek out my company, I would rather not have her shot, now that I have gone to the trouble of reviving her."

Nathan nodded, a sudden vision of Harry the Dog flashing through his mind. His father's pity for the large, odd creature had saved the animal's life, and it seemed that now Billy's pity had saved this hawk. It was also not lost on Nathan that Harry the Dog had gone on to save his own life on several occasions, most recently in the Battle of New Market, which had nearly cost the hound his own life. It had seemed to Nathan that Harry had been heaven-sent to protect him from harm. Perhaps this hawk was likewise some form of divine intervention.

"Yes, very well. I can do that, Billy. Seems like the right thing to do."

"Thank you, Captain," Billy said, then turned and strode back toward where his scouts were continuing to pack up for the march.

𝕯𝕺𝕮𝕾𝕭𝖀𝕯𝕺𝕮𝕾𝕭𝖀𝕯𝕺𝕮𝕾

Billy had not gone more than a few strides when the hawk launched herself into the air, flapping with great, strong beats. Nathan and Tom watched as the bird gained an altitude of several hundred feet, then began to circle. Billy continued to walk briskly toward his company, and it seemed to Nathan that the hawk was following him from above.

He smiled and turned toward Tom. "Tom … you heard what Billy asked for. Please issue the necessary orders to the regiment."

"Certainly, Nathan. But … how shall I explain it? I've never even heard of such an order before. The men will think it's some kind of joke."

"Hmm…" Nathan answered, looking back up at the circling hawk. "Tell them … that the hawk has been trained using old Indian techniques … that she has been taught to spy out the enemy and report their positions to Billy. That ought to do it."

Tom smiled and nodded, "Yep, I think that'll work. I'll issue the orders straightaway."

"Thank you, Tom."

𝕯𝕺𝕮𝕾𝕭𝖀𝕯𝕺𝕮𝕾𝕭𝖀𝕯𝕺𝕮𝕾

Major General David Hunter exchanged a dark look with his adjutant, Major Wilson, as the two brought their horses to a halt at the edge of the roadway. Hunter took a deep breath, then dismounted. Wilson followed as two privates stepped up to grab their horses' reins, snapping salutes as they did.

Hunter could see a small group of Union soldiers standing near a split-rail fence some fifty yards off to the right side of the road across a field of tall grass.

Hunter knew what to expect; he'd already been informed of what the soldiers had discovered, but he needed to see it for himself, with his own eyes.

As he and Wilson approached the two dozen soldiers—one a sergeant and the rest privates—the men snapped to attention and saluted. Hunter stepped up to the sergeant, and returned the salute.

"Sergeant…"

The sergeant nodded, then gestured past the row of soldiers toward the fence, "This way, sir … if you please."

"No … it does not *please* me, Sergeant. But I will see it anyway."

"Yes, sir. As you say."

Hunter stepped past the sergeant and took three steps toward the fence before stopping in his tracks. Though he'd been warned, the sight still shocked and sickened him. Six blue uniformed privates had been tied to the fence with what appeared to be leather straps. All were hung upright with their heads slumped forward against their chests, and each had a black stain spreading down to his belt line—their throats had been cut from ear to ear.

The sergeant stepped up to Hunter. "No reports of any enemy regulars operating in the area, sir."

Hunter nodded, "Bushwhackers … Goddamned, cowardly, murdering marauders."

"Yes. I believe so, sir."

Hunter looked down at his boots and closed his eyes, neither speaking nor moving for several moments. When he looked up, he held a dark frown as he turned toward Wilson. "Major, I am not the type of man to turn the other cheek; I will have hard retribution for this outrage. And send a message that this vile wickedness will not be tolerated."

"Yes, sir."

"There is no way that these villainous scum are operating right under our noses without the tacit aid and support of the locals. I would teach them the price of their treachery.

"Issue the following order … 'Every house and all other property of every secession sympathizer residing within five miles from this place, shall be destroyed by fire … effective immediately.'"

"Yes, sir."

"And further ... post notices throughout every village and town under our control and in the line of our march ... 'Every Union soldier fired upon, wounded, or assassinated by bushwhackers in any neighborhood within the reach of my command shall suffer the same fate as those surrounding this outrage.'"

"It shall be done, sir."

Hunter scowled. "If they wish to unleash hell on our troops, let's see how they like it when we give them the devil's own inferno straight back!"

இஅஇஇஅஇஇஅஇஇஅஇ

Sunday June 12, 1864 – Lexington, Virginia:

With the arrival at Staunton of Generals Crook and Averell on June eighth—their 12,000 men now giving General Hunter a force of more than 20,000—Nathan was certain the army would advance immediately upon Lynchburg. But once again, he was surprised when Hunter ordered an attack on Lexington, Virginia instead.

Though Lexington was not far out of their way, and they met but little resistance from the rebel cavalry tasked with defending it, Hunter decided to remain in the town for three days, during which his penchant for burning and destruction rose to new heights.

Nathan was saddened to learn that Hunter had ordered the burning of the Virginia Military Institute, whose corps of cadets had fought in the Battle of New Market. VMI, whose mission to train military officers was identical to that of the United States Military Academy at West Point where Nathan had studied, was now the school for Confederate officers. But he couldn't argue with the logic that its mission made it a legitimate military target, though the burning of its library and scientific laboratory seemed excessive.

However, the additional burning of two private residences occupied by the families of absent VMI professors, now serving as C.S.A. officers, raised Nathan's ire. Looting was also running rampant, with no apparent effort on Hunter's part to stop it.

Nathan issued an order to his regiment that they would not participate in any burning or "unauthorized acquisition of private property" without his express orders. He couldn't control what the commanding general ordered, nor the behavior of soldiers from other regiments, but he was determined that his own men would behave honorably.

When he learned that Hunter had ordered former governor John Letcher's private residence burned, Nathan was livid, and had to go see it for himself. Tom went with him. When they arrived at the smoldering ruins, they found a woman sitting on the lawn of the house across the street from the one that had been burned. She had her head in her hands, and appeared to be crying. Beside her on the ground lay a trunk of the type that clothes were transported in when going on a lengthy journey.

Nathan dismounted and walked over to the woman, kneeling down in front of her. He removed his hat and spoke to her in soft tones, "Excuse me, ma'am ... are you in need of assistance?"

She glanced up at him and scowled. He could see her eyes were red and puffy from crying. "Not from you villainous Yankees. Haven't you done enough?" She waved her hand toward the still smoking remains of the house.

"Governor Letcher's?" Nathan asked.

"Yes, certainly ... You devils have now had your revenge on my John ... though he never wanted any of this business in the first place, and tried to prevent it."

"John...? Then am I correct in assuming that you are *Mrs.* Letcher?"

"Yes, or what's left of me, with no food, no house, no money, and only the clothes in this trunk, with no way to carry them anywhere."

Nathan frowned, "I am truly sorry for your plight, ma'am. I knew your husband before the war, and can vouch for his desire to prevent the secession and all that has followed. I believe he was a good man—still is, I assume, though no longer the governor, I understand."

43

She gazed up at Nathan and her expression softened. "You knew John before the war?"

"Yes, ma'am. I am Colonel Nathaniel Chambers. I was a state senator for Virginia, and spoke with Governor Letcher on multiple occasions. Worked with him trying to prevent the secession."

"Nathaniel Chambers? I remember John speaking of you a few times. I recall that he was quite impressed with you at the time — how you stood up to that awful Henry Wise and his slave power cronies.

"Ended up fighting for the North, did you, Mr. Chambers? Not surprised, and can't say as I blame you."

"Thank you, ma'am. Yes, my loyalties have always been with the country as a whole, rather than just Virginia.

"What is your *given* name, if I may ask, ma'am?"

"I am Susan."

"Good to meet you, Miss Susan. And please, allow me to help you with your things. May we take you to someplace you can stay … Local friends or family, perhaps?"

"Yes, yes, there are several who would take me in once they learn what has happened. That would be fine; thank you, Colonel Chambers. I am much obliged."

"It's the least I can do, Miss Susan."

𝔰𝔬𝔠𝔰𝔠𝔰𝔟𝔲𝔰𝔬𝔠𝔰𝔠𝔰𝔟𝔲𝔰𝔬𝔠𝔰𝔠𝔰

After depositing Mrs. Letcher at a friend's house, Nathan and Tom rode slowly back to the regiment's camp. Nathan had a sullen look as he puffed on a cigar.

Tom finally broke the silence, "What's eating you, Nathan?"

Nathan didn't immediately answer, as if gathering his thoughts. "Tom … though war has always carried its horrors, tragedies, and atrocities … there has always been a certain … *civility* to the whole matter, as ironic as that seems. The so-called 'rules of war.' But now…"

"You're speaking of Hunter's burning of civilian property?"

"Well, yes … but not *just* that … Those rebel bushwhackers … murdering pro-Union civilians and captured, helpless soldiers.

Then Hunter, rightly or not, retaliates and burns their supporters' houses.

"Is there any doubt the rebels will take offense and do the same to the houses of pro-Union civilians? Then what started as a contest between warring armies devolves into a blood feud of senseless murder and destruction."

Tom nodded, but said, "Maybe that's how it should be."

"What do you mean? Are you saying you approve of this type of brutal, uncivilized behavior from the warring parties?"

"No, no, not at all. I hate seeing it come to that, same as you. But I was just thinking … if war is too neat and tidy to the civilians, whose tax dollars are funding it, then perhaps they have little reason to wish it ended. On the other hand…

"If it affects them directly, and in a terrible way, perhaps they'll push for their government to put a stop to it?"

"Hmm … interesting point, I suppose," Nathan nodded, continuing to smoke the cigar. "But that presumes the civilians actually have any say in the matter. In my experience, government leaders in time of war tend to dismiss the concerns of their citizens, believing the conflict gives them some higher moral authority.

"No … I get what you're saying, Tom, but I will stick with my gut instincts: that breaking the established norms of warfare will only instigate a downward spiral of mindless brutality and destruction—a path of blood, pain, and death, leading straight to hell. Makes me think of Billy's old Indian story."

"Which story was that?"

"The one about the merciless war that raged when everything civilized fell apart, resulting in a nightmarish inferno … the time he called 'The Breaking.'"

જીભ્ય છ૬ ૦૩૭૦ જીભ્ય છ૬ ૦૩૭૦ જીભ્ય છ૬ ૦૩

Saturday June 11, 1864 – Richmond, Virginia:

"Let me make sure I have your account of the matter correct, Miss Alice." Major White gazed down at his neatly penciled notes laid out in front of him on a rough, wooden table, the surface of which had made his note taking difficult and annoying.

Across from him sat the young woman, Alice Spencer, serving an indefinite incarceration for suspected espionage. After her initial arrest, White had moved her to an old, abandoned house he'd requisitioned for just such a purpose, under guard by reliable and discreet men he'd personally selected for the task. He'd feared the enemy spy ring might attempt to assassinate the prisoner to keep her from talking to the Signal Corps if she were kept in any of the normal lockups.

But now after multiple interrogation sessions, he was even more convinced of the correctness of his decision to keep her whereabouts a secret, but for a different reason. He now feared she might suffer the same fate at the hands of someone within his own department.

"You insist you are *not* an enemy agent, but have in fact been cooperating with our own Signal Corps' counterespionage efforts under the direction of one of our own officers, who presented himself to you under the guise of a gentlemen named 'Mr. Gray'?"

"Yes, that's correct, Major."

"And when I arrested you, and brought you to the War Department, you immediately recognized that 'Mr. Gray' was in fact Colonel Grayson of the Confederate Signal Corps? This despite the fact he states he does not know you, and has never seen you before your arrest?"

"Yes ... I would know him anywhere. We ... well," she blushed, "Mr. Gray and I ... uh, that is, *Colonel Grayson* ... we have been ... *intimate* ... on multiple occasions while working together on behalf of the nation."

"Ah. I see," Major White nodded, this new information adding more fuel to the fire of his growing dislike of Grayson and his tactics. And it also helped to explain Grayson's continuing insistence on being informed about Alice's whereabouts, and being allowed to interrogate her himself. Efforts White had stubbornly resisted, even going so far as to enlist the support of Secretary Seddon himself. Seddon, who—for reasons of his own—seemed eager to keep the two officers at odds and conducting separate, rival investigations, had been only too happy to comply.

Alice suddenly teared up and wiped at her eyes, "I just don't understand why he says he doesn't know me ... why would he do that, Major? What have I done to harm him? I realize I ended up in the wrong place at the wrong time ... but doesn't it seem likely that the enemy began to suspect me and so arranged the whole thing to have me arrested?"

"Hmm ... it is a viable theory one might put forward in your defense. But I have no evidence to prove or disprove it one way or the other. At least not at this time," White answered. But what he thought was, *If this woman is our spy queen, then I'm a snake. The only question is, did Grayson set her up to take a fall, or was it the enemy's spies?*

White stood, replaced his hat, and turned toward the door.

"But, Major! You *do* believe me, don't you? You know I'm no enemy spy. Please ... won't you set me free and allow me to return to my family? I'm sure my father, the general, is worried sick about me."

The implied threat from her father, Brigadier General Spencer of Major General Beauregard's staff, was *not* lost on White. But Alice was unaware of how little such things affected him.

He turned and gazed at her a moment, before shaking his head, "I'm sorry, Miss Alice. I can't do that just now." He turned and walked to the door.

Best to keep her here until I know the truth ... And she may still be useful: leverage against Grayson, if nothing else.

In the meantime, I believe it's time to take a fresh look at Miss Evelyn Hanson.

☙✺☙☙✺☙☙✺☙

Saturday June 11, 1864 – Richmond, Virginia:

Evelyn invoked her usual wit and charm as she mingled amongst the dozens of ladies at yet another of Varina Davis's elegant affairs, complete with a fine string quartet, and a sumptuous sideboard.

It occurred to Evelyn that Varina's parties had become ever more frequent and extravagant as the war closed in on Richmond, and the general population increasingly suffered from a lack of supplies of all kinds, especially basic foodstuffs. *One more reason to despise these Confederates and everything they stand for*, she thought, even as she smiled brightly and nibbled at a sweet biscuit.

She was greeted by Mary Richards, who curtsied politely, offering Evelyn treats from a tray. Mary, who was posing as a highly skilled domestic slave for Varina, was actually a freeman, and Evelyn's own planted spy in the Confederate White House.

"Miss Evelyn, so nice to see you again, ma'am."

"Mary … a delight as always. You are well, I trust?"

"Yes, ma'am, so kindly of you to ask. Won't you have another biscuit?"

"Oh, thank you, Mary, but no. I couldn't possibly —"

"I really think you *should* try another, Miss Evelyn … that one nearest you on the tray looks *especially* tasty," Mary gave Evelyn a serious look that belied her casual words.

Evelyn nodded, "Well, I suppose one more wouldn't hurt." She reached out and picked up the treat, noting as she did that there was a tiny slip of paper stuck to the bottom. "Thank you, my dear."

Mary nodded, then turned away with her tray, continuing her route around the room.

Evelyn moved to the side of the room and pretended to nibble on the treat as she surreptitiously pulled off the tiny slip of paper and glanced at it, before slipping it up her sleeve.

The note had contained the letters, "*wtr clst*" in pencil. Evelyn set the biscuit aside on a table, then headed down the hallway toward the water closet.

She'd not gone more than three quarters of the way there when she passed a doorway on the left and heard a sharp noise, "*Pssst…*" She turned, and was not at all shocked to see Hank, Varina's longtime butler, standing there, waving her into the room. She glanced quickly back down the hall before slipping into the room and quietly shutting the door.

"Hello, Hank," she whispered.

"Hello, Miss Evelyn. Sorry for the mystery, but I needed to speak with you."

"That's all right, Hank. What is it about?"

"Miss Evelyn ... you'll recall our agreement ... 'bout you helpin' me get out of Virginia?"

"Yes ... of course, Hank..."

"Well, I figure now's the time. Yankee army closing in ... folks starving in the streets. I don't wanna be in this here house when Grant comes a callin'. Or maybe just hungry folk come to take what they're needin'. I'm ready to go. Now."

"Oh. Very well. I will certainly keep my end of the bargain. But ... are you sure you must go *now*? While Mary is still here, we could certainly use your help—"

"No, Miss Evelyn; now. We made a deal."

The vehemence of his response startled her. And that it seemed to have been triggered by the mention of Mary was a surprise. Evelyn wondered if Hank and Mary had had some sort of falling out, but she decided it was best not to pry.

"Yes, of course Hank," she answered. "I will make the arrangements, and then I'll send Tad around, under some pretense, to share with you the details."

"Good," he said, and then stepped to the door, looked out, then left without another word.

She sighed, continuing to wonder what had triggered *that* all of a sudden. But she shrugged it off and also slipped out of the room, continuing toward the water closet, which she realized she actually did need after all.

❧⳥⳩⳺⳩⳥⳩⳺⳩⳥⳩⳺⳩⳥⳩

Saturday June 11, 1864 – Richmond, Virginia:

Harriet Hanson set her book aside and stood to answer an unexpected knock on her door. It was getting late, with darkness fast approaching, so she could not imagine who it might be at this late hour.

49

When she opened the door, she felt a sudden surge of anxiety when she saw took in the odd, intense gaze of Signal Corps Major White. The man had visited several times in the previous year, quizzing her relentlessly about Evelyn, her friends, acquaintances, social activities, travel, and so on, all the time refusing to say what it was concerning. But he'd not made an appearance for many long months now, and Harriet had begun to think he'd given up his investigation.

"Major White ... what a *pleasant* surprise," but her tone clearly didn't match the words.

"Is it, Miss Harriet? A *surprise*, yes ... but *pleasant?* I seriously doubt that."

"Well, be that as it may, Major ... would you like to come in?" she asked halfheartedly, praying he'd decline.

"Yes, I would; thank you," he said as he stepped inside and removed his hat.

She led him to the tiny sitting room and offered him a seat, which he took with a slight bow.

"Tea, Major?"

"Thank you, but no, Miss Harriet. I should like to get right to business, if you don't mind."

"Certainly, Major. And what business is it that brings you to my door *this* time, sir?"

"The same business as before, Miss Harriet ... I wish to know what your daughter Evelyn is up to."

"I'm sure I don't know what you mean by that, Major. Or what you may be implying ... If you wish to have a conversation, then I'd suggest you speak more plainly, sir."

"Very well ... I will ask you specific questions, and I expect you to answer *truthfully* this time."

"But I—"

"Please, Miss Harriet ... I pride myself in being a keen observer of people, and can almost always tell when someone is lying, telling half-truths, or simply withholding something vital. In the past, you have done all three when it comes to your daughter. This time I wish to know the truth ... the *whole* truth.

"But before we proceed, I would be remiss if I didn't reassure you that I intend your daughter no harm. She is, by all accounts, a very admirable young lady … well-liked by all, and a credit to her family.

"But … sadly she has become involved with certain … *individuals* … who are conspiring to undermine the government and its war efforts. I only wish to speak with her about these individuals, that I may put a stop to their misguided actions. And once she cooperates with me in my efforts, she will no longer be of interest to the government, and can go about her affairs, certain in the knowledge that she will be safe from any further action by the government.

"However, if she does *not* confide in me, and soon, I cannot guarantee her safety; other government officers may be less merciful and understanding than myself."

"Oh … I see…"

"And the same applies to you, Miss Harriet … not that you care about your personal wellbeing as much as that of your daughter, of course … But it is certainly possible that some less scrupulous government agents may seek to vent their righteous wrath against you personally, assuming you are in league with the same nefarious individuals that your daughter has been associating with."

"Oh! Uh … I'm sure I don't know what you may be referring to, Major."

"One more thing, Miss Harriet. I am somewhat reticent to tell you, but I have, as part of my legitimate government investigation, been forced to look into the finances of your daughter, which sadly required me to look into yours as well. And … I am very sorry to see that your monetary resources are in such dire circumstances, Miss Harriet. If I am not mistaken, you are nearly depleted of cash, and very likely are barely able to afford food for your table. For a lady of your station, that must be … a difficult burden to bear."

"Well … that may or may not be, but I don't see what business that is of yours, sir."

"Only this, Miss Harriet … If you help me in my investigation, I have access to certain … *resources* … that could resolve your current money issues, and put you in good standing for some time to come."

"Oh … I see. Still, I have nothing new to tell you concerning Evelyn, though you can ask whatever questions you wish. I know of nothing she is doing that is illegal or goes against the government's war efforts. Nor do I know of anyone she associates with in that regard."

"Very well, but let us proceed with my questions anyway, shall we…?"

ɆɆɆɆɆɆɆɆɆ

Sunday June 12, 1864 – Richmond, Virginia:

> *June 4, 1864*
> *Cold Harbor, Va.*
>
> *My Dear Evelyn,*
>
> *Yesterday I had the very odd experience of feeling sickened and downhearted after a triumph in battle. Always in the past a victory brought on feelings of joy and elation, though almost always tempered by the inevitable losses we would have suffered.*
>
> *But yesterday, the Yankees attacked our dug in position at a little crossroads named Cold Harbor. Words cannot describe the horror of their slaughter on a scale that beggars belief. And the suffering of their wounded! Many of us had to stuff cotton in our ears after darkness fell so that we'd not have to hear their heart-rending groans and screams that went on all night unabated.*
>
> *Their General Grant must be a man with no conscience and no heart, is all I can fathom. He threw the Yankee soldiers against our unbreakable position as if he gave no thought as to how many lives he might lose. Thousands of men he sacrificed, while not gaining an inch of ground,*

*nor inflicting any significant damage on our army. Truly
a horrific waste of humanity. I fear I shall never get the
images of it from my mind.*

*Daily I grow sicker and sicker of this war. It grinds on and
on with no end in sight, at least not one that will turn out
well for our side. I am ready to be done and to return home
to the peaceful life I once knew.*

*Thank you for reading my letters, though I am thinking
they are not so very pleasant. But mostly thank you for
continuing to write to me. That is truly one of the things
that keeps me going and maybe helps keeps me alive in the
midst of all this death.*

*As always, I pray for your continuing good health and
happiness, and that we may one day see each other again.*

Your forever friend,

Jubal Collins
~~1st Lieutenant~~, Captain
27th Virginia

*P.S. I nearly forgot, I am now a captain, as you can see
from my signature. The brigade had lost so many officers
that all those left in charge were only lieutenants, so they
raised me up. It no longer seems like much of an honor,
however.*

Major White carefully folded the sheet of paper and resealed it
with a blob of wax from a simple white candle. As the sender was
a soldier who'd not had access to an identifying stamp for the
wax, there'd been no need to carefully unseal and reseal the letter
so as not to spoil the original wax imprint.

He stood and walked down the hallway, stopping first at the
office of the postmaster to drop off the letter so that it could be
sent on to its original intended recipient, Miss Evelyn Hanson.

He then took the stairs at the end of the hall up to the third
floor, to the War Department proper. There, in a matter of

minutes, he determined where the Twenty-Seventh Virginia Regiment was currently bivouacked —a task made more difficult because they, along with the rest of the old Stonewall Brigade, had been reconfigured into Brigadier General William Terry's brigade, so no longer retained their original regimental numbers. But Captain Collins, as with most soldiers, was apparently a stubborn creature of habit, insisting on using his old regimental identification in his correspondence.

Fortunately for Major White, Captain Collins' unit, whatever he chose to name it, was currently located only a few miles away in the siege lines outside Petersburg.

Two hours later, White pushed back the flap of a tent and ducked inside. A young officer sat up on his bunk, and then, noting the entrance of a superior officer, stood to his feet and saluted. White returned the salute, "Captain Jubal Collins?"

"Yes, Major ... How may I assist you, sir?"

"Please ... sit, Captain, and be at ease. I am Major White of the Signal Corps. I have just come from the War Department, and wished to speak with you concerning a matter I am looking into."

"Oh! All right," Jubal sat back on the bunk and gestured for the major to take the camp chair next to it. "Though I can't imagine what matter the War Department would possibly wish to discuss with a captain out on the front lines."

"It is likely a matter of little importance, Captain ... I just have a few questions for you concerning a woman named Evelyn Hanson, with whom you've had an ongoing correspondence."

White was gratified to see Collins flinch at the mention of *that* name. *Ah! He knows something he shouldn't.*

"Major ... I can't imagine why you'd want to know anything about Miss Evelyn. And to tell the truth ... it concerns me that you even know that she and I have had a *personal* correspondence. We are friends, and that's no one else's business. Nor is what we might discuss."

"*Everything* is the nation's business in time of war, Captain. Even your seemingly innocuous letters to Miss Hanson."

The captain now held a dark frown. "Major ... I must protest in the strongest terms. That you have seemingly read my private, personal letters to Miss Evelyn is ... quite despicable, sir, and inexcusable. I shall file a formal complaint against you with my superiors, you can be sure of that."

"No ... I don't think so, Captain. After all, I am only doing my duty. If you will calm yourself and answer my questions, perhaps we can clear up this matter and I can be on my way and leave you to your duties."

"Very well. What is it you wish to know, Major?"

"Captain, are you aware of any close associates Miss Hanson may have, or activities she may participate in that would go counter to the lawful wartime needs of the Confederate government?"

The captain didn't immediately answer, looking down at the floor. *Another flinch*, White noticed. *He definitely knows something.*

Captain Collins looked back up, "No, Major. Miss Evelyn is a fine, upstanding member of Richmond society. I understand she is even friends with the president's wife and ... betrothed to one of our officers, though I don't know his name. She is the finest, most proper, and decent lady I've ever known. How she could be accused of doing anything detrimental to the government I can't fathom."

Another lie ... and interesting news about a betrothed officer.

"Hmm ... very well. Please now just tell me the dates of any meetings you've had with Miss Hanson in Richmond since the beginning of the war, if you would."

"I've only been back to Richmond once since the war started, Major. That would've been back in mid-September when the Stonewall Brigade was finally back in Virginia, and I got two weeks' leave. I went to her house one afternoon and we chatted for a few hours. Then I left and returned to my parents' house, just outside town, where I stayed until my leave was up and I returned to my regiment."

"I see. So you've only seen her once since you left Richmond to fight in the war?"

"That's the only time I saw her *in Richmond...*"

"Oh? You saw her somewhere else, then?"

"Well, only for a moment, and unfortunately, we never spoke. It was during the Maryland Campaign, early September of '62 … General Lee decided to put on a parade for the loyal people of Frederick town in Maryland. While we were marching down the street, I saw Miss Evelyn for an instant in the crowd. When we spoke of it later, she explained she'd been in Maryland looking after her sick aunt."

"Ah. September of 1862, you say?" White asked, but what he thought was, *I have you now, Miss Evelyn Hanson! You told me you were in North Carolina at that time … I've finally caught you in a lie. Now you are mine!*

"Captain Collins … with this new information, I'm afraid I am going to have to take you with me back to the War Department for further questioning."

"*No.*"

"Excuse me?"

"I said, *no.* I'm not going back to the War Department with you. There's a war on, sir … *remember?* And we've just been handed marching orders for first light tomorrow, heading out west to confront some new Yankee threat out near Lynchburg. I have men to lead in battle, and no time to accompany you to Richmond."

"I'm a superior officer, and a War Department official. I'm ordering you to accompany me. If necessary, I shall place you under arrest."

Rather than answering, Captain Collins stood to his feet, stepped past White to the tent entrance, stuck his head out, and shouted, "Sergeant … come here please!"

In moments, a burly young sergeant with a large bushy dark beard stepped into the tent, then seeing the major stood to attention and started to salute.

But to both the sergeant and the major's surprise, Captain Collins slapped the man's hand down before he could complete the salute.

"Don't salute this man, Sergeant! He's come here to arrest me and take me off to the War Department, dressed in his fancy, perfectly clean and ironed uniform … for reasons known only to himself. Does that sound like someone you ought to be saluting—you being an actual *fighting* soldier who's risked his life on so many occasions he's lost track, and who'd feel naked without a rifle over his shoulder? While this fellow has sat back in Richmond, warm, well-fed, and comfortable on his fat ass ..."

"Uh ... no, sir. It don't."

"That's right, Sergeant. Now, please just step outside and pass the word amongst the men, concerning what I have just told you."

"Yes, sir!" The sergeant saluted Captain Collins, who returned it smartly. But the sergeant turned and scowled at Major White, and this time did *not* salute before leaving the tent.

Collins turned to White, "Now, Major ... within moments, there will be several hundred angry, armed men just outside this tent flap. If you walk out of here with me in shackles—which is the only way you will get me to go with you—well, then I can't be responsible for your safety ... *sir.*"

White gazed up at Collins, slowly nodding, "Very well, Captain. If that's how you wish to play ... I too can play games." He stood and left the tent without further ado. Neither man bothered to salute.

Major White went straight to Brigadier General Terry, figuring he'd cut out any interim commanders and go straight to the brigade commander. But if he'd expected a sympathetic ear from the general, he was quickly disappointed. Terry was busily dealing with staff officers organizing the brigade for marching out in the morning, and gave White little attention, reading through and signing various documents and papers in a stack in front of him.

"Yes, Major ... what is it?"

"Sorry to disturb you, sir, but I'm here from the War Department on an urgent matter of counterespionage."

"Yes ... *and?*"

"And ... we suspect one of your officers is involved. One Captain Jubal Collins, late of the Twenty-Seventh Virginia, now under your command."

Terry's pen stopped, and he looked up at White for the first time. "Major, either this is some sort of jest, for which I'm in no mood, or you are sadly mistaken. Captain Collins was one of the original members of the old Stonewall Brigade. He has a reputation for bravery and heroics under fire that is unmatched in my command—likely we'd pin a medal on him if we had time for such things. As far as I know, he's been in the thick of every major battle the army has fought since the outset of the conflict. The man's been too busy *killing* Yankees to possibly have been spying for them."

"That may be, sir, but—"

"Major … I have no time for this nonsense. I have a brigade to march tomorrow, on General Lee's direct orders. Do you suppose your current task, such as it is, supersedes that?"

"No, sir. But you should know, when I threatened to arrest him, Captain Collins basically ordered his men to shoot me."

"Did he?"

"Yes, sir."

"Well, good for him. If you don't leave my camp immediately, I'll order you shot myself. Good day, sir!"

🙰🙰🙰🙰🙰🙰🙰🙰

Sunday June 12, 1864 – Petersburg, Virginia:

Despite the scramble to prepare the regiment for the march, Jubal felt a growing sense of trepidation over the unnerving visit by the Signal Corps major. Not for himself, of course; at this point, he could think of nothing worse the army could do to him than the duty he was already assigned.

No, his fear was entirely for Evelyn; thinking back on the interrogation, he couldn't figure out what it was he'd said that had been detrimental to her, but it had been clear from the major's reaction that something had been.

With a gnawing feeling of dread, he paused in his packing, reached into his kit, and pulled out paper and pencil. He knelt on the floor and spread the paper on top of a board that had been serving as a sort of bridge across the mud from the tent flap to his cot. Ignoring the dirt that would doubtless smudge the backside of the paper, he began to write:

June 12, 1864
Petersburg, Va.

Dear Evelyn,

*Though I'm preparing to depart for yet another battle, I
feel the greatest sense of urgency to warn you of—*

But mid-stroke, the pencil lead broke from the rough wood
underneath. As he pulled out his penknife to resharpen it, he
paused as a thought hit him. *Damn it, Jubal, think! The major has
been reading our letters ... it's a good bet he'll read this one too.*

With a groan of frustration, he grabbed the sheet of paper,
crumpled it up, tossed it onto the floor, then stomped it into the
mud.

He sat heavily on the board with his head in his hands, trying
to think of what to do. He briefly considered deserting his
regiment and returning to Richmond to warn her. But he knew he
could never leave his men just before a battle. And besides, likely
it would only make matters worse for Evelyn if he was caught
trying to see her.

So, he did the only thing left to him: he said a silent prayer for
her safety and promised himself if anything ill befell her, he'd
track down the major and ensure there'd be a reckoning.

🙰🙰🙰🙰🙰🙰🙰🙰🙰🙰

Monday June 13, 1864 – Richmond, Virginia:

Although he now had proof of Evelyn's prevarication, Major
White wanted more solid evidence of her treason before going to
Secretary Seddon. He needed a witness to testify against her. He
needed her mother, Harriet Hanson.

He arrived at Harriet's house at first light the day after his
meeting with Captain Collins. Though his inability to arrest the
young officer had been a setback, he'd gotten the information he
needed out of Collins, and there was always the possibility of
laying hands on him later when his brigade returned from
whatever mission General Lee was currently sending them on.

Now he just needed to obtain Harriet's cooperation, and with the information he now had in his possession, he meant to force the issue. And he decided that *force* should be the operative word this time.

When Harriet came to the door at his insistent knock, he pushed past her into her house without a word, and did not bother removing his hat. When she turned to gaze at him with a shocked look, he reached past her and slammed the front door shut behind her, causing her to flinch.

For a moment, she stood gazing at him, mouth agape, eyes wide.

"Miss Harriet ... I now have solid proof, in the form of an eyewitness account, that Evelyn has been lying to me, and so have you. I am here to give you one last chance to save yourself and your daughter from a great deal of grief and heartache. And one last chance to accept my more than generous offer of monetary assistance.

"But you *must* tell all that I need to know. Or I shall not be responsible for what happens..."

Harriet gazed at him another long moment, then looked down at the floor. For a moment, White feared she would continue to resist, despite his best efforts at intimidation and persuasion.

But then she sighed, sat down heavily on a small bench in the entryway, and said, "All right ... all right. What is it you wish to know?"

Chapter 3. 'Twas Not to Be

*"Nothing is more expensive
than a missed opportunity."*
- **H. Jackson Brown, Jr.**

Monday June 13, 1864 – Richmond, Virginia:

Once he'd obtained a written and signed statement from Harriet Hanson, Major White returned to the War Department and immediately strode upstairs to call on Secretary of War James Seddon. Because of the previously agreed delicate nature of Evelyn Hanson's standing in Richmond society, and the high level of her government connections, White could not simply arrest her as he'd preferred; the matter would need to be carefully coordinated with Seddon so that no one else knew of it, and so that she could be secreted away somewhere where she could be interrogated until such time as she could no longer provide useful information. After that ... she would simply disappear and never be heard from again.

White fought to control his excitement, knowing he needed to present a calm, unflappable countenance to the habitually intimidating secretary. He stepped up to the secretary's civilian assistant, seated at a desk in front of the short hallway leading to Seddon's office.

"Hello, Major White. How can I be of assistance to you, sir?"

"Good morning, Harvey. I must speak with the secretary straightaway. Please tell him it is of the utmost national urgency, if you would."

"*Oh!* Uh ... that *is* a serious problem, Major ... You see, the secretary left two days ago. He is accompanying General Braxton Bragg on a mission to Atlanta to meet with General Johnston who is in charge of the army out there."

"Oh ... yes, that is a problem. When do you expect the secretary to return?"

"I'm sorry, Major, he didn't say, but I should think several weeks at the least. And normally, I'd say to just send him a telegram on the matter. But the telegraph lines to Atlanta have been extremely problematic of late, what with all the Union Army operations in the area—lines cut, messages intercepted, and so on. The secretary himself ordered that no further telegrams be sent from the War Department to Atlanta lest the Yankees intercept them."

White left the office feeling suddenly deflated of his exultation from only a few moments earlier. A swift arrest and interrogation of Evelyn Hanson was apparently not to be.

Downstairs, he happened to meet Colonel Grayson in the hallway. Grayson gazed at his face a moment, then smiled, "White ... you look like you ate a spoiled fruit ... Something amiss?"

"No, Colonel ... nothing is amiss ... nothing at all," but for once, White was unable to disguise his disappointment, and he knew Grayson would gloat over *that*, not needing to know the reason for it.

෨෬ඎ෮ඎ෨෬ඎ෮ඎ෨෬ඎ෮

Wednesday June 15, 1864 – Liberty, Virginia:

Nathan scowled and chewed vigorously on an unlit cigar as he rode Millie at the head of the Twelfth with Tom riding next to him. Nathan was once again fuming at the delays General Hunter's command had suffered in the last few days. First, there'd been an ultimately unsuccessful side mission to prevent the rebels from burning the bridge across the James River at Buchanan—the Confederates had burned it anyway—and then there'd been the more-difficult-than-expected fording of the swollen Big Otter River just north of the town of Liberty.

The result had been another two days' delay in the march to Lynchburg. Nathan could easily imagine the rebels taking advantage of the respite to rush troops to the obvious Union objective at Lynchburg, and then having time to dig in.

But as he rode, a sight met his eyes that gave him pause, and caused him to raise his right fist in signal for the column to halt. He dismounted and walked a few yards off the right side of the road to a tree there. Tom also dismounted and followed.

The thing that had caught Nathan's attention was that this particular tree had a Union soldier tied to it, by ropes coiled about his midsection and wrapped around the tree trunk. Two bored-looking privates stood by, rifles at their sides, apparently guarding the bound man.

Nathan stepped up to the tree, and the two privates immediately stood to attention and snapped salutes. Nathan returned the salute before turning to gaze at the bound man, who appeared weary, and was sweating profusely in the hot sun, but was otherwise unharmed. Nathan then looked to the private on the right, "What is the meaning of this, Private?"

"Company punishment, sir."

"Ordered by whom?" Nathan asked.

"General Hunter hisself, sir … as I understand it."

"Hmm … and what exactly did the fellow do, to earn such a stern punishment?"

"Don't rightly know, sir. They ain't told us … just said to keep him here 'til all the soldiers of the command had passed this spot … however long that takes."

Nathan slowly nodded, then turned to the tied man, "So … what's your story, Private? Why did the general order you tied to this tree?"

The man slowly shook his head, "Not sure, Colonel … God's truth … Was just sitting over yonder, takin' a break from the march, telling a joke with the boys, and laughing. Then everyone gets all quiet and serious looking of a sudden. When I turn around, I see the general behind me, sittin' on his horse, an angry look on his face. He says, 'If you think the situation is so funny, soldier, let's see how you like it when you're a bit less comfortable.' Then he orders me tied to this here tree, and rides off."

"Hmph," Nathan scowled, and reached behind his back, pulling out the great Bowie knife he kept there in its sheath. He quickly cut through the cords. "Punishment's over."

The tied man slumped to the ground and sat rubbing at his legs in attempt to get some life back into them.

"But, sir ..." the private who'd previously been talking protested, "general's orders..."

"Well, this *colonel* is ordering the punishment done. You two privates help him to his feet and fall in with the Twelfth. After we make camp this evening you can escort him back to his own regiment, and then return to yours."

The privates exchanged a look, then shrugged and did as ordered. "Yes, sir, Colonel."

ঙ৵৩৻৵৩৵৩৻৵৩৵৩৻৵৩৵৩

Friday June 17, 1864 – Lynchburg, Virginia:

As Jubal Collins, along with fifty men of his command, hopped down off the boxcar onto the platform at the rail station in downtown Lynchburg, Virginia, he heard the rumble of Union artillery in the distance, and could see flashes of exploding shells out over the town, followed by their deep echoing *booms*.

Turning to Sergeant Rollins, he said, "Have the men fill their canteens, and see if there's some food for their bellies before we march out to the front lines. Then prepare them to move out at the double-quick on my return. I'm going to locate General Terry to find out what we're facing here and where he wants us positioned."

"Yes, sir! C'mon men, move it along," the sergeant shouted, now looking back toward the grumbling men slowly piling out of the train cars. "I know y'all are stiff and sore from the long ride, but the sooner you're off o' that train, the better you'll feel!"

Jubal trotted off toward the front of the train, where he guessed their general would be, likely receiving his own orders from higher up. As Jubal approached a group of officers gathered near the engine, he wasn't surprised to see their overall

64

commander, Lieutenant General Jubal Early, standing in front of the assembled officers. Early appeared to be addressing them.

Although it wasn't, strictly speaking, his place to join the group, Jubal decided he'd been through enough that he'd earned the right to hear what they were discussing. So without asking permission, he stepped up to the group and slipped in next to a colonel.

"Reports from the locals and our scouts agree that Hunter's got somewheres around twenty thousand troops between infantry and cavalry, just outside town," Early stated, just as Jubal stepped up close enough to hear.

"And thanks to the Goddamned, piss-poor state of our railroads," Early turned and spat to the side, "we'll be lucky to field half that number before the shooting starts in earnest—which looks to be first thing in the morning. Should o' started today by all accounts—then we'd have already lost Lynchburg—but lucky for us, Hunter seems more concerned with burning and looting than with actual fighting... And he also appears to suffer the usual Union general illness of severe foot-dragging. Well, let's see how that works out for him."

Jubal nodded. It did seem like the Union generals always erred on the side of caution, a thing that usually benefited the Confederate side. Excessive caution did not, however, seem to be a problem with the rebel commanders, starting with Stonewall Jackson when he was alive, and continuing with Lee. And General Early seemed to be cut from the same aggressive cloth.

After some discussion back and forth among the generals, Early raised his hand for silence and then stared at the ground for several long moments, seemingly deep in thought.

Then he looked up and said, "Gentlemen, it's clear we haven't the firepower to take on Hunter ... *But* ... luckily, he doesn't know that. We'll use his ignorance and his natural caution to our advantage. First ... y'all spread the word among the troops and townsfolk, that we have just marched twenty-five thousand ... no, make that *thirty* thousand of Lee's best veteran troops into Lynchburg in a move designed to annihilate Hunter as payback for all his burning. It's very likely there's at least a few Union

sympathizers in town that'll report the news to Hunter. And if …
no, make that *when*—as we will be sure to arrange it—they
capture some of our men, they'll say the same. And Hunter will
believe it, because our men will believe it."

"Next … back this train up a few miles … as quietly as
possible, then bring it back into town with all the noise and fanfare
we can muster—whistles blowing, drums beating, bands playing,
and soldiers cheering. Repeat the process as many times as we can
'til the wee hours of the morning.

"Make Hunter believe he's outnumbered and outgunned.
Worked before with McClellan … Let's see if this new Union
general is any smarter… I'm betting he's *not*."

𝕤𝕠𝕔𝕝𝕔𝕤𝕓𝕠𝕤𝕠𝕔𝕝𝕔𝕤𝕓𝕠𝕤𝕠𝕔𝕝𝕔𝕤

Saturday June 18, 1864 – Lynchburg, Virginia:

Colonel Thoburn's brigade, which included the Twelfth West
Virginia, had been assigned the right flank of the Union line for
the assault on Lynchburg, arriving there at first light on Saturday
morning after a short, two-hour march in the pre-dawn darkness.

Nathan ordered his men to dig in behind the far side of the
Bedford Road so as to take advantage of the already existing berm
that highway provided. He'd decided this would make an
excellent position from which to either launch an attack, or to
receive one. A few dozen yards behind them ran a thick wood,
which would provide excellent cover should they need to fall back
for any reason. On the opposite side of the road, past several
pastures and a low rock wall, the rebel line could be seen, dug in
behind a barrier of logs and dirt, five hundred or more yards
away. To Nathan's expert eye, gazing at the rebel position
through his expandable brass spyglass, it seemed the enemy's
earthworks were not particularly strong, as if thrown up in a
haphazard manner in a desperately short period of time.

Once the Twelfth was in position, Nathan ordered Billy to
spread his skirmishers a few hundred yards out in front of the
regiment to keep an eye on the rebels, to harass them as the
opportunity presented itself, and to provide a tripwire in the

66

event of an attack by the enemy. And true to form, not a half-hour after Billy led his men out, the popping of rifle fire could be heard in that direction, with the usual telltale puffs of gun smoke.

Captain Carlin, with his big guns of the Wheeling Battery, was positioned further off to the left of the Twelfth's position, where they could provide covering fire for both Thoburn's position on the right flank and General Hunter's main column in the center. Like Billy, Carlin wasted no time when it came to annoying the rebels, beginning a steady barrage out toward the Confederate lines.

The Twelfth had been given orders to hold their position, guarding the flank as the main column in the center launched its attack. This Hunter did in the early afternoon, around two o'clock. Nathan could hear heavy firing off to their left, though he could see but little of the action from his position.

At first, there was no enemy activity across from their position, but as Nathan gazed intently at the Confederate earthworks, he saw regimental flags raised above it, and the telltale signs of a force gathering for an attack.

"Twelfth will stand to, fix bayonets, and prepare to meet the enemy!" he shouted. These orders were immediately obeyed down the line by his now veteran soldiers. He smiled as he recalled the first time he'd formed up the regiment for a real battle, back when the rebels had attacked the Union forts at Winchester. *That* Twelfth, though more numerous then than this one, had been almost entirely inexperienced in warfare. Now the regiment could probably fight a gunbattle in its sleep, he decided.

Rebel artillery then opened up, and their projectiles came screaming overhead, tearing into the tops of the trees behind where Nathan stood. *Aim's a little high, boys*, Nathan smiled. It was a typical issue with rebel gunners for reasons Nathan wasn't entirely sure about. He suspected it might be that their fear of the Union batteries targeting them may have been causing them to dig in so deeply that they couldn't properly aim their guns. Whatever the reasons, the rebels' big guns were mostly just noise, and to little effect.

Then, just moments after the artillery barrage began, the eerie, high-pitched rebel yell went up, and the Confederates poured up over their earthworks. They came toward the Twelfth at a run, quickly closing the 500-yard gap between the two belligerent armies.

Nathan watched the oncoming wave intently through his spyglass, waiting until they came to within firing range, at just under four hundred yards. *"Present arms! ... Aim! ... Fire!"*

The guns of Thoburn's brigade and the rest of the Union division on the right flank opened up, a cacophonous roaring of fire and smoke.

The order for volley fire was repeated once more, and the roadway was now covered in a thick, gray, choking cloud of gun smoke. A few moments later, as the smoke lifted, the Union soldiers could see that the rebel charge had been decimated, stopped dead in its tracks. A spontaneous cheer rose up from the Union ranks at the glorious sight.

The rebel survivors were fleeing back toward their earthworks, some throwing down their rifles as they ran. Others, more courageous, attempted to drag their wounded back to safety as they went.

Nathan felt a growing sense of satisfaction. If the battle in the center were going half as well as this one on the flank, Lynchburg would soon be in Union hands. But within an hour, the sounds of gunfire off to their left died down, and shortly thereafter Billy sent a scout to inform Nathan that Hunter's attack had faltered, and the Union soldiers were now digging in just a few hundred yards short of the rebel earthworks.

Still, Nathan had to believe if Hunter ordered his flanks to attack at the same time as he launched another frontal assault, surely the enemy would fold under the pressure, especially considering the pounding the rebels to their front had just received.

As afternoon wore on into evening, no order to attack was forthcoming, and Nathan began to wonder if, once more, the Union Army would fail to take advantage of a golden opportunity laid out in front of it. But there was nothing he could do but wait and see ... and stew.

ଈଠ୧୯ଈ୪ଈ୪ଈଠ୧୯ଈ୪ଈ୪ଈଠ୧୯

"Colonel Chambers, sir..." a young lieutenant pulled his horse to a halt in front of Nathan and Tom where they sat upon stumps as the sun slowly sank behind the trees to the west. They were eating a quick bite of hardtack while hidden from the front lines—and the inevitable enemy snipers—by a thicket of low-growing trees. Nathan and Tom stood as the lieutenant snapped a salute, which they returned smartly. The junior officer remained mounted as he held out a folded sheet of paper toward Nathan.

"Orders from General Hunter, sir. I am not required to wait for a response, sir, and have other orders to deliver. So, with your permission, sir—"

"Yes, yes ... dismissed, Lieutenant. Thank you."

Nathan unfolded the paper and quickly read its contents. *"What the ...?"* He scowled and handed the sheet across to Tom, who also read it before returning Nathan's look.

"Withdraw?" Tom asked. *"Why,* in God's name?"

"Yes, why? From what Billy reports, we have them outnumbered all down the line, and the rebs know it. Other than that one brief foray early this morning, they've adopted an entirely defensive posture, clearly fearing to stick their necks out and risk being flanked. One hard push and—"

"It makes no sense, Nathan. Why do you suppose Hunter's doing it?"

"I don't know, Tom. But I mean to find out. Sergeant Hicks ... bring my horse 'round, if you would."

"Yes, sir!"

ଈଠ୧୯ଈ୪ଈ୪ଈଠ୧୯ଈ୪ଈ୪ଈଠ୧୯

Nathan pulled up to General Hunter's headquarters—a small farmhouse a few miles to the northwest of Lynchburg—arriving at the gallop and pulling Millie to a bouncing stop. Before the mare was even fully still, he vaulted from the saddle, and headed for the front stairs of the house at a trot, leaving the well-trained horse to fend for itself.

He exchanged abbreviated salutes with the guards and entered the house, striding down a short hallway to where he saw several officers gathered. Pushing his way through, he entered a room where General Hunter sat behind a table that was currently doing duty as a desk, maps and papers spread generously across its dark surface.

Hunter looked up as Nathan stepped forward and saluted, "Chambers..." Hunter responded, returning the salute but remaining seated. "Don't recall asking you to call on me ... why aren't you with your regiment, preparing for a fallback per your orders?"

"Sir ... I came to speak to you about those orders ... and to beg you to reconsider. From our vantage point on the right flank, the enemy appears ripe for the picking. One hard thrust—"

"Colonel, you are obviously not privy to the intelligence we've been gathering. According to several independent sources—including not only local Union sympathizers, but also rebel prisoners—General Early arrived last night with a considerable force of Lee's veterans—a column estimated to number some thirty thousand."

Nathan scowled, "I don't believe those reports, General. My own officer of scouts, who is in my opinion among the best in the army, has reported no such buildup. I believe those numbers may be an intentional rumor started by Early to make us think he has more capability than he does."

"Well, if that were true, Chambers, then why is it that our own forward scouts observed and heard troop trains arriving at regular intervals all throughout last evening, continuing well into the night?"

"Hmm ... I don't know ... a well-orchestrated *ruse de guerre* perhaps? It seems like something a crafty old veteran like Early would try."

"Highly unlikely. Besides, even if it's *not* true, and Early has a lesser force than the reports say, with the rebel bushwhackers relentlessly raiding and harassing our wagon trains, we are running dangerously low on supplies, especially ammunition."

"All the more reason to press the attack, sir. Vanquish the enemy force, and then seize their supplies to replenish our own."

And though Nathan pleaded his case with great confidence and resolve, Hunter remained unmoved.

"Colonel ... the decision has already been made. We begin the withdrawal at nightfall."

Nathan scowled. "You would give up a possible victory, for fear of Early's *supposed* superior force, without even giving him a real fight?"

But Nathan realized with a sudden, sinking feeling that he was not only failing to persuade the general, but was now pushing his luck with the man.

"Chambers ... you are now bordering on insubordination, sir. And I will choose to ignore your implied accusation of cowardice on my part—for the moment."

Then Hunter leaned forward in his chair and looked Nathan hard in the eye. "You know ... I would think in light of your recent failure to obey my *specific* orders concerning the punishment of shirking soldiers, and the rightful destruction of rebel military property, you might be a bit more reticent in pushing such strong opinions.

"Some might even be inclined to question your loyalty, sir ... you being a Virginian and former slaveholder, after all."

Nathan's face turned stoney cold. "Accuse me of insubordination if you will, General, but I have sacrificed my home, my fortune, and several of my dearest friends fighting for the Union ... and to put an end to the evil scourge of slavery. I will suffer no man to question my loyalty, regardless of the rank the army has seen fit to give him. I *respectfully* request that you recant that crass and reckless statement, *sir.*"

Hunter flinched, seemingly startled by the strength and vehemence of his subordinate's retort. He stood from his chair, and locked eyes with Nathan for a long moment. Finally, he nodded and looked away. "Yes ... yes, you are quite right. I misspoke ... and I stand corrected, Colonel.

"Even so, the order to withdraw stands, Chambers. Prepare to pull your regiment back come nightfall. *Dismissed.*"

ᔒᓄᑫᑯᔒᓄᑫᑯᔒᓄᑫᑯ

Sunday June 19, 1864 – Liberty, Virginia:

Nathan continued to fume over what he saw as the unnecessary and humiliating retreat from Lynchburg, smoking a cigar and holding a grim scowl on his face as he rode Millie at the head of the Twelfth's column.

Tom decided it was best to just leave Nathan alone, and not attempt to engage him in any conversation for the moment. He wondered if Hunter would now be the subject of Nathan's wrath, like Sigel before him. *Well, at least none of our men died this time, so that's one point in Hunter's favor.*

Without Nathan's active engagement, Tom occupied himself with gazing out at a group of several hundred civilians milling about or seated in a field to the side of the road. Most of these were black men, women, and children, many carrying heavy loads of food or clothing with them—runaway slaves, Tom assumed, taking advantage of the presence of the Union Army to make good their escape to the North. *No, not slaves—freemen,* Tom reminded himself. *With Lincoln's emancipation, they are now legally free, and it's our duty to help them to safety.*

Tom considered their plight and decided, *Well, whatever faults he may have, at least General Hunter is sympathetic toward these people and is disposed to provide them with whatever aid and protection he may.*

As he rode slowly next to Nathan, Tom scanned the civilians' faces, curious if they would appear joyful at their escape, fearful of the potentially deadly conflict they might yet get caught up in, or something more ambivalent. He wasn't especially surprised to see a mix of emotions written on the faces he passed.

And then he saw a face that triggered a memory—a black woman in her late thirties or early forties, very pretty, and … *familiar* somehow. His breath caught and his eyes widened at a sudden recognition.

He glanced over at Nathan and said, "I'll be right back …"

Nathan looked at him and nodded, seemingly disinterested in whatever Tom had decided needed doing.

Tom moved to the side of the road, turned Jerry and trotted back to where he'd seen the woman's face. She was seated on the ground in a group of a half dozen men and women.

Tom dismounted, approached the group, and knelt down in front of the woman, removing his hat. She looked up at him with a startled expression.

"Is ... is there something I can do for you, master?" she asked, hesitantly.

"*Lilly?*" Tom asked.

"Why, yes, master ... *how...*" and then Lilly's eyes widened. "*Oh!* Oh, I don't believe it ... *I don't believe it!*" she covered her mouth with her hands, and tears filled her eyes. "You've come back, Mr. Tom ... after all this time, you've come back to free us, even as you promised!"

Tom nodded and beamed, and now fought back tears of his own. "Yes ... yes, I've come back, Lilly. Mr. Lincoln has sent me back for you. He has sent me to bring you to freedom."

𝄞𝄢𝄐𝄡𝄢𝄐𝄡𝄢𝄐𝄡𝄢

Nathan looked up to see Tom trotting back to the front of the column, where he pulled his horse in next to Nathan's. But to Nathan's surprise, Tom now carried a passenger behind him on the horse, a black woman.

Nathan looked at Tom with a raised eyebrow.

"Nathan ... I would like to introduce you to our guest ... this is *Lilly.*"

Nathan gazed at her for a moment in puzzlement, and then in a flood it came to him. "*Oh!* Oh, my goodness ... *Lilly*, yes ... it is good to meet you, Lilly." He dropped the smoldering stub of his cigar to the earth, already forgotten.

She bowed her head, not making eye contact, "Thank you, master. And thank you for sending Mr. Tom to free me."

Nathan gazed at her face for a long moment. Seeing her for the first time, he recognized the familiarity that Tom had spoken of

73

years before, after he'd met her at a farm near Lynchburg during their escape from Richmond.

"Lilly … my name is Colonel Chambers. Does that name mean anything to you?"

She glanced up at his face for a moment, appearing startled. She quickly looked down again. "Yes, master … *could* be."

"Lilly … did you once live at a place called Mountain Meadows Farm?"

"Yes, master … but that was many years ago."

Nathan nodded, then turned to Tom, "Thank you, Tom. Thank you most sincerely for this. I do wish to speak with Lilly at length, but not here, and not now.

"Lilly … I am the commander of the Twelfth West Virginia Infantry of the Union Army. I would very much like it if you would allow us to take you into our protection and if you would accompany us as we journey into the West."

She looked up at him once again, gazing at his face as if to judge his disposition. After a moment she nodded, so Nathan assumed she approved of what she saw. "Yes, master … I would like that very much. But … some others have come away from the farm with me … my friends. Might they come as well?"

"Oh, yes, most certainly. How many are you? The men will have to march with the infantry, of course, but if there aren't too many of you, the women and children can likely find spots in the wagons."

"There are only six others, four men and two women. No children. Thank you very kindly, master."

"You're welcome, Lilly. And please don't call me 'master.' In fact, you needn't call *anyone* 'master' ever again; you are now truly free. Please just call me 'Colonel.'"

She smiled brightly at this statement, "Yes, Colonel. And thank you also for *that*."

৪০০৪ঙ৪৮৪৯০৪ঙ৪৮৪৯০৪ঙ৪

Like a pack of wolves smelling the blood trail of a wounded stag, General Early's cavalry carried out a campaign of harassment that turned the unhappy retreat of Hunter's army into a nightmarish slog with dwindling supplies and rations through a countryside already stripped of food and fodder by rebel guerillas and bushwhackers.

Nathan's regiment had rearguard duty as the army passed through the mountains between Liberty and Fincastle. It was just past noon, and the Twelfth had already fended off the third Confederate cavalry attack of the day as Nathan and Tom rode through a narrow, winding canyon at the head of the column.

Nathan gazed up at the steep walls, then turned to Tom. "Why does this place seem familiar?"

Tom looked up and chuckled, "Because we passed through this very spot when we were escaping Richmond back at the start of the war. You only recall it vaguely because you were barely conscious at the time, having been recently bashed on the head."

"Ah ... yes, now I remember ... *sort of.*"

"Yes ... I remember *this spot* in particular," Tom continued, "because it gave me a nervous, twitchy feeling. A perfect spot for an ambush, I was thinking. We rode through with our pistols drawn—nervous as midnight cats sneaking through a dog kennel."

Nathan nodded, and again gazed up at the tall cliffs surrounding them. "Hmm ... *ambush* you say ... Tom, do you think we could get a couple of big guns up there?"

Tom sat up in his saddle and gazed around. "Well ... yeah, looks like there's a bit of an incline just over there ... a group of men with ropes ought to be able to drag one or two guns up. Set them up ... hmm ... probably over on that ridge there. I'd also send a rifle company up with them, for good measure."

Nathan nodded. "Tom ... I'm getting mighty tired of these rebels following us. Would you be so kind as to dissuade them from their present impolite behavior?"

Tom grinned and saluted. "Yes, sir! With pleasure." He pulled his reins over and trotted his horse back down the line to where a half-dozen artillery carriages and their caissons were being pulled along with the column.

ॐ

Elijah Walters felt a growing sense of frustration. Though the confrontation with the federals at Lynchburg had gone better than anyone could've hoped for, considering General Early's army was badly outnumbered and had begun the battle well strung out behind the town, the subsequent pursuit of the retreating Yankees had been frustratingly sluggish.

To make matters worse, Walters had learned from prisoners they'd captured straggling behind the Union column, that his old nemesis, Nathan Chambers, and his Twelfth West Virginia Regiment had been in the fight—in fact now had the rearguard just ahead of Walters' Thirty-Sixth Virginia Cavalry Battalion, which was in hot pursuit.

But though Chambers was tantalizingly close, and dangerously exposed while on the march, so far Walters had not been able to get enough men positioned to seriously get at him. He hoped once they got through the current narrow mountain pass, they'd be able to use their superior speed and maneuverability to get around the slow, plodding infantry and cut them off. Then, he'd finally have his way with Chambers.

Walters turned his horse off the road to allow the lead elements of his battalion to pass. He had a mind to chastise any stragglers and encourage the troopers to stay tightly together so that they could move quickly once out of the narrow pass.

But even as the middle of his column had passed and he was gazing back to see where the rear was, he flinched at a tremendous blast coming from ahead in the canyon. This was almost immediately followed by another, even louder explosion, and the popping of multiple rifle shots.

In moments, his cavalry troopers at the front of the column were streaming back past him in disarray. Several clutching at wounds, though none appeared serious. When Captain Roberts reached him, he stopped. "They've positioned artillery in the narrow gap above the road—opened up with cannister. We lost a dozen men in mere seconds. It's a death trap, sir, and there's no way past it."

Walters nodded and was thoughtful for a moment. "Pull back the battalion. We may as well return to Liberty at this point; the Yankees will be well away before we can do anything to stop them now."

"Yes, sir. What about the wounded?"

"What about them?"

"I'm sure there are still wounded men up there. Shall we not try to get them out, sir?"

Walters thought for a moment, then shook his head, "Have you seen men hit with cannister, Roberts? Even if they're alive, they won't be for long. Leave them. It's not worth risking more of our men just to bring back men who'll only be a burden, if they live at all. Let the Yankees tend them if they wish."

Roberts nodded his head, but said nothing.

🕮🕮🕮🕮🕮🕮🕮🕮

Saturday June 25, 1864 – Lexington, Virginia:

Captain Jubal Collins and the 247 remaining men of the original Stonewall Brigade stood to attention, facing a large, simple headstone in a cemetery in Lexington, Virginia. The stone was newly carved, one of many lined up in neat rows. This one was only distinctive due to its size and the inscription carved upon it:

> *Lt. Gen. Thomas J. Jackson*
> *Jan. 21, 1824 – May 10, 1863*
> *"He stood firm like a Stonewall"*

When General Jackson was buried, the Stonewall Brigade had been actively engaged in operations against the federals and had been unable to attend any sort of ceremony. So now as they were in Lexington, General Terry agreed to Jubal's request that the

77

remaining members of the original brigade be allowed to conduct their own funeral in their former general's honor.

Jubal stepped out in front of the men assembled and called out, "Attention!" The men of the Stonewall Brigade all saluted, holding that stance as Jubal opened his Bible to the page he'd marked, from which he proceeded to read aloud the Twenty-Third Psalm:

> *The LORD is my shepherd; I shall not want.*
>
> *He maketh me to lie down in green pastures: he leadeth me beside the still waters.*
>
> *He restoreth my soul: he leadeth me in the paths of righteousness for his name's sake.*
>
> *Yea, though I walk through the valley of the shadow of death, I will fear no evil: for thou art with me; thy rod and thy staff they comfort me.*
>
> *Thou preparest a table before me in the presence of mine enemies: thou anointest my head with oil; my cup runneth over.*
>
> *Surely goodness and mercy shall follow me all the days of my life: and I will dwell in the house of the LORD for ever.*
>
> *Amen.*

Jubal closed the book, then turned to Sergeant Rollins and nodded. The sergeant called out, "*Company one ... Present arms ... Fire!*"

Seven rifles fired into the air simultaneously. This was repeated twice more, giving General Jackson the traditional three-volley salute.

And though all those present were hardened veterans of many desperate campaigns and battles, now stretching back over several years, there was not a dry eye in the company as the men marched single file past Stonewall Jackson's grave, each man still holding his salute in the general's honor.

Chapter 4. An Empty House

"A home filled with
nothing but yourself.
It's heavy, that lightness.
It's crushing, that emptiness."
- Margaret Atwood

Saturday June 25, 1864 – Greenbrier County, West Virginia:

It was a hungry, bedraggled, and footsore army that finally arrived at White Sulphur Springs in West Virginia, where it was supposed to meet up with a wagon train of supplies and equipment. But General Hunter was furious to discover that the officer in command of the wagon train had panicked under threat of the rebel guerilla activity in the area, and had retreated west to Gauley Bridge, another seventy miles away.

So instead of much needed provender, Hunter's army was forced to endure yet another night of deprivation. Even the grand Greenbrier Hotel had been stripped bare, having been recently used by the Confederates as a hospital.

Nathan ordered his men to forage for whatever food might be found in the area, and had his officers distribute anything they had saved, including their personal allotments.

Once the Twelfth's camp was established, Nathan approached Tom, and the two shared a meaningful look. "Shall we?" Nathan asked.

Tom nodded, having no need to ask Nathan what he meant by it; Mountain Meadows Farm was only five miles away.

"I'll gather the men," Tom said.

Nathan nodded, knowing exactly which *men* Tom meant. "While you're doing that, I'll invite Lilly, after telling her the place is empty, and … also it might be appropriate to let her know of my father's passing."

Tom nodded his understanding.

"This seems like the right time and place to have my long-awaited conversation with Lilly," Nathan concluded.

Tom smiled at Nathan and patted him on the shoulder. Nathan returned the smile.

Nathan walked through the Big House alone, the others instinctively understanding that he might want a few moments of solitude to take in the great emptiness that was once his home. So Zeke, Billy, and Ollie walked around outside, visiting the various outbuildings and gazing at places the former two hadn't seen in more than three years.

Ollie, of course, had never seen Mountain Meadows before, having grown up in Richmond and spent the first several years of the war serving on the Confederate side. But he had heard about it from Evelyn, and more recently from Nathan's men, so he held a considerable amount of curiosity concerning the place.

Lilly sat on the front step next to Tom, waiting for Nathan to come back outside.

Nathan walked deliberately from room to room, gazing at the empty floors and bare walls. Evelyn had warned him of it, based on her brief visit following their meeting at Harpers Ferry. But it was still shocking that nearly everything had been taken; stripped bare, he assumed by foraging armies, refugees, and looters. Only an old, wooden table he didn't recognize and a few broken chairs remained in the sitting room, and nothing at all in the others.

But he was pleased to see that other than a good accumulation of dust and spider webs, the house in general still seemed to be sound, as did the outbuildings. Most of the windows were still intact, and there had been little in the way of damage to the walls and floors.

And once he'd nearly finished his odd, melancholy tour of the downstairs of the house, he climbed the stairs to his old bedroom. This he also found devoid of all furnishings, as he'd expected. But he'd come here for a specific reason, and despite the dismal setting, he felt an odd, growing excitement. He immediately went to northeast corner of the room and knelt down to examine the baseboard there. He smiled when the board moved at his touch. *Just as she said it would…*

He gently worked the board loose and set it on the floor to the side. There against the wall where the baseboard had been was a small sheet of paper, neatly folded. He picked it up and unfolded it. On a whim he smelled the paper. A shiver went down his spine; he thought he could still faintly smell her perfume on it.

He glanced at the date and shook his head in wonder—she'd written and hidden it here more than two years before.

He stood and held it up in front of the window to have better light in which to read:

June 3, 1862
Mountain Meadows Farm
Greenbrier, Virginia

Dearest Nathan,

I feel such overwhelmingly strong, mixed emotions being inside this house again, seeing it empty and cold, so unlike how it was the last time I was here with you.

Though the last several days have been some of the most difficult in my life, still I can't help feeling that all this death and darkness shall one day pass, that we may once again be together.

You once told me that this place was "almost heaven," except that it held so many people in bondage. Well, now that all its people are free, perhaps one day you and I can return here together and make this place truly a heaven on earth.

I don't know when you will read this message, but if you ever do, I wish you to know that whatever has happened or will happen, I shall always and forever be your true love,

-Evelyn

Nathan had to stop and wipe his eyes on his sleeve before re-reading the message.

Nathan stepped back out the front door onto the veranda, and Tom and Lilly looked up at him. He looked at Tom, then nodded and turned to Lilly. "Lilly, would you like to join me for a moment in the house? I wish to speak with you."

But she surprised him when she looked down and shook her head, "No, Colonel … I would *not* like to go back into that house. No … thank you, sir."

Nathan thought about this a moment, and it occurred to him that, if his suspicions about his father and Lilly were correct, she may have some very unpleasant memories of the inside of this house. He nodded his head, "Very well … Will you walk with me, then? Please?"

She looked back up and nodded, rising to her feet.

He came down the stairs and gestured toward the gravel drive. Lilly stepped down with him, but Tom stayed seated on the steps, allowing the two of them to have their conversation in private.

They walked for several minutes in silence, back toward the slave cabins. Once there, Lilly paused and pointed to the second cabin closest to the Big House, one that was right next to the road. "That was my cabin when I lived here."

"Ah." Nathan was surprised; it had also been Rosa's cabin. He wondered if that was mere coincidence, or something more.

Then Lilly looked up at him and said, "Colonel … where'd they all go? The slaves?"

He smiled, "I freed them, every man, woman, and child. Then we all went North when the war broke out, to escape the slavers. Including Miss Abbey and a few others of the household. Most now live on a farm we purchased up there."

She gazed at him with a look of surprise. "You … you freed them all? Before Mr. Lincoln freed us others?"

"Yes. It was the right thing to do…"

She looked down and nodded. When she looked back up, she held a smile, "You're not anything like your father, you know."

He returned the smile, "Yes, I know. And I'll take that for a compliment."

She nodded, "Yes, sir ... that it is."

Again she looked down at the ground and was silent for a long moment, so Nathan decided to broach the subject that was foremost on his mind.

"Lilly ... your daughter Rosa is there ... at the farm in the North."

Lilly clapped her hands to her mouth, and collapsed to her knees on the road, tears filling her eyes. "Oh, my dear God ... oh sweet Jesus ... my baby ... my little baby still lives. Oh, thank you, Lord ... thank you ... thank you." Her voice faded off to a whisper.

"I have been looking for you since before the war," Nathan continued, "which is part of why Tom ran into you at the farm in Lynchburg. I will now take you to my farm to be reunited with Rosa just as soon as circumstances allow. If you wish it, that is."

"Oh yes! Yes, please, Colonel! That would be the greatest ... the most wonderful thing I can ever imagine. Oh my goodness ... to see my little girl again ... to hold her. Oh my ... oh my."

He chuckled, "Well, she's not so little anymore; a full-grown woman now."

Lilly smiled and slowly shook her head, her eyes aglow.

Nathan sat down in the road next to her. "Lilly ... I have a very important but difficult question to ask you. Normally, I would say this is a question that you needn't answer if you don't wish, but ... I must confess that my desire to know the truth must outweigh such proprieties this time."

"Yes ... what is it, Colonel?"

"Lilly, I must know ... I must know if my daddy, Jacob Chambers, was Rosa's father, as I suspect."

She gazed at him a long time, this time making eye contact and holding it, a thing he greatly admired, understanding the courage it required of her.

"And if I say yes, what will become of Rosa? Will you send her away? Will Miss Abbey hate me and never let me onto your farm?"

"Lilly, please believe me when I tell you, that nothing would please me more than to learn that Rosa is my half-sister. She is strong, intelligent, loyal, and capable—not to mention beautiful like her mother. In short, everything one might wish for in a sister.

"As for Miss Abbey ... I don't know what she knows or suspects, but she has always treated Rosa with respect and affection. And I believe she never got along well with my daddy, so my guess is that she will not be shocked, nor will she blame you."

"Oh, well, that would be a relief. I always liked Miss Abbey, and felt terrible about what happened, though it wasn't by my wishes. Yes ... yes, it was ... it was the master. I was afraid ... too afraid to say no."

She put her head in her hands and sobbed softly. Nathan had to resist a very strong urge to put his arm around her, deciding under the circumstances it might not be appropriate or welcomed.

"It's all right, Lilly. I understand; it is what I had suspected. And never you worry, I will speak with Miss Abbey first thing when we return there, and make sure all is well with her concerning the entire matter."

"Oh thank, thank you so kindly." She sat up straight and wiped her eyes with her sleeve, then smiled through the tears, "I ... I still can't believe it ... I will finally get to see my dear, sweet Rosa again."

He chuckled, "And I can't believe I have another sister!"

"Another?" Lilly asked, "Miss Abbey had another child after I left?"

He shook his head, "Not exactly ... I'll tell you all about my *other* sister, Margaret, as we walk back."

෫෦෨෫෫෩෨෦෫෫෩෨෦෫෫෩෨෦෫෩෫෩

Saturday June 25, 1864 – Richmond, Virginia:

Smoke billowed from the windows on the lower floor of the Confederate White House as Mary Richards hustled Varina Davis out the front door and down the steps to the garden, then out to the street where she would be safe. Dozens of men quickly

84

responded to the emergency, including several soldiers who were just passing by when they heard the screams and saw the smoke.

A bucket brigade was quickly formed, and men lined up along the street to pass water while waiting for the steam pumper to arrive.

Unnoticed in the chaos, a tall black man strolled casually away down the street. Mary Richards stole a quick glance in his direction, watching as he turned the street corner and disappeared from sight. She sighed, wiped a tear from her eye, then turned back toward the house.

A white man that Mary didn't know was just coming out the front door with something black and sodden in his hands. He dumped it unceremoniously on the street in front of the other men, who had ceased their firefighting efforts, as the smoke slowly dissipated.

Of course, Mary already knew what the thing was: some old rags that Hank had set on fire down in the basement — not enough to cause a serious, potentially harmful blaze, but enough to cause a good deal of smoke, smoke that was just the distraction he needed to make good his escape.

ಖೋಡಚಿಆಶುಖೋಡಚಿಆಶುಖೋಡಚಿಆ

When Hank arrived at the back door of Evelyn's house, she was there to greet him, along with one of the usual conductors of the Underground Railroad. Joseph, who was feeling much better, though still moving slowly, had also come — this time dressed as a proper gentleman — to help disguise the well-known butler. Margaret was also there, and offered to assist Joseph in his task.

Joseph ordered Hank to sit in a chair in the kitchen, where he carefully applied makeup, such as was used in the theatre, in order to make Hank look like a much older man. After doctoring Hank's face, he slipped a fake, black tooth-covering over one of Hank's front teeth to make it appear that one was missing. Finally, he spread a special white powder in Hank's hair to make it appear gray.

He then had Hank dress in ragged clothes he'd brought along, then handed him a gnarly, well-worn cane and made him practice walking with a limp.

When Hank was finished with his training, it was nearly dark and time to depart.

Evelyn stepped up to him, "You're a good man, Hank. I'm happy to have had the privilege of knowing you. Thank you for all you've done for me … and for Mary."

At the name "Mary," Hank winced, as if in pain, which surprised Evelyn. But she shrugged it off, "Godspeed on your journey, Hank."

"Thank you, Miss Evelyn … Thank you for helping me today. And good luck to you."

Hank and the conductor slipped out the back door and disappeared into the night.

Rather than return to the front door, Joseph paused. "Evelyn, though my intention was to come only to help in Hank's escape, at the last moment, I was tasked with an even more pressing mission. Jonathan has sent an urgent message with me, and an apology."

"Oh? What is the message? And an apology for what?"

Joseph's brow knit into a dark frown, "He apologizes for not warning you of this matter earlier. You see, he has had several of his men following Major White for some time now — tracking his whereabouts and recording what he was up to. They had been keeping a journal of various places he visited. But when Jonathan reviewed the document, there seemed to be nothing of particular interest in most of it, though White did visit one particular address several times in recent weeks. The address is a for a private residence: 323 Jefferson Street."

Evelyn gasped, "Why … that's Momma's house; White has been talking with her!"

Joseph nodded, "So it seems. Unfortunately, Jonathan didn't recognize the address, and set the information aside to investigate further as time allowed. And so, as such things go, the matter sat longer than it should have; thus, his apology. He only discovered the truth a few minutes before this meeting, and told it to me straightaway that I might warn you."

"Oh, dear ... this is *most* distressing. I must go there at once to see what she may have told him. This could be..." she shook her head and shared a worried look with Joseph.

"I'm coming with you," Joseph said.

"Me too!" Margaret wore a concerned look, such as she'd not had since William's escape to the North.

🙟🙝🙜🙝🙞🙟🙝🙜🙝🙞🙟🙝🙜🙝

Sunday June 26, 1864 – Richmond, Virginia:

Joseph and Margaret loitered outside Harriet's house near the carriage, casually conversing as if they'd not a care in the world—all the while surreptitiously scanning the surrounding neighborhood for any watching eyes or suspicious looking individuals. Joseph rested his hand inside his suit jacket on the handle of the small revolver he'd secreted there.

Inside the house, Evelyn paced the floor and fumed as Harriet sat in a chair in her sitting room, "Momma ... this is *serious* ... more serious than any matter we've ever discussed before. I *know* you talked with Major White, so please don't pretend you don't know of whom I speak."

"And how would you know *that?*" Harriet shot back, "Have you been spying on me?"

"No, Momma ... I thought I could trust *you*. The people I work with have been spying on Major White, not *you*. They noted several visits he made recently to this house. Would you like me to recite the exact date, time, and duration of each? Because I can if you insist on prevarication."

Harriet bowed her head into her hands and sighed, "All right ... all right. Yes, he was here."

"And?"

"And *what?*"

"What did he ask you ... and more importantly, what did you tell him?"

"I … I told him nothing … nothing at all about you … I was afraid you would get into some kind of trouble about … *you know.*"

Evelyn gazed at her mother long and hard, "I don't believe you."

"It's true! I told him nothing, though he quizzed me for hours, on several visits. I told him nothing … until it no longer mattered."

"What do you mean?"

"The last time he came here, he already knew about your activities."

"Oh? And what did he say I had been doing, pray?"

"He … um … he said he knew you were doing something … something against the government … he said he had *proof.* An eyewitness, he said."

Evelyn sighed, and sat heavily into a chair opposite Harriet. She bowed her head and rubbed at her temples for a moment, "So … what did you tell him then?"

"I just … *Oh!* Do you think he was lying to me about having proof against you?"

"Yes, yes … very likely … But please, Momma … you *must* tell me exactly what you told him. It is critically important."

"Oh, dear … I meant well … I never meant any harm to you, dear—"

"Momma! *Please* … just tell me what you said!"

"I told him about the day I came home and found you meeting with those two strange men. And that you then confessed that you had been working with them to help runaway slaves get out of the South. I told him that we then had a falling out and you left my house to live elsewhere."

"You mean you kicked me out of your house…" Evelyn scowled.

"Well, yes … I suppose, though … I thought we had made amends since—"

"Yes … we had … until *now*," Evelyn frowned, gazing up at the ceiling.

"But, my dear..." Harriet shook her head. "He said if I told him what I knew, he'd make sure you were kept safe ... that no harm would come to you. And ... that the government would even help with our finances."

Evelyn looked back at Harriet, mouth agape, "*Our* finances? You're telling me he offered you money to betray me? And you took it?"

"It wasn't like *that* ... He said he would help you ... keep you from getting into serious trouble with *other* government officials. That he was only interested in the men you were working with."

Evelyn stood to her feet, red in the face and fighting to contain her anger, "Momma ... Major White is a dangerous and evil man, who cares nothing for my wellbeing, nor anyone else's. For a handful of silver, you have very likely condemned your only child to torture and death!"

Harriet's eyes widened, and she covered her mouth, but said nothing.

Evelyn turned and stormed from the house, slamming the door behind her.

She strode toward the carriage, pulled open the door, and climbed inside without a word. Margaret immediately climbed in next to her.

Joseph took one last look around the neighborhood, tossed down the stub of his cigar, and stepped up into the carriage, shutting the door behind him.

Evelyn fought to control her emotions; the last thing she wanted to do was to break down and start sobbing as she felt like doing. She needed to keep her head ... to think. *What now?*

She shared a look with Margaret and then Joseph. "Harriet has betrayed me; I dare not return home. Joseph ... please ask the driver to take us directly to the Hughes's house."

☙❧☙❧☙❧☙❧☙❧

"We must get you out of Richmond immediately, my dear," Angeline said after they'd listened to Evelyn's tale. "And likely you, too, Margaret. Someone may have noticed your close relationship with Evelyn."

89

"Yes ... I agree," Jonathan added, a concerned look knitting his brow as he sat in a chair across the sitting room.

Joseph said nothing, but nodded his agreement.

"No." Evelyn frowned.

"No?" Angeline gazed at Evelyn, then over at Jonathan, as if he might've better understood her response. But he just shrugged his shoulders and looked back at Evelyn.

"*No*, Angeline ... To run away is to surrender ... to admit defeat. To let them win. That I will never do. I must continue to do my part in the greater conflict. If I can't do that I ... oh ... I don't wish to be overly dramatic ... Suffice to say, I can't just sit still and do nothing."

"I feel the same," Margaret nodded. "I've intentionally avoided all social functions, so my association with Evelyn is known to only a handful of people, all of whom I trust completely. I'm certain there is no danger to me, only to Evelyn."

Evelyn looked thoughtful a moment, then turned to Margaret and asked, "What about Captain Hill? He knows, and despite your personal relationship, he *is* a Confederate officer, after all."

Margaret looked down at the floor a moment, nodded her head, then looked up at Evelyn, "No ... I don't believe Bob would ever betray me. He risked his life to save me from Walters, and recently his freedom and officer's commission in the army when I was wounded. I can't imagine he would ever willingly harm me, regardless of my sympathies in the war."

Evelyn nodded.

"Well, then it's settled, you two will just have to stay here with us," Angeline decided. "You'll be safe here until the war is over."

But Evelyn shook her head, "I agree that Margaret should move in here with you; that makes complete sense and there is little to no risk in it. But if I stay here, I'll be a virtual prisoner in this house. I'd dare not leave for any reason, and I'd have to hide anytime you had guests. If someone were to see me, you two would be implicated, and everything we've worked for would come crashing down. Not to mention the danger to you personally.

"Besides, I now have a whole house full of freemen who are depending on me to help them carry on with their most admirable efforts to do whatever they can to help free their people from bondage."

Angeline slowly nodded, a smile growing on her lips, "As usual, Evelyn, you prove your courage and self-sacrificing heroism."

Jonathan smiled and nodded his agreement. "Evelyn ... given you won't escape the South, and you won't stay here, shall we not then discuss what you *will* do next?" he offered.

"Yes ... but I must confess, I am at a loss," Evelyn answered. "I know I must go into hiding if I am to remain in Richmond, but I refuse to abandon the freemen who're dependent upon me."

"But Evelyn," Angeline shook her head, a frown creasing her brow, "hiding *you* is one thing ... but hiding a whole household of freemen ...? That will be much more difficult and dangerous. Someone may notice all the comings and goings of such a large group."

"Maybe so," Evelyn answered, "but I won't abandon them."

"Understood." Jonathan nodded and looked down at the floor for a long moment, as if deep in thought. Then he looked up again. "I do have an unused warehouse down near the waterfront ... Normally it would be a veritable beehive of activity this time of year ... but with the Union blockade in effect, it has been sitting empty and idle for months now. It's located a few blocks back from the main thoroughfares, so it should keep you mostly out of sight. But it does have easy ingress and egress. And from there, one should be able to inconspicuously position people to keep a watch out for anyone coming near the building."

"That sounds good..."

"But I must warn you, Evelyn ... it has little in the way of comfort ... running water, yes ... and a stove for cooking meals ... but little else. No heat when it's cold, and it'll be stifling hot in the summer."

"Oh ... so it's much like Libby Prison, from what I've heard. With fewer lice and rats, I presume. I suppose if the poor Union soldiers can endure that, so can I."

Joseph, who'd said nothing up to this point, chuckled, "Don't count on a lack of lice and rats."

Evelyn rolled her eyes, "I'm sure I'll survive, Joseph. Thank you, Jonathan. Now … let's go gather the freemen and move to our new home, such as it is. I fear there may not be a moment to lose. Margaret, please stay here; I will collect your things. If the worst happens, I would not have you caught up in it."

But when Margaret started to protest, Joseph cut her off. "She's right, Margaret; it will serve no good purpose for you to go. But never fear, I will be there to watch over Evelyn." And to emphasize his point, he pulled a small revolver from his pocket, and double-checked that all six cylinders were loaded.

Chapter 5. Joyful Reunion

*"The sweetness of reunion
is the joy of heaven."*
- **Richard Paul Evans**

Monday June 27, 1864 – Richmond, Virginia:

"Excellent work, Major," Secretary of War James Seddon smiled and nodded, a rare sight, from Major White's perspective; his meetings with the secretary were normally serious in nature at best, and often severe.

Seddon reached for a sheet of paper and pencil, then wrote on the page and folded it, handing it across to White. "This is the address for a house I have procured for just such a purpose as this. There's a storage room in the basement made of solid rock, with an iron door that locks with a key. You can secure her there."

He opened a desk drawer, reached inside for something, then held it out for White. "Here's the key. Go ahead and arrest the tart, then take her straight there. But only you and her; take none of your men. No one but you and I must know that she's been arrested and where she's been taken."

"Hmm ... I've had several men watching her house while I've awaited your return, Your Honor."

"Recall them ... tell them she's been cleared and is no longer under suspicion ... then go yourself immediately after they've left the scene and secure her arrest."

"Very good, Mr. Secretary. It shall be done."

Seddon grinned, a wicked looking leer. "Let me know once you've incarcerated her, then I shall personally pay the treacherous Jezebel a visit—but *not* a pleasant social call, I can assure you."

"Yes, Your Excellency."

ಬೊ಄ಶ೫ಬೊ಄ಶ೫ಬೊ಄ಶ೫

Moments after Evelyn arrived, her household was a frenetic beehive of activity, as her people, both black and white, scrambled to pack the bare essentials they would take with them. She ordered them to take only a few changes of practical clothing and any treasured personal items, but to leave everything else, including fine suits and dresses, and all the silver, fine China, and crystal.

Absent from the melee was Joseph, who had immediately upon their arrival slipped out the back door into the gathering darkness. As they were pulling up in the carriage, he had noted several men loitering around the neighborhood, and he wished to keep an eye on them.

Evelyn tossed her jewelry haphazardly into a carpet bag, and then stuffed in a few examples of her most simple clothing; the type she would use when out in the garden tending the flowers.

She sighed when she gazed at the row of fine formal evening gowns hanging in her closet, several of which were the most expensive to be found in Richmond. She shook her head and turned away, trying not to think about the hundreds of dollars those garments represented.

The only thing of sentimental value she grabbed were her letters from Nathan and from Jubal. These she tied together with a string and carefully slipped inside her bag along one side.

She'd just stepped into Margaret's room to grab the few things she had requested when Joseph poked his head in at the door.

"Something is happening, Evelyn ... While I was spying on our 'friends' who've been watching the house, I saw a man in a suit step up, and they exchanged words. Afterward, they all left together."

"*Oh!* What do you suppose *that* means?" she asked.

"Hmm ... not sure, but something about it filled me with dread ... I think we should leave ... *now!*"

⚜⚜⚜⚜⚜⚜

Major White, who'd been watching his men depart from down the block, waited only a few moments to make sure they were well out of sight, then strode purposefully toward Evelyn's house.

He'd watched Evelyn arrive in a fine carriage, escorted by a gentleman. After they'd entered the house, the carriage had driven away. He wished he had some means of having that carriage followed to see who it belonged to, but at the moment, he was alone, so there was nothing he could do.

He stepped up to the front door, and eschewing all pretense of politeness, unholstered his pistol, reached out, turned the doorknob, and stepped inside.

He was surprised that nobody confronted him as he stepped into the foyer. Then he paused and listened … and heard only silence. *No … it can't be.*

Then, toward the back of the house, and seemingly on the ground level, he heard a door slam. He raced down the hallway, and into the kitchen, searching for the stairs to the basement. He pulled open a door, but it was only a pantry. He tried another and found it: a simple wooden staircase leading down into darkness.

He scurried down the stairs, nearly stumbling in the gloom, but caught himself before reaching the bottom. It was so dark here that he had to slowly feel his down a hallway. The hallway turned a corner, and he saw that this led to a door with a small window in it, affording him just enough light to see by.

He rushed to the door, pulled it open, and stepped out into the backyard. Across a wide lawn loomed a thick forest of trees. Out the corner of his eye he caught some movement in the woods, so he ran toward it.

But even as he stepped into the darkness under the first tree, something struck him on the head, and he saw no more.

☙℃℃℗☙℃℃℗☙℃℃

"You mean to tell me the witch has gotten clean away, Major White? Please explain to me how that has happened?"

White shrugged. "Well, as you can clearly see, Your Honor, I was pistol-whipped by a hidden assailant, even as I attempted to effect her arrest." A blood-soaked bandage on the major's head where his hat would normally rest paid mute testimony to the truth of his words.

"But never fear, I shall yet track the harlot down. And when I do … *someone* shall be repaid in spades for my injuries, I can assure you of *that*, Mr. Secretary."

"Yes, I should certainly hope so. A thing like that must not go unanswered. Well, keep me informed of your progress, Major."

"Yes, Your Honor."

ℰⁿℭℬℰⁿℭℬℰⁿℭℬ

After Joseph departed, assuring Evelyn he would check in on her from time to time as his duties allowed, Evelyn sat with her elbows on her knees and her chin in her hands on a rough, wooden bench in a large, empty room, which smelled of dust and axle grease. But at least she'd not yet seen any rats, she consoled herself as she indulged in a heavy sigh.

"Not quite a high-society manor house, is it, Miss Evelyn?" her major-domo Jacob asked with a wry grin, as he swept the floor near where she sat using an old broom he'd found in a storage closet.

She snorted a laugh, but could think of nothing clever to say in answer. So she just shook her head, and slowly gazed around the room, taking measure of her new home. And though the ceiling was low, the room was huge—at least fifty feet wide and over a hundred feet long. Plenty of room to accommodate the ten people, three white and seven black, who were now occupying it.

Finally, she looked back at Jacob and chuckled, "Well, at least it's roomy."

ℰⁿℭℬℰⁿℭℬℰⁿℭℬ

Friday July 1, 1864 – Wheeling, West Virginia:

When General Hunter's army reached Charleston, West Virginia, transportation was arranged via steamships down the Kanawha River to the Ohio, and from there north to Parkersburg, where they could utilize the rail lines for the rest of their journey.

The Twelfth was ordered to report to Martinsburg, West Virginia, there to await further orders, as the situation in West Virginia was uncertain, especially concerning the whereabouts of

General Early and his corps since their unexpected victory over Hunter's troops at Lynchburg.

Nathan thought he might take advantage of the pause in action to head home to Wheeling for a few days, taking Lilly and her recently freed fellow slaves with him. So, when the Twelfth debarked at Grafton and learned that several bridges eastward were down and would require extensive repairs, it seemed the perfect opportunity for him to catch the northwestern line to Wheeling, leaving Tom in temporary command of the regiment.

After paying his respects to Governor Pierpont in downtown Wheeling, Nathan hired a two-horse wagon large enough to hold Lilly and the freemen, then headed south toward Belle Meade Farm. He had no driver, so he drove the wagon himself, with Lilly sitting up next to him.

As he turned into the drive at Belle Meade, he was pleased to see two black men step out into the lane and block his way. The younger one held a rifle, and the other, who was missing an arm, held a revolver.

Nathan stopped the horses, then stood and grinned, "Well, seems this farm has some especially fearsome guardians!"

Phinney beamed up at him, lowering his pistol, "Captain! So good to see you home, sir!"

"The pleasure is all mine, Phinney. Good to see you too, Moses."

After hands were shaken, and introductions made, Nathan turned to Lilly, "Y'all stay here with Phinney for a bit. I'll walk down to the farm and have a talk with Miss Abbey first, so she's not caught by surprise. I'll send someone back to fetch y'all shortly."

"All right. Thank you, Colonel. I can never thank you enough for what you're doin' for us all ... and especially for me." Lilly graced him with a bright smile, with tears shining in her eyes.

He tipped his hat to her and returned the smile, "Never mention it, dear lady; it is my *great* pleasure, believe me."

Minutes later, as he approached the farmhouse, striding along in his blue Union Colonel's uniform, the freemen out in the fields stopped what they were doing to stare and point. He was not surprised to see several drop their hoes and rakes and start moving in his direction.

And then a familiar figure stepped out the front door with what appeared to be an armload of laundry. Megs looked up and saw him, then squealed, dropped her burden right there on the steps, and rushed down the stairs out the driveway toward him, shouting out, "*Miss Abbey! Miss Abbey!* He's home ... *He's home!*"

Megs met Nathan on the drive and wrapped her arms around him. He squeezed her and held her feet off the ground in return. And then Abbey appeared at the door, and she too rushed out to greet him. She too received his enthusiastic embrace. He realized it had been eighteen long, dark months of fighting, fear, danger, and death since he had last seen either of them.

Nathan was soon surrounded by the freemen of the farm — mostly women and children now, with the war on—smiling, laughing, patting him on the back, and greeting him boisterously. He soaked in their heartfelt joy like a flower in the bright sunshine after months of darkness and rain. Among them was Rosa, who also greeted him warmly, to which he responded with a knowing smile.

Adilida and Edouard came out of the house, presumably to see what all the commotion was about, and Tom's son, little Nathaniel, ran forward to leap into Nathan's arms, giving him a hard hug and a kiss on the cheek. Nathan held the boy in his arms as he greeted the others.

Ollie's wife Belinda, the newest member of the Belle Meade family after having fled the Confederacy shortly after her husband's defection, was the last to come out of the house, smiling brightly at Nathan and waving greetings to him. He was so tightly crowded in now that she had no way to reach him.

Minutes later, after the impromptu celebration had somewhat dispersed, and little Nathaniel had trotted off to play, Abbey and Megs led Nathan into the house, sat him down at the kitchen table, and served him out whatever food and refreshments were at hand. He gratefully accepted, as it had generally been poor fare out on campaign.

But after a few moments, he looked up at the two ladies with a serious look, which they immediately mirrored, and it occurred to him that they would assume he had dire news about one of their men.

"Firstly, let me reassure you … all of the men are well. We've thankfully suffered no casualties of our own men on the present campaign. And I've had no news of our freemen in the colored regiments either."

Both women relaxed noticeably at this announcement, but Abbey looked puzzled. "But, Nathan, dear … just now you suddenly had a severe look, as if you had bad news…"

Nathan nodded, "There is a serious matter I wish to discuss with you two ladies, and it may be hurtful to you, Momma. But that being said, I don't consider it a *bad* thing. Not now."

Abbey gazed at him, "Well, now you have me curious. Please, just say what you have to say, Nathan. After all that has happened in recent years, I can't imagine anything short of the death of one of your men that would give me much pause."

"Momma, Megs … do you remember a slave woman at Mountain Meadows named Lilly?"

Abbey tilted her head, "Lilly? I…"

But Nathan noticed Megs suddenly held a dark scowl, but she said nothing.

"She was Rosa's mother," Nathan prompted.

"Oh, yes," Abbey nodded. "Now I remember. Jacob sold her off long ago, when Rosa was still a little girl. I never understood why, and he wouldn't speak of it. I remember being quite puzzled about it at the time, and felt badly for the little girl. I have often tried to give her some special attention to make up for it. The odd thing is … Jacob seemed to also feel badly for her, as I often saw him speaking to her in a kindly way."

Nathan nodded, but was now gazing at Megs, who looked down, and no longer met his eye.

"Megs?"

"Yes, I remember Lilly," Megs answered, but seemed disinclined to elaborate.

It suddenly occurred to Nathan that Megs knew about Lilly and Jacob ... and Rosa. But clearly Miss Abbey had been kept in the dark all these years.

"Momma, I'm just going to come out and say this, praying that you'll be understanding and accepting on the matter. I have been searching for Lilly since even before the war started, ever since I learned Daddy sold her off and separated her from Rosa. And now, by odd chance or divine intervention, I have finally found her. She is here, along with several other freed slaves from the farm she was on."

"Oh! Well that sounds wonderful, Nathan ... but..." Then Abbey became thoughtful, and quiet, as if the truth was beginning to dawn on her.

"Momma, I was searching for Lilly not just out of kindness toward Rosa ... I was searching because I have suspected that Daddy was ... Rosa's father."

"*Oh.* I see..."

"And now, Lilly has confirmed it."

Abbey nodded, then glanced over at Megs. "You knew of this, didn't you, dear?"

Megs frowned, then looked down at her feet. "I'm terrible sorry for not telling you, Abbey. I just couldn't. At first, I was afraid of the master ... that he'd be angry with me and send me away from you like he'd done with Lilly. And later ... I feared it might be hurtful to you, and didn't know what would become of the little girl, who never had harmed anyone."

Abbey nodded, then reached over and patted Megs on the arm. "It's all right, Megs. You did right, I believe. Jacob was ... not a man to be crossed."

Nathan jumped back in, "I have spoken with Lilly at length, and it is my fervent belief that she had no choice in the matter; she was deathly afraid of Daddy, and feared what he'd do to her if she refused him. The whole thing happened shortly after Ned had received his terrible beating, so that frightful event was still fresh in her mind."

Abbey nodded, and suddenly Megs's expression softened. It was Megs who responded, "I … never knew that … I just assumed—"

But Abbey shook her head. "No … now that I think on it, I am certain there is no fault with Lilly. The fault was all Jacob's, I am certain. He was never gentle with me either, and often expressed his … *dissatisfaction* with me in certain regards."

Nathan felt a blush rising on his face and looked away. It was hard to think of his parents in *that* way.

"But, Nathan … you say Lilly is here … yet you arrived alone. Where is she, and the others she brought with her?"

"Phinney is watching them out at the end of the drive. Please just have someone run out and fetch them, if you would."

Minutes later, when the wagon pulled up in front of the farmhouse, driven by Phinney, Nathan stepped over and helped Lilly down from the wagon as the other freemen climbed out the back of the wagon. Nathan looked Lilly in the eye and nodded. She smiled in return.

Nathan led Lilly by the hand up to the front steps, where Abbey waited at the top of the stairs. Megs stood up by the front door, arms folded, watching the scene.

Nathan moved aside, and Lilly stepped up to Miss Abbey holding a tentative smile, and giving a quick curtsey. "Miss Abbey … it is good to see you again, ma'am."

Then to Lilly's complete surprise and everlasting joy, Abbey stepped forward, embraced her, and said, "Welcome home, dear. After all these years … welcome home!"

෨෮ඁ෪ඏ෮ඁ෪ඏ෮ඁ෮෪ඏ

Minutes later, Nathan led Lilly out into the fields where Rosa was hoeing weeds. As Nathan approached, she looked up at him and smiled. He returned the smile, tipped his hat to her, then said, "Rosa, I have brought someone I think you will wish to see."

He stood to the side, and Lilly stepped forward. The two women stood gazing at one another. Lilly with a bright smile, blinking back tears, and Rosa with a puzzled expression.

101

But after a few moments, Rosa's eyes widened, and she whispered, "*Momma?*"

Lilly nodded emphatically, "Yes, my sweet baby girl ... it's me ... your Momma. I've come home."

Then Lilly gazed at Rosa, from head to toe. "Oh my, my ... look at you, baby ... You're all growed up. A beautiful young woman. I can't hardly believe it."

Rosa now had tears streaming down her face. She looked over at Nathan, who beamed back at her and nodded.

Rosa stepped closer, examining Lilly's face as if taking in every detail, "You look ... older, Momma ... but still ... the same. Just exactly the same as I remember." Then she stepped forward and the two women embraced, rocking slowly back and forth, as sobs shook their bodies.

Nathan turned and strode back to the farmhouse, sticking a cigar in his mouth and lighting it as he walked. Lilly had insisted that she would tell Rosa about Jacob, so Nathan left them alone that they might have time to reconnect and discuss all that had happened.

But a few hours later, Nathan was surprised that it was Lilly who first came to speak with him; he had expected Rosa to come and talk to him about their newly discovered kinship. He asked Lilly to sit with him in the library.

Lilly was wide-eyed, almost in shock, "Colonel ... Rosa just told me that Henry was here ... that he's been at this very farm for several years now, until he went off to the war."

"Henry? Well, yes, he's been here for quite some time. A good man. But ... you two *knew* each other, did you—back at the farm in Lynchburg? That is news to me."

"Colonel! We didn't just *know* each other ... Henry is my husband!"

"*Oh!* Oh, my goodness ... how about *that!*" Nathan sat up straight in his chair, tipping his hat back and scratching his scalp. "That's amazing ... I had no idea. Well, this is an even happier homecoming than either of us had imagined beforehand. But, I am sorry he's not here. He and the others are over to Virginia somewhere fighting in the colored regiments."

After Nathan offered to pen a letter for her to Henry, and use his War Department connections to locate him, Lilly departed.

And then it was Rosa's turn to meet with him. She stepped into the library, and he stood to greet her. She wasn't smiling as he'd expected, but held a serious expression. He met her gaze evenly and waited for her to speak first.

She never broke eye contact, but finally said, "Captain ... I always felt something special with you. But I never understood it ... And I always felt a kindness—that no one else did—from the *old* master, your daddy ... *our* daddy. Now I know the why of it. But ... how do *you* feel about it, Captain?"

He smiled, "Rosa ... *sister* ... I couldn't be happier. And please, from now on, you must call me *Nathan*, since it turns out I'm your brother."

She returned his smile, then stepped forward and wrapped her arms around his broad chest, hugging him tightly.

𝕾𝕺𝕮𝕽𝕮𝕱𝕭𝕺𝕾𝕺𝕮𝕽𝕮𝕱𝕭𝕺𝕾𝕺𝕮𝕽𝕮𝕱

Among the many happy duties Nathan undertook during his surprise homecoming was the handing out of personal letters from two of his officers to their wives—in this case from Tom to Adilida, and from Ollie to Belinda. Letters mailed to and from the front lines of the war had a habit of being delayed—often for months or even years—or destroyed altogether in the chaos and combat, so a hand-delivered letter was worth its weight in gold.

When she received hers, Addie squealed for joy and gave Nathan a warm, enthusiastic hug and a kiss on the cheek, which he greatly enjoyed, beaming at the ebullient, sparkling young lady. In that moment, it became readily apparent why Tom had been drawn to her so quickly back in New Orleans. It seemed to Nathan that Addie was everything good to be found in a woman, which—not unexpectedly—caused a vision of Evelyn to appear in his mind's eye. *Yes, my dear ... you are also that type of woman ... and so much more!*

𝕾𝕺𝕮𝕽𝕮𝕱𝕭𝕺𝕾𝕺𝕮𝕽𝕮𝕱𝕭𝕺𝕾𝕺𝕮𝕽𝕮𝕱

Adilida blinked back tears as she read Tom's letter:

103

July 1, 1864
Grafton, West Va.

My Dearest Addie,

Words cannot describe how much I have missed you out here in the war, nor how happy I am to be writing you a letter that I know for certain will be delivered into your very hands.

I hope this letter finds you healthy and happy, along with little Nathaniel and Uncle Edouard. And I hope you aren't too worried about me. Despite what the newspapers may say, I've hardly been anywhere near any action which might harm me. Colonel Chambers keeps me safe as a babe in arms, truly. So, you see, you have nothing to fear and can rest assured it is only a matter of time before I am safely back in your arms.

And what a glorious day that will be. Not much longer now, my love. I can feel that the war is turning in our favor, and will soon be over, to the satisfaction of all.

Please give Nathaniel a kiss from his father, and my very best regards to Miss Abbey and everyone else at Belle Meade.

Your loving husband,
Thomas

∞আওএ৪∞আওএ৪∞আওএ

Belinda's reaction to receiving a letter from Ollie was more subdued but no less appreciative, to Nathan's mind. She graced him with a bright smile and an effusive thank you—not only for the letter, but more importantly for allowing her to take up residence at his farm after her flight from the South.

But since they'd never met before, Belinda did not indulge in an embrace that might appear too forward. It occurred to Nathan that was also a contrast in upbringing and culture—the difference between a lady raised in conservative, upper-class Richmond versus a well-to-do lady of the more demonstrative Cajun culture of New Orleans.

Belinda smiled and nodded as she read Ollie's letter:

July 1, 1864
Grafton, West Va.

Dearest Belinda,

I hope and trust this letter finds you in good health and filled with all happiness.

I am doing very well here, and am happy to feel like I am finally serving on the correct side in the war. The men of the regiment have been most welcoming and accepting of me, and even treat me with some awe and reverence when they learn that I previously worked directly with the famous General Lee when serving on the other side.

And Colonel Chambers has proven to be everything Evelyn always spoke of, and more. A brilliant officer and a warm, kindly gentleman (but don't ever cross him – he has a mighty temper, but only when well deserved!)

Though the fighting doesn't always go our way, I am confident that we will prevail in the end. I am looking forward to settling back into a peaceful life together once the fighting is over.

Please convey my thanks and best wishes to Miss Abbey for taking you in and treating you as family. I can't wait to join you there myself, hopefully someday soon.

With love and sincerity, your husband,
Oliver Boyd
Captain, 12th West Va., Union Army (Praise the Lord!)

Belinda let out a sigh of satisfaction as she finished, lowering the letter into her lap. She pictured her beloved husband's face in her mind, imagining his serious, thoughtful visage as he had penned the letter. She savored the image for a long moment, then raised the letter and immediately reread it.

❧❧❧❧❧❧❧❧❧❧❧

Wednesday July 6, 1864 – Martinsburg, West Virginia:

As the train once again ground to a halt, Tom groaned inwardly, *Don't tell me another bridge is down!*

What should've taken eight hours from Grafton to Martinsburg on the train had already taken six days, as rebel guerillas had damaged or destroyed five different bridges along the line. At each break in the line, the Twelfth had been forced to debark the train, break out shovels, axes, and any other tools at hand, and rebuild or repair the bridge so that the train could pass on to the next break.

Tom never in life thought he would trade being an officer in command of battles for an engineer in charge of building bridges, but such had become the case over the last few days. Fortunately, the newest member of their officer corps, Captain Ollie Boyd, whom they'd "acquired" from Confederate General Lee after he'd helped William and Zeke escape from Libby Prison, proved an invaluable asset in that regard. Ollie had studied engineering before the war, and knew a good deal about bridge structures. And what he didn't know, he was able to puzzle out with his keen intellect.

So Tom happily put Ollie in charge of the construction crew, and put the other officers in charge of felling trees and shaping timbers as needed, so he himself could adopt a more supervisory role.

It had become almost routine, the train coming to an unexpected stop, followed by the conductor entering the car, walking up to Tom, and saying, "Sorry to disturb you, Colonel Clark, but I'm afraid we have another bridge out. Do you think you and your men could—"

"Yes, yes, certainly. We will fix *yet another* bridge," was Tom's typical, not-so-cheery response.

So, when the conductor once again entered the car and strode up to Tom and said, "Good evening, Colonel Clark—" Tom responded grumpily.

"Yes, yes, I know ... *another* bridge down."

But this time the conductor grinned, "Oh, *no,* Colonel Clark ... I have just come to tell you that we have arrived at Martinsburg station."

"*Oh!* In that case, thank you very kindly, Mr. Billings."

And five hours later, just as the Twelfth had nearly finished setting up camp in a field outside town, Tom was *not* entirely surprised when Nathan strode into camp, looking happy and refreshed.

"Well, looks like you've had a better time of it than we have," Tom said. "Fixed five different bridges along the way, making your trip a smooth one, no doubt."

"Well, I thank you for that, Tom. I appreciate you went to all that effort just to ease my travels." The two shared a laugh and a vigorous handshake.

"How did it go back at the farm?" Tom asked.

"It was ... *wonderful,* Tom. Several of the happiest moments I can *ever* recall, in fact."

He handed Tom a letter from Adilida, which he eagerly opened. "She appreciated when I handed her *your* letter, though I expect she was a bit disappointed you didn't come in person."

"So was I," Tom nodded, as he quickly read through Adilida's letter, a smile growing on his face. Then, as if realizing he may have misspoken, he looked up at Nathan, "Oh ... but, no fault to you, Nathan ... Someone had to take command of the regiment, and clearly you needed to accompany Lilly to Belle Meade."

"Thank you for your understanding on it, Tom. If the action slows down at some point, I'll arrange a furlough for you."

Tom shrugged, "If it works out, that would be fine, but ... don't worry yourself about it. We still have work to do."

"Very true, I'm afraid."

Wednesday July 6, 1864 – Petersburg, Virginia:

Cobb put his hands to his ears, knowing what was about to happen. But knowing the blast was coming didn't stifle the involuntary flinch the great concussion always caused. He uncovered his ears and picked up his rifle from where it leaned against his chest by the point of the bayonet. He glanced around the side of Big George so he could watch the dust settle back down from the explosion.

"Move out, men!" came the shouted orders down the line. And in moments, Cobb was moving at a full trot directly toward the large natural depression in the earth in which the bomb had been detonated by the Union engineers—a relatively minor blast not intended to do any real damage, but only to simulate what was planned for some future date at a much larger scale.

It was the third time today that the men of the Twenty-Third Colored Regiment had practiced the same exercise, along with the other colored units of the Fourth Division of General Burnside's IX Corps. And they'd done the same all afternoon the previous day.

A great double-column of soldiers rushed forward, but when they reached the edge of a large depression in the ground, still smoldering from the explosive charge, Cobb's regiment and the other units of the Second Brigade turned and followed the left edge of the crater, while the members of the First Brigade, led by the Forty-Third Colored Regiment, headed off to the right.

After a long day of training, Cobb could feel his weariness; his legs were starting to feel leaden, and his shoulders and back were aching from carrying the heavy rifle plus his pouch of ammunition and canteen of water. His uniform was soaked through with sweat from the sweltering heat, and dust coated his face and hands, giving him and the other men a ghostly appearance. His one consolation was that they didn't have to carry a full pack of supplies as the planned attack was expected to be over swiftly. Even so, he forced himself not to think on the heat and his weariness and instead to focus on George's boots moving up and down in front of him, figuring if the big man could do it, so could he.

When the column reached the center of the depression, still on the outside edge but now just past a wall made of dirt and logs, their officers turned ninety degrees to the left and led them at a charge, bayonets thrust forward, shouting as they went. They rushed forward, completely overwhelming the stunned enemy soldiers defending the earthworks.

Or would've if there'd been any, Cobb thought. He couldn't suppress a wry grin at the thought that they'd so easily defeated their *imaginary* enemies, whose earthworks they'd just breached thanks to the massive hole blown by the engineers. *Won't be so easy when it's the real thing*, he decided. *But maybe we can at least catch them by surprise. One can only hope.*

As they marched back to their starting point, again skirting the edge of the fictitious bomb crater, Cobb saw the group of officers standing on a knoll a few hundred yards back. That was not unusual, as Brigadier General Edward Ferrero, commander of the Fourth Division, had stood there all day observing the training with his staff officers and the regimental commanders. But Cobb noticed now that there were many more officers gathered than before, along with a number of additional horses.

Then Cobb felt the same odd, uncomfortable feeling he'd experienced once before back in Washington City as he and the other men of the Twenty-Third had marched past the president's review stand and he'd seen their commanding officer. Once again, he found himself gazing at that same officer, Major General Ambrose Burnside, and he suffered the same premonition of dread.

ಬಿಂಬಿ ಬಿಂಬಿ ಬಿಂಬಿ ಬಿಂಬಿ

Big George had noticed Cobb's unusual downcast look as they walked back to camp after they'd been dismissed from training for the day. And after a bit of prodding, Cobb admitted to his ongoing trepidation about their commanding general. But George shrugged it off.

"Lookie here, Cobb; they's takin' the time to train us up right for this-here attack," George said. "And I can't find any fault in the idea of it, and we know we can fight when it comes down to it. So, cheer up, brother ... After all, what could possibly go wrong?"

Cobb shook his head, "Only everything."

George laughed, then whacked Cobb on the back, making him cough.

But when they reached camp, Cobb's ill feelings were suddenly swept away by the presence of a surprise visitor; as George and Cobb stepped into camp, now joined by Tony and Henry, who'd trotted up to join them, a Union captain stepped up in front of them.

They stopped and stood to attention, saluting as they did.

The captain returned the salute, then smiled, "Well, gentlemen ... it's been a long road from Belle Meade Farm in Wheeling to here—and a couple of years now, I'll admit—but I'd think you'd still remember an old friend."

Cobb gazed at the man's face a moment, then broke into a grin of his own, "Well now! If it ain't Captain Hawkins of the Bloody Seventh! Bless my soul, Captain, but it's good to see you, sir!"

"Same here, Cobb ... Tony, George, Henry. Good to have you men finally in blue uniforms. And ... *damn* ... you wear them well! Does my heart good see it."

There were smiles all around as they shook hands and began swapping stories of all that had happened since they'd last spent time together back in Wheeling. It was a happy reunion that lasted well into the evening when Hawkins finally returned to his own camp with the Seventh, which had recently arrived to join in the siege of Petersburg.

Chapter 6. Early Is Late

"Early should have attacked
earlier in the morning,
but Early was late."
- Captain Elisha Hunt Rhodes
2nd Rhode Island Regiment

Thursday July 7, 1864 – Martinsburg, West Virginia:

"Ah, there you are, Sergeant Creek." Union Captain Ollie Boyd called out as he spotted Billy across a small meadow of thigh-high grass and scrub, where the scout stood atop a stump gazing into the sky.

Billy neither turned nor answered, so Ollie strode across the meadow until he stood under the stump. He felt no small amount of pride in actually finding Billy, which was never a simple task. Ollie had been led to understand that when the Indian scout served with the army out in Texas, it was the duty of the officer of scouts to always have at least a general idea of where Billy and the other scouts were at any given time. But since the formation of the Twelfth Regiment, Billy *was* the officer of scouts, so he would now know where all the other pickets and skirmishers were at any given time, but there was no one required to keep track of *him*.

So, Ollie had been forced to follow a series of suggestions, hints, rumors, and clues until he finally located his man. He had to admit it had been an interesting intellectual exercise, and as it had not been a pressing matter, the delay had not caused any undue concern.

And though the thing he wished to discuss with Billy was not urgent, Ollie had an ever-present need to satisfy his own overly active mind. It had been the thing that had driven him to become the de facto intelligence officer for General Joseph Johnston and then later for General Lee back when Ollie served the

Confederacy, and now, at times when the regiment was idle, it rarely let him rest even for a few hours.

Fortunately, since switching sides in the war and joining the Twelfth, he'd had very little idle time, him now being a field commander of troops. It was a new experience for Ollie, and the *old* him might've shrunk away from the responsibility, and even the outright fear of leading men in combat. But Colonel Chambers's unwavering confidence in him had affected him in ways he could never have previously imagined. He'd always felt inadequate and inferior beneath the long shadow of his own father, and he'd felt much the same in the presence of experienced military men like General Lee. But Nathan Chambers was a whole different kind of leader. He seemed to sense some ability in Ollie that he didn't recognize himself; Chambers simply *expected* Ollie to perform well. And maybe because of that, he had.

On this particular occasion, with a few hours to occupy, and for reasons he did not understand, his mind had decided to contemplate various tactics and strategies of the regiment's scouts, pickets, and skirmishers, and how these differed when employed in static defense, in offensive action, and when on the march. It had been a topic of some concern to him under Lee, as these forward positioned troops were a vital source of timely intelligence concerning the enemy, but he'd had little opportunity to delve deeply into its practical day-to-day functioning.

He'd been mulling over various things he knew, and others he didn't, when he'd decided the best thing would be to speak with an expert on the subject. And he knew of no greater expert than Billy Creek.

So now Ollie stepped up next to Billy. "Hello, Captain Boyd," Billy finally said, continuing to stare up at the sky.

Ollie stifled a chuckle. Billy was the only soldier he knew who could regularly get away with ignoring military protocol and not turning to salute a superior officer. It was something of an unwritten rule in the Twelfth, and everyone seemed to know it; Colonel Chambers expected everyone in his command to follow strict discipline and protocol … except Billy.

Ollie looked up, but the bright sun dazzled his eyes for a moment, and he had to shade them with his hand. "What're you looking at, Mr. Creek?" he asked.

Billy finally looked down at Ollie. "I am watching how she flies ... and I am puzzled by it."

Ollie looked up again, shading his eyes against the sun from the start so as not to be blinded again. Then he saw the thing that had captured Billy's attention: the shape of a hawk soaring several hundred feet overhead. "Your hawk?"

"Yes ... though she is not mine. She chooses to stay close by me at times, for reasons known only to her, but she does not belong to me, nor is she a tame beast."

Ollie nodded, then looked back up, "Just now you said you were puzzled ... how so?"

"Normally she soars in broad, overlapping circles. Though she seems to fly higher at times and lower at others depending on the terrain below her—hills or valleys, streams or lakes, and so on— she usually soars in perfect circles. But today ... well, see for yourself, Captain."

Ollie reached down for the binoculars that hung around his neck by a strap. He looked up, and in a moment located the hawk. He saw, just as Billy had described, the hawk soaring in a wide arc overhead. At that moment, she was flying in a clockwise direction, coming steadily closer to their current location, though somewhat to their right. Then, suddenly, as she came almost even with their position at the stump, she peeled off in the opposite direction, now flying in the counterclockwise direction. *Hmm ... interesting.*

Ollie continued to watch as the hawk now circled out away from them, then came closer once again, this time off to their left. But then, once again as she came almost even with the stump, she peeled off, returning to the clockwise direction.

Ollie lowered the glasses and looked over at Billy. "She is flying in semi-circles, rather than the full circles you described a moment ago."

"Yes … as I said, it is unusual for her, though I have seen it at times before. This is what I was trying to puzzle out … the *why* of it."

"Ah," Ollie answered, then brought the field glasses back up again and watched the hawk repeat the same odd pattern several more times. Then he jumped up onto another nearby stump and gazed about—first in the direction the hawk seemed to prefer, then slowly turning to his left, scanning the terrain for anything that might account for the hawk's odd behavior. He'd turned nearly 180 degrees, until he was facing in the direction from which he'd come … and then it hit him … He was now facing back toward … *the camp*—a camp filled like a veritable beehive of activity with hundreds of soldiers.

"It's the camp, Billy. I believe she prefers not to fly over our camp."

Billy looked over at Ollie, then back toward the camp and his eyes widened. "Yes … could be…" Then he was quiet for several moments as if contemplating this new revelation. "This is … most interesting. And may prove … *useful*."

Ollie nodded and grinned, pleased with himself for solving the puzzle, though he couldn't quite figure how that might prove useful.

Then Billy looked intently at Ollie, as if really seeing him for the first time. "The Captain has told me that you are a good man, and would prove your worth to the regiment. But I did not know you before. *Now* … now I am seeing what he meant by it."

"Thank you, Sergeant Creek. It has been the greatest pleasure and honor in my life serving under Colonel Chambers. I only hope I can measure up to his expectations.

"Tell me, though, as you now have captured my curiosity concerning this interesting creature overhead, have you not given her a name?"

Billy shrugged, "None of the normal lady names seem to fit a hawk. She is a natural born fighter and a skilled killer. I could think of a few names in Tonkawa that might fit, but then none of the white men would be able to say them. So, I have just been calling her 'she,' and since there are no women in camp, everyone knows who I am meaning."

"Hmm ... doesn't seem proper, not giving her a name, since she's become something of an honorary member of the Twelfth, like Harry the Dog..." Ollie scratched at the stubble on his chin. "But I agree, calling her Betty or Susie, or some such, just wouldn't do. Billy, just now you used the words ... 'lady' and 'hawk' in the same sentence. How about a name that's both straightforward and descriptive, like 'Ladyhawk'?"

Billy thought a moment, then nodded. "Yes, could be... If it pleases you, Captain Boyd."

"Yes ... it does; for some odd reason it seems like something of an honor to name your very remarkable bird ... yes, yes, I know ... she doesn't belong to you. But anyway, I thank you, Billy. This has been most interesting ... much more so than the thing I came out here to discuss with you, I think. Perhaps we shall have *that* talk another day."

ﰮﰮﰮﰮﰮﰮﰮﰮﰮﰮ

The flap of Tom's tent suddenly flew open, and Nathan poked his head in, "C'mon, Tom ... 'rest and refit' is over; we've gotta go, *now!*"

"*What?!* What has happened?" Tom said as he leapt from his seat, snatched up his hat, and started to grab his tunic until he thought better of it; the heat was stifling. He turned and headed out the door after Nathan, who was already striding away. Tom had to trot to catch up.

"It's General Early..." Nathan answered. "While we've all been assuming he headed back to Richmond after the Lynchburg battle, turns out he's instead stolen a march down the valley, headed to ... *guess where...*"

"*Washington City!* Damn it, Nathan. How did *that* happen? Hunter's been telling us to rest up and get ready for another campaign ... and now this? It's Winchester all over again."

"Agreed. Apparently General Hunter has been badly misinformed. We're to march to Harpers Ferry post haste, there

115

to report to General Crook, who's been tasked with chasing after Early."

"How far's Early gotten?"

"Already crossed the Potomac, from what I heard. One can only imagine the mad scramble now going on at Washington to throw something up in front of him."

"Reminds me when we had to try to stop Stonewall Jackson at Harpers Ferry."

"Yep, only this time it's worse. Come on, let's get the men moving."

෨෩෬෭෨෩෬෭෨෩෬෭

Saturday July 9, 1864 – Monocacy Junction, Maryland:

Captain Jubal Collins took one last look through his binoculars knowing the order for the brigade to advance would be forthcoming. General Early had hoped to flank the left side of the federals' line using the cavalry alone, and then have the infantry exploit the breakthrough, but so far that hadn't worked out. Jubal watched as the Confederate cavalry's charge slowed, then came to a halt—never a good sign when confronting dug-in infantry. An initial volley by the Yankees had been followed by independent rifle fire and several shots of cannister from their artillery. The result had been predictable: the cavalry began falling back, leaving the dead and wounded in its wake.

Jubal lowered his glasses and shrugged. It was not a major setback, and he was still confident that General Terry's brigade, of which the remnants of the old Stonewall Brigade were a minor part, would easily sweep aside the enemy to their front. Jubal had been skeptical, to say the least, when he'd learned that General Early meant to instigate a march against the federal capital after breaking off the pursuit of Hunter's army after the victory at Lynchburg. He feared another Antietam or Gettysburg; nothing good had ever come of the army's excursions into the North.

But he had to admit, this time it felt different. With the Union's main army group, the Army of the Potomac, engaged with Lee's army around Petersburg and Richmond, the North had been

116

nearly stripped bare of defenses. Opposition had been light or non-existent during much of the march, and even now, at the critical Monocacy Junction—one road leading to Baltimore and another to Washington City—it was clear the federals were in desperate straits, pushing forward green, disorganized troops, with insufficient, poorly manned artillery. And even had they been hardened veterans, which they clearly were *not*, there were not nearly enough of them to hold back General Early's army for long.

It was a heady feeling, knowing that they only had to push aside this pathetic army facing them and then the road to the enemy's capital would be wide open. If they could seize the capital, the federals would be forced to sue for peace, and then perhaps the war would be over. Jubal felt a growing excitement at the prospect of *that*, a feeling he'd not had since the thrilling victory at the first battle of Manassas, when the brigade and their general had earned their famous moniker.

The order came down the line to prepare to advance, and Jubal relayed the order to his own men, then checked his rifle to make sure everything was in order and to affix the bayonet to the barrel.

He looked up in time to see the cavalry streaming past, looking a bit worse for the wear—ragged and tired, with a number of the troopers nursing fresh wounds. As a cavalry officer—a lieutenant colonel—trotted toward him on his horse, Jubal noticed that the man was missing his left hand. But this was an old wound, well healed over. He glanced up at the officer's face, and something tickled the back of his mind.

Who are you? Where do I know you from...?

Jubal suffered an itchy, unpleasant sensation that suggested there had been something very negative about his earlier interaction with this officer. But with all the marching and fighting, and all the different regiments and officers he'd encountered in the last several years, it was all a jumble in his mind.

He gazed intently at the man's face as the rider came ever closer. *Odd ... though he's clearly just been through some intense and deadly action, the man seems strangely unaffected by it, like he has no feelings at all.*

And then it came back to him like water through a floodgate — the federals' retreat from the encirclement of Winchester, the capture of thousands of Union soldiers. Then a Confederate lieutenant colonel from the cavalry murdering a captive sergeant and nearly shooting a captain. Jubal's own timely intervention to prevent *that* tragedy.

What did the young Union captain say the colonel's name was? Hmm … something with a W … Walker … no … Wallace? No, no … hmm … Walters. Yes, that was it, Walters.

Jubal had filed a formal complaint at the time, but either the paperwork had been lost — they were, after all, on the march to Gettysburg then — or it had been ignored by the War Department. In any case, clearly nothing had been done about it, as Walters was still an officer in the cavalry.

As the colonel approached, Jubal faced him and nearly called out his name, thinking to confront him about what he'd done. But then he thought better of it. *What would I say to him? What would I do? Shoot him? Right here in front of the men … and for no apparent reason?*

As the rider drew up even with Jubal's position, he seemed to notice Jubal's stare and looked in his direction. But if he recognized Jubal at all, he showed no sign of it and quickly turned away, trotting past.

Jubal let out his breath, not realizing he'd been holding it. And then the order to advance came down the line and all thoughts of the murderous Lieutenant Colonel Walters were swept from his mind.

SO)CRCFEU)SO)CRCFEU)SO)CRCF

Monday July 11, 1864 – Fort Stevens - Washington, D.C.:

"Mr. President, please step away from there now, sir…" a stern voice commanded. The voice was not one Lincoln had been expecting, and as such, it gave him pause; he turned from the spectacle he'd been gazing out at to see who this new person

118

might be. He'd anticipated a scolding from Secretary of War Edwin Stanton, or from any one of the half dozen White House staff members who invariably accompanied him wherever he went around the capital—expected it and had been entirely prepared to ignore it. He wished to continue his firsthand observation of the battle scene unfolding before his very eyes out beyond the battlements of Fort Stevens just north of Washington City, despite any potential danger.

The man standing a few yards behind him atop the earthen wall of Fort Stevens was a strongly built, serious-looking sergeant in his late thirties or early forties, cradling a rifle in his arms. Lincoln could immediately sense that this man was an actual, honest-to-God soldier who clearly knew his business. The president suddenly felt presumptuous and self-conscious, and even a bit foolish. He stepped away from his exposed position on the edge of the fort's parapet and stood in front of the soldier.

"If *you* can see the rebels, Mr. President, then *they* can see you. We are within rifle range here, sir, so I would appreciate it if you would not so expose yourself to the danger."

Lincoln nodded to the soldier. "Is that an *order*, Sergeant?" he asked, now with an amused look.

"Oh, *no*, sir. If you were one of my *privates*, it would be ... but you are in fact the Commander in Chief. That makes you my superior officer, and I would never presume to give you orders, sir. I can only *request* that you allow me to do my sworn duty and protect you from the enemy, sir."

Then, as if to underscore the sergeant's concern, the distant popping of rifles could be heard, along with the dull thudding of their projectiles embedding themselves into the thick, dirt walls of the fort. Then they heard a sharp cry of pain and saw that a soldier who'd also been up on the wall a few yards away had been hit and was crawling away to safety. Union rifles returned the fire, but how effective that response might be, was impossible for the president to discern.

Lincoln ducked his head and followed the sergeant down off the wall. Once back on the ground, he stood and faced the man again, "It appears you were quite right, Sergeant, and I stand corrected and properly chastised for it, although ... I can't promise I won't do it again. I have been known to be somewhat impetuous in that regard."

"Yes, sir. And clearly a man of personal courage, if I may say so."

Now Lincoln smiled, "What's your name, Sergeant, and where are you from?"

"Sergeant Major Patrick Murphy, Twelfth New York Volunteer Infantry Regiment, sir. My hometown is in upstate New York—a nice quiet little place called Brockport, right on the Erie Canal."

"Ah ... Twelfth New York, you say? But ... I wasn't aware we even had a veteran infantry regiment in the capital ... I'd been informed we were scrambling to find any man who could shoulder a rifle at this point."

"Uh, yes ... you were correctly informed, sir. Old habits ... I *was* a part of the Twelfth at the start of the conflict. Was wounded at First Bull Run. Caught a piece of shrapnel to the back, and the surgeons have banished me to home-front duty ever since."

"Ah ... I see. And yet, here you are, clearly prepared to fight and defend your nation's capital in its most desperate hour, Sergeant."

"Yes, sir. I heard about the emergency, and gathered what men I could—all of our off-duty prison guards, commissary officers, cooks, and so forth—armed them with rifles, and came at the double-quick. We may not be much—and most of us are here after being wounded too badly to march—but such as we are, we *will* fight, sir. And with the current shortage of officers, they've put me in charge of this section of the wall.

"Which is why I am standing here, *requesting* that the President of the United States not get himself killed by a Confederate sniper on my watch. With all due respect, sir."

Lincoln nodded, "Good man, Sergeant. Well done. But ... you said *prison guards* just now...?"

"Oh, sorry ... yes, sir. Since being wounded, my duty has been to serve as officer of the guard at Old Capitol Prison, though I am a trained soldier, sir, and would prefer to be out in the field."

"Of that I have no doubt, Sergeant Murphy. You appear to be a fellow who knows which is the business end of a gun. And speaking of men who know how to fight, General Grant has informed me that he has four divisions of the VI and XIX Corps already on their way to the capital from City Point by boat. Should be arriving here later this evening. So, if you and the rest of our men can hold the rebels off for the remainder of the day, then all will be well. Otherwise…?" he shrugged.

And then, despite the dire circumstances, Lincoln couldn't resist chuckling at a humorous thought, "Ironically, if you men succeed in holding him off today, our friend *Early* will have arrived one day too *late!*"

Murphy nodded and smiled at the president's attempted humor.

"Come, Sergeant … walk with me a moment, if you would, as I rejoin the secretary and the rest of my party. I'd appreciate if you would take the time to explain the current military situation that I was observing out beyond these walls just now…"

"Yes, sir. It would be my honor, Mr. President."

※)C8C8次)※)C8C8次)※)C8C8

Jubal Collins pushed past General Early's staff officers and stepped right up to the commanding general himself and saluted. But the general was busily gazing out at the city with his field glasses, and didn't seem to notice Jubal's arrival.

"Sir … I'm Captain Collins of the Twenty-Seventh Virginia. I have just come from the forward skirmish lines and wish to report the situation out there, sir."

General Early lowered the glasses and looked down at Jubal with a frown.

"Captain … why have you left your post? Why not send one of your men to give the report? And why not give it to one of my staff officers, as is proper protocol?"

"Because, sir … I wished for there to be no … *misunderstanding* … about what I am seeing out there."

Early raised an eyebrow at this, "Go on, Captain…"

"General … *we have them, sir!* We've caught the federals with their pants completely down this time. The hastily thrown-up breastworks in front of us are manned by the most haphazard looking men I've yet seen in the war. Many are not wearing uniforms, and carry what appear to be common hunting rifles. And most of those who *are* in uniform appear to be their walking wounded; I saw several men sporting large bandages, as if fresh from hospital, and others walking stiffly with canes or crutches. The defenders up on the walls of Fort Stevens itself appear to be a similar hodgepodge collection of men.

"And the few big guns I saw were old smoothbores, and their crews seemed terribly inept at handling them, as if learning on the job. There seem to be few officers to direct these men, and their lines are dangerously thin. Further, our forward scouts report no movement of larger formations anywhere nearby—"

In his excitement, Jubal's words had come out in a tumbling flow, and he suddenly stopped, realizing he'd not allowed the general to respond nor to ask any questions.

"Sorry, sir, I was just …" and then Jubal noticed the general had *not* reacted in the way he'd expected. Not at all.

Early groaned, "*Damn it!* It is as I feared …" he said, and went back to gazing through his binoculars.

"Sir?" Jubal was completely dumbfounded by the commanding general's response.

Early continued to peer through his glasses in silence for several moments.

Jubal was bewildered, and feared perhaps the general had not understood what he was saying. So he decided to chance being a bit more direct, "Sir, I believe with one good hard thrust we will sweep their meager defenses aside and their capital will be ours."

Early lowered the glasses and looked back at Jubal with a scowl. "I *do* understand your report, Captain. Don't presume to teach me my business."

"Sorry, sir, I …"

But Early's frown immediately changed to a look of utter frustration, as if Jubal's indiscretion was already forgotten. "What would you have me do, Captain? Through these field glasses I can see the Capitol dome itself … so close I can almost reach out and touch it. And believe me, I'd like nothing better than to burn the thing to the ground. Hell, I'd happily light that match myself…"

Jubal turned and for the first time looked in the direction of the general's gaze. In the far distance, through a dusty, wavy haze of heat, he could just make out the great white dome, even as Early had said.

"But only half my men have yet arrived … the others are straggled halfway back to Monocacy Junction. It's this infernal heat … With our men half-starved as it is, they're falling out like flies. I've had reports of men staggering out of formation on the march, and simply dying right there on the side of the road from pure heat and exhaustion.

"And of those few who are here, I'd wager less than a quarter have any fight left in them."

Then Early seemed to really notice Jubal for the first time. Though Jubal too was exhausted, and his sweat-soaked uniform was so caked in dust that the yellow piping was indistinguishable from the gray fabric, *he* still had fight left in him.

Early nodded, "*Twenty-Seventh* you say? Stonewall Brigade … old guard … You men are the veterans … You don't know how to quit, even half dead. But these others … *pah!*"

"Then … what shall we do, sir?"

"Collins, return to your skirmish line. Continue to harass the enemy and observe their movements. We must give our men time to arrive, rest, and regroup. Either later this evening, or tomorrow morning at the latest, we will launch our main attack."

"Very good, sir," Jubal saluted, and turned on his heels, preparing to return to his unit.

"Oh, and there is one more thing you can do, Captain …"

Jubal turned back toward the general, "Sir?"

"Pray that Grant is caught napping and delays, giving us just *one* more day…"

"That I will do, sir."

☙❧☙❧☙❧☙❧☙❧☙❧

Monday July 11, 1864 – Harpers Ferry, West Virginia:

By the time Crook's command reached Harpers Ferry, a rumor was circulating that General Early meant to take the town, and that an attack was imminent.

Nathan was skeptical; after all, if Early meant to attack Washington, why would he backtrack to capture Harpers Ferry? But General Crook was concerned enough that he ordered the army to a position atop Maryland Heights, on the north side of the river overlooking the town, and there to dig in.

So there was nothing for Nathan to do but obey his orders, and stew … wondering whether Early was even now attacking Washington as he and the Twelfth sat in a trench on top of a hill, waiting for an attack that might never come.

⚞⚟⚞⚟⚞⚟⚞⚟⚞⚟⚞⚟

Tuesday July 12, 1864 – Fort Stevens - Washington, D.C.:

Though there'd been some sharp skirmishing and an ongoing, moderately heavy artillery duel the afternoon after they'd arrived at Fort Stevens, Jubal had a feeling General Early had been correct: that his men were just too exhausted to conduct any major operations until the following morning.

Jubal was up before dawn, pacing back and forth behind his dug-in line of skirmishers, waiting for it to be light enough out to see what the enemy was up to. When the sun finally peeked into the sky, Jubal raised his field glasses and gazed across at the enemy's earthworks. What he saw made his heart sink, and he let out a low moan: thousands of blue-uniformed soldiers now manned the fortifications along the streets, with thousands more up on the walls of Fort Stevens. Further back, he could see more troops marching forward, rifles on their shoulders, led by Union officers. A large artillery battery moved along behind them, pulled by teams of horses. Ammunition caissons for the big guns followed. Jubal could see these cannons were accompanied by what he assumed were their gun crews. The guns were new-looking—large, shiny, and black—and the crews had a

124

professional appearance, unlike the raggedy ones he'd seen the day before.

Veterans … fresh from the fight down in Virginia, no doubt, Jubal decided.

He turned to the man next to him. "Sergeant Rollins … I wish you to take a message to General Early, straightaway."

"Yes, sir. Do you wish me to write it down?"

"No, that won't be necessary; the message to General Early is quite simple."

"Which is?"

"Just tell him this: 'General Grant has arrived.'"

꽃ꆂꇙꋬꆂꇙꋬ꽃ꆂꇙꋬꆂꇙꋬ꽃ꆂꇙꋬ

Monday July 18, 1864 – Snicker's Ferry, Virginia:

Nathan slowly smoked a cigar, taking several deep breaths to help still his growing frustration as he gazed out from his regiment's position on the west bank of the Shenandoah. Once again, a Confederate general, this time Jubal Early, had invaded the North, wreaked havoc and caused mass panic, then had been allowed to escape virtually intact. Nathan couldn't help but think of the Gettysburg campaign, when the Twelfth had been unsuccessful in cutting off Lee's army, thanks to General Meade's lack of aggression.

And now, in similar fashion, Early had been able to re-cross the Potomac at Leesburg, looting and pillaging with seeming impunity as he went, and now had also successfully crossed the Shenandoah into western Virginia.

The good news this time, Nathan reminded himself, was that the Union Army was in hot pursuit, seemingly determined to catch Early before he could skulk back to Richmond with his ill-gotten gains.

General Crook, in command of the remnants of General Hunter's command, including Nathan's regiment, had joined forces with Major General Wright, whom Grant had sent to Washington along with four divisions of his VI Corps, giving the federal army a formidable force for the pursuit.

The Twelfth had forded the river as part of a brigade under the command of Colonel Joseph Thoburn, a fellow West Virginian with whom Nathan had a cordial, if not overly warm, relationship. Thoburn had been tasked with driving off the rebel pickets that guarded the ford—assumed to be the rearguard of Early's retreating army—and then securing the crossing for the remainder of the Union Army to follow after.

Thoburn had assigned the Twelfth Regiment reserve duty, ordering them to stay behind at the riverbank while he led the remainder of the brigade to a nearby ridgeline topped by a stone wall, where they would take cover just in case the rebels had any ideas of driving them off. Nathan, not taking any chances, ordered his men to also dig in, using the bank of a roadway that ran parallel to the river upon which to build its low breastworks.

Later that afternoon, Tom approached Nathan's position at the center of the Twelfth's line. "Flanks are secured, and all companies report they are prepared to conduct defensive actions as necess—"

Tom's report was interrupted by the sudden sound of rifle fire, seeming to come from out beyond Colonel Thoburn's more advanced position. Nathan and Tom turned in that direction, and Nathan raised his brass spyglass for a look.

"Hmm … no action up at Thoburn's position at the stone wall … must be the skirmishers out in the valley beyond," Nathan said, lowering the glass.

Tom nodded, "But if the only force Early left behind was a mere picket line, or a row of skirmishers, then—"

"Why attack a much stronger Union force?" Nathan finished the question for him. "You're right, Tom, it doesn't make sense … hmm … I suggest we send the word down the line … Prepare for a general engagement."

Tom frowned, then nodded, gave a quick salute, and trotted off to pass the word to the regiment's officers.

ℬ𝒞ℛ𝒞ℬ𝒰ℬ𝒞ℛ𝒞ℬ𝒰ℬ𝒞ℛ𝒞ℬ

By the time Tom returned to Nathan's position, it had become readily apparent that their earlier assumption had been correct;

the enemy force in front of them was greater than had been assumed — *much* greater. After a brief pause in the fighting, which Nathan interpreted as the time it took for Thoburn's skirmishers to beat a hasty retreat back to the main column, fighting had broken out in earnest. Nathan and Tom stood and watched through their field glasses as gun smoke rose in clouds from the Union troops hunkered down behind their stone wall, and the popping and rattling of massed gunfire echoed through the valley.

"Damn it, Tom ... the left flank ... it's not going to hold ... There ... there, you see, they've turned it. The game's up..."

Tom just nodded, having nothing to add. In moments, Union soldiers from the left flank were streaming back toward the river, not bothering to stop at the Twelfth's defensive position but continuing on into the river and across.

"Pah! Green troops," Tom sneered. "Let them go ... not worth the money paid for their uniforms ... They'd just get in our way."

"Agreed," Nathan nodded. "Ah, here comes Colonel Thoburn ... bringing the remaining troops with him. A much more orderly withdrawal, to his credit."

Nathan stood, cupped his hands, and shouted out down the line to his left, then turned and repeated the order to his right, *"Twelfth West Virginia will stand firm and prepare for volley fire, on my command!"*

As Colonel Thoburn approached on horseback, Nathan gestured to him, and the commander turned and spurred in his direction, leaping the horse over the low earthworks the Twelfth had thrown up on the lip of the road by the riverbank. Thoburn immediately dismounted and scrambled back to Nathan's position as the remaining Union forces came on in a steady stream.

Nathan looked over at Thoburn and said, "We will hold them here, Colonel. You might have some men reinforce our right flank, otherwise, I suggest you send the rest of them back across the river. There are at least several enemy brigades out there, and likely more coming."

Thoburn nodded, "Good ... Well done, Chambers, and agreed. With your leave, I will take command on the right flank and will reinforce you as best we can ... Buy time for the rest of the brigade to reach safety."

"*Sir!*" Nathan said with a salute, then as the last of Thoburn's men crossed the Twelfth's line, Nathan raised his spyglass to eye the oncoming enemy, and whistled to himself. *A full infantry division, at the least.*

But the rebels were coming on pell-mell, completely disorganized, shouting in their excitement, assuming the rout was on. Nathan had other ideas.

"*Present arms!*" he yelled out, and a thousand Union rifles came up over the road bank, aimed toward the oncoming rebels. Nathan unshouldered his own Henry rifle and cranked in a round. "*Aim!*" He picked out a target ... a tall, lean fellow, yelling wildly while shaking his rifle above his head ... about three-hundred yards distant ... "*Fire!*" Nathan squeezed the trigger. The Henry barked, pounded his right shoulder, and the barrel jumped as it belched out smoke and flame. A thunderous roar hit his ears as the great rifle volley rolled out from the Union line.

The oncoming rebels were caught completely by surprise, and dozens of men were instantly cut down mid stride.

"*Reload ... Aim ... Fire!*" Another rifle volley pounded the Confederates—no longer surging forward, but now scrambling to get out of the deadly killing field.

By the time the men of the Twelfth had reloaded for a third volley, the field was clear save for the dead and wounded; the rebels had retreated back up the ridgeline, and were now sheltering behind the same stone wall that had previously housed Thoburn's troops.

ᔕᗝᏟᔕᏟᔕᏼᗝᔕᗝᏟᔕᏟᔕᏼᗝᔕᗝᏟᔕᏟᔕ

For the remainder of the day, the rebels launched intermittent attacks at the Twelfth's position, hoping to overrun them or drive them back into the river, but Nathan, Thoburn, and the federal soldiers held firm each time.

Nathan began to suspect that the rebel commanders were rivals of some kind and not disposed to cooperate with each other, as the attacks seemed uncoordinated and piecemeal—first one brigade of Confederates would attack, and then another.

This allowed Nathan and Thoburn to reposition their men as needed to reinforce the line wherever it was most threatened. In this way, they were able to hold the position until nightfall, when they quietly passed the word to fall back across the river under cover of darkness.

As Nathan splashed back to shore—the last member of the Union formation to regain the eastern bank of the Shenandoah— Tom was there to greet him, holding out a hand to help him up out of the stream.

"Well, not exactly a victory..." Tom said with a rueful grin.

"No ... Chalk up another win for their side, sadly. But ... at least we've lived to fight another day."

"Amen to that, Nathan. And sometimes that's the best we can hope to do."

Chapter 7. Back on the Farm

*"I'd rather be on my farm
than be emperor of the world."*
- George Washington

Wednesday July 20, 1864 – Wheeling, West Virginia:

As Adilida sipped her tea in the Belle Meade sitting room, already beginning to warm up though it was only mid-morning, it occurred to her she'd not checked on little Nathaniel in over an hour. Though she wasn't especially worried, she stood and walked to the front door, and stepped out onto the patio to have a look.

She broke into a smile at the scene that greeted her: off to the left of the front stairs, just a few yards back from the driveway, a small group of children sat cross-legged on the grass in the shade of a large elm tree. The "leaders" of the group were two older girls, Annie and Lucy, ages eight and seven—Big George's girls. Nathaniel, now nearly three and a half, sat next to the older girls, gazing up at them in obvious admiration as they played a game of pat-a-cake, expertly clapping their hands against each other's to the rhythm of an old children's song:

> *My father went to sea, sea, sea,*
> *To see what he could see, see, see.*
> *But all that he could see, see, see,*
> *Was the bottom of the deep blue sea, sea, sea.*

When the girls had finished their demonstration, Nathaniel giggled and said, "Let me try!"

The little boy sitting next to Nathaniel also chimed in, "Me too … me too!"

Two little girls in the group also expressed their enthusiasm for joining in the game.

"All right," Annie, who was the older and bossier of the two sisters, replied. "Nathaniel, you sit in front of Lucy, and Samson, you sit in front of me. You two girls sit across from one another…"

The younger children immediately complied, and soon the clapping and singing began again, only this time with plenty of missed claps and the requisite restarts, with the hysterical laughter that accompanied the game's many miscues.

Adilida sighed with satisfaction at the sweetness of the scene—in sharp contrast to the noisy, rambunctious mischief Nathaniel usually managed to get into when he ran around with the other little boys.

And it was not lost on Adilida that Nathaniel sat in a circle of black children, him being the only white child on the entire farm—a fact none of the children ever seemed to give a moment's thought to. Adilida smiled and decided that maybe despite the terrible war raging, perhaps the world was making a turn for the better, at least maybe in some small ways.

She went back into the house just as the freeman maid Sarah was coming down the hallway. "Oh, hello Miss Sarah."

"Miss Adilida."

"Sarah, do you know where Miss Abbey is? I haven't seen her all morning … nor Miss Megs either, for that matter …"

"Oh, yes, Miss Adilida … Them two ladies is out in the corn field for the harvest with the other women folk … and what's left o' the men—those as ain't guardin' the farm 'gainst that old rascal Walters."

"Oh. The ladies are supervising the workers, are they?"

"No … reckon old Toby's doin' *that*—him bein' the resident expert on farmin' and such. No, they's out pickin' corn, same as all the others. Was out there myself yesterday," she held out her hands, and Adilida could see they looked scratched and blistered. "But today's my turn to help fix the meals, so I got house duty— I'm happy to say. You wantin' somethin' to eat, ma'am?"

"No, but thank you kindly, Miss Sarah."

The two exchanged a smile, and Addie headed back down the hallway, intending to finish the cup of tea that she'd left there, hoping it hadn't gone cold yet.

But when she entered the room, she found it was no longer empty; Belinda was now sitting in the chair next to where Addie had been seated, and she too was sipping a cup of tea.

"Hello Addie, how are you this fine morning?" Belinda smiled with genuine warmth. The two young women had made an immediate connection after Belinda's arrival at the farm—both being displaced Southerners whose husbands were now fighting together for the Northern side out in the war.

"Hello, Belle, my dear one. I find I am feeling ... an upwelling of joy this morning—"

"Oh? Please sit, and do tell..."

"Thank you, Belle, but I was going to add ... I also find I am suddenly feeling more than a little bit of guilt—"

Belle tilted her head quizzically as she gestured for Addie to resume her seat. "Now you have me curious ... First, tell me what has pleased you so, and then ... well, then tell me the *other* thing which has clearly given you pause."

Addie sat and resumed sipping her tea while describing, in glowing terms, the vision of idyllic childhood joy she'd just witnessed.

Belinda smiled and nodded as Addie told her tale. "What a pleasure to watch children play, without a care in the world. I am always amazed at how they are filled with such joy at the simplest things."

"True. Hopefully we too can soon feel such carefree happiness ... once our men finish this horrible war," Addie said.

Belinda nodded, suddenly seeming thoughtful.

"Sorry, Belle ... I shouldn't have darkened the mood with the mention of such a thing. Better that we just enjoy a moment of happiness and peace."

"Never mention it, dear. But you haven't said what has made you feel guilty."

"Oh, yes, *that*..." Addie set down her tea and reached out to take hold of Belinda's hands. "Belle ... I find you and I have such a very lot of things in common..."

"Yes, certainly, Addie. Which is why we get along so well."
Belinda chuckled. "So well, in fact, I've been meaning to tell
you ... I feel like you're the sister I never had."

Addie beamed and nodded. "Me too, dear one ... me too.
But ... what I was going to say is, one of those common things we
share is ... we two were raised ... how do you say? Pampered?
Yes, *pampered*. The finest clothes, the grandest houses, wonderful
parties ... like little princesses. Am I right?"

Belinda thought back on the elegant dresses, sumptuous
meals, lavish parties, and servants to meet her every need, and
nodded. "It's true ... we have lived a pampered life, as you say ...
until now, that is."

"Hmm ... do you truly think so? I mean, that we are no longer
pampered?"

"Well, the maids are no longer slaves, so we can't order them
about ... and there are no grand balls or feasts. And the house is ...
comfortable," she shrugged, "but not exactly luxurious."

Addie smiled and nodded, "True, but ... think on it, Belle,
darling ... Here we two sit, sipping our tea, without any duties or
responsibilities whatsoever. Our meals are served to us, and our
beds are made. Oh, I have to somewhat keep an eye on Nathaniel,
it's true ... but between Miss Megs and the two little Washington
girls, it seems I am hardly needed."

Belinda chuckled, and nodded, but then became thoughtful.
"So ... what are you saying, Addie?"

"I'm saying, while we two sit here at our leisure, the two *true*
ladies of the house, Miss Abbey and Miss Megs, are out there in
the fields in the hot sun all day picking the corn until their hands
are worn and blistered."

Belinda's eyes widened at the sudden realization, and the two
women shared a long, serious look. Then Belinda slowly nodded.

Addie stood to her feet and held out her hands to Belinda.
"Come, sister ... let us see if we can find some old, worn clothes
around here to change into..."

Belinda smiled, took Addie's hands, and stood. "Yes, let's do."

The young freeman, Moses, sighed for the second time in as many minutes. Phinney turned toward him and scowled, reaching up to wipe the sweat from his brow on the shirtsleeve of his one remaining arm.

"What's eatin' you, boy?" the older man asked. Though they sat in the shade, a few yards back from the roadway, it was still stiflingly hot.

Moses swatted at a fly before turning toward Phinney with a pouty expression. "Phin ... why we gots to stay here, doing nothin', while the others get to go fight in the war? Feelin' like a worthless sack of dirt, just sittin' here..."

Phinney wasn't surprised by the question, as he'd heard the same from nearly all the young men, and several of the older ones, who'd been forced to stay behind when the other freemen marched off to join the colored regiments.

"Moses, you know damned well the answer. You's only thirteen for God's sake. Though you can work a rifle—I'll give you that—you gotta give yourself a few years to grow 'fore you go 'n get yourself kilt. Or your arm blowed clean off!" He waved his empty sleeve at the young man for emphasis.

"Well, see there, Phin ... least you got somethin' to show when the fightin's over. Nobody's gonna doubt you was in it and was a hero ... But me ... they's gonna figure me for a damned coward is all."

"Now you's just talkin' nonsense, boy. You know damned well I lost this arm right here on this farm, fightin' old Walters and his scoundrels. The same kind o' rascals we's here to guard against even now ... as you well know."

"Maybe so, but I heard you still went out and fought ... in a real battle ... with big ol' cannons and whatnot. Even with one arm. There ain't no way I'm gonna do anything to match up with that."

"Hmph. You forget how it was just a few years back ... back when we was all slaves. Look at you now! Sitting there with a damned rifle across your knees, ready to shoot a hole clean through the next villain that comes down the road to our farm. Moses, that right there's a thing undreamed of by any black man

134

for the last … oh, I don't know … hundred years or more—ever since our folks came over on the damned slaver ships from old Africa. You're a man with a duty … to protect his kinfolk with a deadly weapon against all enemies. And they're *real* enough … I can vouch for that!" Once again, Phinney waved the empty sleeve at Moses, but this time made a comical face.

Moses finally smiled. "Yeah … guess when you say it that way … this here duty ain't so bad."

"You're damned right it ain't. Be proud of where you is, Mose. Even those of us too old or too young … *or too shot up*," he shrugged, "to march in the war, are still real, fighting men— warriors—such as hasn't been true of our folk since they came here to America. So … chin up, boy. And be ready to fight, 'cause it still may come to that—never forget, that devil Walters is still out there somewheres, and he'd like nothin' better than to skin us all alive."

Moses nodded, and though he looked thoughtful, and continued to swat at the swarming flies, Phinney could see he now held a grin, and seemed to sit up a bit straighter than before.

Phinney turned and gazed back down the empty driveway toward the main road that led to Wheeling, reflexively sliding the pistol in its holster to ensure its smooth movement. But for now, as had been the case all that long, hot day, the roadway was empty.

❧❧❧❧❧❧❧❧❧❧❧

The maid Sarah helped Addie and Belinda find suitable clothes to wear, along with straw hats. And once they had changed, they left the house determined to do their part. Addie decided the first person they should seek out was old Toby, since he was said to be in charge of the harvest. After asking around, they located him standing next to a wagon into which the corn cobs were being dumped by the pickers once their baskets were full.

"Well, good afternoon, ladies," he said, grinning brightly as he tipped his hat to them. "What can old Toby be doing for you?"

135

Addie giggled, "Oh, my dear Mr. Toby ... it is not what *you* will be doing for us, but what *we* will be doing for you."

He tilted his head in puzzlement at this statement, so Belinda chimed in, "Yes, that's right, sir ... we wish to do our part and help ... like Miss Abbey and Miss Megs are doing."

"Oh! Well, that is very admirable of you ladies, very admirable, and much appreciated. We got ourselves a whole lotta corn to get picked, and the more hands the quicker it gonna get itself done."

The ladies smiled at this and nodded, then Addie got a more serious expression, "But, sir ... the only difficulty is ... we don't know what to do."

"Oh, never you worry about that ... Old Toby'll show you all you need to know. Step right over here, if you will."

He led them around to the far side of the wagon, where several small baskets lay in a pile. He picked one up and handed it to Adilida.

She saw it was made of straw, with a rough-spun cloth strap attached at the top.

"Just slip that over your shoulder," Toby instructed. "Yeah ... yeah, that's it ... good!" He reached down and picked up another, handing it to Belinda, who looked at how Addie had mounted hers, and followed suit.

"Now ... reckon you'll need a knife..." He rummaged around under the pile of baskets, and soon came up with two short-bladed knives with rough wooden handles.

"Here you go ... Careful now, they's sharp," he said, handing one to each lady, handle first.

"Now, the men often just snap off the cobs, but the ladies find it easier to use the sharp blade to cut 'em loose. C'mon over here and I'll show you."

He led them a few yards away from the wagon, where some unharvested corn stalks stood. He reached out, grabbed an ear of corn on the stalk, bent it over, and neatly cut the stem using his own sharp blade. "Now, you'll need to shuck the ear, like so ..." he demonstrated quickly stripping off the green husk to reveal the golden cob beneath. "Then, just toss it in your basket, and get on with the next 'un. When your basket is full, find the nearest wagon and dump 'er in. That's all there is to it."

Belinda nodded, "That seems easy enough …"

But Addie held a frown, "But sir … down in Thibodaux I have seen the corn harvest on occasion, and I seem to recall the men cutting the stalks down with great curved blades … how do you call them? Scythes? Is this the right word?"

"Oh, yes, ma'am, scythes is often used for the corn harvest, all right. They cut down the stalks, ears 'n all, and haul them back to a drying shed for threshing … Uh, that's where they whack the stalks 'til all the dried kernels come loose. Then they scoop 'em into a pile before loading 'em into a wagon. You do get a better price for the crop that way, for certain."

"Oh … then why are we not doing it *that* way? Don't we want to get more money for our crops?" Addie asked.

"Oh, yes ma'am. And we did do it that way the first year we was here at Belle Meade. But that was when we still had all our men folk on the farm. Them piles o' corn stalks get powerful heavy, and the threshing … *whew* … now that there's a tiresome job. No … with most o' our men off to the war, we just can't manage doing it that way no more—not enough strong hands. So, we go back to the old ways … pickin' by hand, and hauling it off, cobs 'n all. But thankfully, with the army buyin' up all the grain in sight, we'll still get a good enough price."

Addie nodded and returned Toby's infectious grin. She and Belinda thanked him for his help and headed out into the fields to start doing their part. Happily, when they reached the end of the row, they found Rosa and her mother Lilly working, and were greeted with fondness and good humor. And when they looked out toward the next row, they spotted Miss Abbey looking their way, with Megs next to her cutting the ears of corn from a stalk.

They waved at Miss Abbey, and she returned the wave with a nod, smiling brightly as she tipped back her straw hat and wiped at her forehead.

෪෪෪෪෪෪෪෪෪෪෪

"Well, how about *that?*" Megs said, after Abbey pointed out the two young Southern ladies working the corn row next to them. "Guess you was right about them two after all, Abbey."

"Yes, I was, happily. And the best part was, I never had to say a word, though I was sorely tempted. They figured it out all on their own."

"Good thing, too," Megs snorted a laugh, "else I was about to scold the hide right offa them if they'd a waited much longer ..."

Abbey laughed, and reached over to pat Megs on the arm, "You would've done no such thing, dear!"

"Oh, yes I woulda!" Megs answered, then grinned and rolled her eyes.

"Now, we just need to get Edouard out here..." Abbey said with a smirk.

Megs shook her head, "That ain't gonna happen. He reckons himself too *old* for such work."

Abbey chuckled, "Not too old to flirt with every lady in town, though."

Megs nodded, continuing to sport a grin, "You noticed that too, did you? When we was up to Wheeling last time ... the fellow's quite shameless."

Abbey returned Megs's grin, and once again reached out to pat her arm, "Just serves to put an exclamation point on our little agreement ... and makes me so happy we never allowed him to come between us, my dear."

"I say amen to that, Abbey ... Amen to that!"

The two went back to work and were quiet for a time, immersing themselves in the steady rhythm of the work.

A few minutes later, Abbey paused, and said, "You know ... it doesn't seem to matter how busy I am, or how hard I work, or how many distractions; my mind just can't help starting in to worrying over how our men are doing out there ... out in the war."

"Yeah ... I know what you mean, Abbey. They're never far from the front of my mind either. Nor from my prayers. Nathan and all the wonderful men he brought here from Texas ... and of course Tony, Cobb, and all the other freemen."

Abbey nodded her agreement and reached out to grab the next ear of corn, but suddenly stopped short with a gasp.

"What is it?" Megs asked, looking concerned.

"Oh, my lord ... I just realized we'd not included Ned and his men in our thoughts and prayers."

"That's true ... We've hardly spoken of them since the rest of the men joined the fight. And we've never heard a word of them ... Don't even know if they made it to Kansas or not."

Abbey frowned and turned to Megs. "Well, that won't do, dear. That won't do at all! We must locate our beloved lost men and make amends for allowing them to slip from our minds."

"All right, I agree ... But how?"

"Hmm ... if Nathan were here, I'm sure he would know how to find them ... Someone at the War Department would be able to discover if they enlisted out in Kansas, and if so, where they're stationed."

"But Nathan's not here, and even if we could get him a message, he'd likely be too busy with the fighting to do anything about Ned and his men."

"True ... but I know someone who just might be able to help. Megs ... tomorrow let's hitch up the carriage and go pay a visit to Governor Pierpont."

ॐ๑๕๗๖๕๑๕๗๖๕๑๕๗๖๕๑๕๗๖๕๑๕๗๖๕

Megs sat with her back to a small tree near the river's edge, enjoying the cool of the shade and a slight breeze off the water after a long day in the fields. As was often the case, she'd ended up here, rather than back at the farmhouse, on the urgent insistence of little Nathaniel. He simply loved the river, but it was the one place on the farm he could not go by himself or with the other children; his mother was most insistent on that point. So, whenever Megs finished with her other chores, and before dinner was served, he'd invariably take her by the hand and look up with eager eyes, "River? Can we?"

"Oh, all right," she always answered with a grin she could not suppress. And hand in hand, they would stroll down the path to the water. There she would rest under a tree while he threw rocks and sticks into the water or searched for bugs and frogs at the water's edge. It was as peaceful and idyllic a setting as she could imagine, and despite her fatigue from the long day of work, she had to admit it had become one of her great joys in life.

The little boy's curiosity was insatiable, and his stream of questions came almost non-stop. Fortunately, Megs had lived on a farm near streams her whole long life, so there were few things she didn't know something about, and his wide-eyed wonderment at her teachings and explanations gave her great pleasure and satisfaction. And it never failed to stimulate joyful memories of another child by the same name, many years earlier.

This day, however, he asked her a question that surprised her, and for which she did not have an immediate, easy answer, "Auntie … today Momma hugged me and cried. I ask why she was sad. She says no, she's happy 'cause o' seeing me play with *black* children. *Why, Auntie?*"

Megs tilted her head thoughtfully, "Well … used to be that white children and black weren't allowed to play together. Guess your Momma's happy now as that done changed — at least on this-here farm."

"Oh…" He looked down at the ground and stirred the dirt with a stick for a moment. "Auntie … what's *black* children?"

She chuckled. It hadn't occurred to her that he had never even noticed the difference. "Come over and sit here by me, Nathaniel."

He tossed aside the stick, and came to sit next to her, looking up expectantly. "Hold out your arm," she instructed, and he immediately obeyed. "And roll up your shirtsleeve." The boy did as he was told, now grinning as if wondering what new game his Auntie was about to introduce him to.

Then Megs rolled up her own sleeve and held out her arm next to his. "See there now, my arm is black, and yours is white."

Nathaniel gazed at it a moment, then shook his head, "No, Auntie … your arm's brown … mine's pink."

Megs chuckled, "Guess you're right there, Nathaniel. Can't argue with that, no sir. But you see, it ain't the *real* color, it's just what folks calls it … Those with skin like mine, they call 'black,'

140

and those with skin like yours, they call 'white.' I reckon it don't much matter what they calls it; the point is, they's different."

"Oh. Like Momma's green eyes, and Miss Abbey's blue eyes?" Then he gazed up at her face, "And yours are black 'uns?"

Megs laughed, and slowly shook her head, beaming. "Yes, Nathaniel ... maybe so. After all is said and done ... maybe no more different than eyes."

CHAPTER 8. THE HUNTERS ARE HUNTED

*"There is no hunting
like the hunting of man,
and those who have hunted
armed men long enough and liked it,
never care for anything else thereafter."*
— Ernest Hemingway

Sunday July 24, 1864 – Kernstown, Virginia:

"Well ... as much as I *love* Winchester..." Tom rolled his eyes, making it clear he meant exactly the opposite, "tell me again why we're back here?"

Nathan had just returned from a council of war at General Crook's command tent, and Tom was eager to hear what had been discussed.

"Trying to locate General Early, apparently. After the near disaster trying to cross the Shenandoah at Snicker's Ferry, another Union force under General Averell marched from Harpers Ferry and chased Early out of Berryville.

"Apparently, our erstwhile commander General Wright had assumed—as Hunter had after Lynchburg—that Early was retreating back to Richmond. So, unfortunately for us, Wright packed up his VI Corps divisions and returned to General Grant, leaving General Crook to his own devices here in the valley, and us with him.

"But from what our spies have reported, Early has *not* yet returned to Richmond, so..." He shrugged.

"Crook's only plan, at this point," Nathan continued, "seems to be to reconnoiter the valley to figure out where Early is."

"And then?"

"And then ... once he is found ... well, then I suppose we shall have to figure out what to do about him."

Tom shook his head, *"That's* the plan? We're just to *look* for him ... a man who most likely has us outnumbered and outgunned, not to mention out-generaled—but that's just between us—and then hope to God he doesn't give us another pounding?"

Nathan snorted a laugh, "Precisely. In the meantime, let's go ahead with our little inspection. Have you lined the men up?"

"Yes, they're falling in even now."

"Excellent. Thanks, Tom. Ought to be good for morale—meet each man eye to eye, and get a feel for how he's doing."

They turned and strode across the Twelfth's camp to where the men were already falling out in formation for the previously announced inspection.

"Agreed ... ironic though, isn't it?" Tom said. "That the men assume you want to make sure they've properly cleaned their rifle, or have the proper items in their kit, or some such ... But what an officer is really doing is getting their pulse and trying to lift their spirits a bit if he can."

"Yes, true, true ... though I *do* like a clean rifle..." Nathan grinned, then stuck an unlit cigar in his mouth.

As Nathan and Tom strode out in front of the assembled troops, a rider approached at the gallop, came to a bounding stop in front of the colonel, and hopped down from the saddle. After saluting, he handed Nathan a note, then remounted and rode off.

Nathan quickly read the paper and handed it across to Tom. "Seems like we've found Early..."

"Or rather he's found *us!"* Tom groaned after reading the note himself.

Nathan cupped his hands, and shouted, "Twelfth will load rifles, and prepare to march at the double-quick. You will leave all belongings behind ... General Crook is coming under attack!"

☣☣☣☣☣☣☣

When the Twelfth and the rest of Colonel Thoburn's command arrived at the battlefield an hour later, they were positioned on the Union right flank. But to Nathan's expert eye, it was clear that the situation for General Crook's army was already dire. The rebel force in front of them was vastly superior, not only in depth, but also extending well beyond the ends of the Union line. Nathan knew it was going to be a monumental challenge just to keep from being flanked and overrun.

But it was not in his character to quit without putting up a fight. So, he ordered the men into line of battle and waited for the onslaught.

And onward the enemy came, screaming the rebel yell and driving hard against the Union line. Colonel Thoburn's division was pushed back, fighting all the way, constantly moving to the right to prevent being flanked. But the numbers against them were too great, and their attempts to protect their right flank opened a gap between them and the rest of the Union formation, which the rebels poured into.

Once again, in the heat of battle, Colonel Thoburn sought out Nathan, trotting up on his horse and shouting, "We must withdraw, Chambers. Can the Twelfth again buy us some time?"

Nathan scowled, but answered, "We'll do our best, Colonel, but it's going to be a near thing."

Thoburn nodded, then jerked on his reins and galloped off.

Tom and Nathan shared a dark look. "I'll not sacrifice our men this time, Tom. Let's fall back fighting, rather than standing our ground. We'll do what we can to prevent the rout, but then … it's going to be up to the Almighty."

"Agreed."

⊱⊰⊱⊰⊱⊰⊱⊰⊱⊰⊱⊰⊱⊰

"Roberts…" Elijah Walters reined in his horse as his second in command came up at the gallop, pulling his horse to a stop and snapping a salute. It had begun to rain, and Roberts had to shake his head to remove the beads of water streaming off his hat.

"Have you found them?"

Captain Roberts smiled, "Yes, sir! Sorry it took a while … The Union line has all but collapsed, and it's gotten a bit hectic out there … Anyway, yes, I talked to several scouts, finally finding one who reported that Thoburn's brigade is on the Union right

144

flank, our left of course. Last we heard, the Twelfth West Virginia was part of that brigade, so..."

"Let's move, Captain ... Time's wasting!"

"Sir!"

The Thirty-Sixth Virginia Cavalry Battalion rode out at a fast trot, in a long double column, angling to the left as they moved forward, aiming toward where the Union right flank had last been located, before beginning their fall back.

The Thirty-Sixth had been in a reserve position behind the center of the Confederate line, and would now have to skirt the left end of their own infantry in order to pursue the fleeing Twelfth.

Walters felt a growing excitement merged with an anxious sense of urgency, knowing with every passing moment Chambers could be slipping further away.

An hour and a half later, the Thirty-Sixth began to encounter resistance from Union pickets, but these were quickly driven back by their overwhelming numbers. They managed to capture two of the federals, who divulged the information Walters most wanted to know, before he had them both shot: as luck would have it, the Twelfth West Virginia was now the furthest Union formation to the west, apparently assigned to seal that flank during the retreat.

But rather than attack them directly, Walters ordered his men to drive hard into the small gap between the Twelfth and the next closest regiment, one from Ohio. Then he turned his men toward the Twelfth's position, which continued to move ever northward. His goal was to harass Chambers just enough, without seriously engaging him, to drive him ever backward and to the west until he was isolated from the rest of Crook's army. Then...

For three hours the Thirty-Sixth sparred with the Twelfth, continuing to press and pursue them until Walters gestured for Captain Roberts to come to him.

"Sir?" Roberts saluted.

"Roberts ... call off the attack. Pull the men back ... say, a half mile or so."

"But ... sir...?"

"And then," Walters continued, ignoring Roberts's implied objection, "send forward our best scouts to shadow them. I want to know exactly where they go. But ... have them stay well back. They must *not* be seen; Chambers still has that damned Indian."

Roberts' frown turned to a grin, "*Ah ... I see where you're going,* sir. Very clever ... very clever, indeed. Make them think we've given up the chase..."

"Precisely, Mr. Roberts."

ℬↃↄℜↄℭℬↄↅↃℬↃↄℜↄℭℬↄↅↃℬↃↄℜↄℭℬ

"No sign of the rebel cavalry for the last hour," Tom reported as Nathan stood on a stump and gazed out to the south through his spyglass.

Nathan muttered a curse, "Damned rain..." as he lowered the glass and attempted to wipe the moisture off the end with his sleeve, which was also soaked through, so it had little effect.

"All right, Tom. Let's call a rest, but deploy the pickets—out say, a quarter mile. Make sure our friends don't decide to try something tricky in the ... what, half-hour or so left of daylight? Have the men dig in here as best they can, and let's just go ahead and have them sleep on their arms tonight."

"Yes, sir ... but it's going to be a damned uncomfortable night of it, with no food, no tents—not even gum blankets. The only good news is the rain seems to be easing up ... *somewhat.*"

"Yep ... it's going to be uncomfortable, all right. But we're alive, which is a damned sight better than it was looking like a few hours ago. I'll take a bit of discomfort over being dead any day."

Tom returned a rueful grin, "Well, that's certainly putting the best possible light on it, I'd have to say."

Nathan returned the grin, and patted Tom on the shoulder, before striding away.

ℬↃↄℜↄℭℬↄↅↃℬↃↄℜↄℭℬↄↅↃℬↃↄℜↄℭℬ

Jubal Collins marched at the head of his column, leading his men back from the front lines for a well-deserved rest. Troops who'd spent the battle in reserve now pushed forward past them

146

to set up picket lines in case any of the federal formations decided to turn and fight, though Jubal thought it highly unlikely. Crook's army had taken a serious beating today, fighting against overwhelming numbers. He couldn't imagine a scenario in which any of the Yankees would even pause in their headlong flight, let alone turn back to fight.

It had been one of the most lop-sided victories yet, and Jubal realized he should be feeling giddy about that. But somehow, he just felt glum. He was mulling over the reasons for his odd, incongruous feelings when he happened to pass in front of General Terry and his staff officers standing beside the road conversing.

Jubal caught the general's eye, and inwardly groaned, as he would now likely be required to converse, and it was the last thing he wanted at the moment. He held up his hand for the column to halt and turned to the lieutenant next to him, giving him the order to lead the men on into camp. Then Jubal stepped over to the general, stood to attention, and saluted.

Terry returned the salute and held a broad grin. "Good fighting today, Captain Collins. A nice little victory," Terry chuckled. "I expect Crook and his men are still running. Likely won't slow down until they've crossed the Potomac."

Jubal nodded, but could think of nothing to add.

Terry frowned, "What? Not feeling celebratory? Took many casualties, did you?"

"No, sir. None to speak of … Only a few minor wounds … nothing serious."

"Well, then … why the sullen look, Captain?"

"I … I was just thinking, sir … We seem to win a lot of battles against the Yankees."

"Yes … and that is a bad thing, how?"

Jubal frowned. He was struggling to put into words the thoughts he'd been wrestling with, and feared he was unnecessarily irritating the general.

"It's just … we win battles, but never seem any closer to winning the war. I thought we had a chance back at Washington, but then … the chance slipped away, and … well, here we are, back to winning lots of battles but…"

"But not winning the war?"

"Yes, sir … that's what was on my mind. At the beginning of the conflict there was plenty of talk of whupping the Yanks and ending it. Nobody talks that way anymore. So, it makes me wonder how it's ever going to end. How can we ever win, if the federals can lose battle after battle and just keep coming, with a seemingly endless supply of men, weapons, and equipment?"

Terry nodded and looked thoughtful. "Well … they say if we keep winning, then it will make Lincoln look bad. So bad, that he may lose his reelection. Then maybe the next guy will be more agreeable to making peace with us."

"General McClellan, isn't it? Wouldn't a general be inclined to keep fighting?"

"Normally, I would say 'yes,' but the Democrat party that he's running under has a plank in its platform that says they'll negotiate an end to the war. And McClellan himself has made multiple statements over the years opposing abolition and emancipation. So…"

"So … we fight battles, in order to affect an election in a country we no longer recognize as ours? Seems like an odd thing to fight and die for, sir."

Terry nodded, but said, "Maybe … maybe so, but it may be the best we can hope for at this point, Captain. So, if that's what it takes, then that's what we must do. Whatever it takes…"

"Yes, sir. Whatever it takes…"

🙰🙵🙰🙵🙰🙵🙰🙵🙰🙵🙰🙵

Monday July 25, 1864 – north of Winchester, Virginia:

"Come, Tom … I tire of waiting for Billy to find the best route out ahead … Let's climb that rise over there, up onto those rocks. Now that the rain has cleared, let's see if we can't gain an idea as to which path we ought to take through these hills. And maybe get a glimpse of the enemy back down the valley, though our scouts haven't seen anything of them since we disengaged yesterday. Likely nothing to see, but you never know."

"Sounds good, Nathan. But … do you think we should take an escort? A rifle company, maybe?"

"Hmm … no, let them rest for a bit; God knows they've earned it. They've had a long hard slog already today after an even harder fight yesterday, and likely little sleep last night with all the rain. It's … what? Only fifty yards or so? We'll leave the horses and just hike over and be back before anyone even misses us. Besides … it'll be nice to stretch our legs a bit after spending all day yesterday—and half of today—in the saddle."

"I like the sound of that. But…" Tom walked over to where their horses were tied in the shade of a large elm tree and proceeded to pull their Henry rifles from the slings tied to the horses' saddles. He walked back over and tossed one of the rifles, which Nathan caught neatly.

"Just in case," Tom said with a grin, which Nathan returned with a snorted laugh, and a shrug, as he slung the rifle over his shoulder.

A quarter hour later, after a short hike through the woods and a quick scramble up a rise topped by well-worn, rounded rocks that peeked up above the treetops, the two officers turned toward the north. Nathan pulled out his brass spyglass from where he'd tucked it inside his tunic, and Tom pulled up a pair of binoculars he'd hung around his neck by the strap. They carefully examined the terrain ahead of them in hopes of finding a reasonable path through the thick vegetation and across the hilly terrain.

For the next half hour, they discussed various options and possibilities, but could not decide on the proper course.

"I think we'll just have to wait for Billy to complete his reconnoiter," Nathan concluded. "I fear if we just march out blindly, we may lose a lot more time than if we just wait for him to scout out a good course."

Tom nodded. "Agreed. I think—"

His words were cut short when something struck the rock between them with an ear-splitting concussion, showering them with shards of stone. This was followed almost instantly by the report of a rifle.

No words were necessary as both men immediately dropped to the ground and began scrambling away from an eruption of gunfire; hundreds of rifles going off nearly simultaneously.

Nathan and Tom unslung their rifles even as they crawled to a spot where the rock outcropping would cover them. But bullets continued to impact against the rocks, such that they dared not raise their heads to offer any kind of response.

But Nathan was gratified to hear other rifles responding to those first bursts; clearly the Twelfth was answering the challenge, mounting a defense against the sudden surprise attack.

Nathan and Tom shared a dark look as bullets continued to impact the rocks in front of them.

"Damn it, Tom! I've been a fool, staying up here in plain sight for so long … Clearly they've spotted us—two Union officers, strutting around up here like prize peacocks. Too tempting a target for our gray-coated friends to resist."

"Yes, yes, but we can chastise ourselves later," Tom answered. "For now, we've got to get off this rock and into the woods before they flank us."

"Agreed. And it galls me our men our under fire without their commanding officers … We've got to get back to them. Let's move!"

But getting back to the position of the Twelfth proved more difficult than they'd first imagined, as it quickly became apparent they were being actively pursued by a troop of mounted rebel cavalry, even as the battle with the Twelfth raged. Each attempt they made to skirt their pursuers through the woods was quickly cutoff by the faster moving, more numerous riders. And to Nathan's growing frustration, the sounds of the larger battle were growing ever more distant. Clearly the Twelfth was falling back under the pressure from the attack, and the enemy was now in force between the two Union colonels and the regiment they were responsible for leading.

Adding to the frustration, they dared not use their deadly repeating rifles for fear of giving away their position. They were simply too badly outnumbered to risk it. So they scrambled back through the woods, often on hands and knees, as riders pushed past only yards away, gazing around, pistols or carbine rifles in hand.

And as a group of rebels rode past so close that Nathan froze and unconsciously held his breath, he suffered a sight that made his heart sink. The leader of the column gazed in his direction, though under the dark shade of the trees, he and Tom were nearly invisible; but the Confederate officer's face was one Nathan would've known anywhere—*Walters!*

A burning desire welled up inside him to raise the Henry rifle and put a bullet through his hated enemy, but he forcefully resisted the temptation. He'd kill Walters, all right—of that he had no doubt—but he and Tom would also be shot down in the process. So he continued to hold his breath and remain motionless until the riders passed them by.

He turned and looked at Tom, who was wide-eyed; he'd also recognized Walters. The cat and mouse game they'd been playing with the rebel cavalry—which might've only ended in their capture—had suddenly become deadly serious.

೨つ೧ೞೞ೮ೞ೨つ೧ೞೞ೮ೞ೨つ೧ೞೞ

"Where the hell's the colonel?" Zeke shouted at Ollie as they worked to rally the troops, forming them up to return fire against the rebel cavalry that was now targeting the Twelfth from a wooded area next to the field where they'd been resting.

"Don't know…" Ollie shouted back just before squeezing off another round from his Henry rifle.

"Well, then … where's Colonel Clark?"

"Don't know that, either," Ollie answered.

"Well, *Goddamn it!* Who's in charge, then?"

"That'd be you, Zeke!"

Zeke scowled, "Well, of all the fucked up … *Lieutenant Durham!* … Move your company off to the right there … Don't let 'em flank us as we fall back."

"Yes, sir!" Durham called back, and immediately led his sixty-four men off at a trot.

"Ollie, you cover our left. We need to pull back out of this field … Too exposed. Find us some cover. Then, by God, we'll give 'em hell!"

"Yes, *sir!*" Ollie answered with a wry grin and a mock salute that made Zeke roll his eyes, despite their desperate situation.

"Twelfth West Virginia will fall back in good order, with covering fire. Fire at will! And *by God,* don't show them your back! Bring the dead and wounded. Move!" Zeke shouted.

They worked their way through the tall grass back toward the cover of the woods, backing slowly, returning fire all the way, keeping the enemy's heads down with their more powerful and accurate infantry rifles. But even as they moved and fought, Zeke wondered, *What has happened to our colonels? And where the hell's Billy? How could he have let this happen?*

CRICABOSICRACABOSICRICA

As dark settled over the landscape, Nathan and Tom stumbled into a corn field they'd come across unexpectedly as they sprinted across a broad field of grass. They quickly dived into its welcoming cover, then moved cautiously down the row, careful not to disturb the corn stalks to either side so as not to give away their presence.

Though the enemy had never spotted them, there'd been several close calls, and at one point, they were startled by gunfire that was much closer at hand than the far-distant sounds of the ongoing battle. And between gunshots, Nathan thought he heard shouting and screaming. Tom shared a dark look with him, but said nothing; clearly, he'd heard it too.

They were exhausted, and night was coming on, but the corn rows provided poor cover; a rider could easily scan down each row as he moved along the edge of the field at a trot. But happily, this problem was solved for them when they came to a place where the corn had been trampled down into a jumbled, matted pile by the earlier passing of a cavalry troop. So they climbed inside the pile, and collapsed to the ground.

Tom volunteered to take the first watch, which Nathan only half-heartedly argued against before falling asleep almost instantly.

In the dark of morning, with dawn barely just beginning to light the sky, Nathan was awake, taking his turn at the watch, when he heard a soft, subtle sound down the corn row in the direction from which they'd come. He stilled his breathing and listened intently, even as he quietly drew his Colt pistol from its holster at his right hip.

He could see nothing over the pile of corn stalks, but the barely perceptible sound continued, and seemed to draw closer. He had almost decided the sound must be coming from a wild animal of some sort—a fox or a raccoon, perhaps—when a new thought pricked the back of his mind. The thought suggested that he'd heard that particular sound before. Almost on a whim, he put his fingers to his mouth and made the sound of a low bird whistle. The sound was immediately answered by an identical whistle a few yards away.

Nathan grinned and holstered his pistol, even as Tom sat up and gazed at him, wide-eyed. But seeing Nathan's grin, he relaxed. A moment later, Billy joined them inside the cornstalk pile.

🕮🕮🕮🕮🕮🕮🕮🕮🕮

Tom felt a welling of relief and joy at the sight of Billy that he found surprising—something like the feeling a lost child might experience when suddenly found by his parent, he imagined. Billy's calm demeanor in a crisis, his unparalleled woodcraft, and his superior fighting skills greatly increased their chances of surviving their present dire circumstances.

"Good to see you, Billy," Nathan whispered, and reached out to shake Billy's hand with sincere enthusiasm, while still kneeling inside the pile of fallen cornstalks.

Billy grinned, and said aloud, "The rebel cavalry are gone for the moment; you needn't fear being seen or overheard."

"Oh!" Nathan responded in his normal voice, and stood up straight. "Good to know."

153

Tom also stood and extended his hand, which Billy accepted with a firm shake. "Thank God you've arrived, Billy. And thank you most kindly for finding us," he said.

But Billy scowled. "It is of little account, after I have once again failed as a scout, allowing the regiment to be ambushed."

But Nathan shook his head emphatically, "No, Billy. *No.* That was not your fault. I had given you specific orders to secure the route ahead, and the rebel cavalry came up from behind. Even you, with all your great skill, cannot possibly be in two places at once."

Billy did not seem convinced, but Tom thought his expression had softened somewhat as he replied, "Thank you for saying so, Captain … but I am still not happy about it."

But Tom had still not recovered from his amazement over the whole turn of events. "Billy, I knew you were an expert tracker, but *this?*" Tom shook his head. "We dodged the rebel cavalry for the better part of a day, crossing and recrossing their paths multiple times, such that several times we lost all sense of direction. Even now I have little idea of where we are. I can't imagine how even *you* could follow such a muddled trail."

Billy shrugged, then pointed up toward the sky, "She helped." Both Nathan and Tom looked up toward where Billy was pointing and saw the silhouette of a familiar shape in the dim, pre-dawn sky—Billy's red-tailed hawk soaring high above.

Nathan looked back at Billy with a look of startlement. "Your hawk? Some sort of Indian magic, Billy? Or have you somehow trained the creature to do your bidding?"

Billy snorted a laugh. "Neither, Captain. After I had freed her and helped her recover, and fed her when she was starving, she seemed to become attached to me, and I found she would often follow me for hours on end, circling high above wherever I went. Clearly, she was watching me with her keen eyes, and was able to track me even through the thickest woods.

"And then I became very curious about her habits, and began watching her as well, even as I went about my normal scouting and skirmishing duties. After a time, I realized I could tell certain things about the earth around me by watching how she flew.

154

Things about the terrain ahead—a hill versus a valley, or a stream versus a lake, an open field versus a forest, and so on.

"But also, with the help of Captain Boyd, I realized she reacted differently when she saw men ahead. And not just that there were men—even a hint of *how many* men. I realized she behaved differently if it were a couple of men versus a small group versus an army."

Tom's mouth was agape, and he looked toward Nathan, who likewise held a look of astonishment.

"Billy..." Nathan finally said. "That's really quite brilliant."

"Thank you, Captain," Billy answered, then adopted a thoughtful expression. "Captain ... do you remember me telling you once about an ancient leader of the People who was said to be able to look through the eyes of a soaring hawk?"

"Hmm ... yes, I do recall that story, Billy. You believed he had some sort of special godly bond with the creature that made the miracle possible, as I recall."

"Yes, that is correct. Only..." Billy grinned again, "Now I think I know how he did it ... and it required no magic. Only a keen eye to see, and a sharp mind to think."

"Ah!" Nathan nodded his head. "Yes, I see what you mean." Then Nathan became thoughtful for a moment, slowly nodding his head. "This could prove very useful, Billy. Very useful indeed."

"Agreed, Captain; it already has."

ଈଓଔଓଃଔଓଃଔଓଈଓଔଓଃଔଓ

Though Nathan and Tom had only the most vague, general notion of which way to turn in order to reunite with the regiment, Billy knew exactly where to go. "When I heard the fighting, of course I returned to the regiment. And though they'd been ambushed, they had recovered quickly, retreating in good order to a defensible position."

"Good to hear, though not surprising," Nathan said, nodding appreciatively.

"I was shocked that you two officers were not there. No one knew where you were. One private reported seeing you walk

155

away from camp just before the battle. So I followed. But first, I talked with Zeke. We spoke of where he would take the regiment after the battle."

"*Zeke?*" Tom asked.

But it was Nathan who answered, "With us being AWOL, Georgie and Jamie gone, and Stan, Jim, and William back with the wounded, that left Zeke the most senior officer."

"Ah, yes … of course. How was he doing with the command, Billy?" Tom asked.

Billy shrugged, "He *was* a farmer, now he is a warrior; he fights."

Nathan chuckled, "Not surprised. He's a good man."

Billy smiled, "Anyway … I talked with Zeke; we decided he must make for Harpers Ferry, while I stay and look for you two lost sheep."

"Good thinking … I approve," Nathan answered. "Billy, let's see if we can't evade these rebels and join him there, shall we?"

But to Tom's surprise, Billy didn't immediately respond, nor take off to lead the way. He hesitated, and suddenly had a serious look.

"What is it, Billy?" Nathan asked.

"There is … a thing you should see before we leave this place. I … wish not to say more," Billy finally answered, slowly shaking his head, continuing to hold onto a dark frown. "Best I show you, that you see it with your own eyes. Come, sirs…"

He led them back out of the corn field in the direction from which they'd come, directly into the rising sun. When they reached the place where the tall corn stalks gave way to the broad field of tall grass, Billy turned to the left and led them north. Tom noticed they were now following a well-worn trail that had recently been trod by the hooves of multiple horses—most likely those of the rebel cavalry.

They passed through a tall rail fence of the type used to contain horses or cattle. They could see that the gate had been opened violently. Its iron latch had broken off, the gate itself halfway collapsed to the side, still dangling from one twisted hinge. Of the livestock there was no sign; Tom assumed if there had been any, the Confederates must've taken them.

A few hundred yards from the gate, they saw a small farmhouse, neatly painted white with black shutters. Though it had all the signs of recent occupation, there was no smoke coming from the chimney, and no lights in the windows. The front door stood halfway open, moving slightly in the light breeze.

As they stepped up to within a few dozen yards of the farmhouse Tom, saw the thing that had caused Billy such angst, and he shuddered; the driveway and lawn in front of the house were littered with bodies — black men mostly, a dozen or more — but also the bodies of three black women. All were covered in blood from wounds that were consistent with gunshots. *Thankfully, no children*, Tom thought, and said a quick prayer for the dead.

Tom looked at Nathan and saw a familiar steely gleam in his friend's eyes — a look that meant someone would pay for this ... that someone was going to die for it.

"Two are better dressed than the others," Billy noted, pointing at where a young man and woman lay near each other, both covered in blood.

Nathan's grave stare held fast as he nodded. "Freemen farmers, I guess ... The owners of this place, most likely."

"Yes, that makes sense," Tom agreed. "And the others were runaway slaves that the farmers were sheltering?"

Nathan nodded, then turned to Billy, "Walters?"

Billy nodded. "I arrived just as they shot the last man, too late for me to help. The riders were ... hmm ... two dozen, maybe. I was thinking ... with the Henry rifle — keeping to cover — I might kill them all before they kill me. But since the black men were already dead, I thought it better to find you instead. And, yes, Walters was there. Sitting on his horse ... watching." Billy snorted derisively and frowned once again. "No decency nor self-respect ... not doing the deed himself. Ordered his men to do it. Like a coward."

Nathan shook his head, scowling fiercely. "No, not a coward ... evil, heartless, cruel. A despicable butcher ... but *not* a coward, unfortunately. If he were truly a coward, he'd not be out here himself trying to kill me."

He was thoughtful for a moment, and then added, "And it must take some level of courage to so brazenly disregard God's eventual judgement, knowing what's surely in store for him in the end."

Billy just shrugged as if unwilling to agree with Nathan, but also not wishing to argue the point.

"Shall we bury the poor souls, do you think?" Tom asked.

Nathan was quiet for a moment, continuing to gaze at the bodies. Then he slowly shook his head. "No ... I think not, Tom, though it galls me to say so. They certainly deserve a decent burial ... It seems the least we can do for them. But burying them would take too long, and I'm feeling a sudden urgency. Something Billy said just now ... about taking the rebels out with his Henry. It has me thinking of a much better way to honor the dead... And I have a feeling they would approve, if they could say so."

He turned and gave them a hard look. "With Billy's arrival, we have superior firepower and the greater skill ... I believe it's time the hunted became the hunters. Gentlemen, I mean to track down these murderers and rain down swift, deadly justice upon their heads. Especially one *Elijah Walters*."

ℬ❀☙ℰ☙ℬ❀☙ℰ☙ℬ❀☙

For the first few hours, they made swift progress following their enemies, despite the seeming disadvantage of being afoot chasing after men on horseback. But the thickly tangled woods and steep terrain impeded the riders much more so than the walkers, and Billy reported they were steadily gaining and should close the gap within a few short hours. And though the hawk circled overhead, Billy did not seem to need her help this time, focusing his attention on the ground in front of him.

When Tom asked him about it, Billy snorted derisively. "Men on horseback? Even you could follow this trail, Sergeant Clark."

Tom just smiled and shook his head.

But shortly after that, they hit their first setback, as Billy reported that a half-dozen riders had split off from the others, moving in a more northerly direction, while the main group continued in a generally eastward direction, seemingly intending to meet back up with the main column that had engaged the Twelfth.

After a brief discussion, Nathan decided to follow the main group and not to split themselves up. It was the wisest course, he argued. But he had serious misgivings ... What if Walters was one of those who had split off?

And then, an hour later, Nathan began to regret his choice of words when he'd first decided to pursue the fleeing cavalry troopers—to "rain" down justice on the heads of their enemies. Heavy clouds, that'd been steadily building since morning, began to drizzle. The drizzle soon became a steady rain, which quickly turned into a torrential downpour accompanied by winds that drove the rain sideways, making it difficult to find any kind of shelter, even under the thick canopy of the forest.

And then, as they stood shivering under a tree, huddled together in a vain attempt to stay warm and dry, they heard a rustling in the branches. Nathan looked up and saw a large bird settling in a few feet above them, looking wet, wretched, and angry, ruffling its sodden feathers in a vain attempt to dry itself.

Nathan looked over at Billy, who had also noticed the hawk's arrival. Billy snorted a laugh.

"Not fit out for man nor beast, apparently," Nathan said.

Billy just nodded, which motion only served to cause the water accumulating on the brim of his hat to stream down onto his face.

And then, as if to emphasize Nathan's statement, the sky lit up, and thunder echoed across the landscape. This was immediately followed by a roaring sound, as hailstones nearly the size of silver dollars hammered the forest all around them, quickly piling up into a thick blanket of white beneath the boughs of the trees.

Though the fury of the lightning and hailstones soon passed, the rain did not, now a heavy deluge that seemed to have no end.

Several hours later, as the rain finally began to ease somewhat, the daylight was waning. Billy went out to see if he might still be able to follow the trail, but he came back in a few minutes to report that it had been obliterated, and they'd have to wait for bright daylight to have any hope of finding it again.

They settled in under the tree and tried to get some sleep — the only positive being there was no need to keep a watch for their enemies under such adverse weather conditions.

ℬↃᙆℭℬↄↃᙆℭℬↄℬↃᙆℭↄ

The following morning dawned dark, gloomy, and miserably wet, with rain continuing to fall in steady a stream such that they could see no more than a few yards in any direction.

But the good news, such as it was, was that the rain had melted the previous day's accumulation of hail so that Billy could once again examine the ground. He immediately headed out to see if he could relocate the trail of their enemies. Nathan and Tom remained where they were, there being no sense in them tagging along behind Billy until he figured out the proper course.

Nathan chuckled when he looked up and saw that the hawk had remained on her perch above them, despite Billy's departure. Her feathers were ruffled up, and she held a sour expression Nathan could only interpret as a look of disgust. For reasons of her own, either common sense or instinct, she had apparently decided against venturing out in weather that would render her aerial vantage point moot, and would likely only leave her sodden and miserable.

A few hours later, Billy returned, ducking back under the relative dryness of the tree's branches. And though he was clearly soaked to the bone, he seemed unconcerned about it. "I have found the trail … at least some hint of it. Shocking how the storm has covered the trail of horses. But ahead the ground rises and grows rocky; even the heavy animals leave but little sign. Come, sirs…"

"But, Billy … you are thoroughly drenched. Shall we not light a fire and warm you a bit first?" Tom asked.

160

Billy just shrugged, "It will do little good, Sergeant Clark ... I will only get wet again. Best way to keep warm is to keep moving." With that, he stood and stepped back out into the rain.

Nathan and Tom scrambled to their feet and followed. As they stepped away, they heard a rustling in the branches behind them. Nathan looked back and saw the hawk launching herself from a branch above. But rather than beat her wings up into the sky as he'd expected, she beat her wings twice, then landed on Billy's head, mashing down his hat. There she seemed to settle in, and once again fluffed up her feathers, looking highly annoyed. Billy just grinned, then turned to continue on his way, looking comical, but otherwise unconcerned. Though the hawk was large for her kind, she weighed but little, being built for flight, so did not make for any appreciable burden.

Nathan and Tom exchanged a look of surprise and a quick grin, then turned to follow.

It was the beginning of a long, cold, dreary day of climbing over rocks, traversing fallen logs, and scrambling in and out of gullies and ravines. And the difficult terrain wasn't the only thing slowing them; Billy continued to struggle with a trail that seemed to disappear and reappear at random intervals, sometimes causing them to have to pause and wait for him to reconnoiter, or even to backtrack several painful miles to recover the track.

But despite the irregular terrain, it had become obvious that they were in general gaining altitude, heading steadily up into the mountains, which made their discomfort all the greater as the temperature continued to drop.

At one point, they reached a place where the ground leveled off, and the trees opened up, such that they could see little around them but tall rock sticking up through the mist. Nathan looked around and suddenly experienced an odd sensation ... like he'd been here before.

"Tom ... why does this place look familiar?"

Tom gazed around, but shrugged.

It was Billy who turned to answer Nathan's question. "It is because we have been here before, Captain. This is the same mountain pass we crossed to escape from the other Winchester battle."

Nathan's mouth dropped and he again gazed about, recalling the meeting with the odd girl, Anna, who had helped lead the regiment to safety. A girl that Nathan had suspected might have been more than she appeared.

He wondered if she might still be here, up on the mountain pass; though this time, he did not see the small house he assumed she lived in. *Odd*, he thought.

And then, as if in answer to his thoughts, a person appeared directly ahead of them on the trail, though through the thick, swirling mist, they could not make out anything beyond a silhouette.

But Nathan noticed the form was slender and had long, flowing hair. He fancied he could almost see a young woman's smiling face on the dark form. "*Anna?*" he said.

Then the figure stepped forward, and he saw that it was not so. This was a man, but to Nathan's shock, no ordinary man—this man had a tanned, lean face, and wore the traditional garb of an Indian! He held a small pistol in his right fist, though his arms were folded across his chest.

Five other men now stepped forward, all Indians, dressed like the first. These men held rifles, pointed at Nathan, Tom, and Billy. The hawk let out a loud squawk and launched itself into the air, away from the newcomers, disappearing into the mist, even as Billy and Tom reached for their pistols.

But Nathan shouted, "*Peace!* Leave your weapons be. If these men meant us harm, we'd be dead already."

Tom and Billy immediately obeyed, slowly moving their hands away from their weapons, but keeping their eyes on the strangers.

The leader then stepped up to within a pace of Nathan and looked him in the eye. Nathan could now see the man was much older than he, with deep wrinkles lining his face. He'd either lost all his hair or had shaved it, but a spiky tuft of brightly colored feathers stuck straight up from the crown of his head. Other long, softer feathers hung down around his shoulders—what Nathan had mistaken for hair through the thick mist. He also wore a small nose ring of a white-colored metal. But despite his years, he had a hard look that belied his age, leaving Nathan with little doubt that this was a man to be reckoned with.

"You are wise for one of your people," the man said.

Nathan nodded, but said nothing, thinking it best to allow the Indian to say whatever he'd come to say.

But then the man turned toward Billy and said something in a language Nathan did not recognize.

Billy gazed back at the man and shrugged. "I do not know this tongue," he answered.

The man was quiet for a moment, then said, "Though we may look the same, we are not of the same people."

Billy nodded. "My people are called Tonkawa by the white men. We are from far out in the West, and have never lived in this place called Virginia. I am the only one."

The man nodded, then said, "We are of the people called Shawnee. I was speaking in that tongue, thinking you would know it."

Billy then said something in Tonkawa. Nathan had lived among the Tonkawa scouts out in Texas long enough that he picked up the gist of it; he interpreted it as, *Do you recognize any of the People's words?*

But the stranger just shrugged. "I do not know your tongue either. So we will speak in the white man's tongue, that we might understand each other."

"It is good," Billy agreed.

"You are a spirit talker," the man said. "This is what I was saying before in my own tongue."

"I ... do not know what you mean by it," Billy answered.

"The hawk ... you have the ancient skill of speaking to his spirit. I have only heard of such things from the old ones ... never before have I seen it with my own eyes."

Billy shrugged. "It is no magic. I don't know why the creature chooses to follow me. I have no special skill for such things."

The man was quiet for a moment and looked thoughtful. "I do not see any deceit in you, but still ... what you say is *not* true. You

163

we have seen before at times on our travels. And it seems to me you have much of the old ways in you. Though maybe they are such a part of you that you don't see them."

He turned back toward Nathan. "We have also seen you before, though I think you have not seen us."

Nathan nodded. "Then perhaps you know that I mean you no harm, and would rather befriend you than be your enemy."

The man seemed to ponder this for a moment. "I do not know you. But the wise ones say you may judge a man by his enemies. And we have seen that your enemies are evil. I speak not of the gray soldiers ... or the blue ... We have little knowledge of what makes such men fight one another. And care even less who may prevail. I speak of men who are merciless killers of the helpless: unarmed men, women, and even children."

Nathan nodded, "Yes, I am the sworn enemy of such men, and will strike them down whenever I may."

The man was quiet again for a long moment, then said, "I am called Wolf-in-the-Mountain, in your tongue."

"I am honored to meet you, Wolf-in-the-Mountain. I am called Nathan Chambers. This is Tom Clark, and Billy Creek."

Wolf-in-the-Mountain gazed steadily into Nathan's eyes for another long moment, then said, "Come."

Without waiting for a reply, Wolf-in-the-Mountain turned and strode away, his men lowering their rifles and following in his wake.

Nathan turned and shared a look with his men, then shrugged and followed after the Indian.

ﾞﾞﾞﾞﾞﾞﾞﾞﾞﾞﾞﾞ

Wolf-in-the-Mountain led them by a steep, twisting path that appeared to have been made by deer or other game animals. After about half an hour, they came to a place where the trail appeared to simply end at the face of a sheer cliff, looming some hundreds of feet above their heads. And even as Nathan had begun to wonder if the Indians intended to scale the cliff, Wolf-in-the-Mountain appeared to simply vanish ahead of them, followed almost immediately by the other Indians in the party.

But there was no magic to it; when Nathan reached the cliff face, he saw that there was a thin vertical shaft to his right, an opening which could not be seen from the trail. He slipped inside, followed by Billy and Tom. After only a few strides, the thin passage gave way to a wide cave, whose ceiling disappeared overhead off into the darkness.

The hall was dimly illuminated by a small campfire in the very center, which had burned down to just glowing coals. But already one of the Indians was kneeling down next to it, stoking the coals with small sticks of wood and blowing into the fire until the light from its flames danced on the surrounding cave walls. It was a most cheerful and welcome sight to the cold, weary, sodden travelers, who quickly gathered around the fire, not waiting for an invitation.

Then, to the delight of Nathan and his men, two of the Indians brought out the carcasses of several small animals, already skinned and cleaned—rabbits or small marmots, perhaps—and proceeded to skewer and roast them over the fire. Within a few minutes, the steaming hot meat was shared around.

The smell of the meat had made Nathan realize just how hungry he was, having had little to eat since they'd parted from the regiment two days earlier—only what little hardtack Billy had brought in his pack, and a few blackberries they'd found along one ridgeline. So he and his men attacked the proffered meal with great enthusiasm and heartfelt appreciation.

When the meal was finished, all the men gathered around the fire, sitting cross-legged on the floor. To Nathan's surprise, it was Billy who started the general conversation, looking straight at Wolf-in-the-Mountain and saying, "I have seen your tracks before, in the mountains near the farm where we lived before the war." Nathan noted that it was a statement, and not a question.

Wolf-in-the-Mountain nodded slowly, "Yes … one of my men saw you, and was greatly surprised by it. Then we watched you for a time, trying to puzzle out who you were, and how you came to be in this land. We were amazed when you discovered our trail … and we knew you recognized it. Few now among us still have such skill … It is a dying art."

Billy nodded. "And were you also out in the snows when I hunted the evil men with the giant man of our party? *Someone* killed one of the enemy with an arrow that was not one of ours."

This time it wasn't Wolf-in-the-Mountain who answered, but another of the Indians, a young, fierce looking man, who snorted a short, humorless laugh before he spoke. "*I* killed him, though I have paid the price of pain for it. Still, it seemed to me you needed my bow. And ... I would do it again," he concluded and gave Wolf-in-the-Mountain a meaningful glare.

Wolf-in-the-Mountain shrugged, then looked at Nathan, "We may not kill white men for any reason, lest we invoke their wrath, and they hunt us down like wild beasts. Only in the most desperate self-defense may we do it. Dark Bear broke our law, and has paid the price."

Billy looked at Dark Bear and said, "I thank you. And owe you the price of the pain you suffered for it."

Dark Bear shrugged, and said, "There is nothing owed. The pleasure to kill an evil one was worth the suffering. That it helped you, a fellow Indian," he shrugged. "It is good."

Billy nodded. "It is good."

Then Nathan turned to Wolf-in-the-Mountain. "Please ... tell me how it is your people have come to be in these mountains. As far as I knew, there have been none of your people here for many years—since my father was a young man, certainly."

Wolf-in-the-Mountain was quiet for a time, then said, "You are among a handful of white men who know of us." He shrugged, "There are a few others—wild men, mostly, who live alone in the mountains and trade with us. Men we know we can trust with our secrets, though no white man may know where our women and children dwell." He paused and was silent a long moment before continuing.

"Of course, none of us alive today was born in the *before-time*, but it was told to me by my father, which he had heard from his father before him, that there was a time when there were no white men in these lands, and the different Indian peoples fought wars amongst themselves for the best hunting grounds, and the most fertile valleys in which to live.

"And then when the white men came, we continued to fight each other, giving little thought to the new people—they were few and widely scattered—except when they offered to use their powerful weapons to aid one set of people against another.

"Not until it was too late, and the white men were too numerous to fight, did the Indians realize who the *real* enemy was. By then, all the people were being driven from these lands. Those of us you call Shawnee were among the people who left this place long ago, traveling to a land where the white men said they could live in peace, far out beyond the setting sun.

"But some among our people refused to leave, including my father. I was but a boy at the time, and did not know the reasons why. They hid away in the high places, among the great trees, where few white men ever tread. We and a handful of others are all that remains of these people—still practicing the old ways, living in hiding among the high mountains and in the deep woods."

"It is an amazing story, Wolf-in-the-Mountain. I am honored that you have entrusted the tale to me."

"Amazing? Maybe ... but I fear it is a story with no good ending. Each year, the farms, towns, and lumber camps come closer to our wild places. The war has given us a rest. But that must one day end. Then the day will come when we are discovered. And then ...? Many among us are now thinking we should try to find the others of our people out past the setting sun." He sighed and fell silent.

Nathan felt great empathy for these hardy, brave souls, fighting a long, hopeless battle against unwinnable odds.

But he could think of no answer to this dilemma, so to break the sad awkwardness of the moment, he said, "Wolf-in-the-Mountain, I am very grateful to you for aiding us in our hour of need—feeding us and giving us shelter from the storm."

Wolf-in-the-Mountain said, "I would not have done this thing, risking our secrets, just to aid you in your discomfort. You are *men ... warriors*. You can endure *much*. More than you have this day. No, we have brought you here for another purpose.

"We too are enemies of these evil men you seek, though they know it not. We have seen their senseless killings, and know they are men who will hunt us down in the wilds when the war is done—murder our women and children, even in their sleep. Such men must be killed. But *we* cannot do it … unless they attack us first. Then it may be too late.

"In the morning we will show you where these men have gone… And then *you* will kill them."

Nathan nodded, and then grinned for the first time since Wolf-in-the-Mountain had first appeared before him on the mountain pass. "That I *can* do, Wolf-in-the-Mountain. And that I *will* do."

☙❧☙❧☙❧☙❧☙❧

True to his word, Wolf-in-the-Mountain and the other Indians led Nathan and company down the mountain in the pre-dawn darkness, as the sky continued its dreary downpour. He guided them to a place where a lonely, one-story farmhouse stood next to a wide field. From the look of the place, it had long since been abandoned; the roof showed several gaping holes and weeds grew tall all around. But smoke streamed from the chimney, and a large group of hobbled horses grazed in the pasture near the house.

When they arrived, just as the sun was beginning to lighten the eastern horizon, they were greeted by three Indians who'd not been at the previous evening's fire. Clearly these men had been keeping an eye on the enemy in the farmhouse, awaiting the arrival of their fellows.

One of them spoke to Wolf-in-the-Mountain quietly in their own tongue. Then the Indian leader turned to Nathan, speaking in low tones, "He says the enemy soldiers are still inside. None have yet come out this morning, though their fire was stoked a few moments ago."

"And they stationed no pickets outside?" Nathan asked.

"*Pickets?* I do not know this word."

"Oh, sorry … guards … men to keep watch outside against approaching enemies."

"Ah," Wolf-in-the-Mountain nodded. Then he spoke a few words to his men, one of which snorted a short laugh before answering.

"He says, no pickets. That the evil ones must believe the bad weather guards them."

Nathan looked up at the dark clouds and nodded. "Guess they don't know who they're up against."

Wolf-in-the-Mountain snorted a laugh.

"Hmm ... how many are they, did he say?" Nathan asked.

The two Indians exchanged more words, then Wolf-in-the-Mountain answered, "He says they have counted ten and eight more."

"And doors?"

"The one in front that you can see, and one more in back."

"All right. Billy, you take the back door, and Tom, you'll have the front. I'll move around there on the side and sneak up to that window. When I break it in and start firing, I expect them to come streaming out the doors. Give them a proper 'good morning,' will you?"

"Yes, sir!" Tom answered, and Billy just grinned and headed out.

"And, Wolf-in-the-Mountain..." Nathan turned back around to speak to the Indian ... but he was gone. They were all gone.

Nathan turned back toward the house but now grinned, *Guess he figured we wouldn't need him. And I expect he was right.*

Moments later, Nathan slipped up to the side of the house where he slowly raised his head up and peeked in the window. He saw a large, open room with a fireplace on the far end. Two men stood in front of the glowing fire while others lay on the floor, a dozen or more, still asleep, covered in blankets.

Nathan hesitated for only a moment, long enough to recall the image of the murdered freemen and runaway slaves, covered in blood, left to rot on the ground. The burning rage returned, and he lifted his rifle and punched the buttstock hard into window, shattering the glass. He immediately reversed the gun, shoved the barrel into the opening, and fired twice, downing the two men standing by the fire. Quickly working the lever action, he pumped more rounds into the room as men scrambled for cover.

Some of the men reached for guns leaned against the wall, and these he targeted first. One man aimed a pistol at him and fired, but it missed, and Nathan made sure the man didn't get off a second shot.

He heard the front door opening, and then the back, knowing that men would now be streaming out. Then he heard the familiar sound of a Henry rifle out in front of the house — *Tom*. And then a second Henry was firing rapidly from the back — *Billy*.

Nathan ducked back down between firing shots, trying not to make an easy target. But after a few moments, he could find no more targets in the room. And after a few more shots, the gunfire went silent. So he crept along the side of the house and peered around the corner toward the front door. Starting at the front stoop, and extending out several dozen yards, were the bodies of eight men. One man had apparently had the idea of getting the drop on Nathan and had been heading in his direction when he'd been felled.

Nathan whistled loudly, then trotted up to the front door and pushed it open, ducking his head inside for a quick look. Seeing no one, he was ready to rush in when Tom banged into the outside wall on the opposite side of the doorway from him.

"Anyone in there?" Tom asked between gasps for breath.

"Not that I could see. Ready?"

"Yep."

"I'll take the left side, you take the right. Go!"

They jumped inside, each pivoting in their assigned directions. Nathan's side was clear, but he heard a gunshot behind him, and turned to see a rebel slumping to the ground, his unfired rifle dropping from lifeless arms with a clatter.

Then they heard two more rifle shots inside the house, out toward the back. So they moved down the short hallway in that direction, ready for any resistance. They passed the large room with the fireplace, and quickly checked it, but all inside were dead, scattered about the room, slumped to the ground. The white walls were now spattered with blood.

Then they heard a quick whistle, and both men relaxed, recognizing the "all clear" from Billy. In a moment, the scout stepped up to them, leading a captive—a young, skinny rebel with stringy unkempt hair and only the wisp of a beard, his hands held high in the air.

"Take him outside, Billy, while Tom and I check the rest of the house. I want to find Walters."

ⵏⵓⵛⵃⵀⵓⵏⵓⵛⵃⵀⵓⵏⵓⵛⵃⵀ

A quarter of an hour later, Nathan and Tom stepped out the front door to where Billy and their captive awaited them. Nathan could not disguise his disappointment; when they'd searched the bodies, Walters wasn't among them.

He stepped right up to the captive and said, "Where's Walters?"

At first the man looked puzzled, then said, "Uh ... do you mean *Colonel* Walters, sir?"

"Yes, yes ... *Lieutenant Colonel Elijah Walters.* Where is he?"

"Oh, uh ... he and Captain Roberts and a couple of other fellas left us a few days back. The colonel said he had new orders to head north, so he went to reconnoiter the route. We was to make our way back to rejoin the rest of the battalion, and then he'd send for us to join him up to the north, somewhere just this side o' the river. Sergeant Drucker was in command o' us as was left behind ... though he's now ... *kilt* ... I suppose."

Nathan groaned. As he'd feared, Walters had been among the small party of horsemen who'd split off from the others several days back. The small group Nathan had decided not to pursue. The group that was now beyond all hope of catching.

"Damn it. Damn it to hell!" Nathan spat as the turned away from the private and stared at the ground. His anger surged again. Despite all the killing, Walters had once again eluded him.

He turned back toward the rebel and said, "And what do you have to say for yourself, reb? Mercilessly shooting down those unarmed black men and women back at that farm..."

171

"I ... I ... I ... was just followin' orders, sir," the man stammered, now holding a fearful expression, correctly reading the anger in Nathan's eyes.

"*Just ... following ... orders?* Wrong answer!" Nathan snarled as he drew out his pistol, pulled back the hammer, pointed it at the private's face, and...

He paused and stared at the young man's face. Nathan realized the fellow was not much more than a boy. Barely yet needing to shave ... and he was clearly frightened out of his mind.

Nathan took a deep breath, lowered the hammer, and re-holstered the pistol. "Get out of my sight. I have no desire to take you prisoner; in fact, I never wish to lay eyes on you again. On your long walk back, pray to God for forgiveness for the evil things you have done. And thank him on bended knee for sparing your life just now."

"Yes, sir, Colonel. Yes, sir, that I *will* do ... And thank you very kindly, sir ... for not shooting me!"

Nathan scowled and turned away.

Not waiting for Nathan to change his mind, the Confederate private turned and ran, never looking back.

Tom stepped up to Nathan and the two locked eyes for a long moment. Then Tom reached out and patted Nathan on the shoulder before striding away to join Billy in rounding up the rebels' horses.

ॐ෴ॐ෴ॐ෴ॐ෴ॐ෴

Walters had been as frustrated as he could ever recall by his inability to locate and lay hands on Nathan Chambers; the man was just too experienced and crafty, and Walters' own men, conversely, too incompetent.

He had been somewhat mollified by the capture and extermination of the runaway slaves they'd come across in the area of the search. It was made all the sweeter by the knowledge that Chambers was bound to find the bodies. And when he did, he'd be galled to know that he'd not only been helpless to prevent it, but had even helped to cause it by fleeing in that direction, leading Walters and his men straight to the blacks.

And as he rode northeastward on a course to rejoin his battalion, Walters was further buoyed by his new orders and the prospect of wreaking havoc once more over on the north side of the Potomac. He'd received his orders from General Early, to leave off pursuing the federals who were fleeing the Kernstown rout, and to instead join with the cavalry brigade of Brigadier General John McCausland in a vengeful raid into the North. And because the bulk of the federals were either occupied in northern Virginia, guarding Washington City, or scattered out west of the Shenandoah Valley, it was expected the raid would face little or no resistance—just the sort of thing Walters and his battalion excelled at.

He resisted a strong urge to smile at the thought of helpless Yankee civilians he'd have at his mercy, knowing that *mercy* was the *last* thing they could expect from him.

❦❧☙❧❦☙❧❦☙

Thursday July 28, 1864 – Halltown, West Virginia:

"Atten … *shun!*" Several hundred soldiers snapped to attention and saluted as one, even as Nathan, Tom, and Billy rode slowly into camp, leading a long line of rebel horses. The three men were dirty, hungry, footsore, and nearly exhausted, though grateful the last part of their journey had been on horseback.

The Twelfth's pickets, stationed a few miles out from their camp on the outskirts of Halltown, had reported the missing officers' impending arrival a half hour earlier. This had allowed Zeke time to arrange a proper reception for them.

They made their way up the dirt road between two rows of soldiers, all still standing at salute, as Nathan and Tom nodded in acknowledgment. At the end of the rows of soldiers stood the officers of the Twelfth: Zeke, Ollie, Durham, and the four other lieutenants.

The three weary travelers stopped in front of the officers and returned their salutes.

Nathan dismounted and stepped up in front of Zeke, reaching out to shake his hand. "Well done, Mr. Benton. From what

Sergeant Creek tells me, and by the look of this regiment, it's clear you've done a splendid job at command in what must've been a *very* tight spot."

"Thank you, sir," Zeke answered, clearly fighting off a grin. "Though I must say, I am very happy … *very happy indeed*, to give the command back to you, Colonel.

"And … you may be happy to hear, sir, that I've not yet filed charges against you two colonels for going AWOL in the face of the enemy."

Nathan grinned, and Tom snorted a laugh. Zeke could no longer maintain his composure, and beamed brightly.

"Good to hear, Mr. Benton … and much obliged," Nathan answered. "And it is *very* good to be back, Captain Benton," Nathan concluded, and even as he said it, he realized that this particular statement was *most* sincere and heartfelt.

$$\text{\textb#}$$

Sunday July 31, 1864 – Harpers Ferry, West Virginia:

The sun was just setting as Nathan strode through the tents of the Twelfth West Virginia's camp at the top of the rise on Bolivar Heights just outside Harpers Ferry. He had a mind to sit with Tom for a few minutes before retiring for the evening, though he had nothing specific to discuss.

He'd found that their relationship seemed to have risen to a new level following the incident where they'd come to blows after the disastrous New Market Battle. Just having Tom call him by his given name had made a huge difference. Tom was much more likely to put his own opinion forward and to bring up his own ideas than he'd been in the past. And he now readily joined in discussions with higher ranking officers rather than taking a deferential position.

It was a change Nathan enjoyed, and it had made for a much tighter camaraderie between the two men.

He was within a few feet of Tom's tent and just reaching out to pull open its flap when he caught a blur of motion out of the corner of his right eye. Before he could react, something large and heavy hit him on the side with such force that he was knocked to the ground. The thing landed hard on top of him, nearly knocking the wind out of him.

Nathan realized that his unknown assailant was an animal, covered in thick fur—a large wolf, or possibly even a bear. He squirmed to extricate himself and pulled his Bowie knife from its sheath behind his back. But then a great wetness hit him in the face, and continued splattering him with a warm, gooey liquid.

He heard a boisterous laugh; booming and unmistakable. Nathan couldn't help chuckling himself as Harry the Dog licked his face with great, slobbery enthusiasm, and Stan stood over them, hands on hips, chortling with delight.

Tom came out of his tent, pistol in his fist, but then lowered it and joined in the laughter, reaching over to shake Stan's huge hand. "Welcome back, Stan. You look well!"

"Is good to be back, Colonel Clark!" the big man grinned and gripped Tom on the shoulders before giving him a good shake. Then he looked back at Nathan, still trying to extract himself from beneath the great, enthusiastic hound. "Is good to see you, too, Colonel. Harry thinks so too."

"Yes, well …" Nathan wiped his face with his sleeve, "in future, I wish you could keep this four-legged soldier under better control, Mr. Volkov. It won't do to have him going around assaulting superior officers." Nathan was now sitting up, stroking Harry's prodigious neck, and grinning.

"Da, da … is true, Colonel. But Private Harry doesn't understand company punishment," he chuckled. "In fact, he doesn't believe in punishment at all—does as he pleases." He shrugged, still holding a broad grin.

Nathan reached out his hand, and Stan lifted him to his feet. The two men embraced, but Stan refrained from lifting his commanding officer off the ground as he would've done to anyone else.

"And yes, it is good to see you too, Stan. How are you feeling, and what about Jim and William?"

175

"Hmm ... still a little stiff and sore in places, but nothing to speak of. You know me, after a time I tire of sitting around with nothing to do and start itching to kill somebody. So ... here I am!"

Then he had a more serious expression. "Jim, he is ... not so good. Though William has kept wound from festering, he can do little for the inside," Stan pointed at his heart. "Is difficult for Jim to accept that he cannot do all things he is used to ... like soldiering."

Nathan nodded. "Yes ... I can imagine he's not taking *that* too well. He's another one who longs for a good fight, on occasion."

"Da, da ... Jim is fighter, none better."

"And William?"

"He is good, but won't leave Jim like he is. I told him stay and do what he can. But William told me to say to you, he wishes to be here."

Nathan nodded, "Yes, of that I have no doubt. Well, come on into the tent and we will catch up on things. I'll just have someone go track down Billy so he can join us and make this Texas reunion complete."

"Is good, Colonel. Is very good."

Chapter 9. Union Inferno

"Hell is empty, and
all the devils are here."
- **William Shakespeare**
(The Tempest)

Friday July 29, 1864 – City Point, Virginia:

Union Major General Ambrose Burnside strode into the farmhouse that served as Major General Meade's headquarters, and without preamble or a proper exchange of salutes, launched into the subject that had heated him more than any in recent memory. "Meade ... what's the meaning of this order?"

Burnside set a sheet of paper down in front of Meade where he sat at a desk, gazing up. Meade glanced down at the paper and shrugged, "Just as it says, Burnside ... the Fourth Division is *not* to lead the attack when the rebel fortifications at Petersburg are blown open tomorrow."

"But, why, sir? The Fourth has been training for weeks for this very engagement. They are fit and ready."

"Yes, yes ... I'm sure they are. But another of your divisions can serve just as well, I have no doubt. One of your ... *white* divisions."

"What? But, sir ... with all due respect, the colored divisions have proven they can fight. They're ready and willing to lead the assault. I have every confidence they will succeed in grand fashion."

Meade slowly nodded, "So you say ... but what if they don't?"

"What do you mean?"

"What if the attack is a failure? What then? How do you think it will look for the president if we send thousands of black soldiers into the breach, and they get cut off and slaughtered?"

"Why should they fail?" Burnside asked. "It's a good plan, and they are well prepared and equipped. Or do you still believe they can't fight because they're black?"

Meade slowly shook his head. "No, no … it's not *that*. But think of the political repercussions…"

Burnside's temper had already been simmering, but he could now feel the heat rising, and knew his face was becoming red. "General … I don't give a good Goddamn about political anything … I just want to finally win a battle here. And the colored regiments of the Fourth Division are prepared to do just that. I beg of you, sir, to reconsider and allow the original plan to move forward."

"Burnside, the decision has already been made. Kindly return to your camp and select another division to carry out the attack tomorrow, as I have ordered."

Burnside stood to his feet. "I protest this order, sir! I think it only fair to tell you I intend to appeal directly to General Grant."

But if Meade was surprised or concerned by Burnside's threat, he didn't betray it, shrugging his shoulders. "Do whatever pleases you, Burnside. But General Grant will back me up on this matter, I assure you."

"We'll see about that!" Burnside pivoted and stomped out of Meade's office.

But an hour later, a downcast General Burnside returned to the spot where his staff officers awaited him, after an unsuccessful visit with commanding General Grant. Though Grant had been sympathetic, and didn't disagree with him, he'd been unwilling to override his subordinate, General Meade, whom he'd placed in command of the siege.

෧◑◖◔஭◐◑◖◔஭◐◑◖◔

When Burnside returned to the camp of the IX Corps, he asked his three other divisional commanders for a volunteer to lead the attack the next morning. All three declined, so he had them draw lots. The lot fell upon the First Division, commanded by Brigadier General James Ledlie. Burnside briefed Ledlie on the plan of action: how his men should advance as soon as they heard the explosion, that they should split into two columns, skirting the edges of the crater. Then, once past the rebel earthworks, they should attack its defenders and secure the fortification so that

178

other units might follow up and flow through the breach unimpeded.

Ledlie nodded vigorously, and expressed his full understanding, even repeating the plan back to Burnside. But when he returned to his command tent, Ledlie found he was weary, and also feeling anxious about the impending action. Having no desire for a general meeting with his subordinate commanders, and all the discussion and bickering that typically entailed, he pulled the cork from a bottle he kept in his kit and had several long sips as he wrote out orders to his regimental commanders:

> *All regiments of 1st Division are to sleep on their arms. At approximately 3:45 a.m. the engineers will detonate an explosive mine beneath the rebel earthworks to our front, which is intended to create a great breach. Once the dust has settled from the explosion, the 1st will launch an attack through the gap and destroy any enemy formations still intact within, leading to an overall Union victory.*
>
> *Good luck and Godspeed,*
> *Brig. Genl. J.H. Ledlie*
> *Commanding, 1st Division, IX Corps*

༺ა๑ดฺ౧ปฺ౧ปฺ๑ดฺ౧ปฺ๑ดฺ౧ปฺ౧ปฺ๑ดฺ༻

Saturday July 30, 1864 – Chambersburg, Pennsylvania:

"No, sir, General McCausland, I will *not* obey this command! Never in life, sir! On whose authority is this outrageous order given?" C.S.A. Colonel William Peters, commander of the Twenty-First Virginia Cavalry regiment, was red in the face as he stood in his wrath before his commanding general in the middle of Main Street in the center of the Union town of Chambersburg, Pennsylvania. Next to him stood two other officers, Peters' subordinate, Major Lewis Taylor of the Twenty-First, and Lieutenant Colonel Elijah Walters, commander of the Thirty-Sixth Virginia Cavalry Battalion.

Peters and his regiment had driven out the modest federal contingent earlier in the morning and had taken command of the small town with professional efficiency, an act requiring no bloodshed from his soldiers. Walters's battalion had arrived shortly after to help secure the town.

But when Peters had been summoned by McCausland, he'd been shocked by the orders he'd received; he was to burn the defenseless town to the ground!

"I have written orders from Lieutenant General Jubal Early himself, Colonel. His orders are not only legal, but I believe highly justified—as reasonable retribution for federal General David Hunter's recent wanton and despicable destruction of the Virginia Military Institute as well as the burning of the private home of former governor Letcher, among several others. Here … read the orders for yourself…" McCausland handed Colonel Peters a single sheet of folded paper.

Peters removed his leather gauntlets and tucked them into his belt before snatching the paper from his general.

He quickly read through it, then looked up. "He has ordered the town's citizens to pay a ransom?"

"Yes, that's right … Either $100,000 in gold, or $500,000 in greenbacks, in exchange for sparing their town from the torch. I have, of course, asked this of the town's citizens … what few I could find. But they have refused."

Peters scowled, "They would have no way of paying this great sum, and General Early knows it. This is not retribution, general; this is just plain thievery, extortion, and brazen wickedness."

But McCausland just shrugged as Peters handed the sheet of paper back to him. "This is not a matter for debate, Colonel. I have my orders, and now you have yours; you will gather your men at the courthouse, arm them with torches, and fire the town," McCausland concluded.

"No, *sir!* I am a soldier and a gentleman. I have never shirked my duty regardless of the hardship, and no man alive has dared accuse me of cowardice; the battle scars I bear give mute testament to that!

"But I will *not*, sir, under any circumstances, wage war on innocent, defenseless women and children; I would sooner break my sword and toss it away!"

McCausland scowled, his own anger beginning to build, "Then consider yourself under arrest for insubordination, Colonel. And remove your regiment from this town forthwith."

Peters glared at McCausland another moment, fairly twitching in tightly restrained anger. Then he stood up straight, snapped a salute, and said, "Well, at least this time you have given me an order I can obey..." Then without waiting for McCausland to answer or return the salute, he snapped his arm down, did an about-face, and marched off—Major Taylor following in his wake.

General McCausland held a dark frown as he began to turn away.

"Excuse me, General..." a voice said.

McCausland looked back, and for the first time, noticed Walters standing there, an unreadable expression on his face.

"Yes, Colonel?"

"May I, sir?" Walters asked, extending his right hand.

"*What?* Oh ... yes, certainly," McCausland answered, handing General Early's orders across to Walters.

Walters took the paper and unfolded it, a task made somewhat awkward by his missing left hand. He read through it, nodded, and handed it back to the general. "I will carry out these orders, sir," he said in even tones.

McCausland smiled, then nodded.

ෂාශ්‍රිෂ්‍රියාශ්‍රිෂ්‍රියාශ්‍රිෂ්‍රිෂ්

Walters's men torched the courthouse first, then the town hall, followed by a large warehouse nearby. While these fires raged, the battalion was formed into squads, which were sent out from the center of town like the spokes of a wheel, leaving a trail of devastation in their wake.

As the rebels moved from house to house, doors were kicked in or beaten down with axes. Rooms were rifled for valuables: jewelry, silverware, greenbacks, coins. Then kerosene was poured over bedding or clothing, and furniture was broken up for firewood before everything was set ablaze.

The ladies of the town, especially those of the highest class, met the attack with shock and incredulity; on previous occasions when Confederate troops had passed through, the soldiers had behaved as the very model of civility, purchasing any goods they required, and going out of their way to treat the civilians politely. General Lee had even, while on the march to Gettysburg the year before, issued stern warnings to his men that any misbehavior against civilians would be severely punished.

But now the women could only beg that they be allowed to collect a few belongings before their homes were torched. A few were allowed to do so; most others were not. Terrorized women wandered the streets, looking for some place of safety, holding the hands of their dazed and bewildered children. The few men in town were old and bent, unable to resist, and were forced to take aid from the women to escape from harm's way.

Elijah Walters rode his horse slowly through the town, silently thrilled at the sight of so much destruction and despair. As he turned one corner, he saw a young woman confronting several of his men, each of whom bore a torch. When the woman saw Walters approaching, she rushed up to him, clutched at his pant leg, and fairly screamed, "Oh, Colonel ... thank God you've arrived! These men mean to burn my home! Please make them stop, sir. I am a widow, and if they burn down my house, I will have nothing."

Walters gazed down at her without expression, but asked, "And what of your husband? How did he die?"

"He was a Union soldier, sir ... killed at the battle in Gettysburg."

Walters nodded, "Hmm ... *Yankee* soldier..."

Then he turned toward the men, who'd been watching his interaction with the woman, and said, "You heard the lady ... Her husband was a damned cowardly Yankee ... burn her house down. But before you do, be sure to *confiscate* any valuables she may have inside."

"*Nooo … have mercy,*" she screamed as she sank to the ground at the feet of Walters's horse and began to sob. But he casually kicked his mount into motion and slowly moved on.

As the day wore on, looting and destruction ran rampant, with groups of the men now staggering around drunken—having imbibed stolen liquor as they went. They sang bawdy songs while wearing all sorts of odd articles of acquired clothing, sometimes even including women's garments. What had started out as an orderly, well-organized operation had devolved into a drunken orgy of chaotic devastation.

But Walters was unconcerned. The more drunken and disorderly his men were, the worse it would go for these Yankee vermin. As he reached the edge of town, he turned his horse and gazed back at the blazing town, taking in the entire inferno. It was, he decided, a most glorious sight, a vision that thoroughly warmed his heart. And he thought it fitting that the town he'd just burned—*Chambersburg*—shared its name with his most hated enemy. It seemed somehow auspicious, perhaps even prophetic. He had a quick look around to make sure no one was watching before allowing himself to indulge in a wicked smile.

ஐஐ௸ஐ௸ஐஐ௸ஐ௸ஐஐ௸ஐ

Saturday July 30, 1864 – Petersburg, Virginia:

Cobb had been shocked when they'd received the word just after dinner the night before, that the Fourth Division would *not* be leading the attack first thing in the morning, as they'd trained and practiced for. He'd exchanged a hard look with Big George, who'd just shrugged. Their role now was to stand by as the reserve and be ready to advance when ordered.

But they had decided, along with Tony and Henry, to get up early and watch the show. The four men stood together at their position on the Union earthworks, peering up over the top, at half past three in the morning, anticipating that the explosion would happen at any moment.

And then … nothing happened. A half hour went by … and then another half hour. Finally, as Tony turned to the others and

183

said, "I wonder what happ—" a tremendous, deafening noise erupted, forcing all four men to cover their ears. At the same time, the earth shook and rumbled as in an earthquake.

Cobb looked out toward the rebel earthworks and saw a sight that beggared belief: the entire hill upon which the rebel fort was built seemed to heave up into the air before a gigantic tongue of flame shot hundreds of feet skyward, spreading into a rolling ball as it rose. The fire was followed by a huge plume of smoke that billowed up like a cloud, even as the ground erupted with a monstrous fountain of red dirt, sailing high into the air, sending timbers, boards, men, and guns whirling upward with it.

In moments, the debris began raining back down with such force that the earth shook once again.

And before the dust could settle, hundreds of Union cannon and mortars opened up all along the line. Once again, the noise was deafening, and the earth trembled beneath the pounding. To Cobb and the others watching, it seemed like it would be impossible for any rebels to recover enough from these shocking blows to put up any kind of fight.

From their vantage point, they could see the trenches of the First Division a bit to their front, off to the left. It would afford them a good view of the attack when it came. But then, instead of immediately jumping up and charging forward, as the Fourth Division had been trained to do, the First Division soldiers seemed to hesitate. A full ten minutes went by before they began to move.

And then Cobb realized something he hadn't before; the First Division was on the wrong side of their own defenses. The plan for the Fourth had been to sneak out in front of the Union earthworks under cover of darkness, so they'd have an unimpeded path to the rebel lines. But the First hadn't done this, so they had to scramble down into their own trenches, then climb up and over their own earthworks before forming up for the advance.

Cobb and George again exchanged a look, and Cobb shook his head. *This ain't a good start*, he thought. But he still had high hopes for the assault. The blast alone must've killed every rebel for hundreds of yards around.

But then Tony cried out, "Oh, no! Don't do that. What're they doing?"

The others looked out and saw what had so upset Tony. "They's goin' down into the crater ... what they doin' that for? They's supposed to go around the sides. They gonna get stuck down in there!" Tony continued.

"Yep. That ain't good," Cobb agreed.

They watched in disbelief as more and more of the Union soldiers charged down into the deep hole, which Cobb could now see was probably a hundred feet wide, two hundred feet long, and thirty or more feet deep. And then he groaned when he noticed how steep the sides were. "They's goin' straight into a death trap."

They watched in horror, unable to do anything to prevent what appeared to be a looming disaster. But then for several minutes, all seemed well; there was little or no rebel resistance, as if the entire Confederate army had been blown away. Union soldiers reached the far side of the hole and had begun climbing out again when they met their first resistance. The surviving rebel soldiers began firing on them from whatever hiding holes they could find. And instead of surging forward and overrunning the lightly defended rebel positions, the Union soldiers took cover within the slope of the crater and began returning fire.

George groaned, "They ought not be doin' that! They needs to move on outta there. Damn it ... don't lay down, *move!* Where's the damned officers? Who's out there tellin' them boys to lay down like that?"

As they watched helplessly, Union soldiers of the First Division continued to flow into the crater until it was too full for them to move. And now the gunfire from the rebels intensified as they recovered from their shock, and they sent in troops from their reserves. The Union soldiers were now caught in a steep-sided trap, most unable to fight back. For more than an hour, the three freemen watched in helpless anguish as the slaughter continued.

Then came the word: the Fourth Division had been ordered to move forward, into the crater, to help support the stalled First Division assault.

Cobb turned to George and said, "I told you I had a bad feeling about this. It's that General Burnside ... somehow he's managed to wreck this whole thing ... and likely get us all killed in the process."

☙☞☙☞☙☞☙☞☙☞☙☞☙☞☙☞

Union Lieutenant Colonel Charles Loring of General Burnside's staff, happened to be standing next to General Ferrero, commander of the Fourth Division, observing the disastrous battle out in front of them through field glasses, when Ferrero's orders from General Burnside were delivered by a courier.

Ferrero read the orders, then gave Loring a hard look before handing him the paper. Loring took it and quickly read through it.

"Oh! No ... this can't be, General ..."

"Seems pretty clear, Loring ... General Burnside has ordered us to advance into the crater with all dispatch."

"Well ... it'll be suicide. The crater's already overcrowded with our men. More will only make matters worse. Clearly the general is unaware of what is happening out here. Belay that order, General. I'll take the responsibility ... I'll return to headquarters straightaway and appeal to the general to countermand that order."

"Very well, Loring. On your orders, as a member of Burnside's staff, I will delay my advance until I receive further orders one way or the other."

"Thank you, General."

Loring jumped on his horse and galloped the half mile back to Burnside's headquarters. There he dismounted and went straight to the general, bearing the paper with General Ferrero's orders to advance.

After a quick salute, Loring, still out of breath from his hurried arrival, gasped out, "General, sir ... please belay the order to advance the Fourth. The battle is already lost, sir. Sending in more men will only get them slaughtered, and will likely do more harm than good to those within the crater. I beg of you, sir … give the order to withdraw instead."

But Burnside just stood, stared at Loring a moment, then turned away, gazing at the wall of the bomb-proof, dugout room that currently served as headquarters for the IX Corps. "I've lost too many battles already in this war, Loring. My reputation hangs by a thread … I'll not lose another and have them say that I didn't have the guts to stick it out … that I quit just because the going got tough and I was weak. No … the orders stand. Send in the Fourth."

"But—"

Burnside didn't turn back around, just pointed his finger at the door. "Dismissed, Loring."

"Yes, sir."

ℬ⊃ℭℰℬ⊃ℬ⊃ℭℰℬ⊃ℬ⊃ℭℰℭℰ

Though Henry hadn't shared Cobb's sense of dread up to this point, he had to admit this situation wasn't looking good. Not at all.

The only good news for the Twenty-Third was that they weren't the regiment in the lead in the Fourth Division's attack; rather, they were closer to the back. As they approached the scene at the double-quick, they could see that the regiments in front of them were already taking a terrible beating and had lost all semblance of order and organization.

Blood-spattered bodies, both black and white, lay everywhere, thick upon the ground, as rebels continued to pour rifle fire down into the crowded crater. To make matters worse, and even more horrific, the rebels had brought up artillery, and now grapeshot and cannister were conducting a horrific slaughter. The scene was the most hellish Henry had ever witnessed.

But Colonel Cleaveland Campbell, commanding officer of the Twenty-Third, chose not to blindly follow his orders, and instead turned at the last moment, pointed up the hill to their right, and shouted, "Charge!" He led the bayonet charge with his saber, as the Twenty-Third surged up the hill, skirting the perimeter of the

187

crater to the right, even as the original plan had called for. This move, which was carried out with great gusto and enthusiasm by the men of the Twenty-Third, seemed to catch the rebels on that side of the crater by surprise. Henry found himself and the men of his rifle company in pitched hand-to-hand combat with the enemy. He yelled as he thrust with his bayonet and pounded with the buttstock of his rifle.

The rebels fell back before them, and during a brief respite, Henry looked back and saw that the two regiments that'd been behind the Twenty-Third, the Thirty-First and the Twenty-Ninth Colored, had also joined them in the attack. And now this considerable force was driving the rebels back into the remains of their earthworks along the right side.

But a half hour later, Henry was forced to take cover as the rebels had rallied and were now pouring rifle fire into the Union soldiers from every hole, cranny, and trench of the extensive, torn-up fortress. Soon, the men in front of Henry were falling back, forced to withdraw under growing pressure from the enemy.

A few minutes later, two men rushed past carrying a white officer between them. Henry looked over and suffered a shock; the man they carried was Colonel Campbell himself. Though his eyes were open, they were wide and unseeing, and he clutched at a bloody wound in his chest as the men hurried past.

In a day that had somehow gone horribly wrong, Henry wondered how bad it was going to get … and then he found out.

෯෨෬෫෮෭෯෨෬෫෮෭෯෨෬෫

General Burnside sat at his desk in his headquarters, reading the latest dispatch from the front, when a burly man covered in dust pushed his way past the milling staff officers and stood in front of Burnside's desk, glaring down at him.

Burnside looked up and gasped, then stood to attention, "General Grant!"

"Burnside … withdraw your men at once! I've been out to the front, dodging bullets; this is a total disaster!"

"But … I thought, perhaps … one last hard push …"

188

"No, Burnside … it's too late for that. The opportunity is lost; there is no longer any chance of success. The troops must be immediately withdrawn; to leave them out there is pure slaughter!"

"Yes, sir!" Burnside then looked across at his staff officers, "You heard the general, issue the necessary orders. Pull them out. Pull them *all* out … now!"

Burnside's staff officers scrambled to obey, and soon Burnside and Grant were alone in the room. Grant sighed, then sat down heavily in a spare chair to the side of the desk.

"Burnside … I'll admit now that you were right about following the original plan of sending the colored regiments in first, and that Meade was wrong—and me with him.

"But, when a battle goes sour, you've got to know when to give it up and save your men. Believe me, I've learned that the *hard* way. And I'd rather we didn't repeat that mistake."

Burnside nodded, then leaned forward over the desk and put his head in his hands.

ͼϾͼϾͼϾͼϾͼϾͼϾͼϾͼϾ

By the time the order finally reached them to withdraw, Henry's company, and the rest of the Twenty-Third, had been pushed back almost to the place where they'd started their initial charge. Henry had seen so many of their men lying dead, torn by bullets or ripped apart by cannister fire, that he felt a sickening knot in his stomach. He wondered if he'd ever get those images from his mind, or if they'd be a permanent fixture, along with the horror of it.

He turned once again to fall back to another point of cover, leapfrogging with the remaining men of his rifle company so they could provide what cover they could for each other. He scrambled, ran, then jumped over a waist-high mound of dirt, crawling in behind it, immediately beginning to reload his rifle. He noticed a dead soldier next to him, sitting up with his back to the dirt pile, a large, bloody hole in the center of his chest. But he'd seen so many dead men today, he paid this one little heed. Then

189

he noticed the sergeant's chevron on the dead man's sleeve out of the corner of his eye, and turned to take a closer look at the face.

He groaned and wiped his eyes, not moving for a moment. Then he dropped his rifle, reached over, and lifted the man onto his shoulders before standing up with a grunt. He immediately trotted off down the hill, praying he'd not be shot in the back as he went. But though Cobb was dead, Henry was never going to leave him there in that horrible place. Not while he, Henry, still drew breath.

He'd made it halfway back to camp, now staggering under the weight of his exhaustion, grief, and the body of his dead comrade, when he felt a strong hand take hold of his left arm.

He glanced in that direction and saw it was Big George, with Tony next to him. "I'll take him now, Henry," was all George said. Henry just nodded, and allowed George to lift Cobb's lifeless body from his shoulder.

Tony stepped up and put his arm around Henry's shoulder as they walked.

Henry wanted to say something to Tony, but he couldn't think of the words, and likely nothing would've come out anyway.

ℰꙨ℃ℛℰℬℭℯℰꙨ℃ℛℰℬℭℯℰꙨ℃ℛℭℯ

Sunday July 31, 1864 – Petersburg, Virginia:

Henry sat on a stump near the camp of the Twenty-Third, feeling as glum and downcast as he could ever remember, and that was saying a lot, considering he'd spent most of his life as a slave, and had been forcibly separated from his wife in the process. The death of Cobb and the dozens of other men of the regiment including Amos, Will, Jimbo, and Eli of the Mountain Meadows men had been horrifying and nightmarish. He could not shake the terrible images from his mind, neither sleeping nor awake. He wondered if he ever would.

As he sat there, he began to wonder what the point of life was. It seemed as if it was a never-ending series of heartaches and disasters, punctuated by a war that would likely claim himself and all his friends before it was over. Without conscious thought,

190

he found himself holding his Colt revolver, though he couldn't remember unholstering it. He spun the cylinders absently, noting it was fully loaded as expected. And then he paused and gazed at the weapon. It occurred to him that this simple device could put an end to his hard, sad, painful life in less than a second, with a single squeeze of the trigger…

But in the midst of this dark reverie, he heard a voice, "Ah, Henry … there you are…"

He looked up and saw a tall, neatly groomed, dark-haired officer approaching and recognized Lieutenant Kaufman, one of the white officers of the Twenty-Third. Henry stood, holstered the pistol, and saluted as Kaufman came to a halt in front of him. Kaufman returned the salute casually.

"I didn't know where you were, Henry. I was looking for you in the camp, and then Tony said he thought he saw you out here by the woods." The lieutenant reached inside his tunic and pulled out a folded sheet of paper. "I was over at the postmaster's for mail call, and saw there was a letter for you. So I thought I'd deliver it myself."

"A letter?" Henry took the paper, and saw that it had writing on one side, and was sealed on the back with a blob of red wax, stamped with an image that looked like a mountain. He gazed up at the lieutenant. "Thank you kindly, sir."

"Never mention it," Kaufman said, and began to step away, then paused. "Oh … Henry … would you … like me to read it out for you?"

"Oh, yes please, sir. That would be most kindly of you. Ain't never had time to learn my letters before the war."

"Understood. No shame in it, certainly."

Lieutenant Kaufman took the letter back, broke the seal, unfolded it, and read aloud:

July 6, 1864
Wheeling, West Va.

Dear Henry,

You are not going to believe this; I can hardly believe it myself, but this letter is from your loving wife, Lilly. Colonel Chambers is writing it for me from inside of his house at his farm called Belle Meade in West Virginia.

Yesterday I had the happiest moment in life when I got to hug my Rosa again for the first time since she was a babe.

And then I've been getting reacquainted with all the folks I knew back at Mountain Meadows, and can hardly believe they're all freemen now. Guess I am too, since Colonel Chambers and Colonel Clark found me near Lynchburg during the recent fighting there. What a happy moment that was! I still can hardly believe it, and thank the Lord Jesus every day for it.

Then imagine my joy and surprise when Rosa told me that you, my dear husband, had also been living here with Colonel Chambers and his family. Truly God has blessed us; praise the Lord!

So, here I am, with Colonel Chambers penning this letter so I can tell you that I love you, hope you are keeping safe and doing well, and that I can't wait for the war to be over so we can be a family once again, this time with Rosa there too.

You keep your head down now, Henry, do you hear? I need you to come on back home safe now, as soon as you can.

With love from your wife,
Lilly

P.S. This is Colonel Chambers, Henry. My best wishes to you and my congratulations on your reunion with Lilly, distant though it may be at the moment. And please give

*my regards to the rest of our men in the 23rd. I pray you
are all staying safe, and I know you all are doing your duty
with the great courage and skill you have always shown
me.*

Henry gazed up at the sky, tears streaming unashamedly from
his eyes. Lieutenant Kaufman handed him the letter, shared a nod
and a bright smile with him, then turned and strode away.

Henry gazed at the wonderful piece of paper for a long
moment, then once again looked up toward the sky, "Dear sweet
Jesus … thank you ever so much … for bringin' my Lilly back to
me. And … for givin' me reason to go on livin'. Thank you, thank
you, thank you."

ĐƆƠ൳ CℬƱƟƆƠ൳ CℬƱƟƆƠ൳ Cℬ

Sunday July 31, 1864 – Fort Smith, Arkansas:

In the predawn darkness, a full hour before reveille, Union
Sergeant Ned Turner, of the First Kansas Colored Regiment, was
shocked awake by a harsh light shining in his eyes.

He sat up in his bunk and held his hand up to shade his eyes
from the offensively bright glow.

Before his eyes could adjust, he heard a familiar chuckle.
"C'mon, Sergeant Turner … we got visitors … and *not* the friendly
kind, to my thinking," Lieutenant Auggie Gordon informed him,
holding an oil lamp in his hand.

Ned was suddenly wide awake, throwing back the covers and
planting his bare feet on the wood floor. "Rebs?"

"Yep … whole damned column of them, coming up from the
south. They say they're led by that Comanche General, Stand
Watie, who's now working for the Confederates. And they've got
'em some big guns, I heard. Drove in the Sixth Kansas Cavalry
down by Fort Number Two. Lookin' to overrun us here at the
main fort, I reckon."

"But we ain't gonna let 'em, *are* we Lieutenant?"

193

"Nope. You can bet your brass buttons on that, Sergeant. Rouse the men and form 'em up. We got ourselves a battle to fight!"

And then, despite his orders to Ned, Auggie couldn't help shouting out, "Up and at 'em men! We got us some rebs to kill! Woohoo!"

This announcement was immediately answered by a mad scramble, as men hurried to pull on their britches and boots and secure their packs.

❦❧☙❦❧☙❦❧☙

By the time Ned and his company lined up in the yard, fully dressed, rifles in hand, the entire population of the fort was streaming out to assemble into their respective formations. Ned caught Auggie's eye, and the two exchanged a quick grin. There'd been little enough action since returning from the disastrous Camden campaign back in April, and now they were feeling the glow of excitement and the surge of adrenaline that always presaged an armed engagement with the enemy.

Ned glanced down the line at his rifle company, making sure all was in order, before gazing out toward the front. There he saw the fort's commandant, Brigadier General John Thayer, speaking with the First Kansas's own commander, Colonel James Williams. Williams was listening and nodding as Thayer spoke. Then the two exchanged a salute, and Williams turned and strode in Ned's direction.

Before the colonel reached their position, an aide came trotting out, holding the reins of the commander's horse. Williams mounted, then trotted the horse toward the formed-up infantry.

Colonel Williams stopped in front of the formation, cupped his hands, and shouted, "The First and Sixth Kansas Infantries will follow me at the double-quick down to Fort Number Four. Gentlemen ... be prepared to engage the enemy!"

But even as he turned the horse's reins, bullets impacted against the side of the barracks behind them, followed a few seconds later by the popping of distant rifle fire. Then a deep, booming rumble rolled out, and a lead ball screamed overhead, impacting somewhere toward the back of the parade ground, well beyond the assembled troops. The Battle of Fort Smith was on.

The men of Colonel Williams' brigade took positions along the firing steps of the small but sturdy redoubt, referred to simply as Fort Number Four, a few hundred yards to the south of the main fort where the enlisted barracks and officers' quarters were surrounded by sturdy rock walls. The gunfire hitting the main fort, they'd determined, was coming from the northwest, across the Arkansas River. Since the rebels were unlikely to attempt fording the broad river, General Thayer had concentrated his men to the south and east of the main fort, with only Union artillery bothering to answer the rebels on the far bank of the river.

As Ned gazed out, sighted his rifle, and squeezed off another round at the rebel line, formed up three or four-hundred yards further south out along the Fort Towson Road, Union gunners set to work with two howitzers they'd brought along.

Ned grinned as he recalled the first battle he'd been in where the sound of the big guns had made him flinch with trepidation. Now, he thrilled to the thunderous sound when it came from their *own* side; it meant they had a good chance at victory. And today was no exception; the Union gunners set to their task with great vigor and enthusiasm, targeting the Confederate gunners with superior Union rifled cannons. Within fifteen minutes, the rebel guns fell silent, either destroyed or pulled back out of range for fear of the federal artillery.

Apparently, Colonel Williams took this as his cue to move against the enemy. He ordered the fort's gates thrown wide, and still atop his horse, pulled out his saber and shouted, "The brigade will fix bayonets and prepare to charge!"

Moments later, Ned was sprinting toward where the rebel line had been, followed closely by the men of his rifle company, and surrounded by the nearly two thousand men of Colonel William's brigade.

But when they reached the rebel position, expecting a desperate, hand-to-hand engagement, they found the rebels were already gone. In the fog of artillery and rifle smoke, they'd abandoned the field to the Union soldiers.

Ned couldn't decide if he was happy for the easy victory, or disappointed they'd not been able to come to grips with the enemy.

As he marched back to the main fort, Auggie stepped up to him and patted him on the back, grinning. "Too bad the rebs didn't stick around for the party," the lieutenant said.

"Yeah … too bad. We woulda whupped 'em," Ned nodded.

"True enough … but we can at least take solace in knowing we've secured Fort Smith, likely for good. After the show of force we just gave 'em, I doubt they'll try it again."

Ned thought about that and decided it was good that they'd saved the fort without a major battle, and the casualties that would've cost them. But he still felt a twinge of disappointment that they'd not had another serious go at the hated enemy.

Chapter 10. Living with the Enemy

"Beware not the enemy from 'without'
but the enemy from 'within.'"
- Douglas MacArthur

Sunday July 31, 1864 – Richmond, Virginia:

Though Evelyn's lifestyle had changed dramatically since she was forced to abandon her fine house and take up residence in an old warehouse owned by Jonathan Hughes, she quickly adapted, and continued her espionage efforts on behalf of the Union Army. Now slightly over a month into her new living arrangement, she had switched her focus from obtaining information from government officials, high-ranking officers, and their wives, to directly spying on Confederate troop movements and defensive works.

But her first order of business, before indulging in any espionage, had been one of self-preservation. Remembering her earlier adventures with Nigel Hughes, she had dyed her hair black and tied it up in a bun each morning. She now wore only the plain clothes of the lowest ranks of society, and her regular "makeup" was now a subtle coating of dirt she applied anytime she planned to leave the warehouse.

Jacob and several other trusted men supplied by the Hugheses set up a subtle yet sophisticated ring of what the army would call "pickets," but who appeared only as street derelicts to the casual observer. These pickets surrounded the warehouse in every direction, and were deployed in depth, so if someone suspicious penetrated one level, the next level would be there to report it and take action, quickly getting word to Evelyn.

Through her freemen, posing as slaves who'd been sent on errands, Evelyn kept in regular contact with the Hugheses, Elizabeth Van Lew, and Margaret. And of course, Joseph checked in on her from time to time, often making a game of eluding her pickets and appearing unannounced.

But on one of Joseph's visits, he surprised her by bringing a guest. To Evelyn's delight, it was Varina's former butler, Hank.

"Oh my goodness, Hank! It is so good to see you again," she beamed. She embraced him, making him grin with an embarrassed look.

"It is good to see you again as well, Miss Evelyn," he answered.

"But, Hank … I thought you were leaving Virginia for good and never coming back … Why are you here?"

"I thought I was too, Miss Evelyn. I got all the way to the Potomac, and even had arranged for a man to ferry me across in a rowboat the next morning. But that night I started in to thinking … something someone said to me once … that when all was said and done, I'd feel a whole lot better about myself knowing I'd done something to help … you know … the others. Those still held as slaves. So, I turned back to the last Underground Railroad stop, and stayed there to help out."

"That was most admirable of you, Hank. I'm pleased, but not surprised. But that still doesn't answer why you're back here in Richmond."

"That's on account of *you*, Miss Evelyn. A couple of weeks back, one of the conductors let slip something about 'Miss Eve,' and when I said I knew you and asked what it was about, he told me what had happened—that you had been forced out of your home and were now in hiding down by the docks. Seemed like you might need some help, so … here I am, to do whatever I can."

"Oh my goodness, Hank. I can't tell you how much that means to me. I know you will be a tremendous help; your strong presence itself will prove a great comfort to those of us doing a difficult and dangerous task."

"Thank you for saying so, Miss Evelyn."

ॐ๏ॐ๏ॐ๏ॐ๏ॐ๏ॐ๏ॐ

Once Evelyn finished giving Hank a quick tour of their warehouse home, and assigned him a space to bed down and store his things, she held a quick private meeting with Joseph, per his request.

"What is it you wished to discuss, Joseph?" she prompted as the two of them sat in the alleyway outside the warehouse, with their backs leaned up against the wall. The spot afforded them a bit of shade from the intense heat of the afternoon sun, and also more privacy than inside the large, echoing building that had become Evelyn's home. It was also surreptitiously guarded by Evelyn's freemen helpers, so there was no possibility of someone eavesdropping on their conversation.

"Something I've been mulling over for some weeks now…" he answered cryptically.

"Oh?"

"Evelyn, do you recall my rather unpleasant visit with the Confederate Signal Corps a couple of months ago?"

"Well, yes, of course. The *animals* … they nearly beat you to death, from which you've only recently fully recovered. How could I possibly forget about *that*?"

"Yes, how indeed. But I must correct you; there was no 'they' to it; only one man participated in my prolonged torture."

"Ah, yes … I recall you mentioning a specific colonel…"

"Colonel *Grayson*."

Evelyn nodded, but waited for Joseph to say what was on his mind.

"And do you recall, as we rode home in the carriage, what I said I would do concerning this certain colonel?"

Evelyn frowned, "You said you would kill him."

Joseph nodded, "And your answer was…?"

Evelyn folded her arms in front of her and slowly nodded, "Yes … well, I suppose … in a moment of weakness and anger … I may have said I would help you."

Joseph now grinned mischievously. "Indeed you did, my dear."

⁂

Later that afternoon, after Joseph had departed and Evelyn had brough Hank up to speed on all of their clandestine activities and plans, she broached the subject that had been prodding at her curiosity for many months.

"Hank ... if you don't mind my asking ... why did you suddenly decide you had to leave Virginia when you did? You seemed reluctant to discuss it at the time, and I didn't wish to pry, since I had promised to help, but I've been unsuccessful puzzling it out."

He looked at her a moment, then down to the floor, as if still reluctant to speak of it.

"It's all right ... If you don't wish to discuss it, I understand," she said.

"No ... it's okay, Miss Evelyn. I ... I was just ... well, to be honest, it was because of Mary."

"Mary? But I thought you two were getting along splendidly ... Did you have a falling out?"

"No!" he said, with such emphasis it surprised her. But then he continued in a quieter tone, "No ... the opposite actually ... we were getting along *very* well. Too well."

"Then ... I don't understand, Hank ... what happened?"

"I ... found myself having ... you know ... *feelings* for her. She's so smart and capable..."

"And beautiful ..." Evelyn prodded.

"Yes, that too," Hank admitted, with a wry grin.

"But, Miss Evelyn ... she's a married woman. So, I just had to leave before ... before I was tempted to do something that just wouldn't be right."

Evelyn gasped, and shook her head, holding her hand over her mouth. "Oh, my good gracious, Hank! Mary *was* married, back at the time of the secession—to a freeman named Bowser. I don't know all the details, but ... suffice to say the man turned out to be something other than what she had assumed, and their marriage was annulled."

Hanks eyes widened, and he gazed up at the ceiling, taking in a long, deep breath.

"You mean to say ... all this time, I thought she was a married woman, but she wasn't? Oh, my Lord ... what a fool I've been."

"But Hank ... didn't she tell you?"

"Well ... no ... someone just said she'd married some fellow back at the start of the war ... and I ... I never asked."

"Oh, Hank ... I'm so sorry you suffered so, and for no reason. But ... oh, my goodness ... wait here a moment, I'll be right back ..."

Evelyn slipped out a side door of the warehouse. In a few moments, she stepped back in, beaming brightly. Hank saw she was leading someone by the hand, who was following behind her.

When they approached within a few steps, Evelyn stepped aside, and Hank saw it was Mary. They gazed at each other for a moment, as if in shock. Then Mary looked down at the floor, "Hank ... you're back."

"Yes, Mary ... I'm back."

There was a long, awkward pause, as neither seemed to be able to find the words they wanted to say.

Evelyn looked from one to the other, smiled, then turned and left the room without a word, softly closing the door behind her.

"Mary, I ... I need to apologize ... for leaving like I did..."

"No, Hank. No slave should ever apologize for trying to get free. No man should be a slave ... and especially not a *really* good man like you, Hank."

He smiled for the first time since she'd arrived. "Mary ... I ... I've been so foolish. You see, I heard you was married and I ... I couldn't continue being around you knowing ... knowing you were married to some other man."

Now it was her turn to smile. "Oh, Hank ... that was years ago, and was only a foolish mistake that was quickly ended ... didn't you know?"

"No, not until just now when Miss Evelyn told me."

"Oh. And ... you were having *feelings* for me, Hank?" She looked down and slowly shook her head, but a smile was growing on her lips. "Here all this time I thought it was just me."

He stepped up to her and took one of her hands in his. "You were feeling the same, Mary?"

"Yes ... but then you just left, and ... I didn't know what I'd done wrong, but I was sure you had left because of me."

"Well, yes ... I left because of you, but not on account of you doing anything wrong, only on account of me being foolish."

She reached up and gave him a quick kiss on the cheek, then smiled. "No, Hank. Not foolish, honorable. You didn't know, and thought you were doing the right thing. But now…"

"Now … well, now, Mary, we can see what might be."

"Yes, now we can, Hank. Oh, I'm so happy you came back."

He laughed. "Me too, Mary. Me too!"

࿐࿐࿐࿐࿐࿐࿐࿐࿐

Despite Dr. McCaw's orders, the Union wounded at Chimborazo Hospital continued to be slighted by the nurses, several of whom simply didn't show up to tend to the Union soldiers when it was their shift. But since most of the nurses were volunteers, there was little Dr. McCaw could do about it.

But Margaret decided that actually worked out in her favor, as she became the de facto head nurse for the Union wounded, being the most reliable to just show up. She now spent the majority of her time in amongst the conical five-bed Sibley tents that'd been added for general overflow, but were now used to house the Yankees.

Not that she had anything against helping the Confederate soldiers—she had, after all, originally volunteered to do just that—somehow, aiding the federal soldiers made her feel more like she was doing something positive for her *own* side in the conflict. And because the task had fallen upon her by default, she had little fear of being accused of being a Union sympathizer. Only Phoebe Pember knew of her connection to William, and she seemed entirely unconcerned about it, and appreciative of the help.

And the more Margaret became comfortable with nursing, the more she became aware of an unintended consequence: she now had a better understanding and appreciation for the things William did as a physician. Somehow that made her feel closer to him, despite their long, forced separation. And when she daydreamed of how things might be after the war, she could now envision the two of them running a medical practice or a hospital together, whereas before she'd always assumed they might teach at a school. It was an interesting train of thought, and helped fill the long, lonely hours of her night shifts.

Monday, August 1, 1864 – Richmond, Virginia:

Colonel Ira Grayson of the Confederate Signal Corps strode down the street in the direction of the Richmond waterfront. And though he walked with a cane, he'd recovered sufficiently from his wounds suffered at the first Manassas battle, such that his limp was now barely noticeable.

Tonight, he wore his finest civilian garb, donning his typical persona as "Mr. Gray." He'd received communication earlier in the day from one of his operatives requesting a meeting down by the docks, that the man might pass on some vital intelligence concerning the infamous Union spy boss, known only as "The Employer."

Grayson had been itching to identify the traitor for months, and now perhaps he would finally get the intel he needed to finish the job. He felt a growing excitement at the possibility.

It was still daylight, but the shadows were growing long as he approached a street corner. Rounding the corner ahead of him and coming his way up the street was a fine-looking couple: an older gentleman, nicely dressed with a neatly-trimmed dark beard, and a younger, dark-haired lady as pretty as any he could ever recall seeing.

The man seemed vaguely familiar to him, though he couldn't immediately put a name to the face. *Hmm ... some government official? Or some gentleman I've met at a social event, perhaps?*

The lady met eyes with him as they approached, and then graced him with a dazzling smile that nearly took his breath away.

Though it wouldn't be proper to acknowledge her look, given she was currently being escorted by the gentleman, it did cross his mind that he was far younger and more handsome than her current escort. So he nodded subtly to acknowledge the look she'd given him, and raised his walking stick as he did so.

And that simple, reflexive, almost unconscious action saved his life; it blocked the gentleman's arm and the blade it held, just inches from Grayson's throat.

And in that moment, the assassin's identity came to him in a flash, and he suffered a second shock: this was the same Union spy he'd tortured and who'd later escaped ... the so-called vagrant!

ℬ)(ℛ)(ℬℬ)(ℛ)(ℬℬ)(ℛ)(ℬ

Though Joseph was an experienced fighter and had been in many scrapes, Colonel Grayson was no ordinary target. By pure bad luck, Grayson had blocked Joseph's killing blow with his walking stick, and now the two men grappled. And it was quickly becoming apparent that Joseph was outmatched by the younger, stronger man, who was also a trained and experienced military man.

With a sharp, painful twist of Grayson's iron-hard grip on his wrist, Joseph was forced to release his knife, which clattered to the ground. Then Grayson stepped back, grinned wickedly as he yanked on the handle of his walking stick with its silver lion's head for a knob. A slim, ten-inch blade slid free from the cane.

Grayson reversed his grip, then plunged the knife down toward Joseph's chest. Joseph caught Grayson's wrist in both hands and held the blade inches from impact. But Grayson used his other arm, applying all his strength, pushing downward on the weapon.

Joseph knew with a sinking certainty that there was nothing he could do to stop the blade's inexorable path to his heart, and that in the next few moments he was surely going to die.

And then, suddenly the pressure was gone. Grayson was slumping to the ground, and Joseph's ears were ringing from a deafening concussion. Smoke swirled up, burning his eyes and forcing a stinging cough from his throat.

He looked over his shoulder and saw Evelyn standing there holding a grim expression, her tiny .22-caliber Smith and Wesson revolver in her hand, smoke still curling up from its barrel.

He looked down at Grayson, and now noticed a tiny hole in the center of the man's forehead. His eyes were glazed over, and he was not moving, though a pool of dark red liquid was spreading out under his head.

❧❦❧❦❧❦❧❦❧❦❧❦❧

Monday, August 8, 1864 – Richmond, Virginia:

Margaret's heart ached for the soldiers who had sickened and died from their wounds, and for those who would be permanently disabled, unable to walk or even stand on their own. But she was consoled and uplifted by those who were progressively recovering and getting stronger and healthier day by day.

Among these were two brothers from Parkersburg, West Virginia, Bill and Ben Higgins. They'd fought side by side for the Seventh West Virginia Regiment in the recent fighting outside Petersburg, and both had been wounded by the same artillery shell. Bill had lost his right arm just below the elbow, and Ben his left arm *above* the elbow.

But despite these devastating injuries, the two young men in their early twenties managed to maintain a bright, positive outlook that seemed almost infectious, to the point where Margaret found herself looking forward to seeing them each day.

"Here I am supposed to be the one buoying up *your* spirits, and yet you two make me smile and laugh every day," she said to them, shaking her head with amusement. The two men sat on Ben's bunk, playing a card game in which they'd figured out how to shuffle the deck by doing it cooperatively, each using his one good hand.

"You're so durned purty and smart, Miss Margaret—we can't hardly keep from laughing and joking with you," Ben answered, to which Bill nodded his agreement, grinning ear to ear. The two men weren't twins—Ben being a year older—but they may as well have been. They had very similar features, coloration, and builds, such that it was sometimes difficult for her to tell them apart.

205

But one day, when Margaret stepped into their tent, she immediately could tell something had changed. Ben and Bill did not greet her with their usual upbeat banter. They both lay on their bunks, staring up at the ceiling, wearing dark expressions on their faces.

"What is it? Are you ill?" Margaret asked, stepping up to their bunks.

"I'm not," Bill answered, "but Ben's been feeling a bit poorly…"

"Oh? Is the wound hurting you, Ben?" she asked, moving over to sit on the bed next to him.

"No, it ain't that, Miss Margaret. I just seem to be having a bit of a cough, and the chills. Also having a hard time keeping down my rations."

"Oh, dear! I will speak with the surgeon about it straightaway." Then she turned to the second brother. "But at least you aren't also feeling ill, Bill?"

To her surprise, he held a glum look. "Might be better if I was."

"What do you mean?" She moved over to a stool between their beds and sat, now gazing at Bill.

"Nurse Sally just told us they's fixin' to discharge me from the hospital in the next couple o' days on account o' the surgeon says I'm doing so well."

"But … that's wonderful!"

Bill nodded, but said nothing, maintaining his glum look, staring up at the ceiling of the tent. Finally, he looked over at her and said, "They's fixin' to split us up, and send me straight over to Belle Isle Prison, Miss Margaret. And Nurse Sally, bein' the nasty Yankee hater she is, seemed to enjoy telling us all about its horrors."

"Oh … I see," Margaret frowned. "Well, yes, I hate to agree with Sally—and rarely do—but … yes, a friend of mine who is a physician once visited there and told me of it … I'm afraid the stories are true. It is … well, *hellish* would not be too strong a term."

Bill nodded. "After all we been through, Miss Margaret, they's gonna send us one by one over to that place just so's we can die—

starved, frozen, or burned up by some deadly consumption. And worst of all, with them splittin' us up, we'll likely each die alone and never see each other again. Don't seem fair, Miss Margaret."

Margaret felt devastated, and her heart ached for these wonderful, brave young men who were facing the prospect of dying in an inferno of hell on earth. A place William had described as many times more horrific and deadly even than the dreadful Libby Prison.

Then at the thought of William and Libby Prison, an idea leapt into her mind almost unbidden: *If William could escape … why not these brothers?*

She stood and graced them with a smile. "Keep your chins up, gentlemen. There is always *hope* … and … sometimes you have friends unknown, who will aid you when the night is darkest, and all seems lost."

She gave them a meaningful look, and though they seemed puzzled by this statement, they each nodded and said, "Yes, ma'am. Yes, Miss Margaret."

And at the end of her shift, rather than walk back to Angeline's house as she normally would, Margaret turned and headed down toward the waterfront and its warehouse district.

⁂⁂⁂⁂⁂⁂⁂⁂⁂⁂

Margaret sighed heavily as she penned the required paperwork:

> *- Bill Higgins, Private. Hometown: Parkersburg, Va., Regiment: Federal 7th W. Va., died of infection from wounds Aug. 10, 1864.*

> *- Ben Higgins, Private. Hometown: Parkersburg, Va., Regiment: Federal 7th W. Va., died of consumption Aug. 10, 1864.*

Two Confederate privates came in and lifted Ben from his bunk. Margaret winced as they lifted his limp, lifeless body. His face was deathly pale, and his closed eyes looked dark and sunken. Such a stark contrast to just a few days ago, she thought.

"Can't hardly believe it, Miss Margaret. I know the one'd been doin' a bit poorly lately, but the other'n always looked so vigorous. I'd o' bet money on him bein' a fella who'd make it," one of the privates said.

"You can never tell with festering wounds, Private. One day you look perfectly well, and the next ..." She shook her head sadly.

"Yes, ma'am. As you say."

Margaret accompanied the soldiers outside, where they unceremoniously laid Ben's body in the back of a wagon next to his brother Bill's. The wagon also contained the day's amputations: several hands, feet, arms, and legs. Some still dripped blood, though most had long since drained out. The sight no longer sickened Margaret, though she did quickly look away.

The first time she'd witnessed bodies being handled in such a cavalier manner, she'd been appalled, and had complained to Dr. McCaw about it. But the surgeon-in-chief had shrugged it off. "I am a doctor, not a priest, Miss Margaret; the dead are not my concern, only the living. There are shortages of lumber and of workers, both carpenters to build caskets and men to dig graves. So one must forgo the usual niceties of peacetime when it comes to such matters." And though she'd had no argument for him, the conversation had stuck in her mind.

The driver of the wagon, a teamster who appeared to be in his forties, turned to Margaret and smiled, tipping his hat, "Ma'am."

She looked at him and nodded, but said nothing, turning away and striding back to the Sibley tent to clean up after the deceased.

ℰᎇᏟᏸᏸᏌℰᎇᏟᏸᏟᏸᏌℰᎇᏟᏸᏟᏸ

One of the soldiers, who was leaning against the wagon wheel catching his breath after carrying the heavy bodies, looked up at the wagon driver and said, "Ain't seen you here before ... Where's Jesse anyway?"

"Took ill, as I understand it. Ain't nothin' too serious, I believe. Likely he'll be back tomorrow ... or maybe the day after."

"Oh. All right. I'm Private Jones, by the way. Abel Jones."

"Good to meet you, Private. Name's Joseph ... Joseph Smith."

208

Moments later, as the wagon rumbled down the cobbled street leading away from the hospital, Joseph called out over his shoulder, "Hope you dead men are comfortable back there." Then he chuckled. "Have no fear, I'll have you back among the living shortly."

And then a voice called out from the bed of the wagon, "Much obliged, mister."

CRICEROBOROBCROCEROBOROCROCE

Wednesday, August 10, 1864 – Richmond, Virginia:

Confederate Signal Corps Major Charles White sat at the late Colonel Grayson's desk as he carefully examined the man's files. Following the colonel's untimely demise, he'd not been especially surprised when Secretary Seddon ordered him to take charge of the entire counter-espionage operation, and further, to look into whatever leads Grayson had been pursuing.

Nor had he been especially surprised about Grayson's assassination; after all, he himself had nearly been killed, presumably by the same people, when he'd gone to arrest Evelyn Hanson.

White had been at the task for several hours now, and had seen enough evidence to conclude two important things: one, that Grayson's belief in the existence of a mysterious spy called "The Employer" was not only plausible, but highly likely; and two, that Alice Spencer had indeed been working for Grayson, as she professed, and was certainly *not* a Union spy.

Unfortunately, there was little else to go on. Clearly, he would have to now expand his investigation to include looking into Grayson's track of inquiry. For several moments, he pondered whether or not his line of inquiry, now centered on Evelyn Hanson, and Grayson's were somehow connected. He soon decided it was highly likely. It seemed inconceivable to him that there would be two pro-Union spy rings working simultaneously in Richmond with no connection to each other. If he bagged one, he decided, he would likely get both.

There being nothing more he could do on *that* matter for the moment, he turned his attention to what to do with Alice Spencer. Though she was clearly *not* a Union spy, she was certainly now a liability. If not to the Confederacy itself, at least to himself. If she blamed him for wrongly incarcerating her, there could be serious repercussions up the chain of command, including with the secretary himself.

Further, if she were wandering around free, there was no telling what she might let slip concerning his investigation and Grayson's, which could alert the Union spies.

He briefly toyed with the idea of simply killing her and burying the evidence, but then decided against it. The risk was just too great; if her father the general learned of it, White would certainly suffer a similar fate.

No, he decided; better to just put her away for the remainder of the war, in a place where she would no longer be a threat.

So he pulled out pen and paper and drafted two documents. The first was an order remanding Alice to Castle Thunder Prison in Richmond, where female prisoners of the Confederacy were being housed.

The second was a letter to the prison warden. The letter read:

Aug. 10, 1864
Richmond, Va.

Warden William Hamilton,

The prisoner I have ordered into your custody is a recently captured Union spy. She has been going by the name of Alice Spencer, and claims to be the daughter of one of our own generals. Don't believe her. Her real name is Anna Smith, and we have gone to great lengths to apprehend her, and put an end to her nefarious treachery.

Please keep her as isolated as possible, and under no circumstances allow her to communicate with anyone outside of the prison.

And then, despite his usual stoicism, White couldn't help but chuckle quietly to himself as he signed both documents, "*Colonel Ira Grayson, C.S.A. Signal Corps.*"

Chapter 11. Battle for the Shenandoah

*"Once a fair land of peace and plenty
the Shenandoah Valley was now
a desolate land, battle-scarred and
laid waste by the conflicts
of contending armies."*
- **William Hewitt**
Twelfth West Virginia Regiment

Wednesday August 10, 1864 – Harpers Ferry, West Virginia:

"Come in, Colonel Chambers," a voice called out, as a sergeant held back the tent flap for Nathan with a bow.

Nathan motioned for Harry to stay outside, then entered the tent and stepped forward toward where a man sat behind a folding camp table. But to Nathan's surprise, even before he could come to attention and salute, the man was already on his feet to greet him. *Hmm ... that's new. Major Generals rarely think to stand when greeting a colonel.*

And even standing, the man was nearly a foot shorter than Nathan. But his dark hair and eyes, and his stern, hawk-like visage belied his small stature, leaving little doubt that Major General Philip Sheridan was a man to be reckoned with.

"General, welcome to the Shenandoah Valley, sir," Nathan said once they'd exchanged salutes.

But to his surprise, Sheridan immediately held out his hand, though he retained his serious demeanor. "Thank you, Colonel," he answered, even as Nathan took the proffered hand in his and shook it firmly.

"Please, be seated, Colonel Chambers."

"Thank you, sir."

General Sheridan gazed at Nathan for several moments before speaking, never breaking eye contact.

"Chambers ... I've been briefed by the War Department on all my regimental commanders, but wished to speak to each in turn, so that we will have a feeling for each other before we find ourselves immersed in combat."

"Seems prudent, sir."

Sheridan nodded. "To be blunt, Colonel, your record is somewhat concerning."

Nathan tilted his head questioningly, but allowed the general to continue.

"There have been reports of you arguing decisions with your previous commanding generals, bordering on insubordination."

Nathan shrugged, but since he'd not been asked a specific question, he didn't feel inclined to respond.

Sheridan gazed at him intently for several moments, as if gauging the truth of the reports he'd read.

"But also," the general continued, "though you have your detractors, you also seemingly have supporters. There is apparently a letter of recommendation in your file from Quartermaster General Rufus Saxton praising your command abilities and recommending you for a general officer's commission. And a similar letter from General Rosecrans. Even more telling, there is another from Major General Winfield Scott Hancock, one of the heroes of the Gettysburg campaign, recommending you for the two-star rank. You're a decorated veteran of the Mexican War ... served with distinction against hostiles in Texas..."

Sheridan paused and looked at Nathan as if he expected a response.

"Sorry, General ... was there a question there that I missed?"

Sheridan nodded and snorted a mirthless laugh. "Very well, Colonel, if you insist... Which is it, then? Argumentative, insubordinate officer, or extremely capable, invaluable commander who by rights ought to be promoted to general officer?"

Nathan gazed up at the ceiling of the tent a moment, considering his answer while fighting down a very strong urge to pull out a cigar and light it.

Finally, he looked back down at the general.

"Both, I'd say," he answered.

Sheridan raised an eyebrow, but said nothing, clearly expecting an explanation.

"If the commanding general is acting foolishly, in a manner likely to cost lives and lose a winnable battle, I'm not a man who's good at holding his tongue; that I will freely admit. The two commanding generals you speak of were inexperienced at best, incompetent at worst. Both lost battles that should've been won. If General Sigel or General Hunter speak ill of me ... I, for one, take little stock in it.

"As for my capabilities ... I know how to train and lead men and how to fight a battle," he shrugged.

Sheridan nodded his head, but continued to lock eyes with Nathan, his expression unreadable.

Suddenly, the general stood, and Nathan did likewise.

"Chambers ... though General Hunter left a recommendation for your removal from command, I'm inclined to keep you on ... under one condition..."

"Which is ...?" Nathan assumed Sheridan was about to put him on a short leash concerning any perceived insubordination.

"That if *I* do anything *stupid* in this command, you will not hesitate to tell me so—though ideally in private. God knows I don't claim to be the center of all military wisdom and expertise; I'll take all the experienced, knowledgeable men I can get to advise me. Please consider that an *order*, Colonel."

"Yes, sir. Though I'm thinking ... with *you*, that'll very likely prove unnecessary, General."

Sheridan then smiled for the first time, and again they shook hands. "Dismissed, Colonel."

When Nathan returned to his tent, he wasn't surprised to find Tom inside, anxiously awaiting the results of Nathan's meeting with their new commanding general.

"Well? How did it go?" Tom asked, as Nathan pulled out a cigar and lit it up before removing his hat and taking a seat.

"Very well, I believe," Nathan answered. "Sheridan is ... totally different from Sigel or Hunter, that's certain. A real, serious, professional soldier, from all I've heard and seen. I think we may finally have a man who can lead us to victory here in the valley."

"Yes, yes ... that sounds good. *And...?*"

"And ... as we suspected, both Sigel and Hunter had written me up for an insubordinate officer and recommended I be sacked."

Tom snorted derisively.

"But ... it turns out several other generals have written me up in the most glowing terms, and I do have a good record from the previous war and from out in Texas. I think Sheridan weighed the pros and cons and decided that I was worth keeping around after all. But he knows I don't happily suffer fools, especially when they're commanding generals."

Tom smiled at this and nodded, "There's a true statement if ever I heard one."

Nathan nodded, then they shared a laugh, and a handshake.

∞⊗⊙∞∞⊗⊙∞∞⊗⊙∞

Saturday August 20, 1864 – Charlestown, West Virginia:

Tom strode through camp in an upbeat mood. Though there'd not been any real action since General Sheridan's arrival, his take-charge attitude had stimulated a tangible improvement in morale throughout the entire army—a general feeling that finally something good was about to happen. A sense that this new general was a man who would finally lead them to victory over the rebels.

But the moment Tom entered Nathan's tent, he knew something was terribly wrong. Nathan sat behind his folding camp table, absently stroking Harry's neck with an expression Tom had rarely seen; not the usual anger, frustration, or concern, but rather, a deeply pained sorrow.

Tom stepped in, removed his hat, and sat across from Nathan, gazing into his eyes without speaking. Nathan stared back for a moment, then reached out and picked up a folded sheet of paper in front of him and handed it over to Tom.

Tom unfolded the sheet and read:

August 14, 1864
Wheeling, West Va.

Dearest Nathan,

First, I wish to tell you the happy news that we have just yesterday received a reply to Lilly's letter from Henry. I must say it was one of the most heartwarming things I have ever read in my life. The joyfulness of those two reuniting is almost beyond words. Even as I am writing this, I am tearing up just thinking about it.

But, now I must, with a most painful, heavy heart, inform you of the loss of several of your dear men from the farm. According to Henry, there was a tremendous battle down by Petersburg, Virginia, in which the colored regiments were heavily involved, including our own 23rd. He says the battle did not go well, and many Union soldiers were killed, both black and white, sadly including Amos, Will, Jimbo, Eli, and most devastating of all, Cobb, who was always very special to me.

After reading this sad news I was forced to suffer one of the most painful moments in life when I had to tell his wife Hetty of his loss. I cannot count the tears I have shed with her over it. Not since the passing of Georgie and Jamie have I felt such a loss. Thankfully I was not tasked with having to inform their loved ones in that case.

I know you will also feel this loss deeply, and I wish there was some way to comfort you in this moment, but I know it is something we each must suffer through in our own way in our own hearts.

I hope and trust that you, Tom, and the other men are in good health. I pray daily for your safety, and for the end to this terrible war.

Your loving Mother,

Tom set the paper back down in the desk, looked across at Nathan, and shared a nod, then buried his face in his hands, there being nothing to be said.

❧❧❧❧❧❧❧❧

The following day, as Nathan strode back toward his tent, Harry hard on his heels, he noticed a commotion up ahead; a circle of soldiers, hooting and hollering, as two men tussled in their center.

Nathan shook his head and scowled. Soldiers fighting with each other was nothing unusual, and he was typically inclined to just let them have it out and get it over with, which also had the positive side effect of allowing the rest of the men a few minutes of much needed entertainment and distraction.

But as he stepped up closer, he noted the men fighting wore officers' uniforms with captains' bars on the shoulders, then he realized one of them was *very* large: Stan. *This can't be good*, he decided, and rushed forward.

Nathan pushed his way through the circle and stepped up to the fighters. Stan, not surprisingly, was getting the better of his opponent, and was currently on top, punching down at the man of the ground.

"Stand down, Mr. Volkov!" Nathan shouted. But Stan seemed not to notice and continued throwing punches at his adversary, who was doing his best to cover his face and deflect the blows. To his credit, the man on the ground was kicking and squirming, continuing to resist despite the unequal fight.

"Peace, Captain Volkov!" Nathan yelled again, but to no avail. So he stepped in and grabbed Stan's right arm as the big man pulled back for another swing. Stan shook off Nathan's grasp like the latter was a child, then landed another blow.

Nathan sighed, balled up his right fist and punched Stan hard on the side of his face, putting all his weight into it. Stan tumbled sideways to the ground, and for a moment seemed stunned by the blow. But he was no ordinary fighter; not only was he gigantic and quick as a cat, but before joining the army, Stan had been a highly skilled professional fighter. He gave his face a quick rub, then was back on his feet, facing his new opponent with a dark scowl.

But Nathan now had his dander up as well, and wasn't about to back down. He balled up his fists and glared at Stan. "I said … *stand down*, Captain!"

Suddenly Stan's features softened, as recognition took hold. "Oh … it's *you*, Colonel. I … I will never fight you … *never*." He shook his head slowly, and then looked down at his feet as if suddenly ashamed.

"I'm surprised at you, Captain Volkov … picking a fight with a fellow officer."

"No, no … it's not his fault, Colonel," he heard another man say. When he turned in the direction of the voice, he saw it was Stan's opponent, now sitting up on the ground and rubbing at a seriously bruised face. "It's my fault," Zeke said. "He was just making a joke, as he always does. But I … I wasn't in the mood for it and took offense. Got saucy with him. And when he continued, I threw a punch. Reckon I got what I had coming to me … Sorry, Stan."

"Is *me* who is sorry, Zeke. I am just being dumb sometimes," Stan answered, slowly shaking his great head.

Stan stepped up to Zeke and extended his hand. Zeke took it and the big man hoisted him to his feet. The two exchanged a look and a nod, then Stan turned and strode away.

The disappointed soldiers were already dispersing, realizing now that the colonel had things in hand, the fun was over. Harry the Dog, who'd been watching the proceedings with curiosity but seemingly no great concern, sat down and started scratching an itch, the excitement of a few moments earlier already forgotten.

Nathan looked at Zeke a moment, then said, "Walk with me, Captain Benton."

They walked through the camp for several moments in silence, side by side, Harry tagging along behind, before Nathan said, "There's been a change in you since you returned from prison, Zeke."

"Yes, sir. I know."

"On the one hand, you do seem more … determined. And your fighting has certainly seemed more … intense, somehow. Even bordering on reckless at times. It seems there's a dark anger in you that wasn't there before."

Zeke looked at him, then looked down at the ground, "Yes, sir. I reckon so."

"So … what's going on with you, Zeke? Something eating at you?"

"Not sure, sir … 'spose it's on account o' not gettin' much sleep. Been having bad dreams … being locked in a box, buried alive … starved, beaten … that sort of thing. Wake up in a cold sweat most times. Sometimes with a shout, I'm told.

"Once that happens, I just go ahead and get up and get dressed, even when it's the middle of the night, knowin' there ain't gonna be any more sleep to be had. Sometimes just walk around the camp, tryin' to shake off the bad feelings, or go out to check on the sentries.

"Then I get into feelin' short tempered later in the day. Try not to take it out on the men. But when I get a chance to have a go at them rebels … oh boy! You can bet I let 'em have it after what they done to me, Phillipe, and William."

"Yes, I can understand that. Hmm … I expect the dreams are the lingering effects of your time at Libby. That was a living nightmare by all accounts, so it's no surprise it has stayed with you this long in your dreams."

"I expect you're right, Colonel. Not sure what to do about it, though."

"I don't know either, Zeke. But I'll tell you what … I'm often awake in the middle of the night, feeling restless thinking about the next action, looking at maps, and whatnot. If you're up after one of these spells, come on over to my tent. If you see the light on, then just come on in and sit with me. We can chat a bit, and maybe you can help me with my planning—help you take your mind off of … *other things*."

Zeke's face brightened. "I'll do that … I believe that would be a help, now that you suggest it. Thank you kindly, sir."

"Never mention it, Zeke. I'll be looking forward to your late-night visits."

Tuesday August 23, 1864 – Halltown, West Virginia:

Nathan scowled as he pushed his way past the burly young soldier guarding General Sheridan's door. "Out of my way, Sergeant."

He stepped into the command office—the kitchen of a requisitioned farmhouse—where Sheridan sat behind a table, surrounded by his half-dozen staff officers, most of whom outranked Nathan.

Sheridan looked up at Nathan. "Colonel Chambers … as you can see, we are in conference here."

Nathan stopped and saluted, but Sheridan looked annoyed, not bothering to return the salute.

"I am here on orders, sir," Nathan answered, lowering his hand but continuing to stand at attention, holding a severe expression.

"Whose orders?" Sheridan demanded.

"*Yours*, sir … orders from our first meeting several weeks ago. I am here on your *explicit* orders … *sir.*"

Sheridan looked puzzled for a moment, and then his eyes widened. "*Ah…*"

He turned and addressed his staff officers. "Let us take a brief respite … Please give me a moment to speak with Colonel Chambers … alone, please."

The staff officers pushed back their chairs and rose. Nathan received several dark looks and a few puzzled ones, all of which he ignored.

Sheridan stood and gestured to one of the chairs, "Chambers … sit, please."

Nathan removed his hat, and took a seat opposite the general, "Thank you, sir."

"So ... you have something you wish to say to me, I presume?" Sheridan wasted no time getting straight to the heart of the matter, which was to Nathan's liking.

"Yes, sir. You came to this command with a reputation for aggressive, bold action, which was to my liking and in my opinion sorely needed in this theatre of the war. But —"

"But so far you've not seen it," the general finished the sentence for him. "You do cut to the quick, Chambers ... in keeping with your reputation, I might add."

"Yes, sir. That *is* my manner, for better or worse. General ... why are we allowing Early to dictate this campaign? You have built up a formidable force here, and even after Lee sent General Anderson to reinforce Early, he cannot hope to match us in the field. And yet ... here we are, driven nearly back to Harpers Ferry, dug into our own defenses, like nervous mice fearing the housecat."

The general frowned, then stood and strode across the room, stopping to stare out the window. He stood there a long moment, leaving Nathan wondering how this was going to end. In his mind, there were two possible outcomes—one good and one very, very bad—and he figured the odds about even on either one.

Finally, Sheridan sighed, then turned back toward Nathan and locked eyes with him. "Believe me, Colonel, it galls me more than it does you. And I am fairly itching to give Early the pounding he so richly deserves!"

"Then ... why not give it to him, sir? You have the men to do it."

Sheridan returned to the table, and retook his seat, staring down at the surface. "It's these damned orders..."

"Orders, sir?"

"Yes ... when General Grant gave me this command, his first order was quite simple. I was to 'get south of Early, cut him off from Richmond, then pursue him to the death!'"

"Well ... that's sounds just fine to me, if I may be so bold," Nathan nodded.

"Yes, I thought so too, and undertook with great enthusiasm reorganizing this department for that very task. But then shortly after came his *second* command ... Following the news that Lee had sent General Anderson's corps to reinforce Early, the administration apparently got nervous. General Grant ordered me to avoid a disaster at all cost. To *not* pursue an aggressive posture against Early lest we suffer a devastating defeat, which might harm the president's chances for reelection. And I think we can agree that if Lincoln loses and we get George McClellan for commander in chief ... well, that would be an unimaginable catastrophe for the Union."

Nathan nodded. He of all people could not disagree with *that* statement.

"So, you can see, Chambers ... I have been presented with a conundrum ... crush Early and put him out of the war on the one hand ... but at the same time, don't take any chances that might lead to a disastrous defeat."

Nathan resisted a very strong desire to pull out a cigar and light it as he digested this news. After a few moments, he answered, "General, I have a very high regard for President Lincoln ... In fact, I believe he is the greatest president we've ever had, save only General Washington himself. But ... I can't agree with directing war strategy based on an election. If we win here in the valley, it will likely benefit the president's chances, true ... but if we are crushed in a humiliating defeat ... well, from all I've seen, Mr. Lincoln is the most savvy politician of our age ... He will figure a way to deal with that ... and still win the election."

Sheridan slowly nodded, continuing to lock eyes with Nathan.

"General ... I've been in the army a long time ... and have come to view conflicting orders from a superior as an *opportunity*, rather than a *dilemma*."

"Opportunity? How so?"

"If you're given two orders that are contradictory, but the second has not explicitly countermanded the first—as I believe is the case here—then you can't possibly follow both orders, and you must decide your own course.

"So ... General Sheridan ... *choose one*." Nathan graced Sheridan with a grin that made it clear which option he would prefer.

Sheridan gazed down at the rough wood surface of the table for a long moment. Then without warning he banged his fist against it, and Nathan saw a hard look in his eyes.

"You're right, Chambers. Absolutely right! I'm going to crush Early, if it's the last thing I do. And if that costs the president the election, then so be it. That's not my responsibility."

Sheridan stood and extended his hand to Nathan, who shook it firmly.

"Chambers, you have correctly fulfilled your orders, and are dismissed."

"Yes, sir!" Nathan stood and saluted, which Sheridan returned this time.

Then the general grinned and with a gleam in his eye, said, "And ... I thank you, sir!"

Nathan returned the grin, "Never mention it, General. See you on the battlefield, sir."

🙰ᘒᘒᘒ🙰ᘒᘒ🙰ᘒᘒ🙰ᘒᘒ

Monday September 19, 1864 – Opequon Creek, Virginia:

Although the battle had raged all morning, beginning just after sunrise, General Crook's Army of West Virginia, including Nathan's Twelfth Regiment, had been kept in reserve by General Sheridan thus far. And though it made Nathan anxious and irritable to be kept out of the fighting, he knew the West Virginians had earned the respite. They'd been fighting almost non-stop since the ill-fated Battle of New Market back in May.

But he also agreed with General Crook, whom he had overheard say to Colonel Thoburn, "I cannot seem to find a four-leaf clover ... so I suppose we shall have to fight today after all."

Nathan also knew from the number of wounded streaming back from the front, that it had not been easy going thus far, though he was gratified that General Sheridan seemed to have taken his advice concerning General Grant's conflicting orders. Since the day of their meeting, the Union general had pressed Jubal Early relentlessly, driving him inexorably southward, finally forcing this day's showdown on the banks of Opequon Creek just outside Winchester.

But Early was as wily a general as any in the war, and not easily cornered nor subdued. So despite their superior numbers, the Union Army under Sheridan had been unable to gain any ground this day, and were taking a serious pounding from the determined, dug-in rebels.

Nathan was not surprised when the order came to march just after noon. Crook's Army of West Virginia headed to the right flank of the Union line, through thick woods. At one point, the march was slowed to a near crawl by the growing number of retreating Union soldiers bogging down the roadway — men who'd clearly abandoned their hard-pressed units to seek safety at the rear. And not only did they represent an impediment to the regiment's progress, they dampened morale with the tales of woe they spread as they went. "We're whipped, boys ... the rebs are on our heels ... Run for it ... save yourselves," they cried out as Crook's men marched past.

Nathan's veterans greeted these pathetic cries with taunts and curses, calling the retreating men greenhorns, shirkers, and cowards. Nathan, though annoyed at the delay and the potential detriment to morale, couldn't suppress a grin at the response from his own men; they clearly weren't buying it, and if anything, seemed even more determined to show what *real* men could do in a battle.

Colonel Thoburn's First Division, of which the Twelfth was a part, arrived on the far-right of the Union line, facing west toward Winchester, with a small stream called Red Bud Run running east to west as the anchor for their right flank. After forming up the regiment, Nathan went to confer with his immediate superior, Colonel George Wells, their brigade commander.

He was not at all disappointed to find Wells already in conference with their superior, Colonel Thoburn, as Nathan could then contribute to whatever discussion they were having. They had only just exchanged salutes when General Crook himself arrived on his horse with the Second Division commander, Colonel Isaac Duval, in tow, along with the army's staff officers.

"Ah, good ... Gentlemen," Crook said as he dismounted and joined the group, followed by Duval. "Let's have a quick council, shall we?"

But despite his words to the contrary, General Crook did not immediately instigate a discussion. Instead, he raised his field glasses and turned west, toward where the Confederates were dug in behind Opequon Creek, some five hundred yards or more distant. He slowly panned from left to right, until his gaze seemed to rest upon the banks of Red Bud Run off in that direction.

"Hmm ... Duval, I'm thinking if we turn back east, and head upstream a ways out of the enemy's view, we can cross over, then march west through those woods at the double-quick past Early's left flank. Re-cross the stream with a charge, catching them with their pants down.

"Thoburn ... you'll launch your attack from here. Be ready to move, but stay put until you hear the sound of Duval's guns pounding the enemy from the north. Then move out and hit them like a hammer from this side. With any luck, we'll catch them in a crossfire and the entire left side of Early's line will completely collapse."

"And ... where will you be, sir?" Thoburn asked.

"I ..." Crook paused, and once again panned the field with his binoculars. "I shall accompany Colonel Duval's division on the north side of the stream. Thoburn, you'll be in command on this side. Send word to General Sheridan of our plan. Questions? Comments? Good, then let's move, gentlemen. And Godspeed."

But only a few minutes after Crook and Duval departed with Duval's division, and well before any message from Colonel Thoburn could've reached him, General Sheridan himself rode up on his horse, pulling to a bounding stop in front of Thoburn, who quickly saluted the general.

"Colonel ... what's the situation here ... and where's General Crook?"

"Sir ... General Crook has taken Second Division upstream on the Red Bud, where he intends to cross, then turn and proceed downstream again, there to cross over and surprise the rebels, hitting them in the flank. My division is ordered to stand by until we hear Duval's guns signaling their attack. Then we are to launch our own attack straight ahead, against the enemy's left flank."

Sheridan nodded his head a moment, then turned and looked out toward the battlefield, "Hmm ... yes, yes ... excellent. Excellent, indeed. That should work nicely. In fact ... I believe Crook's maneuver will be the key to breaking the entire rebel line."

Then he looked back at Thoburn and said, "Colonel ... I believe I shall stay here and observe the action until you launch your assault."

Then Sheridan looked around at the other officers assembled and met eyes with Nathan. Though he said nothing, he nodded, and Nathan thought he detected a smile at the corners of the general's mouth. Nathan returned the nod, saluted, then took his leave.

When Nathan returned to the Twelfth, he reported Crook's plan to Tom, who spread the word to the other officers of the regiment. There followed a long, anxious period of waiting, hunkered down against enemy snipers with only the Twelfth's forward skirmish line engaging the enemy in a deadly long-range cat and mouse game of harassment.

After nearly two hours of fretful waiting, Nathan finally saw signs of Crook's attack from across the river a quarter mile ahead and to the north. The attack seemed to start slowly at first, with only a smattering of rifle fire and telltale puffs of smoke. But then the intensity seemed to grow, and Nathan wondered if the crossing of the stream had been more difficult than expected downstream, slowing the attack. He watched through his spyglass as the rebels scrambled to turn their line and meet the new threat. *Time to go*, Nathan thought, lowering the glass. *"Twelfth will prepare to march at the double-quick!"* he called out.

And within a few minutes, Thoburn's entire division was on the move. Nathan led his men afoot, as was his preference in battle, and rather than leading with the saber, he unslung the Henry rifle from his shoulder.

When the Twelfth passed the place where the officers had held their meeting with General Crook, Colonel Thoburn and General

Sheridan were still there, sitting on their horses, watching the Army of West Virginia trot past on their way to the front.

But General Sheridan was no reserved, stoic commander, sitting quietly as his men passed; he held his hat in his hand and waved it vigorously at the passing troops, beaming brightly and shouting a non-stop stream of enthusiastic, encouraging profanity at them: *"Go get 'em men! Give those sorry rebel sons-of-bitches hell, boys! Give them a fuckin' pounding, my bold fellows! Show those shit-eating rascals what real men are made of! Blow their Goddamned heads clean off, boys! Give them the bayonet right up the ass, men. Pull their guts out and stomp on them! Those cowardly gray bastards can't stand up to you beautiful blue sons-of-bitches..."* And on and on he went, laughing, shouting, and waving, never seeming to tire of the sport.

Nathan smiled and shook his head. *Not even Jim Wiggins can compete with that!*

The men of the Twelfth laughed to hear their commanding general swearing like a teamster, and a spontaneous cheer went up for Sheridan as they passed. The soldiers waved their caps and shook their bayonet-mounted rifles at him in salute.

When Captain Stan Volkov heard the general, he laughed aloud, then turned to the sergeant next to him, "General speaks with much all-oh-quence ... is this correct word? *Alloquence?*"

"How would I know?" the sergeant answered. "I ain't never made it past third grade. Don't never use none o' them fancy words..."

Stan nodded. "I think is right word..."

He turned back toward the general and shouted, "Hey ... for a general who speaks with such alloquence, I will gut those sons of bitches myself!" And he pulled out his hunting knife and waved it for emphasis, as he sported his great, toothsome grin.

Sheridan leaned back his head and guffawed. Then he looked back at Stan, his eyes sparkling with amusement. "Son ... you look like you could lick the whole damned rebel army yourself!"

Stan laughed with him, "Maybe so, General ... maybe so. Will give it good try, anyhow!"

Sheridan continued to smile, and waved a salute at Stan as he passed by, which Stan returned with a flourish.

But once past their animated commanding general, the dire, desperate nature of their situation quickly became clear. Though the rebels had been caught by surprise, and were reeling from Crook's flanking, they were hard, veteran fighters and fought with great skill, tenacity, and courage, stubbornly refusing to give ground, firing desperate volleys into Thoburn's advancing federals.

Thoburn had ordered the advance with only the bayonet — so that the division could move forward at the double-quick to within one hundred yards and then charge, never stopping to fire their guns. In this way, he hoped to multiply the impact of the sudden onslaught and give the enemy little time to react.

Though Nathan had been skeptical, the gambit seemed to work; although the rebels raked the oncoming Yankees with rifle fire, the Union soldiers closed up ranks and kept coming at great speed, giving their enemies little time to reload.

As Nathan reached the rebel earthworks, he leapt up the log wall, and vaulted over the top into the enemy midst beyond. Harry the Dog was right on his heels, as was Tom Clark.

A startled rebel sergeant tried to skewer him with a bayonet, but his move was too slow, and Nathan smashed him in the face with the butt of the Henry, knocking him out of the fight. Nathan glanced to his right as Tom landed next to him and ran his saber through the defender standing there.

Hearing a scream behind him, Nathan turned and saw that Harry had ahold of a rebel by his left arm, biting down hard, and growling furiously. Though the man had dropped his rifle, he pulled a knife from a sheath at his belt and stabbed down at the dog's neck. But before he could land the blow, Nathan fired a shot at the soldier with his Henry, hitting him in the chest, knocking him to the ground. Harry released the dead man's arm, panting heavily, as he looked over at Nathan, who nodded in return. "You're welcome, buddy … and it's about damned time I returned the favor for all the times you've done that for me!"

In a moment, blue uniformed men came pouring over the wall like a great wave, and the rebels were scrambling back in disarray.

But the rebel commander, General Gordon, was an experienced fighter and a bold leader of men, and he quickly rallied his troops, pulling them back, compacting their line, and organizing them into an inverted "L" shape so they could face Crook's attack from the north at the same time as Thoburn's from the east. The rebels fell back to a stone wall, where they dug in and began hammering the oncoming Yankees with rifle fire.

And then, the Confederate artillery joined the fight; though they'd initially been caught out of position by the surprise flank attack, they'd now been repositioned, back behind the infantry lines, and began raking the federals with grapeshot and cannister, forcing men to take cover lest they be torn to pieces.

Nathan ordered his men down, and halted the advance for the moment—moving forward through the hailstorm of lead would clearly be suicidal until more federal units pressed forward to take some of the pressure off.

And then, as if in answer to Nathan's unspoken wish, Sheridan launched the remainder of his army against the rebels in a massed attack off to the left of Nathan's position. The pressure from the onslaught forced the rebels steadily backward, though they were not yet broken.

At the same time, Union artillery opened fire, targeting the Confederates' big guns. Once again, Captain DuPont, who'd helped the Twelfth escape from the New Market battle, proved his prowess, systematically destroying one rebel cannon after another.

In answer to the easing pressure to their front, Thoburn ordered another advance, this time more slowly paced, with regular stops for volley fire. The attack gained the rebel's stone wall, but the Confederates had already fallen back to a new position, several hundred yards further to the southwest. So Thoburn led the division a little further to the west where they rejoined General Crook and Colonel Duval's Second division. The re-joined Army of West Virginia now pivoted to the south and attacked the new Confederate line, this time hitting the northern side of the "L."

But the more the rebels were pushed back, the more compact their lines became, and the more difficult they were to dislodge. And as they were pushed back toward downtown Winchester, their big guns back at the former Union forts on the high ground west of town could be brought to bear, which the smaller, more portable Union guns were unable to answer.

The Twelfth, along with the rest of Crook's army, went to ground less than a hundred yards from the Confederates, and for the next hour, exchanged rifle fire with Early's intransigent infantrymen. Looking off to his left, Nathan could see that the VI and XIX Corps of Sheridan's army were also bogged down, and seemed likewise unable to advance. He knew that something would have to break the stalemate, and soon; stopping here would mean conceding the field to the Confederates, and once again admitting that the Union Army was incapable of defeating the Army of Northern Virginia within its own territory.

And then, even as Nathan was feeling a growing sense of desperation and despair, a great noise off to his right made him turn and look, along with most of his men, who paused in their firing to gaze at the spectacle. And then Nathan beheld a sight so glorious that he was certain it would stay with him the rest of his days.

A great host of blue-coated cavalry, sabers flashing in the sun, came thundering toward the rebel line at full gallop. The formation was led by a handsome young officer, his sword outstretched and his long blond hair floating behind him in his speed; Nathan recognized him instantly as the brilliant, courageous, and flamboyant General George Armstrong Custer.

The Union cavalry crashed into the rebel formation like an unstoppable wave, breaching their lines and pouring through the resulting gap in great numbers. Thousands of glittering swords slashed left and right as rebels scrambled for safety. And then the sound of trumpets and drums reached Nathan's ears, but this was not the sounding of the cavalry charge; Custer had ordered his band to play a marshal tune even as they launched their surprise attack to smash the rebel line.

The men of the Twelfth gave out a great cheer, and without orders, leapt to their feet as one and rushed forward with a yell. Nathan shared a quick look with Tom, who shrugged, grinned, then jumped up and sprinted after them. Nathan did likewise, along with the rest of Thoburn's division.

The Union infantry surged toward the Confederate earthworks. Following a feeble smattering of ineffectual rifle fire, the rebels abandoned their guns and fled in the face of the oncoming blue tide. Soon they were streaming away from the fight in great numbers, rushing back through the town of Winchester in a great flood, discarding rifles, ammunition, and equipment as they ran.

But the Confederate guns positioned in the old Union forts on the hillsides stubbornly continued to target the federals, preventing them from following up the breakthrough with an all-out rout of the enemy's infantry. It took another half hour of hard fighting to dislodge and capture the rebel guns, but by then, Early's main force had escaped.

Early's army was beaten, but not yet destroyed. They would live to fight another day.

And although the Union Army enjoyed a boisterous, joyous evening basking in the glow of a great victory over Early's army, the celebration was tempered by the realization that the job was not yet done.

☣❬❫❬❫☣☣❬❫❬❫☣

Wednesday September 21, 1864 – Fisher's Hill, Virginia:

Despite the overwhelming victory at Winchester, Union Major General Philip Sheridan had been in no mood to celebrate, and had made that fact known to his subordinate generals in no uncertain terms, with much cursing and haranguing. So by five the following morning, the Army of the Shenandoah was already on the march, following in the wake of Early's retreating soldiers.

Now, two days later, Sheridan stood on a prominence some twenty miles south of Winchester, looking out across the Shenandoah Valley at the rebel earthworks on Fisher's Hill. Early had fortified the position earlier in the year as an impregnable redoubt in the case of an emergency. Now that emergency had arrived, and Early had not hesitated in deciding upon his fallback point.

And formidable it was: steep-sided, with overlapping defensive lines in great depth, its eastern flank was anchored on the river, and its western edge on Little North Mountain. And it was now manned by some of the toughest, most experienced veterans in the Confederate Army, including the remnants of the old Stonewall Brigade.

Major General Horatio Wright, commander of VI Corps, Brigadier General William Emory, of XIX Corps, and Brigadier General George Crook of the Army of West Virginia stood with Sheridan. Filling the entire valley behind them was the vast Army of the Shenandoah, twenty-thousand strong, with nearly a hundred artillery pieces in tow.

But despite the power at his command, Sheridan hesitated. He lowered his field glasses and turned to his subordinates. "Hmm … that's gonna be a tough nut to crack, gentlemen…"

Emory nodded. "Aye, sir … looks damned near impregnable. Word is Early's had all year to prepare the position, and he appears to have made the most of the time."

Wright agreed, "Yes … an assault would be costly. We could easily lose half our force trying to take the place. Even then there'd be no guarantees. What about a siege, General? Would take longer, but…" He shrugged.

Sheridan nodded, a frown creasing his brow. He turned back toward the sight and noticed that Crook was still gazing out with his binoculars. The two were old friends, having known each other from their days growing up in Ohio. Sheridan often consulted with Crook, more than he typically would a subordinate officer.

"George … you've been oddly reticent. What're you thinking?"

But Crook did not immediately answer; instead, he slowly panned his glasses to the right and there he paused for a long moment. Finally, he lowered the binoculars and turned toward Sheridan, who was surprised to see Crook held a grin.

"I am thinking … might be time for another flanking attack, General."

"Well, yes, that is always a given," Sheridan scowled, "but … *how?* With the river on his right, and the mountain on his left, just how do you propose doing it?"

Crook was undeterred. "You forget, sir, my army is made up mostly of West Virginians. These men have lived their whole lives in these mountains; they know how to move quickly and quietly through steep terrain and deep woods. And to fight there when needed.

"We can make our way through the forest to the west, then cross between the end of their lines and the peak of the mountain. With luck, we'll be at the end of their line before they even know we've marched."

Sheridan gazed out at the mountain for a moment, then smiled for the first time that day. He turned back to Crook and snorted a laugh. "I've met a few of your West Virginians, General. Some damned tough sons-of-bitches, that's certain; and those boys love nothin' better'n a good fight as far as I can tell."

Crook smiled and nodded, "It's true, General, it's true. And I say, it's time to give our boys what they want!"

⁕⁕⁕

Thursday September 22, 1864 – Fisher's Hill, Virginia:

C.S.A. Captain Jubal Collins gazed out at an awe-inspiring sight, which nearly took his breath away, and at the same time filled him with great dread. Veteran soldier though he was, he'd rarely been in a position such as this, with a view looking out across the Shenandoah Valley from a great height at the gathering Union Army below. Tens of thousands of blue uniformed soldiers marched down the valley, rifles on their shoulders, flags flying, drums drumming, and trumpets sounding. And behind them rolled dozens of artillery pieces followed by long lines of ammunition caissons. It was a truly magnificent, truly frightful sight.

And though he knew their defensive position was a strong one—likely the best he'd ever occupied—he couldn't envision a scenario where they could prevail indefinitely against the odds now coming against them, especially after the drubbing they'd suffered just days earlier at Winchester. It had been the first time the army had been thoroughly beaten by an attacking Union force, and the effect on Confederate morale had been devastating.

True, they'd supposedly "lost" the battles of Antietam and Gettysburg, but in those battles, they'd been on the offensive, taking the fight to the Northerners in their home territory, and very nearly beating them despite being outnumbered. The Union had only "won" those battles by surviving the Confederate onslaught.

This time had been different. This time, the Yankees had been aggressive and well led, applying good solid strategy, and proper tactics. This time, they'd been an unstoppable tide, and the new Union General Sheridan, like Grant, seemed to be cut from a whole different cloth than his predecessors. Jubal knew it did *not* bode well for the future.

Jubal turned to look at Sergeant Rollins, and knew his own expression reflected the sergeant's fearful visage.

"Don't see this'n turnin' out well for us, Cap'n," Rollins said.

Jubal slowly shook his head, but could think of nothing to say, so turned back toward the view. They'd know soon enough.

ᔥᑭᏟᔢᏸᎤᔥᑭᏟᔢᏸᎤᔥᑭᏟᔢ

For Nathan and the men of the Twelfth, it had already been a long, tiring day of scrambling through brush, crossing deep ravines, clambering over rocks, and scaling steep embankments, all through a woods so thick one could rarely see anything beyond the next tree trunk. But all the while, despite the difficulties and physical challenges, the officers had enforced strict silence among the men—no cursing, no shouting, and no handling of weapons,

234

lest there be an accidental discharge that might give away their position.

The day had started before dawn, with no bugles, no drums, and no fires allowed, not even to warm up their coffee. General Crook quietly led his corps up into the trees well back from the Union front lines while Sheridan used the rest of the Army of the Shenandoah as a distraction, attacking the enemy's forward outposts, driving in his skirmishers, positioning Union artillery, and marching great formations of infantry about, as if preparing for an all-out frontal assault. Which, in fact, he was—but only as a follow-up to the planned *real* attack on the rebels' left flank by Crook's West Virginians.

Now in the late afternoon, Crook's army finally emerged from the trees to a sight more wonderful than anything Nathan had ever witnessed in all his years in the military. The scene spread out below them, over a stretch of nearly open ground, gently sloping downward, was a panoramic view of General Early's entire army, well dug-in, heavily defended by earthworks, rock walls, and dozens of artillery pieces. And every single man of them, and every single gun, was facing the wrong direction! The men of the Army of West Virginia had, against all odds, managed to slip unnoticed completely around the left flank of the Confederate Army and were now staring at their foes' backsides.

With no orders being given, men quietly mounted bayonets and formed up in ranks. General Crook himself, for once without his mount as the trek had been too rough for horses, jogged out in front of the assembled ranks, swept out his sword with a flourish, turned toward the enemy, and swiped downward.

As one man, the Army of West Virginia rushed forward down the hillside, and then what had started as a silent run, swiftly turned into a deafening roar, as men's voices seemed to spew forth of their own volition, caught up in the thrill of the moment. Nathan found he too was shouting at the top of his lungs, though he couldn't remember a conscious decision to do so.

He ran as fast as his legs would go, with Harry the Dog loping along beside him, but he noticed a large man out to his right side outpacing him—Stan, of course, shaking his rifle above his head like a spear and bellowing like a bull as he ran.

A rebel cavalry battalion was the first to realize the threat, and to recognize the futility of standing against such an onslaught. A few feeble, sporadic shots were fired before the Confederate troopers wheeled and galloped back toward the center of their defensive line.

Rebel infantry on the near end of the line tried to turn and meet the threat, but they were immediately rolled over like pebbles on the seashore. Hundreds simply threw down their weapons and raised their hands in surrender. Nathan ignored them and rushed on, firing the Henry at anyone who tried to stand in his way. When the rifle was emptied, he slung it over his back, unholstered his revolvers, and kept going. He could now see off to his left that Sheridan had also launched his assault; the entire Union Army was rushing forward, storming the enemy's earthworks, pouring up the hillside, crushing all resistance in its way. The assault was so overwhelming that Union soldiers climbing up the hill were soon merging with Crook's men rushing along behind the enemy's earthworks.

At one point, Nathan had to stop in his tracks to keep from crashing into a saber-wielding Union officer who leapt down in front of him from the earthworks above and to his left.

"Oops, sorry there, my good man! Nearly skewered you!" the officer said. And when he turned and they met eyes, Nathan grinned.

"*Keifer!*" He'd instantly recognized his old friend, Colonel Joseph Warren Keifer of Ohio, whom he'd served with under General Milroy during the ill-fated Second Battle of Winchester.

"*Chambers!* Well met, sir. Well met, indeed! Shall we finish these rebels first, and then enjoy a happy reunion?"

"Indeed, we shall, sir!" Nathan answered, reaching out to give Keifer a quick pat on the back after holstering his now-empty pistols. He swept out his saber, and the two colonels now rushed forward, side by side, swords in hand, with Harry the Dog close behind.

But after only a few more moments of action, they found there was no longer anyone left to fight. The Confederates who hadn't surrendered or been killed outright had fled the fight, discarding their weapons and equipment and simply running, singly or in groups, through the thick trees and underbrush heading south.

Nathan and Keifer sheathed their swords and stood side by side, panting as vigorously as Harry, all three trying to catch their breath after their exertions. Tom Clark came trotting up, and immediately shook hands and exchanged greetings with Keifer, and then gave Nathan a hearty handshake and a beaming grin.

The victory had been stunning. Never had Nathan seen anything like it, and couldn't imagine a more thorough, lopsided victory against a tough, well-dug-in opponent. And never had he seen a battle where the plan had worked so near to perfection as this one, leaving the Union with almost no casualties, and the enemy thoroughly devastated and completely routed from the field.

The only downside, if there was any, was that it had happened so quickly and so thoroughly that the rebels had not had a chance to rally or fight back, and so had fled the field in great numbers rather than being completely surrounded and destroyed. Despite the jubilation around him, Nathan retained the tiniest inkling of a doubt that they'd not yet seen the last of Confederate Lieutenant General Jubal Anderson Early.

☙◊☙◊☙◊☙◊☙◊☙◊☙◊☙◊☙◊

When Lieutenant Colonel Elijah Walters heard a great shout coming from behind and to the left of where his cavalry battalion was positioned, he turned and immediately took in a scene that sent a chill down his spine. It was one of the few times in life he knew for certain that if he didn't act quickly, he was gazing upon the approach of his own death.

Thousands of Union infantry soldiers, bayonets fixed, rushed unimpeded down the gentle slope of the hillside, straight toward where he was sitting on his horse.

He turned back toward his men and shouted, "We are under attack, follow me!"

And if his men expected him to lead a charge at the attacking enemy in an attempt to hold them back and buy time for General Early's army, they were quickly disabused of the notion. Walters pulled hard on his reins and spurred his horse in the opposite direction, back toward the center of the Confederate lines. But when he came up even with the place where the infantry was dug in behind its great earthworks, he didn't pause and wheel about to meet the enemy, as one might have expected. Instead, he turned to the right, heading south along a dirt path that led into the woods and down into the valley. He led his men without pause, nor with even a backward glance.

He did not think of himself as a coward, but rather as an intelligent and practical man, who knew a certain defeat when he saw one. He could see no reason to get himself, and the men serving him, killed in a futile, unwinnable fight. Better to make his escape and live to fight another day. His only regret was he was fairly certain Chambers was out there somewhere, and he would miss a chance to take a shot at his old enemy. But there would always be a next time for that.

🙰🙵🙰🙵🙰🙵🙰🙵🙰🙵

Monday October 10, 1864 – Winchester, Virginia:

Unlike his previous meeting with Sheridan, in which he'd bullied his way past the sergeant guarding the general's door, this time, Nathan waited patiently in the foyer until he was summoned.

When he finally entered Sheridan's office, currently in the parlor of an elegant home in downtown Winchester, the commanding general stood to greet him and smiled, extending his hand, eschewing the usual salute.

"Colonel Chambers ... do come in, my good man," he said, gesturing toward the chair opposite his desk. Nathan took the offered seat, and Sheridan returned to his.

"So ... come to once again serve as my conscience?" Sheridan said with a playful grin.

Nathan decided the general looked much more at ease and less anxious than he'd ever seen him before. He felt a slight twinge of guilt that his sole purpose for being here was an attempt to unsettle the general.

"No, sir. You've no need of that. I've seen you at work, and I'm convinced your conscience is functioning quite correctly." Nathan returned the grin.

Sheridan chuckled. "Well, then, what is it I can do for you, sir? Much as I've enjoyed our previous little meetings, it is … a bit of a breach in protocol, considering there are … hmm … at least three levels of commanders between us in the hierarchy."

Nathan shrugged. "Again, I must fall back upon your original orders to me, General. Orders that were open-ended and never countermanded, I might add."

"Ah, I see. Perhaps I should do something about that."

"As you wish, General. But I have come here with … *advice* … if you would hear it."

"Well, you are already here, and ostensibly at my own request, I must admit, so … speak away."

"Well, firstly, of course, congratulations are in order on your most recent victory yesterday at Tom's Brook. I understand General Custer has once again proven his mettle by routing the rebel cavalry in the valley."

"Yes … they'd become quite the nuisance lately, harassing our troops as they went about the business of destroying the agricultural capability of the valley."

"You mean burning crops, barns, and farms?" Nathan shot back.

Sheridan waved his hand. "However you like to call it, I'm under orders from General Grant on the matter, however personally distasteful I might find it. He believes it will help hasten the end of the war by depriving Lee's troops of much needed provender. Was that what you wished to speak with me about, Chambers? The burning of the valley?"

"Not specifically, sir, though as you say, I'm not a huge proponent of the practice, especially when it seems to distract the army from what it *ought* to be doing."

239

"Oh? And what might that be, in your estimation, Colonel?"

"Going after Early, sir. I've sent my best scout, Sergeant Creek, to spy out Early's camp down at Rockfish Gap."

"Your Indian scout?"

"Yes. And Sergeant Creek reports that Early still retains the core of his army, depleted though it may be, and he has recently been receiving large quantities of supplies from the east."

"*Pah!* Early is done. We so thoroughly whipped him at Winchester, then again at Fisher's Hill, that he'd be ashamed to show his face in the valley again. And now, add Custer's thorough dismantling of the rebel cavalry yesterday, and you must conclude that Early is truly done."

"No, General, I do not. With all due respect ... I believe the presence of Early's cavalry in the valley, despite their recent defeat, is proof he is *not* yet finished with us. I fear he is plotting some sort of counterattack. If Richmond were to reinforce him—"

Sheridan stood. "But that's not going to happen, Chambers. General Grant assures me that Lee has his hands full trying to counter the constant pressure on Richmond's defenses from the Army of the Potomac. He'll not dare to deplete his own forces just to bail out Early. No ... this time I must disagree; Early is done for. And I'll not go chasing after him, only to have him flee further into Virginia, leading us on a wild goose chase. We will finish the job here, and then get ourselves organized to join General Grant's attack on the rebel capital."

Nathan stood, and saluted the general, understanding that he'd pushed his luck this time, and ought not to wait until he was formally dismissed. But he had a sinking feeling that Sheridan was underestimating Early, as other Union generals had done, to their regret.

💙Ѳ☞ѳ💱💙Ѳ☞ѳ💱💙Ѳ☞ѳ

Wednesday October 19, 1864 – Winchester, Virginia:

For Nathan, the day started out promising to be one of the unnumerable dull, mundane days that were many times more common in the army than the action-filled ones. This day, the men of the Twelfth West Virginia Regiment had been assigned the duty of escorting a supply wagon train from Winchester down to the army's bivouac near Cedar Creek, some fifteen miles to the south along the Valley Pike. There they would rejoin General Crook's Army of West Virginia, from which they'd been detached two days earlier for the wagon guarding duty, it being their turn in the rotation.

They headed out of Winchester even as dawn was just touching the eastern horizon. As was his standing order, the officers of the Twelfth marched on their own two feet, same as the enlisted soldiers, the difference being the officers led their horses behind them, in case they were needed in battle.

And Nathan was not startled nor alarmed when he heard the distant rumble of artillery fire coming from the south. He'd been warned to expect it; VI Corps would be conducting a minor operation to root out some rebel skirmishers who'd reportedly taken up Early's old position on Fisher's Hill. The rebel snipers had become an annoyance to Union cavalry patrols in the area, so General Wright had decided to send out a regiment or two with a few artillery pieces to exterminate them.

But an hour and a half later, Nathan was starting to become concerned; the artillery fire had intensified, much more so than would be expected from the minor action he'd been warned about. He exchanged a dark look with Tom, who was walking next to him. Tom nodded, but as yet there was nothing to be said.

So Nathan was not especially surprised when Billy came trotting up on his horse a quarter hour later and pulled up beside him, snapping a salute.

"Billy…"

"Captain … as you can hear, something is amiss. Large numbers of our soldiers are coming this way up the road. They are disorganized without officers, and many are without weapons."

"Damn shirkers," Tom grumbled.

"Yes, Colonel Clark," Billy answered. "I questioned several, but it is hard to get a clear story from cowards who run at the first sound of gunfire."

"Yes, yes ... but what are they saying? How bad is it?" Nathan asked, sticking a cigar in his mouth and chewing on it. As had become his recent habit when meeting up with Billy, Nathan glanced up at the sky, and was not surprised to see the silhouette of a hawk soaring high above.

"Bad," Billy answered. "They say the rebels launched a surprise attack on the camps at first light. Many soldiers were still in their beds. Our own army of General Crook's was the first hit, and is falling back in great disarray."

"It's General Early again, I'd bet money on it ..." Nathan muttered. "Damn him."

Nathan immediately mounted up on Millie, and Tom did likewise on his horse, Jerry. "Tom, get those wagons off the road and parked, then form up a skirmish line across this road. Spread the word, looks like we've got ourselves a battle up ahead. Have the skirmishers fix bayonets and stop those shirkers—with a pointy steel prod, if necessary. I'll not have them stampeding back through Winchester causing a panic."

"Yes, sir!" Tom turned his horse and trotted off to carry out his orders. Without waiting for instructions, Billy turned his horse and galloped back the way he'd come.

A half hour later, the first stragglers began to arrive. Nathan noted with a scowl that these men showed no wounds, nor did they carry rifles. And the new arrivals seemed shocked when the veterans of the Twelfth ordered them to stop at the threat of being stabbed with an eighteen-inch steel blade mounted at the end of a rifle. And Nathan was pleased to see that his men were entirely unmoved by the pathetic pleas and cries of the deserters. "Shut yer fuckin' mouth, *coward*," was a typical reply from his glowering West Virginians.

But soon the trickle became a flood, which threatened to overwhelm the men on the skirmish line, and Nathan was forced to send more men out to reinforce them. Tom wisely put Stan in charge of the effort, and his huge, menacing presence atop his great, intimidating stallion brought things under control—at least for the moment.

Another half hour passed, and now nearly a thousand disorganized Union soldiers milled about in front of the Twelfth's position. Not all of them were unarmed, and there was a growing sense of fear, frustration, and anger among them; shouting matches were threatening to turn violent. Nathan was anxious to get moving to join the battle and did not relish the prospect of ordering his men to open fire on fellow Union soldiers.

But then Nathan heard a growing noise behind him, coming from his own men ... an entirely incongruous sound under the present circumstances; the men of the Twelfth, as with one thunderous voice, were cheering!

Nathan turned his horse in bewilderment even as his hat-waving, hollering men parted to each side of the roadway, allowing a small group of officers to ride through them, heading straight toward Nathan.

The officer in the lead pulled to a stop, and Nathan sat up straight in the saddle and saluted, *"General Sheridan!* I can honestly say I've never been happier to see someone, sir." And it was true, Nathan felt a wave of relief wash over him at being able to turn this problem over to his superior. And Sheridan had a fire in his eyes that left little doubt he would be up to the task.

"Colonel Chambers ... what's the situation here?"

"Well, as you can see, General..." He turned and gestured out toward the milling mob of soldiers in front of the Twelfth's bristling bayonets. "We appear to have a large number of soldiers who ... seem to have gotten themselves turned in the wrong direction."

"Ah ... I see ... Chambers, we've no time for this business, our men down at Cedar Creek are under attack."

"Yes, sir. So we've heard."

"Part your men and let me through," Sheridan ordered, and a lane was quickly cleared even as the general pushed his horse through, followed closely by his half-dozen staff officers. Nathan followed.

Without hesitation, Sheridan rode right into the midst of the milling throng of soldiers. He stopped and stood in his saddle, glaring about at the men gathered there, and suddenly all eyes were one him, and a silence fell over the scene.

"My men..." he called out, "If I'd been here, this debacle would *not* have happened. I will take the blame for my absence. But I am here *now!* And *BY GOD* we are going to turn around and whip these damned rebel sons of bitches!"

And to Nathan's undying amazement, such was the power and electricity of Sheridan's personality that the whole lot of seemingly craven deserters began to cheer him along with the men of the Twelfth.

Sheridan held up his hands for silence, then continued, "Now, men ... I know you've become separated from your units in the confusion and fog of war, so we will form you up into a new, temporary regiment that you can get back into the fight, as I know you so desperately wish to do. Colonel Chambers will take command and assign his good officers to lead you.

"*About face!* Form up into lines ... let's *move*, men, time's a wasting. We're gonna slaughter them rebs before the sun is down, or die trying!"

Another great cheer went up, and the erstwhile deserters scrambled into lines. Tom Clark was already sending his sergeants and lieutenants out to start taking charge of the new, impromptu formation. And Nathan gave Stan the command of the new regiment, for good measure.

Sheridan turned back toward Nathan, "Chambers, I'll see you at the battle." But then he paused, "Oh, and Chambers..."

"Sir?"

"You were right about Early."

"So it would seem. But I take no pleasure in it, sir. Godspeed to you."

"Thank you, Colonel," Sheridan turned his horse and galloped off with his staff officers, cheered on once again by the gathered soldiers. Nathan sat where he was for a moment, slowly shaking his head in wonder. *Never seen anything like it ... The man's a pure force of nature!*

ಬಂದೆಬಂದೆಬಂದೆಬಂದೆಬಂದೆ

When the Twelfth and Stan's impromptu, unnamed regiment arrived at Cedar Creek in the mid-afternoon, the scene that greeted them was much more encouraging than Nathan had expected. It was clear to him that Sheridan's infectious energy had not only inspired the shirkers, but had re-energized the sagging spirits of the men who'd stayed to fight. The army seemed to be reasonably well organized, arranged in a broad front running east to west across the valley, with the flanks guarded by the cavalry. And though the field hospitals that'd been hastily erected seemed to be doing a brisk business, those remaining in the ranks exuded a confidence that belied the pounding they'd received earlier in the day.

As the Twelfth approached the line, Billy came trotting up once again to give his report.

"Captain ... General Crook's army is positioned behind the left flank. I am told they are to be the reserve force in the coming battle."

"Reserve?"

Billy shrugged. "They were the hardest hit by the rebels. Caught still in their tents, mostly. Many casualties. Colonel Thoburn and Colonel Wells were both killed I am told, among many, many others."

Nathan winced at that news, "*Damn* ... sorry to hear that. And what of the rebs?"

"So far, they have had their way in the battle. But for reasons I don't understand, they have stopped for the moment. I have spied on them rifling the abandoned Union camps. I think maybe they are starving, and search for food."

Nathan nodded, "Well, whatever the reason, we can be grateful for the temporary reprieve. And where is General Sheridan?"

Billy snorted a laugh. "Everywhere. He has even spoken with me for a moment. He rides like the wind, from one unit to the next, shouting and cursing. The men love him. They cheer wherever he goes."

Nathan smiled, remembering the immediate impact Sheridan's presence had had on the deserters. "Not surprised."

"Captain ... if you wish, I will lead you to where General Crook's army is positioned."

But Nathan didn't immediately answer. Instead, he reached into his pocket, pulled out a cigar, and lit it. He took a couple of long puffs and gazed up at the sky. He was not especially surprised that Billy's hawk was nowhere to be seen this time, remembering that Billy had said the creature was shy of large formations of men, and likely had a strong dislike of gunfire.

After a moment, Nathan looked over at Tom, "Colonel Clark, I do believe we are still officially on detached duty, assigned to guard the wagons."

Tom nodded. "Yes, Colonel Chambers ... I believe you are quite correct there."

"And so ... since we have not yet fulfilled that duty, we are under no obligation to report to General Crook in the reserve position," Nathan continued.

Tom grinned. "Once again, I believe you are correct, sir. And ... may I add ... it was my understanding that General Sheridan himself ordered us to move forward, along with our new regiment of erstwhile shirkers, and join the line of battle."

Nathan returned the grin. "I believe you have the right of it, Colonel Clark." He took another puff on the cigar, before standing in the stirrups and gazing out at the Union battle lines. "*Oh!* I believe I see our old friend Colonel Keifer ahead, just to the right of that gap in the line."

Tom turned and looked where Nathan was pointing. "Yes ... that's him. I recognize his battle flag."

As they were gazing out at Keifer's Ohio brigade, Stan came trotting up on Groz. "Colonels ... greetings. I have come to ask what is it you wish me to do in coming battle."

"Ah ... hello, Stan. Thanks for taking charge of our miscreants, by the way," Nathan said, waving his hand back toward where Stan's new regiment waited.

Stan just shrugged, "Is of no matter. I will make sure they fight ... whether they like it or not!" He grinned his great, toothy grin.

"But most of them have no rifles ..." Tom said.

"Is okay … I have told them to find heavy stick or rock, if they have nothing else. And when shooting starts, pick up rifle from dead man in front of you, and keep fighting. They seem to get the idea. Or maybe no one has enough balls to question me."

Nathan grinned and shook his head. "All right, Stan. That sounds as good a plan as any. Tom, I think we'll slip into that position on Keifer's left flank, assuming he's agreeable. Stan, you just have your regiment fall in behind the Twelfth. That way, as you say, when the shooting starts, your boys will likely have more fallen rifles to choose from."

Stan nodded. "Is good, Colonel." He saluted, then rode back to get his troops repositioned.

"Let's get moving, Tom. I'll meet you over there after I have a quick chat with Colonel Keifer."

Moments later, Nathan pulled up Millie next to Colonel Keifer where he sat on his dappled gray and gave him a salute. Keifer returned the salute with a broad grin. "Ah, Colonel Chambers, we meet again! This is becoming quite a pleasant habit, sir."

"Agreed, Colonel Keifer. I've just arrived down the pike with a couple of regiments. Mind if we slip into line on your left?"

"*Mind?* Well … I'd be delighted, Chambers. It will be a great comfort, and an honor, to once again have you guarding my flank, and vice versa. We made a good team back at Second Winchester; it's always good to know you can trust the fellow next to you."

"Likewise, Keifer. That being decided, I must return to my command, and wish you well in the coming engagement."

"Same, Chambers. See you on the other side. This time perhaps we will finally finish Early for good."

"Let's hope so. See you then."

❧❦❧❦❧❦❧❦❧❦

Sheridan began the march shortly after 4:30 in the afternoon. The Army of the Shenandoah marched forward in a broad front nearly two miles wide, heading in a southwesterly direction up the valley. Once they were finally in motion, Nathan spread the Twelfth out in a wide double row, with Zeke in command of the left flank, and Ollie on the right. Tom would be in command in the middle once the fighting started. Nathan himself would, for once, hold back so he could observe the direction the battle went, and then send in Stan's unit, or parts of it, wherever they might be most needed.

Within a half mile, they began to encounter the rebels' skirmish line, but this was quickly driven in by the vast Union skirmish line Sheridan had sent out ahead of the advance.

A mile later, they found the enemy. Early's inexplicable pause in the rebel advance had been the break Sheridan had needed to rally his forces, get them reorganized, and launch the counterattack.

Nathan could clearly see that the tables were now turned, and obviously Early knew it too. He was no longer on the offensive, but his troops were now dug in, with dozens of artillery pieces for support.

But Sheridan also had big guns at his disposal, and these he quickly arranged to target the enemy, including the few guns Captain DuPont had managed to rescue from the morning's disaster. In moments, the big shells were thundering across the valley in both directions, and the opposing infantry formations began exchanging rifle volleys.

Nathan, who never believed in fighting a battle from out in the open, ordered his men to take what cover they could as they fired their rifles.

And though the Confederates once again found themselves outnumbered and outgunned, they stubbornly held their ground, as was their proclivity. As a result, Sheridan's infantry attack stalled, and could advance no further.

And then, as at Winchester, the Union cavalry made its presence known. Rather than holding his cavalry back to guard the army's flanks, as military doctrine would demand, Sheridan launched his horse troopers at the enemy in a coordinated charge from both flanks at once, in a move designed to penetrate their lines and encircle them.

When Nathan saw what was happening, he raised his spyglass and watched as the cavalry galloped forward, once again with the gallant General Custer leading the charge. They hit the

Confederate line like a hammer, and then, rather than turning to engage the enemy behind his works, they continued on past, intent on completing an encircling movement, thus cutting off their escape.

Nathan, veteran commander that he was, immediately recognized his opportunity and ordered an all-out attack by the Twelfth. He was gratified to see the other Union infantry commanders doing the same, including Colonel Keifer on his right.

Nathan watched through his spyglass as Zeke led his rifle companies up to a low rock wall the rebels had been sheltering behind, bayonets thrust forward. Over the wall the Union soldiers went, and the fighting was hand to hand. At almost the same moment, Tom's men hit the center of the rebel line, and after a brief fight, they too vaulted the wall to engage the rebels. To the right, Ollie's men met stiffer resistance, as the rebels on that side had a taller wall and fired their rifles with deadly efficiency.

So Nathan turned to Stan, who was watching him intently like a leashed hound waiting for a chance to go after the hare. Nathan motioned to the right, and Stan nodded, then turned to his men and shouted an order. The entire regiment rushed forward with a shout. Nathan saw that many of the men carried no rifles, but rather all manner of odd weapons they'd picked up along the march—hammers, pitchforks, axes ... even poles and rocks. And yet, despite this, they surged forward with gusto, seemingly swept up in the excitement of the moment. When Stan reached the wall, he was up and over it in seconds, with scores of blue-clad soldiers following.

Then, with no conscious thought, Nathan found himself standing atop the rock wall, gazing out across the field. Harry the Dog hopped up beside him. And though he knew it was an exceedingly dangerous place for an officer to stand, he could not help but pause and take in the glorious sight.

He could see that the charge by the Union cavalry had been the break that had caused the dike to give way; the rout was on, and Confederate infantrymen were throwing down their arms and either surrendering or sprinting away from the field in any direction available.

But as he started to raise his spyglass for a closer look, he felt the distinctive *hiss* and sudden blast of air from a bullet zipping past his right ear, only inches away. Though he instinctively flinched, he resisted the urge to jump back off the wall; whoever had fired the shot would take time to reload, so there was no immediate danger.

Instead, he raised the spyglass and slowly scanned the field until he found what he was seeking. He paused, refocusing on the image before him. In the midst of the chaos, a burly looking Confederate officer sat on his horse holding a rifle, aimed directly at Nathan. A telltale puff of smoke rose up from the barrel of the gun. Nathan watched as the officer calmly tossed the rifle to the ground, then raised his left fist and shook it, before turning his horse and trotting away. The fist had been missing its hand. *Walters!*

Then Nathan scanned across the battlefield, looking for the thing he'd originally been seeking. For a moment, all he could see was a great wave of blue-clad soldiers surging forward in pursuit of the fleeing enemy, and he feared his search would be in vain.

And then he saw it, several hundred yards away, still within the crumbling rebel lines; there upon his horse sat the crotchety General Jubal Early himself, "Old Jube" as he was called, waving his sword, yelling and gesticulating at the men running past him. Nathan could only imagine the profane vitriol the general was spewing forth in his vain attempt to rally his troops. But it was to no avail; Nathan envisioned the quixotic general tilting at windmills, which paid him no mind whatever.

Finally, another officer approached on horseback, seemed to speak a few words to the general, then pointed frantically to the south. After a moment, Early nodded, lowered his sword, then dropped it on the ground. He bowed his head, slowly turned his horse, and allowed the officer to lead him from the field.

Nathan lowered the spyglass and nodded with gratification. The general had the look of a broken man who'd been thoroughly beaten and humiliated. Nathan's heart told him that this was a blow from which Early would never recover.

With a deep breath of satisfaction Nathan basked in the certain knowledge that their great enemy, whom they'd battled for the better part of two years, ever since the Second Battle of Winchester, was finally defeated for good.

Chapter 12. Beginning of the End

"Now this is not the end.
It is not even the beginning of the end.
But it is, perhaps, the end of the beginning."
*- **Winston Churchill***
Prime Minister of England

Thursday October 20, 1864 – Strasburg, Virginia:

The day after the devastating defeat at Cedar Creek, Captain Jubal Collins marched with the broken remnants of General Terry's division. The drizzling rain and thick, sticky mud caking his boots seemed a fitting reflection of his downcast mood. He could not remember ever feeling so demoralized. The once proud Army of Northern Virginia, Second Corps had been thoroughly defeated in three straight battles. This time, there would be no recovering, no counterattack, no rebuilding. This time, General Early's Army of the Valley was done.

Jubal wasn't sure if General Terry had decided on his own to return to Richmond or if he was following orders, but he knew from all the grumbling he'd heard among the officers, that they'd generally lost faith in Early. Likely Terry had just decided he'd had enough and was going home, which was fine by Jubal.

He'd had enough too. Enough marching, enough starving, enough fighting. All the way to Washington and back again. *And for what?* he wondered. Then he realized he couldn't answer his own question, except maybe to say, *For nothing.*

𝔸𝔹

Saturday October 29, 1864 – Staunton, Virginia:

Elijah Walters found himself in a bit of a quandary. During the retreat back toward eastern Virginia, Walters had received orders to report to the earthworks at Petersburg. The orders had come, ostensibly, from General Early himself. But Walters could see that

Early's army was now completely shattered, and that the general himself was a beaten man. As a result, the chain of command had been considerably muddied, and Early was said to be out of favor with high command.

Walters had no desire to participate in the grimy, grinding stalemate that rumor said was the current state of affairs outside Petersburg, just south of Richmond.

So, when they reached Staunton, after a ride of nearly a hundred miles with the scattered remnants of Early's army, instead of turning southeast toward Richmond with the other Confederate soldiers, he continued on the road to the southwest, toward Lexington, with the goal of returning to Lewisburg.

Time to go home for a spell, he decided. *Time to see how things are back on the farm. Make sure everything is still in order. And, hmm ... maybe ... see what the situation is over at Mountain Meadows Farm.*

෨෬෪෬෨෬෪෨෬෪

Thursday, November 10, 1864 – Newtown, Virginia:

"Nathan!" Tom poked his head in the command tent, and Nathan noted a wide grin on his comrade's face. "I just heard the news."

"News?" Nathan feigned ignorance of what Tom meant, but a grin betrayed him.

Tom shook his head, but stepped forward and extended his hand, which Nathan took and shook firmly.

"Brigade command! Congratulations, Nathan."

"Thanks, Tom. Though I am sorry it comes as a result of the unfortunate death of Colonel Wells at Cedar Creek. They've given me First Brigade, which means the Twelfth will still be under me, fortunately. Oh, and congratulations to you as well, of course ... You're now the official commander of the Twelfth."

"Thanks ... I guess." Tom rolled his eyes, and they shared a chuckle. "But ... no general's star with the promotion?"

Nathan shook his head. "No ... If you'll recall, when they gave Colonel Thoburn command of First Division, they didn't bother giving him his star, which I thought odd at the time. The word is that Grant has put a moratorium on any new brigadiers—thinks there are already too many of them, and that most of them aren't worth much."

Tom chuckled. "Can't disagree with that … But anyway, with your promotion, and finally whipping Early to secure the valley once and for all, it seems we have a lot to celebrate."

"True … and don't forget President Lincoln's landslide reelection. With all the battles going on, we've hardly had time to savor that victory."

"Yes, though I suspect winning our battles helped secure a few votes," Tom nodded.

"That along with General Sherman's success down in Georgia … And all the sweeter to think it was at George McClellan's expense." Nathan grinned as he stuck an unlit cigar in his mouth.

Tom snorted a laugh. "That reminds me … did you hear about the poll the brigade conducted after they'd voted?"

"No … do tell, Tom."

Tom shook his head as he chuckled. "Well, as I understand it, out of the thousands of votes cast by the brigade, only four or five men voted for McClellan!"

Nathan feigned shock, "So many? What's wrong with those five men, anyway?"

They shared a laugh.

"The other good news of the day is we are finally shipping out to the east, just as soon as the transportation can be arranged," Nathan announced. "There we'll join with the Army of the Potomac as they attempt to break through to Richmond."

"Good! Maybe we can help Grant finally put an end to this thing," Tom said.

"Amen to that, Tom. Amen to that. Hey, since we're in a celebrating mood … I've had a thought…"

Nathan went over to his trunk and dug inside for a moment before coming away with a bottle containing a brown colored liquid.

"Since we are, for the moment, out of active duty and awaiting transfer, seems like an appropriate time for a celebratory drink, with everything we have to be thankful for."

"I couldn't agree more ... and it's been ... I can't even remember the last time I had a sip of whiskey."

"Neither can I ... Let's break that dry spell, shall we?"

"Agreed."

A few minutes later, the two newly promoted officers were enjoying a cigar and a well-earned sip of whiskey.

"Nathan ... when you were a little boy, did you ever imagine that one day you would be leading thousands of men into battle?"

Nathan nodded. "In fact, yes, I did."

"Oh?"

"Yes ... I don't think I've mentioned it to you before, Tom, but my great grandfather, *Ethan* Chambers, fought in the Revolutionary War. He was one of Daniel Morgan's men. He wrote a book of his adventures, which he titled *The Road to Revolution*. It's in the library back at the farm, written out in his own hand. Hmm ... I ought to look into having it published after the war, though I suspect it needs a bit of editing first..."

"Anyway, it was one of my favorites when I was a boy, along with *The Adventures of King Arthur*. Megs used to read it to me so often she likely had it memorized at some point. So, I grew up with tales of Grandad Ethan's adventures in the war, and dreamed of one day being a soldier like him."

"Ethan Chambers ... why does that name sound familiar?"

Nathan chuckled, "I borrowed great granddaddy's name when I first came to Fort Davis, Texas, disguised as a private. You recall I wished to arrive incognito so I could learn how things stood at the fort. I initially rostered in as Ethan *Chamberlain*."

"Ah yes, now I recall. But I never knew it was an actual family name."

"Yep ... One of these days, I'll have to tell you some of his wild adventures with General Morgan."

"I'll drink to that."

Billy tilted precariously, clinging to the top of a pine tree at the peak of a ridgeline. He could see the town spread out below him to his left, its houses belching smoke into the chill winter air. He noted a few larger buildings down its main street, but its most prominent feature was its train station, currently packed to overflowing with soldiers preparing to board a train for the fighting in the east.

Off to his right, a great pine forest spread until it was lost to sight in the misty distance.

He'd not seen Ladyhawk for more than a week due to the great crowd of men gathered in and around the town, compounded by the recent foul weather, which had likely kept the bird mostly grounded.

He was surprised how troubled he was by the thought of leaving town without ever seeing her again. He shook his head and smiled ruefully at the idea of becoming so attached to an animal, a thing that had never happened to him before; now he finally understood how the Captain and Stan felt about Harry the Dog.

He carefully released the branch gripped in his left hand, continuing to hang on tightly with his right, then grasped the binoculars hanging from his neck, deliberately raising them to his eyes. Billy then panned slowly across the forest in the valley below, looking for any sign of a large bird sitting atop a tree.

He silently thanked the Tonkawa God of Storms that today there'd been a break in the weather. Though the air had a bite to it and the sky was overcast, this day had been devoid of snow or rain.

As he scanned the forest's canopy, he paused at a large dark lump near the top of an especially tall pine. He lowered the binoculars, cupped his hands to his mouth, and made the distinctive, shrill call of a red-tailed hawk. To his satisfaction, the lump stirred, stretched, and launched itself off the branch, disappearing for a moment behind a great towering tree before reappearing in the sky above.

A few minutes later, the branch next to Billy shook and bounced at the impact of the large bird's taloned feet. For a moment, she bobbed up and down while the branch steadied itself, and Billy clung to his precarious perch.

Then, for several seconds man and bird gazed steadily into each other's eyes. Billy thought back to the time he'd first looked into those eyes, the day he'd found her tangled in a fence. The fierce look of defiance she'd displayed had touched something in him and had ultimately saved her life.

But now the look he saw, though just as bold and stern, seemed somehow softer, and he imagined it held respect and perhaps even affection, if such a thing were possible with a hawk.

He smiled at her and nodded. She gazed at him a moment longer, then spread her wings and launched herself back down into the valley, slowly disappearing from his sight.

Goodbye, friend hawk, Billy said silently as he watched her glide away. *Perhaps we will meet again one day...*

☞☜☞☜☞☜☞☜☞☜☞☜

Thursday December 8, 1864 – Richmond, Virginia:

A gust of cold wind caught the back of Margaret's bonnet, nearly yanking it off her head, even as she ducked into the door of the Chimborazo Hospital administrative office building. "Brrrr ... nasty out today," she shivered, and rubbed at her arms as Phoebe Pember stepped up to greet her.

"Yes, there's definitely been a turn for the worse in the weather, dear. You may want to just keep your shawl on today. The Sibley tents aren't much warmer than the outside, I'm afraid, despite the stoves being fully stoked."

"Seems like sound advice. Thank you, Phoebe."

Phoebe began to turn away, then paused and turned back toward Margaret, "Oh, I nearly forgot ... you have a visitor waiting to see you. He's sitting in the office down the hall. Second door on the right."

"Oh? Who is he?"

Phoebe gave Margaret an inscrutable look, then said, "Best you just go see for yourself, dear."

"Oh, all right."

When Margaret entered the room, a Confederate officer rose to his feet and stepped forward to greet her.

"Bob! What a surprise!"

"Miss Margaret!" Bob Hill beamed as he stepped forward and briefly took her hand and nodded. "It is such a pleasure to see you again … and a joy to see you looking so well after … *you know.*"

"Yes, I am feeling much better, thank you. Nearly as good as before. And much of that is thanks to you, Bob. I know I've thanked you before in letters, but … it is so nice to finally do so in person."

Bob smiled sheepishly, "Never mention it, Miss Margaret."

"No, truly, Bob … if you'd not allowed Captain Jenkins to care for me when I was wounded, and then asked Miss Phoebe to send her nurses to aid me … well, who knows what may have happened."

"I'm pleased I could help, Miss Margaret." Bob continued to smile and nod, and Margaret noticed a blush on his face, and then he looked down and he seemed anxious about something.

Suddenly there was an awkward silence between them, so Margaret tried to fill the gap with a polite platitude, "So … to what do I owe the pleasure, Bob? And why have you come here to the hospital?"

"I … I know you have reassured me of your good health in letters, but I … just wished to see for myself. As for coming here to the hospital … my last letter to you was returned and the postmaster said there was no longer anyone living at Miss Evelyn's residence. I didn't know how to find you, so I asked Miss Phoebe if she was still sending nurses to aid you, and if so, where you were. Though she didn't know where you lived, I was surprised when she told me you were now volunteering here at Chimborazo."

Margaret smiled, "It seemed the least I could do after all Miss Phoebe and the nurses had done for me."

"Very admirable of you, Miss Margaret."

"Thank you, Bob. Uh ... and are you still assigned to the prison?"

Bob frowned. "Yes, unfortunately. It's a very unhappy duty for me. The condition and treatment of the prisoners is, as you know ..." He slowly shook his head and sighed. "I struggle daily with a desire to leave, and return to my unit in the field, versus a feeling I should stay and do what I can to improve the lot of those poor souls who are being so terribly mistreated."

"And now it is *you* who is being so very admirable, Bob." Margaret graced him with a genuine, sincere smile, which made him beam.

"Kind of you to say."

"No, truly, Bob. You are such a good man, as I have known ever since you helped me escape from Walters."

Bob smiled, and nodded, then turned, and gestured toward the chairs surrounding simple wooden table in the middle of the room. "May we sit for a moment?"

Margaret nodded, then took a seat, with Bob taking the chair next to her, and turning it so the chairs were facing each other. But then once again he fell silent, and seemed oddly uncomfortable, to Margaret's thinking, as if struggling with something he wished to say.

"Was there ... something else you wanted to talk about, Bob?"

"Well ... yes, actually. I ... I've been thinking about ... uh ... well, I know that you have a certain ... *friendship* ... with Captain Jenkins."

"Yes."

"But I ... well, to be perfectly honest, and at the risk of seeming forward ... I have a very great admiration for you, Miss Margaret, starting back during the time when you were forced to endure confinement in your own home."

Margaret suffered a sudden realization of Bob's intentions, and her heart sank. She now recalled Evelyn's flippant remark, months ago, about Bob being in love with her. She'd dismissed it at the time as nothing more than a playful tease on Evelyn's part. Now, suddenly Evelyn's suggestion no longer seemed so far-fetched. She didn't know what to say, so allowed Bob to continue, though her heart went out to him for his obvious discomfort.

"And … I was hoping that we … well, that we might … that *you* might …" He paused, and shook his head. "Sorry, I'm no good at this sort of thing, having never had much practice, so I'll just say it." He breathed a sigh, then continued, "Miss Margaret, I would be greatly honored if you would agree to allow me to court you … with the most honorable of intentions, of course."

He ended with such a pleading look that it nearly melted Margaret's heart. She reached out and took his hands in hers, and looked him in the eyes. "Oh, Bob … you've been so good to me … have done so much for me. I can never thank you enough. But my heart belongs to another, and nothing is going to change that."

He looked down, and no longer made eye contact, slowly withdrawing his hands from hers. "I … understand, Miss Margaret. And I believe Captain Jenkins to be a good man, though I don't know him well." He stood, and tipped his hat. "I wish you all happiness in life, Margaret. You deserve it. But … I should go now."

She stood, and all she could think to say was, "I'm so sorry, Bob…"

He nodded, then turned and walked out of the room.

Margaret sank back into the chair, put her face in her hands, and cried.

ॐ৹ৎ৸ঌ৹ॐ৹ৎ৸ঌ৹ॐ৹ৎ৸

Later that afternoon, Bob stepped into the guardroom at Libby, still feeling glum about his meeting with Margaret, but happy to be out of the frigid outdoors after the long, uncomfortable walk. He was surprised to see the prison commandant, Major Thomas Turner sitting at the duty officer's desk. The major was a clean-shaven young officer with a face that was stern and unsmiling—matching his serious demeanor as an officer who'd been enrolled at West Point when the war broke out. He seemed to consider himself more important than he actually was, in Bob's opinion.

Bob stopped, stood to attention, and saluted, which Turner returned without rising.

260

"Have a seat, Captain Hill." Turner gestured to the simple wooden chair opposite the desk.

Bob removed his hat and took a seat, looking up at Turner expectantly.

Turner gazed at Bob for a long moment, holding a frown on his brow. "Bob ... once again I have received word from the War Department that you have filed an official complaint about this prison."

Bob nodded his head. *So, that's what this is about ... Not surprised he'd be unhappy about that.*

"I have to say ... I'm disappointed in you, Bob. We have discussed this very matter on at least two other occasions, and I thought we had come to an ... *understanding* about it."

"Yes, Major, it's true you have mentioned your displeasure about my submitting complaints in the past, but it is *not* true that we have ever reached an 'understanding' on the matter. I have told you before that I object to the maltreatment of the Union prisoners, on moral and humanitarian grounds, and have never agreed to your wish that I would stop speaking out about the matter."

Turner slowly nodded, the frown turning to a scowl. "I see... Well, then, Captain Hill ... allow me to make myself more clearly understood this time. If you submit even one more additional complaint—even concerning the taste of the soup—I promise I will arrange for your immediate transfer to the front lines, where I'm told—given the current dire state of the war—the odds of living more than a few weeks have become quite slim."

Bob pushed back his chair, and stood to his feet. "I'll save you the bother, Major. I'll pack my things and depart for my old unit this very afternoon. I have no desire to serve in this rat-infested hellhole any longer. And I've had a belly-full of officers who relish other men's suffering while they sit back in their warm offices, in their clean uniforms, sneering down their noses at those out doing the actual fighting! Good day to you, *sir!*"

Without waiting for a reply, Bob saluted, pivoted on his heels and marched out of the office, leaving Major Turner with his mouth hanging open.

Friday December 9, 1864 – Petersburg, Virginia:

C.S.A. Brigadier General Terry, and the remnants of the old Stonewall Brigade, including Captain Jubal Collins' two companies from the old Twenty-Seventh Virginia, finally arrived back in eastern Virginia after their long slogging return from General Early's disastrous campaign in the Shenandoah Valley.

Jubal prayed it was the last time he'd ever have to fight out west, or up north for that matter. After all the combat and marching, he had no enthusiasm for any more of it. But as they marched into Richmond, any illusions he might've entertained of spending even a few days there, and possibly gaining leave to visit Evelyn and check on her wellbeing, were quickly dispelled as they were ordered to immediately continue on to Petersburg.

He fought hard against the dark foreboding concerning her that haunted him daily after the confrontation with the Signal Corps major, made worse by the lack of any answer to any of the letters he'd sent her during the current campaign. And with no time in Richmond, once again all he could do was continue to write, and to pray.

So after a brief halt to refill their canteens and gather food, ammunition, and other supplies, they marched south to Petersburg, then straight through that town out to the massive defensive earthworks, designed to prevent General Grant from seizing the critical rail infrastructure at Petersburg—rail lines that were essential for keeping Richmond in the war.

But if Jubal had felt the marching and fighting were difficult, dangerous, and tiresome almost beyond bearing, the place he found himself in now was horrific beyond words—a living hell on earth. Men were forced to live in man-made caves underground to survive the regular Union bombardments. The soldiers who'd not been wounded or fallen sick to dysentery, typhoid fever, or any number of other potentially fatal diseases, were worn down and emaciated. The earthworks reeked of sweat, vomit, and sewage. Rats scurried everywhere.

A frigid wind blew through a camp where shelter was primitive, and firewood was in dangerously short supply. Men huddled together in the trenches for warmth, and when it rained, those unlucky enough to be on duty at the walls simply bowed their heads and endured.

Jubal stood knee deep in the mud of a trench and looked up at a dark sky as frigid rain drops spilled down on his face. He wondered if God was even there to hear his prayers. He decided to say them anyway. *Dear God, have mercy on us poor souls suffering down here. Please bring a swift end to this war, one way or the other. And please keep Evelyn safe ... And if I live through this, and if you can find it in your heart, please allow the two of us to somehow, some way, be together when it's all over. Amen.*

But later that evening, as Jubal shivered in a bombproof hut, trying in vain to warm himself next to the sputtering camp stove, whose supply of wood was green and damp, creating more smoke than heat, his prayers seemed to be answered at least to some degree, though not in a way he'd expected.

The rough wooden door of the bombproof suddenly popped open, letting in a cold gust, but it was quickly pulled shut again by the man who'd entered. In the gloom, Jubal couldn't make out a face, but he could see that the man wore a captain's uniform.

"Come on in, Captain," Jubal offered. "The stove's not puttin' out much heat, but I expect it's a might better'n outside."

"Thank you kindly, Jubal," the man said, and then as he squatted on the floor, the flickering light from the wood stove illuminated his features.

Jubal gasped with surprise, then surged forward and embraced the newcomer, nearly knocking him backward. "Captain Hill ... you're back ... I can't hardly believe it!"

And as the two men embraced, Jubal began to sob. And after a moment, Bob also wept, as the two men rocked back and forth, sharing the desperate joy of reuniting with a friend after so many had been lost. And for a few happy moments, Jubal was oblivious to their hellish environs.

❧☙❦❧☙❦❧☙❦

Tuesday December 20 – Petersburg, Virginia:

Captain Hawkins of the Seventh West Virginia leaned back in his camp chair and gazed up at the ceiling of his tent, a contented smile spreading across his lips.

Well, 'bout damned time! That's the best news I've had since … well, since Gettysburg, at least. Maybe, just maybe, Colonel Chambers can now figure a way to break through this stalemate … If anyone can do it, surely he can.

He sat back up, pulled the oil lamp close, and re-read the telegram he'd just received, this time savoring it:

> *Washington, D.C.*
> *Dec. 20, 1864*
>
> *Captain James Hawkins*
> *7th West Va. Regiment*
> *Union Camp, Petersburg, Va.:*
>
> *Dear James, I have been promoted to command of a brigade, including the 12th West Va. We are to report to the siege at Petersburg as soon as transport from this place may be arranged.*
>
> *Looking forward to seeing you shortly, and finally putting an end to Lee and the rebellion.*
>
> *Nathaniel Chambers,*
> *Brigade Commander,*
> *Colonel, 12th W. Va. Infantry*

ℬↃℭℨℬↃℬↃℭℨℭℬↃℬↃℭℨ

Tuesday December 20, 1864 – Petersburg, Virginia:

"Hey, listen up here, fellas," Tony waved a sheet of paper over his head.

"What you all-fired excited about?" George asked, looking up from his seat by the fire. "We got new marching orders … *again?*" There was no mistaking George's tone; ever since the Twenty-Third Colored Regiment had arrived at the so-called "siege" of

Petersburg, they'd seen almost non-stop action against the enemy—one engagement after another. Following the disaster at the crater, they'd fought at Weldon Railroad back in August, Fort Sedgewick and Poplar Grove Church in September, and at Boydton Plank Road and then at Hatcher's Run in October. It was a hard, grinding duty that was slowly wearing down morale and depleting the ranks of their best-trained veteran fighters.

"Nope; this here's even better," Tony answered, entirely missing the sarcastic tone of George's question. "Wait'll you hear."

Henry was also there, along with several other of their men from Mountain Meadows, gathered around a campfire amongst the tents, a mile or so behind the front lines.

"Uh ... as Sergeant Miller is a fairly good hand when it comes to his letters, I've asked him to read it out for us. Sergeant?"

A short, round black man in his mid-twenties, sporting a wispy beard, stepped forward, took the sheet of paper from Tony, then turned his back toward the fire so he'd have light with which to read.

"Ahem ... This here telegram is from a man named Nathaniel Chambers, Colonel of the Twelfth West Virginia..."

There were murmurs of startlement and excitement at this announcement, but the company quickly fell silent, eager to hear what the telegram said. The sergeant read:

> *Washington, D.C.*
> *Dec. 20, 1864*
>
> *Sergeant Mark Anthony*
> *23rd US Colored Regiment*
> *Union Camp, Petersburg, Va.:*
>
> *Dear Tony, et. al., am now in command of brigade including the 12th WV. Presently in Washington, but shortly joining you in Petersburg to finish Lee. The men here are eager to fight side by side with you men once again.*

Nathaniel Chambers,
Brigade Commander,
Colonel, 12th W. Va. Infantry

A cheer went up from the gathered men, and there were happy handshakes and pats on the back all around the campfire, as they absorbed this happy news, the general consensus being that with the imminent arrival of Colonel Chambers and his men, the war was surely now as good as won.

❧❧❧❧❧❧❧

Tuesday December 20, 1864 – Fort Smith, Arkansas:

"Hey, Ned … there you are; I've been lookin' all over for you. Don't you ever check in at the mail call?" Auggie held an odd, inscrutable grin as he strode up to where Ned was standing on guard duty.

Ned gave him a puzzled look. "Mail call? What I ever need to go an' do *that* for? Ain't nobody ever writ' me any mail…"

Auggie laughed, "Well, now they have … and here it is!" He held out a letter, sealed on the back with a red wax stamp.

Ned took it and saw his own name written on the front, along with some other writing that he assumed was the name of the fort where he was currently stationed, and likely also the regiment's number. He flipped it over to look at the red wax seal and his eyes widened. Though he'd never received a letter before, he'd seen enough of the outgoing posts over the years to recognize the fanciful, mountain shaped letter "M," which stood for Mountain Meadows.

He gazed at it for a long moment until Auggie said, "Well, ain't you gonna open it?"

But still Ned hesitated. "Won't do no good," he finally answered, and gazed up at Auggie. "Ain't never learned my letters."

"Oh, hell, is that all? Here, give it to me; I'll read it for you … if you wish."

"Oh … yes please, Lieutenant … That would be right fine. Thank you."

Auggie took the envelope, opened it, and read aloud:

November 30, 1864
Wheeling, West Va.

Dear Ned,

I apologize that this letter is so late in the writing. Though we at Belle Meade have thought of you and the other of our men often, I have had the devil's own time finding out where exactly you were. There is maddingly little news here concerning anything happening out West.

I finally had to ask Governor Pierpont to help, and he used his contacts in the War Department to find out where the First Kansas Colored was stationed. If you are reading this, then we have finally been successful, and I hope this letter finds you all in good health.

I thought you men might enjoy some news from this side of the country. Mr. Chambers is now a colonel, and has taken charge of one of the new West Virginia regiments, the 12th, along with the rest of his old soldiers. They are doing well in the fighting, having just won several large battles down in the Shenandoah Valley to drive out the rebs from there, hopefully for good.

Most of our freemen of fighting age, some twenty or so, went over to Washington City and joined up with the US 23rd Colored Regiment, to get into the fight. They have been stationed down in Petersburg, Va. Sadly, there was a great battle fought there recently, and several of our men were killed, including Cobb, Amos, Will, Jimbo, and Eli.

Everyone is doing well back here on the farm, with the women working extra hard to do all the farming, what with most of the men off to the war, though Phinney and a few of the younger men keep watch against rebel bushwhackers, which are always a potential nuisance.

I guess with all the fighting you haven't yet had time to learn your letters, but if you would have one of the other soldiers pen us a letter telling us how you, Sammy, Caleb, Jack, and Sid are doing, we would be most grateful and happy to hear from you all.

I expect by the time you receive this it will be nearly Christmas, or possibly New Years, so I will wish you all happiness of the holidays.

Sincerely,
Miss Abbey

When Auggie finished reading, Ned sat quietly for several minutes, taking it all in. He was touched that Miss Abbey had taken the time to track him down and to write him a letter, though he was saddened to hear about the deaths of men he'd known his whole life.

Though he'd been curious about what was going on back home, he never thought he'd hear any news. And then he suffered a twinge of guilt; it had never occurred to him to try to send a letter back east, not even to tell of the death of their men, Jack and Sid.

Auggie just sat and gazed at him a moment, then said, "Sorry for the loss of those men, but that was most kindly of her to write you ... Who is she, anyway?"

"She's the wife of my *old* master, who was the father of Captain Chambers ... my old master who—" he was about to describe the horrific beating he'd received at the hands of Jacob Chambers. But then he thought better of it. The person who had suffered that whipping was no longer someone he knew or recognized: like a different man from a different lifetime. "My old master from when I was a boy," he finished, and smiled at Auggie, who returned the smile.

"Nice lady ..." Auggie nodded. "You want me to pen a letter to her for you? You say whatever you want to say, and I'll just write it down, word for word."

Ned thought a moment, then nodded, "Yes, I would like that; thank you kindly, Lieutenant."

Sunday December 25, 1864 – Petersburg, Virginia:

Despite a joyful, exuberant reunion with the freemen of the Twenty-Third Colored Regiment two days earlier, and a happy Christmas Eve get together with Captain James Hawkins and the officers of the Seventh West Virginia the previous night, Nathan could not fight off a dark melancholy as he and Tom celebrated a cold, wet, Christmas Day in the brigade's command tent, sipping on hot cups of coffee in a vain attempt to stay warm.

Nathan was feeling a gnawing frustration that the war seemed to have ground to a halt even as the Union Army neared its goal of capturing Richmond.

"I suppose it was to be expected; that the enemy would dig in and fight all the harder the closer we came to his capital," Nathan finally said, more to have something to discuss than out of any real interest in the topic.

Tom just nodded and grunted as he took another sip of his coffee.

Once again, a silence fell over the room, only broken by the soft snoring of Harry from where he lay under the table. Nathan knew his glum mood had more to do with missing Evelyn than anything to do with the actual war. Another Christmas come and gone with their forced separation still firmly ensconced. Her absence had become an endless aching need, only driven into the background for short periods of time by the distraction of some dangerous, desperate action—a thing decidedly missing from the current state of siege warfare. Nathan took out a cigar, stuck it in his mouth, and chewed on it.

But the silence was interrupted when the dog snorted in mid-snore and sat upright, banging his huge head on the underside of the camp table, nearly spilling it. Harry scrambled out from underneath and bolted out the tent flap.

"Stan is here, maybe?" Tom asked.

But then they heard a robust voice that was not Stan's. But it was one they knew well, though they'd not heard it in many months, "Well, Harry … good to see you too, you big ol' ugly gol-durned mangy creature!"

They sprang to their feet, wide-eyed, and rushed out the door. There they found Jim Wiggins, sitting up on a horse in his Union major's uniform, beaming with a cigar clenched in his teeth, as water streamed off the brim of his hat. William stood next to him, holding his own horse's reins while he stroked Harry on the head. The dog's tail wagged vigorously, whacking into the legs of the horse on one side and then the other, and his tongue lolled out to the side.

Both Jim and William snapped salutes at Nathan and Tom, but couldn't help grinning brightly.

After handshakes and embraces, Nathan looked up at Jim questioningly. "I couldn't be more pleased to see you, Jim, but…"

"Yeah, I don't expect you thought you'd *ever* see me back in uniform again after gettin' my durn foot shot clean off at New Market. Well, I didn't figure I would either, but William …" He looked over at William, and the two exchanged a smile. "Well, let's just say William don't take 'no' for an answer. Sat down and drew up a wooden foot with metal hinges, leather straps, and so on … damned odd-looking contraption, but he had a local mechanic build the thing, and damned if it don't work. Course I can't march all day like I used to, but I can get around camp okay, and can still ride a horse. And I damned sure can still work a rifle!" He turned to the side and spat to emphasize his point, then snorted a chuckle. And then to prove the truth of his story, he dismounted and walked over to the tent, turned and walked back with hardly a limp.

"That's wonderful," Tom said.

"Truly," Nathan nodded. He noted Jim's boot on that side came up to his knee and appeared to be tightly strapped on. He also noted a wince of pain that Jim tried to hide, but he said nothing about that.

After Tom sent one of the sergeants out to gather the rest of their officers, they moved into the command tent to get out of the rain. And though they would imbibe no whiskey, being in an active combat zone, Nathan shared out cigars all around to celebrate the joyful surprise arrival.

A short time later, the entire company of the Twelfth's officer corps—plus Billy—were crowded into the tent, laughing, joking, and exchanging happy Christmas greetings all around. Nathan felt like there was finally something to celebrate and said a quick, silent prayer of thanks for sending the very thing he needed to bolster his sagging spirits.

And in a quiet moment later in the festivities, William leaned over and looked Nathan in the eye. "Colonel, I find it an odd sensation ... knowing Margaret is only a short distance away—hmm ... some twenty or thirty miles, I guess—and yet impossible to get to. I'm sure you are feeling much the same about Evelyn."

"Yes, yes ... I know *exactly* what you mean, William. It burns in me every day ... frustration and yearning almost beyond bearing."

William nodded, then said, "Colonel, what say we end this thing and take our ladies home?"

"I say amen to that, William. Amen to that."

ℬↄⅭℬↄↄⅭℬↄℬↄⅭℬↄↄⅭℬↄⅭℬↄↄⅭℬↄ

Saturday December 31, 1864 – Richmond, Virginia:

Though the surroundings were as elegant as any she'd ever known, Margaret understood that the present New Year's celebration at the Hugheses' manor house was much more subdued than was their norm. No musicians, no dancing, and nobody in attendance who wasn't a member of their very closest circle of trusted friends—friends so close that they were either well aware of the type of clandestine activity the Hugheses were involved in, or were themselves participants. So few guests, in fact, that all twenty-some fit comfortably at the great table in the dining hall.

One unexpected guest from Margaret's perspective was Jonathan and Angeline's eldest son, Gareth, now a captain in the Union Army, though currently sitting at table in fine civilian garb.

271

He was presently among the federal troops assigned to the siege of Petersburg. How Jonathan had managed to smuggle Gareth across warring lines and into Richmond for the New Year's celebration was a mystery, but his presence had made the affair much more joyful and uplifting than it otherwise would've been.

And yet still, there was an unspoken acknowledgement of those who were missing, which served to dampen the festive mood. Even as the remains of the meal were being swept away by the freemen staff, and the brandy and whiskey was being offered around, Jonathan seemed to sense the mood, and clinked a spoon against his crystal glass. "Ladies and gentlemen, it is an honor and a privilege to have each of you—our dearest friends and family …" he nodded at Gareth and smiled, "here with us on this auspicious occasion."

Gareth returned the nod and raised his glass in response, as Angeline beamed.

"But I would be remiss," he continued, "if I didn't recognize our dear loved ones who are absent from the festivities this evening … starting with Gareth's younger brother Edward, who is serving in the Union army under General Sherman out in the West, may he stay safely from harm's way."

Jonathan then acknowledged several other families who had men out fighting, not surprisingly, all for the Union side, though this was not common knowledge. He included Margaret in this, mentioning her "special friend" Captain William Jenkins, and her brother, Colonel Nathaniel Chambers.

Then he raised his glass. "And then there is our dear friend and ally, Joseph, whom many of you know. He is presently somewhere out there …" Jonathan waved his hand in the general direction of the ongoing siege. "As usual, risking life and limb on our behalf, never asking for anything in return.

"And last, but certainly not least, I wish to send out my very fondest regards to our dearest friend Evelyn, who has been like a daughter to Angeline and myself these past several years. May she find some measure of peace and joy on this New Year's Day.

"Ladies and gentlemen … a toast … to those loved ones who are absent, and especially … to the coming end of the war, that we may all soon be reunited in peace and happiness!"

Margaret took a sip of her brandy and thought of William. She prayed it was true, that the war might soon be over, that they might be forever reunited. The thought gave her a glow, reflected by the warmth of the brandy she sipped.

But then to her chagrin, the ever-present dark cloud loomed like a distant thunderhead, threatening her joy; Walters was still out there somewhere. And while he was, she would never truly be at peace.

ഇരുന്ന

Saturday December 31, 1864 – Greenbrier County, West Virginia:

Elijah Walters sat on his horse, gazing across the valley at Mountain Meadows Farm spread out below. Captain Roberts sat next to him, also mounted. Seventy other riders, the ragged remnants of the Thirty-Sixth Virginia Cavalry Battalion, had been left bivouacked at Walters Farm, where they'd been since their long retreat from the disastrous Battle of Cedar Creek in the Shenandoah Valley.

Walters had spent the first month and more of his return getting his farm re-organized and cleaned up, using his cavalry troopers for labor, having discovered that the caretaker he'd left in charge had abandoned the place, along with all the slaves, presumably having run away when Hunter's Union army had passed through back in June.

But in the past month, he'd begun to consider what to do about his old nemesis, Nathan Chambers, and his farm Mountain Meadows. Though he could imagine numerous pleasurable resolutions to the problem, he'd not yet made up his mind on it. So, it being New Year's Eve, he'd decided it was an auspicious day to ride out and survey his enemy's farm, with the hopes of coming to a decision on the matter.

"So … this is Chambers's farm? Pretty place …" Roberts gazed out at the weed-filled fields and abandoned slave cabins and various outbuildings, all beginning to show signs of neglect. But the great picturesque white manor house, shining in the distance, appeared to have held up well.

"Yes … this is it. Last time I was here, it was just after Chambers abandoned the place. I held a torch in my hand and intended to burn the whole thing to the ground … but ironically, a Confederate colonel stopped me."

A vision of the rising flames engulfing Chambersburg, Pennsylvania appeared before Walters's mind's eye, and he immediately envisioned that highly satisfying conflagration raging here at Chambers's own home.

Roberts gazed at Walters and shrugged. "You want us to finish the job now, sir?" He chuckled. "The men are well versed in the business by now. I can gather a few dozen and come back here straightaway. We'll make short work of it."

Walters nodded, very nearly cracking a smile at the thought of the wanton destruction his men had recently wreaked against the helpless Yankee town, and what they could do here as well. But he didn't immediately answer, thinking on what the future might bring, and how he might still turn events in the war to his advantage.

Though today was the long-anticipated hour of his revenge against Nathan Chambers, to his own surprise, he hesitated; burning the place would give some measure of satisfaction, true. But he knew it would never be enough … not as long as the man himself yet lived, along with all his disgustingly loyal men.

"Sir? Shall we burn the farm down for you?" Roberts repeated the question.

"Hmm … Thank you, Roberts … but *no*. I have just thought of a better use for the place."

"Oh? What's that, sir? If you don't mind my asking…"

Walters turned to Roberts, gracing his subordinate with his usual odd, bland expression, "*Bait*, Mr. Roberts. Bait."

☙❧☙❧☙❧☙❧☙❧

For Evelyn it was an odd, melancholy New Year's celebration. She shook her head when she thought of the irony. The last New Year's she'd spent at Jonathan and Angeline's house, feeling more than a little guilty for indulging in sumptuous excess. And the year before that, she'd been at the Confederate White House, dressed in her finest, mingling with the elite of Richmond. She'd spent much of that evening sitting at a table with President Davis himself, and the first lady, Varina.

Now she sat alone at one end of a large, open room in an old warehouse, with only a folding screen separating her "bedroom" from the others of her people occupying various corners of the same room. She had no brandy, and only a single candle burning in its holder, sitting on her simple, rough wooden table. The room was cold and drafty, with only a single large fireplace midway down one wall. She clutched a knitted shawl tightly about her shoulders to keep from shivering.

In her mind's eye she pictured the gathering at the Hugheses' house this night. She shook her head ruefully at the contrast with her current humble circumstances. She'd been invited, of course, but Joseph had stopped by earlier in the day to warn her that Major White was still out there, actively seeking her, and had been seen visiting Miss Harriet on several occasions. That, of course, was of little concern to Evelyn, as her mother was now the last person she would confide in concerning her present whereabouts. But it did emphasize the point that she dared not go anywhere near Jonathan and Angeline, lest she be caught and give away their connection. So, here she sat, alone on New Year's Eve.

But despite her present situation, she smiled, and could feel a warm glow on the inside in sharp contrast to her chilliness on the outside. And as was often the case, her feeling of peace and joy emanated from thoughts of Nathan. And though she'd not heard from him directly, she'd received news *of* him this very afternoon, in a note from Angeline:

My dearest E.,

We have received news today that should brighten your day. Our people have confirmed that N. has been placed in command of a brigade which has been transferred to the siege of Petersburg. So, it may bring you some measure of encouragement and good cheer to know that your dear one is now within a mere 25 miles of the very place where you will be bringing in the new year.

We miss you so, but now have great hopes for a new year that will surely see the end of this conflict, and our own happy reunion, as well as the reuniting of a nation, a people, and not least by any means, you and N.

Affectionately yours,

A.

And she took comfort in knowing that from now on, whenever she heard the rumbling of artillery in the distance off to the south toward Petersburg, it would be as if Nathan himself were calling out to her, announcing his impending arrival, and the long-awaited end to the war.

ᔑᓭᔑᓭᔑᓭᔑᓭᔑᓭᔑᓭ

Saturday December 31, 1864 – Petersburg, Virginia:

Nathan trudged purposefully down the length of the trench, four feet deep and just wide enough for two men to walk abreast, it contained another four feet of thick timbers above. The drainage was woefully inadequate, such that the bottom several inches was perpetual muck this time of year, and Nathan was grateful for his riding boots, which, when his trousers were tucked inside, kept him reasonably dry and free of mud splatter. Still, it made for a tiresome slog to travel any distance at all.

He briefly wondered if this dug-in trench warfare would be the future of warfare, where deadly accurate, rifled guns had made frontal assaults by large formations of soldiers against well-fortified defensive positions almost entirely suicidal. Grant's switch to siege warfare seemed to indicate that he, at least, had learned that hard lesson at Cold Harbor.

Nathan reached the place he'd been making for, where the artillery spotters had erected a series of ladders and scaffoldings from which they could watch the impact of the Union's large siege guns as they targeted the enemy's positions across "no-man's land" in their redoubt on the outskirts of Petersburg, Virginia.

Though he had no legitimate military reason for being here, Nathan had a very *personal* reason. Tonight was New Year's Eve, and he knew the guns would go silent at sundown. Then he'd be able to do what he came to do.

He climbed a ladder and stepped onto the scaffolding, and for a few moments, watched the remainder of the day's show, as heavy Union artillery rumbled from its hiding place a half mile or more behind the trenches, sending projectiles streaking through the sky overhead to impact a mile or more away toward the rebels' own earthworks—there to either impact with the resounding *thud* of solid shot against earthen walls, or the deep *boom* of high explosive shells detonating overhead.

The rebels had long since given off answering these bombardments; clearly, they wished to ration their limited supply of ammunition and powder. He assumed they would save their big guns and their precious projectiles for when the Union attempted an advance in earnest.

He pulled out his pocket watch and checked the time. The sun would set in a few moments, though that would only mean that the gloom would get darker; there had been no sun for days. He waited.

With a last great, concussive blast echoing across the valley, the big guns fell silent, and darkness settled across the Union entrenchments.

Nathan climbed a few more steps to the very top of the earthworks, that he might look out over the top. He pulled out his brass spyglass and pointed it to the north, but not toward the enemy's redoubt in front of Petersburg, nor yet in the direction of the town's lights beyond. Rather he gazed out toward the faint glow on the horizon, twenty miles and more beyond. To Richmond. To the very center of his beating heart. To *her*.

He knew Evelyn was there, within but a single day's march. And the thought of her tantalizing closeness burned inside him like a torch; he longed to see her face, to hold her, to kiss her lips. The aching need of her brought a tear to his eye. And he thought back on all the lonely New Years they'd spent apart, recalling their last brief, joyful meeting in Washington just after the Emancipation, now nearly two long years past.

Oh, Evelyn … my dearest love … I am coming for you. Like an irresistible tide, I am coming! Nothing short of death will stop me now … maybe not even that.

<END OF BOOK 9>

If you enjoyed *Inferno*
please post a review.

Inferno – Facts vs. Fiction

I get asked all the time whether this or that person or event in one of my books was factual, or invented for dramatic effect. This volume, like the others in the series, contains a good number of interesting historical facts and circumstances that may, at first, seem made up. I thought you might enjoy the following enumeration and explanation of these details. – *Chris Bennett*

- **Civil War's descent into "total war"** – by 1864, the American Civil War had devolved from a typical European-style "Gentleman's War" at the outset in 1861, to a brutal, hellish war of destruction and annihilation as depicted in this book (thus the title.) **Bushwhackers**, who regularly targeted civilians and murdered captured soldiers, enraged Union generals such as **David Hunter**, who reciprocated by burning houses of private citizens suspected of aiding and abetting the rebels (along with generally destroying anything that might remotely aid the Confederate cause.) **Confederate General Jubal Early** was thus inspired to return the favor by infamously burning the Northern town of **Chambersburg, Pennsylvania** as depicted in this book (and **Confederate Colonel William Peters**, commander of the Twenty-First Virginia Cavalry regiment did in fact courageously and honorably refuse his orders to do the deed, as described herein.) **Union General Philip Sheridan**, under orders from **General Grant**, extensively destroyed the agricultural and other production capacity in the upper Shenandoah Valley in what came to be known as "The Burning." And most famously, **General William Tecumseh Sherman's** infamous march through Georgia left a fifty-mile-wide path of destruction across most of the state.
- **Fire at the Confederate Whitehouse** – in 1864, a slave butler named "Henry" (I have been calling him

"Hank" to eliminate confusion with the Henry who is one of Nathan's freemen) escaped one night after allegedly building a fire in the mansion's basement to divert attention.

- **Twelfth West Virginia building bridges** – on General Hunter's retreat from Lynchburg, the Twelfth eventually ended up at Parkersburg on the Ohio River. From there they should've been able to reach Martinsburg by rail in less than a day. But to Tom Clark's consternation in this book, the journey took six days because the regiment was forced to rebuild or repair five bridges along the way.

- **General Jubal Early's attack on Washington D.C.** – in the aftermath of his victory at **Lynchburg**, Early surprised the federals by marching north rather than returning to aid Lee back in Richmond. His bold march on Washington caused a panic, and forced the administration to put Union wounded and civilians on the firing line while awaiting reinforcements. And President Lincoln did in fact stand on the parapets at **Fort Stevens** until admonished by an unnamed Union officer to get down out of harm's way (and a soldier was shot a few yards away while the president stood there.) But Grant sent reinforcements from Virginia by boat, and Early was stymied. If he would've arrived one day earlier, the capital would've been his for the taking, but Early was indeed, late.

- **Battle of Snicker's Ferry** – this relatively minor engagement, depicted accurately in this book, not only has a humorous-sounding name, but also has the distinction of having more aliases than almost any other battle in the war. It is also known as the Battle of Cool Spring, Battle of Castleman's Ferry, Battle of Island Ford, Battle of Parker's Ford, and Battle of Snicker's Gap.

- **Two Union colonels getting separated from their regiment** – this may seem like a far-fetched piece of fiction, but it actually happened. During the Union retreat from General Crook's defeat by Jubal Early at the Second Battle of Kernstown, Colonel Thoburn (First Division commander) and Colonel Curtis (Twelfth West Virginia commander) somehow became separated from their commands in the confusion of battle, and were forced to escape together from pursuing cavalry patrols, at one point crawling through a cornfield and surviving on blackberries and whatever they had on them for four days, until they made it back to Martinsburg to rejoin their units. In *Inferno*, I have depicted this scene using Nathan and Tom, and had the rebel cavalry led by Elijah Walters.

- **Indians in the Civil War** – most people are surprised at the involvement of American Indians in the Civil War. While the mysterious Shawnees depicted herein, and of course the Tonkawa scout Billy Creek are fictional, Indian regiments fought on both sides out west (as described in book eight - *War*), and shockingly the Confederate Army did in fact employ a Cherokee Indian, **General Stand Watie,** who led the rebels in the **Battle of Fort Smith** as described in *Inferno*.

- **Battle of the Crater** – the depiction herein is accurate; what started as an excellent plan and very likely would've resulted in a dramatic Union breakthrough at Petersburg was botched because Union higher-ups got cold feet about sending in the colored regiments first. Instead, they sent them in last, after the battle was already lost, needlessly sacrificing hundreds of lives.

- **Union victories in the Shenandoah Valley** – the three dramatic Union victories at **Opequon Creek** (a.k.a., **Third Winchester**), **Fisher's Hill**, and **Cedar Creek**, led by **Major General Philip Sheridan** were the first time the federals were successful in an offensive action against a corps of Lee's Army of Northern Virginia on their home territory. These successive victories led to the elimination of Lieutenant General Jubal Early's Army of the Valley, and the wily general's eventual loss of command. And **Sheridan's dramatic ride from Winchester to Cedar Creek** to turn around his army's fortunes in the battle was a singularly heroic moment that captured the nation's imagination at the time and still endures today as one of the most memorable feats of the war.

As the Civil War grinds to a ruinous conclusion, Nathan faces a showdown against his hated adversary, Elijah Walters, and Evelyn desperately seeks to escape the evil Confederate Major White as Richmond burns down all around them.

Don't miss the thrilling final volume of the Road to the Breaking series in:

RESOLVE
ROAD TO THE BREAKING BOOK 10

coming spring 2025.

❧✦❧✦❧✦❧✦❧✦❧✦

While awaiting *Resolve*, don't miss the free sneak preview of the new series featuring Nathan Chambers' great grandfather
Ethan Chambers
and
real-life Revolutionary War hero Daniel Morgan
In

TROUBLES

A SHORT STORY
FROM
THE ROAD TO REVOLUTION SERIES

coming fall 2024

To download your **free copy** of the short story TROUBLES, please use the web address below:

https://www.chrisabennett.com/troubles

Acknowledgments

Special thanks as always to my editor, Ericka McIntyre, who keeps me honest and on track, and my proofreader and fellow Tolkien fanatic Travis Tynan, who makes sure everything is done correctly!

And, as always, I can't thank her enough for all she does for the Road to the Breaking team—our "head coach" and my most excellent partner in crime, Keri-Rae Barnum. *You are the best!*

Recommended Reading

For excellent nonfiction accounts of the people and events in this book, whose titles speak for themselves, please see:

- *Lincoln's Abolitionist General: The Biography of David Hunter,* by Edward A. Miller, Jr.

- *History of the Twelfth West Virginia Volunteer Infantry: The Part It Took in the War of the Rebellion, 1861 – 1865,* by William Hewitt

- *The Last Battle of Winchester: Phil Sheridan, Jubal Early, and the Shenandoah Valley Campaign, August 7 – September 19, 1864,* by Scott Charles Patchan

Get Exclusive Free Content

The most enjoyable part of writing books is talking about them with readers like you. In my case that means all things related to *Road to the Breaking*—the story and characters, themes, and concepts. And of course, Civil War history in general, and West Virginia history in particular.

If you sign up for my mailing list, you'll receive some free bonus material I think you'll enjoy:

- A fully illustrated *Road to the Breaking* **Fact vs. Fiction Quiz.** Test your knowledge of history with this short quiz on the people, places, and things in the book (did they really exist in 1860, or are they purely fictional?)

- **Cut scenes from *Road to the Breaking*.** One of the hazards of writing a novel is word and page count. At some point you realize you need to trim it back to give the reader a faster-paced, more engaging experience. However, now you've finished reading the book, wouldn't you like to know a little more detail about some of your favorite characters? Here's your chance to take a peek behind the curtain!

- I'll ʼoccasionally put out a **newsletter with information about the Road to the Breaking Series**—new book releases, news and information about the author, etc. I promise not to inundate you with spam (it's one of my personal pet peeves, so why would I propagate it?)

To sign up, visit my website:
http://www.ChrisABennett.com

ROAD TO THE BREAKING SERIES:

Made in the USA
Middletown, DE
10 March 2024

51211097R00175